In this story of covert
Halkin has written a
producer, he has travel
in Singapore. His ear
horror novel *Slither*.
with his wife Irmgard in Richmond, Surrey.

JOHN HALKIN

Hantu

GRAFTON BOOKS

A Division of the Collins Publishing Group

LONDON GLASGOW
TORONTO SYDNEY AUCKLAND

Grafton Books
A Division of the Collins Publishing Group
8 Grafton Street, London W1X 3LA

Published by Grafton Books 1990

First published in Great Britain by
The Bodley Head Ltd 1988

ISBN 0-586-20800-3

The passage on page 242 is extracted from
Keesing's Contemporary Archives,
Keesing's Publications Ltd, 1950

Printed and bound in Great Britain by
Collins, Glasgow

Set in Times

To Irmel and Christoph
remembering Singapore years

Author's Notes

All characters and events described in this book are fictional.

Historical Data

1949   September. First USSR atomic bomb tested. USA no longer sole nuclear power.

October. Chinese People's Republic proclaimed.

December. War Crimes trial of Japanese officers at Khabarovsk, USSR.

1950   June. Start of Korean War.

November. President Truman reveals use of atomic bomb under consideration.

December. British Prime Minister, Clement Attlee, in Washington for urgent talks with President Truman.

Russian Security Organizations

In the 1930s the NKVD (People's Commissariat of Internal Affairs) exercised wide control over state security, but during World War Two the section concerned with political police split away to become the NKGB (People's Commissariat for State Security). The two commissariats became ministries in 1946: the MVD and the MGB. (*Note:* After Stalin's death in 1953 they merged again to become the KGB.)

Military intelligence, whose interests included all technical and weapons developments, was the responsibility of the GRU, the Chief Intelligence Directorate of the Soviet General Staff.

Chinese Spelling
This story is set in 1950. The spelling of Chinese names follows the normal practice at that date.

Glossary

amah: Chinese nursemaid

atap: thatched roof, usually of palm leaves

cheongsam: Chinese dress with high neck and side-slits in skirt

chop: personal seal or stamp

dhobi: washing; person who does washing

dua stingah: two whisky sodas

godown: warehouse

hao-a?   good?

kang: a hard, shelf-like, built-in bed

kampong: village

klong: canal

lathi: long bamboo stick often used by police

makan: eat

mari sini: come here

mati: dead

padang: open space; in the story, the Padang is the green on the Singapore waterfront

sakit: ill

samfu: Chinese high-necked tunic and slacks worn by women

sarong: wrap-around cloth worn as a skirt by Malays, men or women

ta: not

taipan: wealthy Chinese businessman

tuan: sir; usual form of address to Europeans at time of story

Prologue

Peking 1950

That morning the new ordinance had come into force liberating the rickshaw men from their traditional, degrading occupation. As a result people had to trudge to work, making the streets even more crowded than usual. Only a few had bicycles.

Colonel Borkin sat patiently in the back of his staff car, marvelling that no one in the crush was knocked down or fell under the wheels as they inched forward. He was a stocky, middle-aged man whose career in the GRU – the Intelligence Service of the Soviet General Staff – had been long and varied. This posting to Peking had come as an unpleasant surprise. A German specialist, he had expected Berlin or Vienna; almost nightly he lay awake till the small hours wondering whom he might have offended – which perhaps explained his tired, defeated air as he stepped out of the car before the anonymous headquarters of the Chinese People's Intelligence Bureau.

Straightening his shoulders, he acknowledged his driver's salute and then strode up the steps. Comrade Tung, dressed as always in a humble, faded blue boiler suit, waited in the entrance hall to conduct him through the security checks.

'A little late today, comrade,' he apologized.

'With rickshaws the traffic moved faster,' his Chinese colleague agreed. 'But we aim to rid China of all such injustices, so they had to go.'

Because neither knew the other's native tongue they

spoke English together, the Chinese more fluently than the colonel. At least it made co-operation possible.

It was no more than a few short months since Chairman Mao's formal inauguration of the Chinese People's Republic and the Soviet Union had naturally been the first to recognize the new regime. Immediately, negotiations started between the two countries to determine what help China needed for the task of building socialism in a land torn by decades of civil war and despoliation by the Japanese. The resulting treaty contained certain clauses, necessarily secret, covering the exchange of intelligence information.

An archivist's job, he thought bitterly as they climbed the stairs, ignoring the shaky old lift. The stage they were at, a junior librarian could have managed it.

'You'll have some tea, Comrade Colonel?'

Comrade Tung lit the spirit stove. While the water was heating he unlocked the safe to take out the day's files, heaping them up on the rough table beneath the obligatory portraits of Mao Tse-tung and Stalin.

He could not deny there had been some rich pickings. Even Moscow would be forced to acknowledge that much. All the American records for a start. Once Generalissimo Chiang Kai-shek's discredited Nationalist government had fled to the island of Formosa with their trunk-loads of jewellery and bullion, the Americans had pulled out in a hurry, leaving more intact files behind than they had intended.

But this week they were concentrating on the Tai-li archives, an extensive collection of papers and dog-eared index cards in Chinese script for which Comrade Tung had to provide rough, off-the-cuff translations.

'I've done some cross-references on the White Russians living in Shanghai,' Comrade Tung announced as he poured the pale-coloured tea into two small, handleless cups, 'with very interesting results. Your authorities may wish to repatriate some of these people.'

'This Tai-li must have been very thorough.'

'He and his agents were much feared. Even Chiang Kai-shek couldn't command him, though he made him a general. He controlled the most ruthless secret intelligence organization ever known in China. To cross him was to die. When the American military came after Pearl Harbor he was so powerful, he negotiated his own terms with them. But he double-crossed them as well, which is why the agents of the US Office of Strategic Services killed him – that was the rumour. Fixed a limpet mine to his plane. It exploded in mid-air.' Comrade Tung picked up the teapot. 'Have some more?'

It tasted little better than hot water, despite a musty tang, but Colonel Borkin nodded. He didn't want to offend the man. 'Is all that true?' he said. 'You talk like a Chinese Tolstoy.'

They worked on the files most of the day. It was all routine stuff, even the details of the White Russians who had escaped to China after the Revolution. But he noted it all down; someone in Moscow might feel it should be followed up. Not till half-way through the afternoon did Comrade Tung turn up a file which genuinely aroused his interest.

On the cover of the tattered cardboard folder was the name Andrei Nikolayovich Burzov, with other members of his family listed beneath. Nothing very special about any of them except one daughter, Tanya, described as a 'dancer and bar-girl', for many years the kept mistress of a British tea merchant called Ross. Ross's son Peter – not Ross himself, he noted – was the subject of a separate file of his own.

Tung had the Ross file ready to hand. Clipped to it were three small photographs.

13

Peter Ross, Colonel Borkin thought, remembering. *Berlin*.

'You see,' said Tung, 'the notes start while the subject is still at school. It takes a mind like Tai-li's to decide it is worth starting a file on a mere schoolboy.'

'This Russian family – do we have other details?' he asked, accustomed to proceeding methodically. 'Present whereabouts? Are they still in Shanghai?'

'These Burzovs, they have no significance.'

'Moscow may feel that they have.'

Laboriously he copied the contents of the file into his notebook, even the reference number of a recent Shanghai police report affirming that the two members of the family to survive the war had both now left China for the United States.

'Addresses in America?'

'Not given.'

'Very well, comrade. Now for this Ross.'

'Peter Ross, born in Shanghai, British parents both now dead. The notes say that as a boy he spoke fluent Chinese, unusual among the International Concession brats. Not Shanghaiese either. His amah was a Peking woman. In school holidays he stayed with the Burzov family where the language was Russian. Ah, and here's a note on his schoolwork. Below average. What d'you make of that, Comrade Colonel? Fluent English, Chinese and Russian, yet he's bad at school!'

'Anything else?'

'Father killed in an air raid . . . The next entry's several years later, different handwriting. He turns up in Malaya in the Japanese occupation. British liaison officer with jungle freedom fighters. Then Singapore, 1945. Reported died in hospital, London 1946.'

Borkin wrote it all down, not contradicting, though

14

Berlin came after 1946. 'I'll take another look at the photographs.'

He unclipped them from the file and laid them out side by side on the table. Producing a folding magnifying glass from his pocket, he examined each one closely. The first was a family snapshot showing a boy, about ten, with a tall, spare man who could easily have been his father. Then came a full-face passport picture at the age of perhaps fifteen or sixteen. It was the third photo that interested him most, obviously the same person, but now grown up and wearing a British army tropical uniform, sergeant's stripes, and facing the sun which was causing him to screw up his eyes. On the back was written: Singapore, 1945.

'This one I shall send to Moscow.' He placed it in an envelope from his briefcase. 'It will be returned with any extra facts we find.'

Comrade Tung did not argue. He made a note on the file and then went on to the next White Russian on his list.

Some six weeks later the Ross file reached Comrade Chuan's desk in the requisitioned Christian mission school which his department had been allocated. To the notes in his own handwriting on the Malayan campaign, Tung had added a few lines of more recent information. Source: Moscow.

He sat and thought about it for an hour or more, staring at the mark left by the crucifix which had previously decorated the opposite wall. Pictures of Mao Tse-tung and Chou En-lai had now replaced it.

So Hantu was still alive. The news hardly surprised him after all. Despite his oddly diffident manner, the man was devious enough to have spread the rumours of his death in hospital himself. No doubt arranged a funeral, too. With himself as chief mourner.

But something had to be done about it. Gradually an idea began to take shape, though at that stage it was no more substantial than the morning's spring snow which had melted as it touched the ground.

The hard details could come later, he decided. Taking a sheet of paper he wrote out a cryptic request for an interview at the highest level. He sealed the wallet twice, using his personal chop, and then called for a despatch rider.

1

The hammering split Ross's head, driving down into the very core of his consciousness, never faltering, never ceasing, that steady *bang-bang-bang-bang-bang* remorsely destroying him till his lips mouthed some painful gibberish response to the torture.

Repeatedly he tried to turn his face away from the intense light hurting his eyes, but his head was strapped so tightly, it couldn't move. The lamps were focused directly at him, blinding him even through closed eyelids. There was no escape, no way out but to surrender to insanity; yet his cursed irrational life-instinct refused to allow him even such small relief.

Then the hammering stopped.

Stopped!

Abruptly. Without warning.

He could not accept it at first. His mind must be deceiving him. It was hallucination. Something had snapped. He imagined he could still hear the blows – yearned for them, to reassure himself – those hard, metallic blows reverberating through his entire body.

'Let's try again, old man – shall we?'

It was the sadistic bastard's turn, the upper class one, Eton and Oxford, Harrow and Sandhurst, some such places where they sent their brats. 'You arrived in Moscow and made contact as instructed – let's start from there, shall we?'

A kind of reply must have croaked from his parched throat because the voice sharpened like a whipcrack.

'What was that, Ross? If you've something to say, speak up!'

Strapped to the chair, time meaningless, questions meaningless, passing his swollen tongue over cracked lips. White walls, clinical. High-powered lamps. The stink of his own excreta. Limbs numb by now, cramp pains long since gone. Two interrogators alternating – stroppy public school type, and the other with a more homely, Hovis touch.

These were facts he could hold on to. All this he knew.

'No good, old chap. Not really trying, are you?' The voice was relentless. 'On the same side, aren't we? Work for the same outfit. So welcome home an' all that! Now tell us what happened. Really screwed it up, didn't you? Is that what we're to believe?'

Again he must have reacted without wishing to.

'Drink?' They were taunting him. 'Spill the dirt, old boy, an' you can have any drink you like. Water – think of it! Cool, fresh water. Then a bath . . . sleep . . . real bed . . . lights out . . . darkness . . . quiet . . .'

The hammering started up again, each blow smashing through his skull, rattling his brain, splintering the bones, bursting the eardrums . . .

'Mr Ross! Are you there, Mr Ross?'

Jesus, who the hell was it?

His head was throbbing. He'd been reliving that interrogation again – oh bloody hell, would he never get rid of it? Would it never leave him in peace?

The details were always the same, always accurate, just as it had happened. A spot of de-briefing, old chap: secured to that chair for God knows how many days; ceaseless questioning; the lights; the amplified hammering noise to drive him out of his mind.

His *colleagues*, or so they insisted on telling him.

That would be one of them assaulting the door of his flat now. Two o'clock in the morning.

'Mr Ross?'

He ignored them but sat patiently in the dark until they had gone away.

By rights, as he knew only too well, he should have been lying dead in a Russian ditch, his decomposing body a prey to state-owned flies on some Soviet collective. They couldn't forgive him for being back in London, September 1950, the year no one had expected him to see, himself least of all.

But in London he was, taking his early walk in St James's Park, a daily habit since his release from their interrogation centre. Usually he had the park to himself at this hour. No nannies with prams yet; no toddlers disturbing his thoughts. Though few people observing him at the lakeside feeding the ducks would have given him a second look. He was taller than average, well over six feet, and his lean, angular face bore a faint scar just beneath the left jaw, but he had a diffident manner. His reach-me-down brown sports jacket and shapeless corduroy trousers contributed to the general impression of anonymity which had helped keep him alive.

He took the paper bag of old bread from his pocket. At first the ducks showed little interest but gradually he lured them closer to the bank, throwing each handful of crumbs closer than the previous one until they were almost pecking at his feet. They trusted him, not seeming to understand fear. Not as he understood it.

'Ah, Mr Ross.'

At the sound of the high-pitched voice behind him he swung round, suddenly tense. It was Potts, from 'Records'. He turned back to the ducks, embarrassed at his instinctive reaction.

19

'You're jumpy,' Potts observed. 'And you weren't at home last night. Not in your flat. We were searching for you. You're wanted.'

The Section had rented the flat for him over a shop near Victoria station, just two rooms with a stained washbasin and peeling wallpaper. An open prison. If he wanted to go away for a day or two he was expected to ask permission.

'I was to say it's urgent, Mr Ross. You're to go there now, sir. After I've gone, please. Once I'm out of sight.'

He extracted another slice of bread from the bag, breaking it between his fingers before tossing it into the water. The ducks squawked excitedly as they competed for it.

This was the first time he had met Potts out of doors. His usual habitat was among the battered wooden filing cabinets and chipped teacups of the Section's Records department. He was a legend there for his phenomenal recall of facts and faces – a fat little man in a worn brown suit which he never changed, shreds of pipe tobacco on his bulging waistcoat. Here in the park, in his stained fawn raincoat and shabby bowler, he had the appearance of a man who haunted cinema matinees hoping to find a lonely girl to sit next to.

'You married, Potts?' It was a random thought, inspired perhaps by the raincoat.

Potts, on the point of leaving, froze. An expression of astonishment flushed across his face. 'Oh, yes,' he admitted awkwardly. 'Dear me, yes. Now you will get a move on, won't you, sir? As soon as I'm clear?'

Without moving from the spot Ross watched him go. An early autumn mist softened the outlines of the pedestrian bridge over the lake. A few yellowing leaves were already falling. He valued these quiet moments.

* * *

Along Whitehall the drab crowds streamed off tall red buses to hurry towards their civil service desks. Ross forced a way through them like a salmon battling upstream as he headed for Charing Cross wondering what the Section wanted with him. They couldn't discharge him; he was too much of an embarrassment, they had made that clear enough. Perhaps they would bury him in one of these offices where they could keep an eye on him. He might even find himself working for Potts.

True, in such Whitehall offices great decisions were taken which sent men to their deaths. This was where the power lay. Here was the fulcrum of the British Empire on which the sun never set, as a woman had told him boastfully when he had first arrived in the country. He had mistaken these imposing buildings for museums – no machine-guns in sight, not even a rifle or revolver, only an elderly commissionaire at each ministry doorway, a single unarmed policeman at 10 Downing Street, and at the War Office – the very seat of military might – a nominal guard of two red-coated soldiers on horseback equipped with shining swords. This more than anything made Ross conscious of being a foreigner here, despite his British nationality, this arrogant assumption of unchallengeable power. It was only possible in a country smugly confident of its own place on the map.

Though now the sun *was* beginning to set on the great Empire. With India and Burma gone, and the traditional treaty ports of China abolished, those splashes of red in the school atlases were already fewer.

In Charing Cross station he bought a paper. Heavy fighting in Korea, Communist offensive against Pusan perimeter, casualty toll high: the headlines gave him all he wanted to know, but for a moment he stood on the street pretending to read while he scanned the people nearby. When he felt ready he wandered off along the

21

Strand, checking the shop window reflections to make certain he was not being followed before he plunged into the maze of narrow roads leading towards the Embankment.

The Section had its offices in a row of Georgian houses with uncurtained windows through which, on the ground floor at least, only closed wooden shutters were visible. Along the entire row, protruding from a low stone balustrade, was a line of shorn iron stumps left when the railings had been cut down to help the war effort. Ross went to number 7, the sole functional entrance, and pressed the bell.

Then he waited.

On the chipped steps stood the same dirty milk bottle as on his previous visit three weeks earlier. The metal plaque on the door bearing the names of the companies supposedly occupying the house – an exports firm on the ground level, commercial consultants above them, and the accountants at the top – had still not been cleaned.

He rang the bell again.

The doorkeeper who grumblingly let him in – a burly ex-Royal Navy chief petty officer Ross chatted with on occasion – told him he could go straight on up. He was expected.

At the head of the narrow, lino-covered stairs Mrs Smith greeted him from her cubby hole with a warm toothy smile like a dentist's receptionist. 'Oh, Mr Ross! I'll just tell him you're here!'

'What's it about?'

She gave a coy giggle. 'Oh, I never know what goes on behind those doors. They don't confide in me.'

She plugged a jack into the archaic switchboard, rumoured to be on loan from the Science Museum, and murmured into her mouthpiece. He caught only his own name. There couldn't be much happening in the Section that she didn't know about, sitting there behind that partition day in, day out, usually knitting, always ready for a quick word with anyone who came through. A comfortable sort of person with whom everyone felt at home. War widow, she'd once confided in him; husband killed at Dunkirk.

'He'll see you right away, Mr Ross.' She tugged the jack free. 'End office. Ask me, he's not well.'

She pressed the hidden button which unlocked the partition door and he went through.

Head of Section's office was at the far end of a long corridor running through all four houses. It was a large, elegant room overlooking the street but furnished with scuffed War Office surplus. Even the desk was scored and ink-stained. Seated behind it, HOS glared at Ross with undisguised irritation.

'Potts found you at last?'

'I *am* on leave,' Ross reminded him. 'On ice. Said so yourself.'

'Leave? Good God man, none of us can ever be on leave. Thought you knew that by now. I pull the string, you jerk – and don't you forget it.'

Patiently, Ross waited while HOS went through the usual ritual of asserting his authority before coming to the point. Missed the army, probably; though his civilian clothes were as much a declaration of caste as any officer's uniform: medium grey suit, waistcoat, Jermyn Street striped shirt with white collar and old school tie, the complete clubman's rig. But Mrs Smith was right; with those bloated features he did not look healthy.

'Sit down, man, sit down!' HOS took a cigarette from the Players Full Strength packet before him, tapping the end against the desk before lighting it. 'Been doing a spot of freebooting, have you? It's what I hear.'

'Freebooting?'

23

'Working on your own, man! Freebooting. Freelancing. Privately, on the side.' His voice had a smoker's grating edge to it. 'Have you?'

'No.'

'I hope you don't intend making this difficult for both of us.' A fit of coughing seized him. For a moment he seemed on the point of choking but he recovered sufficiently to gulp some water from the glass that stood ready. 'It's this damned cigarette. Only wish I could give 'em up.'

'You should see a doctor,' Ross commented without interest.

HOS dropped the Players packet into a drawer and shut it. The fox-like look returned to his eyes. 'Know very little about each other, you and I, do we? You were recruited by my predecessor, may his soul rest in whatever bunkhole he found for himself. Before my posting.' He took another sip of water. 'Born in Shanghai, weren't you?'

'So were many thousands of others.'

'Father and mother both British?'

'It's on the file.'

'*White* British?'

'True blue.'

A quick frown. 'Get on well with Chinamen?'

'Chinese,' Ross corrected him automatically. 'What are you getting at?'

'I ask the questions, Ross.' His hand reached into the drawer for a cigarette. He played with it nervously, then put it back. 'Been in contact with any since you left Shanghai?'

'Not recently.'

'Meaning?'

'Force 136. Ask Potts. He keeps the records.'

His face flushing a deep scarlet, HOS stood up abruptly

24

and brought his hand down hard on the desk. 'I want straight answers, Ross. I warn you, don't mess me about.'

Ross stared back at him with intense dislike. The orders for the interrogation must have come from him, no one else. 'I was held for three months in your sanitized prison,' he said bitterly. 'Treated like shit.'

'A normal de-briefing.'

'You call that normal?'

'We use specialists for these jobs. They reported you were holding back information. You can't blame them for becoming impatient. You said yourself it went on for three months.'

'Because I couldn't give the kind of answer they wanted.'

'You know better than that, Ross. Now let's not lose our tempers. What Chinks have you seen in the last few weeks since you came out of interrogation?'

'They're called Chinese. I've seen none.'

'Some decent Chinese restaurants in London. Haven't you tried them?'

'No. Should I? Is that an instruction?'

'How have you filled your time? Get to Lord's at all?' Now he was trying the conversational touch. 'That's what I'd have done in your shoes. The whole summer free. I envy you.'

'I'm afraid I never understood cricket.'

HOS's eyebrows rose. 'You did say your parents were British?'

The black telephone rang and HOS grunted into it, then replaced the receiver.

'The admiral's on his way over,' he announced. 'Before he gets here, Ross, I'd just like to say this. Don't try anything on. If there's one thing that the admiral can't tolerate it's people who try it on. He doesn't approve of freebooters either. Come to that, nor do I.'

Whoever this admiral might be, he obviously put the fear of God into HOS. It was one point in his favour, not that Ross had heard of him before. When he arrived he turned out to be a tall, lean-faced man who wore authority with the unselfconscious ease of someone accustomed to being obeyed from the cradle. In his expensively cut suit he might have stepped from the pages of *Tatler*. To Ross's amusement HOS emerged from behind the desk to offer him an armchair which not even the blind could have missed.

'I apologize for my lateness,' the admiral said briskly. He ignored the chair. 'Been closeted with the minister. To put it mildly he's perplexed, as I think we all are. Had it been one of the Allies – the United States, or France even – that might have been a different matter. As it is . . . Well, I don't know what to make of it. This is Ross, I take it?'

'Yes, sir. We found him.'

'Put him in the picture?'

'About to, sir. When you arrived.'

'Well, Ross.' The admiral turned to him, looking him up and down. 'Not been playing footsie with any Chinese recently, I hope.'

'I've asked him that question, sir. He denies it, but of course he would in any case.'

'Ross?'

He replied truthfully that he did not know any Chinese in London. What the hell was biting them, he wondered.

'Someone knows you. How would you feel about being seconded to China?'

The question caught him off-guard. What the hell were they trying on now?

'Which China?' he asked cautiously.

'Oh, not Chiang Kai-shek's Nationalist lot on Formosa

26

if that's what you're thinking. It's Peking. We've had a request for you. By name.'

'The question is,' HOS rasped, 'how did they get hold of your name? And the fact you work for the Section?'

'First I've heard of it. And the answer's no.'

'Don't be too hasty, Ross.' The admiral regarded him thoughtfully, as though uncertain about him. 'Before any decisions are taken we've demanded a meeting – just you and their man, face to face. You do speak Chinese, don't you? No one else in the Section does. Damned few Englishmen anywhere.'

'Oh, Ross is quite a linguist.' HOS make it sound like an unattractive disease. Plumes of blue-grey cigarette smoke hovered around his lips as he spoke. 'But I'd still like to know how these Chinamen picked him out.'

'Chinese.' This time it was the admiral who patiently put him right. 'His Majesty's Government have formally recognized the new Chinese administration, unlike our American friends who have some difficulty about it. Of course this request has not come through diplomatic channels, but we should like to honour it in so far as it is consistent with our own interests.'

'They're backing North Korea,' Ross probed. 'Aren't we about to go to war with them?'

'All the more reason to discover what's on their minds. Do you still refuse?'

'Nobody in this Section refuses anything,' HOS intervened.

'When do I meet him, and where?'

'Neutral ground for the first meeting,' the admiral said. 'Somewhere in the Far East probably. We're trying to fix that up now though communications are very slow. Be ready to travel at short notice, will you? Arrangements all made, HOS?'

'Yes, sir.' HOS straightened up as he barked out his

orders. 'Report downstairs to "Exports", Ross. They'll fix you up with a passport and tell you where to go for your jabs – smallpox, yellow fever, TAB, cholera, all the usual. And don't wander off this time. Stay where we can reach you. Off you go.'

They were lying, Ross brooded sourly as he stepped out into the corridor.

They were bloody lying, still trying to catch him out, a repeat performance of those first months back in Britain when they had incarcerated him in their Spartan Hampshire 'nursing home' for their ceaseless questioning – how had he got out of Russia after so long, how had he survived, had he done a deal with the MGB – he was working for them, wasn't he? Wasn't he? Till he felt his eyes were bursting out of their sockets with exhaustion under the glare of the lamps and he'd been on the very edge of losing control and screaming in their faces, a mindless, valve-blowing scream.

But he had held back, too proud to let go, and that was how it was going to be this time, he promised himself. Once let them win and nothing would be left, only the long walk in the dark.

'Oh, you're due in "Exports" now, Mr Ross!' Mrs Smith instructed him with a quick smile. He found himself back at the end of the corridor. 'Use the rear stairs, they're more convenient.'

With her was a man he thought he recognized: sensitive features, almost fastidious. 'We've not met formally, Ross, but I'm Richards.' He stretched out a hand and his long, delicate fingers seemed to get lost in Ross's stronger grip. 'I'll show you the way. Can't risk mislaying you a second time.'

'I'm sure you can't.' Ross followed him back along the corridor.

About half-way along Richards paused and pushed

open an unmarked door. 'Stairs are through here,' he explained, leading the way. 'We're in number 5 now. Number 3 is for top brass only, hence we call five the rear stairs, which they are not. Just been tête-à-tête with the admiral, I hear?'

'Something like that. Who is he?'

'They didn't tell you? That's typical of them. Oh, he's very top brass. He's CIS, Controller Intelligence Services. Doesn't encourage folk to use the initials though. Prefers the old naval rank. Whiff of the briny. Look, you must be a bit lonely here in London, not encouraged to make outside friends an' all that. Why don't you an' I have a spot of dinner one evening? Let our hair down?'

'Could do.' Ross was non-committal. The Naval Air Base, that was where he had seen Richards before, hovering in the darkness on the fringes of the 'welcoming' committee the night he had been flown in. Now the casual, friendly approach – didn't miss a trick, did they?

In the office, the admiral turned to stare out of the window, waiting with distaste for HOS's coughing fit to end. Walsh may have been a good army officer in his day but he was not the man he would have chosen as Head of Section, not the way things stood with the Russians one step ahead all the time. It was turning out to be one hell of a year, what with Britain's top atomic scientist Klaus Fuchs being found guilty of espionage, and then the balloon going up in Korea.

And now Ross. Not an easy man to assess, but then none of these Thirty-nine Steps types ever were.

Despite over six years now in various branches of intelligence work, the admiral still instinctively thought of himself as a sailor. Every generation of his family for the past 200 years had served at sea. His father and grandfather had both attained the rank of admiral in their day, and one ancestor had commanded a ship-of-the-line at Trafalgar, but he was the first to be shunted into this undercover world of spies and counter-spies.

After some of his experiences, very little could surprise him any longer, but this request from the Red Chinese certainly did, whatever they wanted. He wished he could handle the meeting himself rather than send Ross. As a midshipman he had spent some months on the China Station. He'd been eighteen then, fresh-faced, tall, good at sport, and pre-war Shanghai had been a paradise. He remembered days at the races, tennis, tea dances, intimate nightclubs, girls . . . He'd had the pick of the expatriate community's available daughters: quite an initiation for an innocent young middy. Wasted his time in some ways too. He had learned little enough about China itself, hardly noticed the poverty, and acquired no Chinese, only half a dozen words of pidgin.

'Get Potts in here, will you, HOS?' The man had stopped coughing at last. 'Tell him to bring Ross's file.'

They had requested him by name, that was the vital point. How had they known about him? The Section had only a patchy presence in the Far East, nothing Ross had ever been connected with, and it did not cover mainland China.

'Ross, sir?' said Potts, laying the file on HOS's desk. 'I remember him being recruited. Late 1946. Colonel Archer was HOS. Went to Berlin himself to interview Sergeant Ross.'

'You did the paper work?'

'Ran the traces, yes. Not easy. Shanghai details are mostly Ross's own account, uncorroborated. I'm not saying they're not true. But from 1939 the documentation is more comprehensive. Arrived in Britain, first time. Joined the Army, commando training, service in Ceylon, recruited to Special Operations Executive – it's all there in the file. He was landed in Malaya as part of Force 136 to liaise with anti-Jap resistance and remained there till the war ended. Shall I go on, sir?'

'Come to Berlin.'

'1946. SOE had folded up so he was put into I-Corps and sent to Germany, British zone. Helped sort out these Russians the Nazis had deported as slave labour. Later he was in Berlin monitoring Red Army phone calls, which is when our people got on to him. Impressed by his Russian, Colonel Archer was.'

'So they dressed him up in a Soviet uniform?'

'Trouble in a camp for Soviet officers, POWs since the first German offensive. They weren't too confident about what lay in store for them when they got home. Ross was infiltrated to find out what he could. You'll see there's a note he wasn't too happy with the assignment.'

'Had the devil's own luck getting away with it,' HOS grunted. He lit another cigarette.

'Talent for it, sir. They sent him into other camps later. That's how we got him into the Soviet Union. He travelled with them. Then the file becomes vague again. As instructed, he made contact with the Moscow circle. After that, silence.'

'Almost the entire circle was rounded up, but not friend Ross.' Another coughing fit seized HOS, but through it he managed to splutter: 'Call that luck if you like!'

'His task was to contact the German V2 scientists who had been taken off to work in the Soviet Union,' Potts said precisely. He tapped the file with his unlit pipe. 'When eventually he got back to the West – '

'Two whole years later!' HOS croaked.

' – he brought detailed intelligence of the new rocket they had developed and tested. Of course he refused to tell us anything else. Nothing about how he survived all that time in Russia.'

31

'You witnessed the interrogation?' the admiral asked.

'Through the one-way glass.' Potts smirked. 'A very stubborn man. Of course it's possible the Russians could have turned him, but I'd be surprised. They'd have fed him some sort of story. Unless it happened a long time ago before he joined the Section. In Shanghai even.'

'That's something we now have to decide,' the admiral summed up. 'Have they turned him? If so, Moscow must have stage-managed the whole thing. If not – well, in that case the man we're discussing is clearly one of our very best operatives. We'll go through the file now in detail. Thank you, Mr Potts. We've no need to take up any more of your time.'

Once Potts had left, closing the door quietly behind him, HOS cleared his throat noisily. '*Was*, not *is*, if you ask my opinion. The man's burnt out. You've only to look at him.'

Several days later, in a rear upstairs room at 10 Downing Street, the admiral waited while the prime minister sat at his desk toying with a paper knife. Of course intelligence reports were part of any head of government's daily diet, but only a raving lunatic would ever allow them to get their hands on operational details. On this occasion – with China involved and the Korean business going badly – the admiral had taken a sober decision to be that lunatic.

No premier could have been more unlike his predecessor, he thought. Churchill would hardly have given him time to complete his report before barking out a decision. These long silences would have been unthinkable. It was difficult to believe this man led the party whose MPs had joining in singing the 'Red Flag' on their first day in the new House of Commons. Flushed with victory. Ready to reform the world.

He was a small, shy man, more like an insurance clerk

than a prime minister, balding and with a mouse-like face, mild-mannered, yet each time the admiral met him his respect grew. Enigmatic he might be, but they understood each other.

A slight clearing of the throat. 'I'm in no doubt we must find out what the Chinese have on their minds. Can your man be trusted?'

'Head of Section is of the opinion he's burnt out.'

'And what do you think? You've met him.'

'He's resentful. But then good operatives are like race horses. Highly strung.'

'Mm.'

'Our Chinese source insists they won't talk to anyone else. We sent a message trying to persuade them but they stonewalled.'

'And what does our man say?'

'As puzzled as we are, or seems to be. We've had him under surveillance on and off since his de-briefing, and round the clock at the moment. No Chinese contacts that we can see. He's something of an odd-ball. Sits in London Zoo, sketching the animals. Pencil sketches, but in a kind of Chinese style.'

'Good?'

'Better than I could manage. Prime Minister, I've no evidence one way or the other, but it's my hunch we should go along with this. We gain nothing by slamming the door in their faces.'

'I think I agree.'

On the wall was a large-scale map of Korea constantly updated to show the North Korean advance. The area around Pusan in the extreme south-east was now all that was left to the South Koreans and the United Nations – mainly American – reinforcements. The prime minister came over to stare at it gloomily.

'General MacArthur is demanding the right to bomb

33

north of the Yalu river,' he said. 'Chinese territory. Perhaps you don't agree with me, Admiral, I don't know. But there's a feeling abroad we're on the verge of world war. The third in my generation. We must not make any wrong moves.'

'Nor any weak moves, Prime Minister. The Russians' main strength has always been their inexhaustible manpower, but now they have the atomic bomb and their own V2 weapons . . .'

'And the power of the idea, never underestimate that. To people suffering from deprivation and oppression, Communist ideas will always seem to offer hope, and we must never forget what that means. Communist insurgency in French Indo-China, Malaya, Indonesia, the Philippines – it can't all be explained away as a Russian conspiracy, however much the Russians may draw advantage from it.'

The prime minister returned to his desk and pressed the bell. 'As soon as you've news I'd like to hear directly,' he instructed. 'By that I mean personally. I think we should keep the wraps on this one. The fewer who know, the better.'

A knock on the door and a personal secretary came in, a young man with a shock of ginger hair. He showed the admiral out.

It was to be Singapore, that was the decision in the end. Ross protested, but HOS brushed his arguments aside impatiently. Even the admiral, suave and courteous though he was, refused to reconsider.

Ross sat in Lyons Corner House afterwards, brooding over his lunch.

'Singapore's the safest place for it,' the admiral had tried to persuade him. 'British crown colony. No undue risks, not for you – though for their side it's the lion's mouth, I'll admit. We were surprised when they agreed. Perhaps if you could tell us what's on your mind . . .'

But he couldn't tell them what was on his mind. Those memories he had to keep to himself – the jungle suddenly holding its breath, warning him . . . unexpected gunfire rattling through the high trees . . . the flash of the Jap officer's sword as it descended . . . blood spurting crimson . . .

And later when it was all over, the eyes watching him . . . accusing eyes . . . blaming him for the ambush. In Singapore too.

Over five years ago now. He could guess their reaction in the office if he confessed those fears – ghosts that might return to haunt him if he ever went back. A chitty to go and see the trick cyclist. The head-shrinker. Back to Hampshire to be kept securely under lock and key till life petered out.

The aesthetic Richards came tacking between the crowded tables towards him. Ross pushed a chair back with his foot, inviting him to sit down.

'Hear you're off?' Richards enquired.

'So they say.'

'Anywhere interesting?'

'Could be.' Find out for yourself, he thought. It was not the first time Richards had tried to probe. 'Why not get yourself some lunch and join me. It's not bad here.'

Richards eyed his plate: baked beans on toast, sausage, and fried egg. Cheap and substantial. 'I usually lunch at my club where there's time,' he excused himself. 'What you need, Ross, is a friend at court, someone back here in the office who can do you the occasional favour while you're away. What about dinner this evening? We could talk it over.'

'Talk now.'

'Bit public, isn't it? A drink then. Six o'clock?'

'Have to let you know.'

Richards left. The Section was like a wasps' nest, crawling with intrigue, every casual remark scrutinized for hidden meanings, hints of promotions, who was the new favourite, who would take over if HOS really was ill. In that respect the jungle had been a healthier place.

It was something, he supposed.

2

Ross blinked in the fierce glare of the sun as he stepped out of the plane at Kallang Airport, Singapore. The oven-heat wrapped itself around him like a padded strait-jacket, smelling of death. He had to remind himself that five years had passed since he was last here; by now those pinch-faced Nips had returned home to Kyoto or wherever: that war was over. Perhaps, too, by now its ghosts were laid.

At the top of the rickety steps he paused, relieved to be able to stretch again after a long, cramping flight. His KLM Constellation had landed two hours late and he was not in the best of moods. Bloody Singapore, stinking hot as ever. If the admiral had his way this was to be the base for the entire operation. That was how the bastards had devised his cover. No consultation of course; no ears for his objections.

A recent storm had left pools of rainwater on the tarmac, forcing the straggle of passengers to detour as they headed on foot to the three-tiered airport building. Clouds of fine steam hovered over the hot ground like morning mist. Within seconds the sweat was soaking through his shirt.

It was a sort of welcome.

Though Ross was not aware of it at the time, three men took special note of his arrival in Singapore that afternoon.

The first was Ah Lim, a stocky, muscular airport baggage handler who was wheeling his truck towards the plane when he had spotted the Englishman emerging on to the steps. He had no doubts about that broad-shouldered, tall figure. It was Hantu, long rumoured dead but now visibly resurrected.

Ah Lim had never known his real name. In the jungle they had called him 'Hantu' – a Malay word meaning ghost – for his skill in creeping up silently behind Jap sentries to despatch them to join their ancestors. A quick knife-blade between the ribs or across the jugular, that was his style. Among jungle fighters he became a legend. The Japs put a price on his head, though they never caught him; no Three Star Army comrade would ever betray him, however viciously they might be tortured.

But the war ended and Hantu went the way of all the other British, old loyalties forgotten. He had last been seen spruced up in a new khaki drill uniform, indistinguishable from the rest as they boarded a troopship in Singapore harbour. It was about a year later that news began to circulate about his death in a military hospital and Ah Lim had believed it . . . until a few days ago when the warning came to watch out for him.

The second man to notice Ross's arrival was Alun Browne of the Department of Internal Security.

Browne was on a routine visit to Kallang Airport. Twice a week he came out, sometimes more often, to keep people on their toes, and he was in the office behind the immigration desk when the KLM passengers began to file into the building. In appearance he was not untypical of the post-war Colonial Service: long, starched white shorts brushing against his ungainly knees, white knee-socks, polished black shoes, and a pale blue shirt with buttoned pockets. His most prominent feature was his Adam's apple; plus, perhaps, the permanent five o'clock shadow which darkened his lean cheeks.

A thoughtful man, such was his view of himself. He had taken a decent degree at Oxford in 1940, then joined the RAF and picked up a wartime non-flying commission. Mainly administrative duties, with regular hours and some time to read. Even now in Singapore he still kept up his Latin: ten lines of Virgil before bed every night. It calmed the soul.

As for the Colonial Service – well, maybe its appeal was largely romantic, the lure of exotic places, though the political problems could be a genuine challenge. And he was single, nothing to tie him down to some grey job in Britain.

'Anything interesting?' he enquired as the freckled young immigration officer returned to the office bearing a pile of passports and entry application forms.

'Usual mixture. No one on the prohibited list as far as I can see.'

Idly, Browne looked over his shoulder. He liked Phil McCarthy. Worked hard, played hard. A good all-rounder who should go far.

Nothing remarkable about the entry forms, not this batch. A couple of doctors bound for a Johore hospital. Three teachers travelling together. Other young men coming out to join the Singapore offices of various commercial firms, banks, Cable & Wireless . . . A rubber planter and his wife, poor sods, posted to an upcountry rubber plantation – wasn't that the area where three white planters had recently been ambushed and murdered?

Then his eye caught a name: *Ross, Peter.*

He examined the form and a half-memory stirred. He'd come across that name before, a few days ago, though not on any watch list, nor on the notice of expected arrivals.

The passport was new, issued only a week before, date-stamped Foreign Office, London. Peter Ross, Shanghai born . . . Profession, salesman.

'Know him?' Phil had noticed his interest.

'According to his form he's employed by a typewriter company. Worth checking if he can back that up.'

Phil went out to the counter and Browne heard him call the man across. He returned with two letters on headed paper – one from the company's London head office certifying that Ross had been appointed to represent them throughout the Far East; the other being a note from the Hongkong & Shanghai Banking Corporation confirming a transfer of funds in his name. Browne tucked them into the man's passport which he added to the pile on the desk.

'Everything in order?' Phil asked.

'Thought I'd come across him in the RAF.' A white lie. He remembered now where he must have seen the name, but decided to keep it to himself. 'Not the same man though.'

'Common enough name.' Phil began stamping the passports. 'See you at the club later on?'

'Loser buys first round.' The breeze from the ceiling fan sent a form skating across the desk. Browne rescued it for him. 'You owe me a game.'

Ah Lim piled up the luggage in the centre of the customs hall, then steered his truck casually to its usual spot behind the building. From here he could easily slip unnoticed through a gate in the wire fence. Outside on the main driveway the taxi drivers were playing cards, squatting on their haunches beneath the shade of the spreading trees. As he'd expected, his cousin was among them. He settled down to watch.

Seeing Hantu again stirred memories of the weeks after Japan surrendered, when the British were so certain of their welcome they invited all Three Star Army freedom fighters to hand in their weapons at an imperialist victory parade – Union Jack, 'God Save the King', all the symbols of Empire. Ah Lim had been there, and his cousin too, watching the white masters smile as he threw his gun on the heap, a rusty shotgun which had never been fired. Their Sten guns and modern Japanese rifles had been quietly buried beforehand, for use again when the time was ripe.

It was ripe now. The armed struggle had been resumed, this time against the British themselves, but he had been ordered to keep his airport job. As a member of Min Yuen, the eyes and ears of the Party, he was in a key position there.

'*Ayee!*'

A great shout from the card players announced the end of the game. His cousin triumphantly scooped up the stake money.

'Third time I win today,' he grinned, noticing Ah Lim.

Together they went over to the battered black Austin parked fourth in the row and Ah Lim described briefly what he must do.

'Eh, if I agree, I lose more dollars than I win. And how do I know him, this Hantu?'

'Watch for my signal,' he said. His cousin had served farther east, in Kelantan, and would never have encountered Hantu.

It had taken the combined savings of the entire family to buy this taxi, rescued from a scrap heap by a Hokkien genius with a set of tools and spare parts cannibalized from other wrecks. The grant of a Government of Singapore Licence to Ply for Hire as a Hackney Carriage was proof of Hokkien skill.

'If you don't take him, we lose him,' Ah Lim insisted. 'We have orders about this man.'

His cousin agreed reluctantly. 'I take him.'

Ah Lim retired to squat in the shade of the airport

41

building with his back against a wall where he had a clear view of the main exit. Hantu was one of the first passengers to emerge, which only confirmed his suspicions. VIP treatment, that was obvious. He rubbed the side of his neck, giving the pre-arranged signal that this was their man.

As his cousin ran forward to grab Hantu's suitcase the other drivers set up a clamour of objections. Luckily a dozen or more passengers came out at that moment, among them families with children, more than enough to fill all the taxis in the line. Ah Lim waited for Hantu to be driven away before he went back to his truck.

It was after nine o'clock that evening when he met his cousin again and learned that Hantu had checked in at the Padang Hotel. Two room boys employed there, both reliable, had been tipped off to keep an eye on him. Leaving his cousin to wash and eat, Ah Lim made his way to Bugis Street, following a devious route to make sure he was not observed. He slipped through the crowds at the food stalls and entered one of the shabby houses, climbing up two flights of stairs to the room where his Min Yuen contact was waiting.

The third man to take an interest in Ross did not learn of his arrival till the following morning. Thomas Pereira, a Eurasian of middling build with a pock-scarred face and eyes that sulked behind heavy glasses, was a clerk in the Internal Security Department. He lived in government quarters and drew a salary most of his friends would have envied; nevertheless he was bitterly aware that he had risen about as high in the civil service as he was ever likely to get, given his meagre qualifications and racial origins.

That morning, as always, he was the first to turn up in the office. He removed the dust cover from his typewriter, checked the out tray, unlocked the stationery cupboard, and then went into Browne's room for a discreet nose around.

Which was when he discovered the notes on Ross.

Not that his superior had left them carelessly lying about. No, as usual he had either filed his papers in the heavy cabinet to which only he kept a key, or else burned them, using his old Ronson lighter. Pereira had often witnessed the ceremony. Browne would hold up each sheet by a corner until the flame reached his fingers, then let it float down to the worn timber floor where he'd crush the fragile cinders beneath his shoe.

What he always overlooked was that the pressure of his pencil on the paper produced clear indentations on the sheet beneath. These Pereira read as a matter of course.

At first his motive had been curiosity. Laudable curiosity, in fact; the information he gleaned made him more efficient in his work. Several times Browne praised him for having relevant files so quickly to hand.

'Keep it up, Pereira, there's a good chap!' he'd said more than once, sucking on his pipe and filling the room with smoke for the fan to disperse. 'Glad you're getting the hang of things!'

Browne despised him, that was obvious. Regarded him at best as second class: neither white nor Asian; a nobody. Not that he was unusual in that. They all looked down on him. They barred him from their clubs; they walked into the office without seeing him; they brushed past him in the street as if he didn't exist. It gnawed into his soul like a slow, corrosive acid.

He began to read Browne's secrets more systematically.

By holding the paper at right-angles to the light the indentations became easily legible. The notes on Ross were brief: his arrival on the KLM flight, the usual details, then the key passage – <u>Served Force 136. No record previous visit to Colony since repatriation 1945. Old</u>

43

<u>China Hand, almost certain fluent Chinese. Possibly use?
Query with military.</u>

Underlined, too.

Pereira went through it once again to make quite
certain he had not missed anything. Then, hearing
Browne's voice from the staircase, he screwed up the
paper and dropped it in the wastepaper basket. It was the
one place Browne would never check.

'Good morning, sir.' He was back at his own desk,
apparently deep in his work.

'Eh? Oh . . . morning, Pereira. Here . . .' He produced
his keys. 'Get me the 136 file, there's a good chap. Oh,
and see if Major Wentworth is available.'

'By telephone, sir?'

'Of course by telephone, you idiot!' Browne exploded,
his obvious hangover momentarily getting the upper
hand. 'Working again, isn't it? Though I sometimes wish
Alexander Bell had never invented the damned thing!'

Pereira found the file for him, but then had some
difficulty persuading the squaddy on the army switchboard
to put him through the Major Wentworth's office. 'Geezer
with a wog accent,' he heard him saying in the background. Browne became impatient, grabbed the receiver
from him and waved him out of the room.

The office building had been constructed in the pre-war
colonial heyday when privacy was regarded as being less
important than staying cool. In place of glass, wire mesh
filled the window frames, and all interior doors were of
the ranch type, with generous gaps at top and bottom to
allow for the circulation of air. Eavesdropping presented
no problem.

'Ah Jimmy, how's the head this morning?' A chuckle.
'Me? No, I'm fine, you know me. Wish I could say the
same for young McCarthy. That was quite a session last
night!'

Pereira waited patiently, guessing that Browne must have some more serious reason for making the call than boasting about his drinking habits. He was right.

'Wondered by the way if you'd run across a chap called Ross,' he came to the point at last. 'One of the wartime 136 lot. Peter Ross. He's on my file here as having been landed from a sub just north of Malacca . . . you have him? That's the man – repatriated 1945, December. No idea what he's been up to since, have you?'

Another pause, this time much longer.

'Anything you can find out really,' Browne resumed, a note of curiosity creeping into his voice. 'For example, those family links with China, now. I mean, he is pukka, is he? You realize he's back in Singapore? Flew in yesterday. Yes. Yes, maybe we should meet over this one. Too good to miss if he really *is* pukka.'

Then a full-bodied laugh as he listened to Major Wentworth's reply. 'Pull him back into the Army? You bastard, I wouldn't put it past you!'

Pereira nodded to himself, satisfied. Yes, this could be a corker, he decided. It was a favourite expression with his now-deceased father, and one which fitted the bill exactly. A real corker.

A couple of days later, Pereira arranged a family visit to see his sister and her husband who was headmaster of a school on the city outskirts. As usual, he took his wife and two small daughters with him. They had tea on the veranda. Afterwards, the two men retired into the house for a private word, leaving their wives comparing dress-making notes while the children played tag around the palm trees.

The following Sunday the headmaster made a special trip into Singapore to drop an airmail letter in the box at the main post office. It was addressed to an old friend from his student days, now a teacher in Bangkok. A stranger reading it might have found its style pretentious with its odd mixture of literary references and old-boy gossip; only someone knowing the correct book code would be able to understand its true meaning.

But the recipient of the letter in Bangkok gave it hardly more than a glance. Within two hours he had passed it on to a pale, nervous young Russian whom he met by arrangement in a mosquito-infested bar backing on to a *klong* near the Oriental Hotel. The Russian checked the letter carefully before stuffing it into his pocket. His hand shook and beads of sweat dropped into his untasted beer. He slid an envelope along the bench.

The Bangkok teacher waited till he was back in his room before opening the envelope. As agreed, it contained several used notes – ten-dollar bills, most of them, in US currency. He would take his cut, and pass the rest back down the line.

As for the contents of the letter, he felt no curiosity whatsoever.

'First time in Singapore, Mr Ross?'

'First time, that's right.'

The lie made things seem simpler; a fresh start with a clean slate. As instructed, Ross had reported to the offices of the Typewriter & Allied Engineering Products Company Limited which part-occupied the first floor of a dilapidated building in the commercial heart of the city – not among the European-owned businesses of Orchard Road and Raffles Place, but in the bustling Chinese quarter where Peking man, whoever he might be, should find it easier to contact him discreetly. It was a genuine, London-registered firm which was long-established in the Far East; through one of its British directors he had temporary accreditation as a roving sales representative which offered him all the freedom of movement he needed.

The offices might well make a good base. On his first day this thin-faced, middle-aged Chinese had introduced himself as Mr Peng, head clerk, though he seemed to be alone there. The local manager Tim Moody was, he knew, in hospital. A letter had been in his pigeon-hole when he checked into the Padang Hotel:

Dear Ross,
Sorry I'm not around to extend the wonted hand of greeting but the quack has ordered me into hospital to have my leg drained. Our head clerk Mr Peng will help you find your bearings in the office. If you have a moment to harry the Oriental Telephone & Electric Co. about our phone (out of order for two months now) I'd be grateful. The thing is to keep nagging them.

Yours
Tim Moody

P.S. Welcome to Singapore.

Moody's hint was sound. For the next few days he immersed himself in files and office routines, demonstrating at least to Mr Peng that he intended to put some pep into the company. It was the best cover for him while waiting for contact to be made. Never take cover for granted, he remembered the instructor insisting. Work at it. It also helped him subdue those memories, though everything about Singapore screamed at him not to forget – the steam heat, the smells as he passed the food stalls, the familiar babble of Cantonese, Hokkien, Malay, Tamil, and sing-song English. I give you special price, tuan. How much you wan'? Taxi, tuan, where you go?

Five days later they had still not been in touch. By now he felt he had become an expert on the typewriter situation in the Malayan peninsula. He was wasting his time.

Unless . . .

Unless the whole business were some elaborate hoax dreamed up by the Section to observe his reactions. They would be watching him, checking if he sent any messages. Their distrust had been undisguised, the question marks about him obvious in their minds. Several times he had sensed he was being followed.

He sat at Moody's desk thinking about it. The electricity was off again, the ceiling fan motionless. Not so much as a whisper of breeze came through the unglazed windows, only the usual sour stench from Singapore river, redolent of decomposition.

Mr Peng came in, pausing by the half-doors to try the switches. 'Still no current?'

'No, and it's stinking hot. Like a Turkish bath.'

Mr Peng managed a discreet smile. 'You will get used to it. I shall go now to the Oriental Telephone Company again. If you leave the office, Mr Ross, please remember to lock the door. Mr Moody plans to take on more staff, but London has not yet authorized.'

Left alone, Ross closed the file he had been checking and went to the window. Along the road a Chinese food hawker approached, half-walking, half-running, bent under the weight of a charcoal stove and other containers which he carried suspended from the ends of the bamboo pole balanced across his shoulder. His obvious pitch would be under the trees farther along; instead, he chose to set up shop in a scrap of shade by the godown wall opposite.

Ross watched him curiously. He'd not seen a hawker there before.

In the outer office, Mr Peng's domain, he had a better view of the man. From that position the hawker could observe the doorway and any callers. It was a good surveillance post, though he'd need a runner, of course; maybe he had several.

Ross locked the door, though its timbers were so worn, a good kick would burst it open. Outside, the high sun licked his pale skin like an eager flame. As he stepped across the deep drain, slimy with rotting garbage, a taxi shaved past him sounding its horn stridently.

The hawker betrayed no interest in him, not even looking up from stirring the chicken and noodles cooking in a flat pan on the charcoal stove. Glazed eyes, sunken cheeks, emaciated body making him seem older than he probably was: opium smoker, Ross guessed. No room for him in the New China.

'I'll have some of that,' Ross said in English, pointing.

A woman customer was already there, squatting in the shade, her loose black trouser legs pulled up over her knees. She held the small bowl close to her lips, her chopsticks flashing as she shovelled the food into her mouth. They could weave a web around him, Ross thought, and he would never know.

To eat, he stood with his back to the godown wall and kept an eye on the road. Lesson one: Guard Your Back. The dark taste of soya in the food recalled his childhood, sending his mind wandering down half-forgotten lanes till an unexpected cackle from the woman brought him back into the present.

'*Hao-a?*' the hawker encouraged him, grinning broadly.

The woman laughed again, loudly, revealing gold fillings.

His chopsticks, he realized. Without thinking, he was using them Chinese-style, not awkwardly as they'd expect of a European. The months on ice in London had blunted his instincts and those bastards in the Section must have known it. Was that their little intrigue – hoping he'd trip himself up?

To cover his mistake he briefly joined in the woman's

laughter, then went on eating. That sort of slip would cost him his life one day.

But before he could brood over it a car drew up alongside him, a maroon-coloured Riley in showroom condition, brand-new and glistening in the intense sunlight. A lean British face peered out.

'I say, you're Ross, aren't you?'

A high-voltage charge shot through him at the sound of his name being bawled out in the open street. He felt exposed . . . naked and vulnerable. He stepped towards the car, instinctively wanting to shut the man up. Or turn and run.

'On my way to call on you at your office,' the man bumbled on cheerfully without moderating his voice. 'Lucky I spotted you here. But don't hurry. Finish your – whatever it is – while I find somewhere to park.'

The car purred away, leaving Ross seething with anger. He handed back his bowl of food half-finished. Who the hell this colonial idiot might be he'd no idea. Not anyone he could remember ever having seen before, that was certain. Not Moody either; only that morning he'd heard it would be another three or four days before Moody was out of hospital.

When the man reappeared on foot Ross examined him carefully. Spotless white shorts, knee socks, striped tie . . . Colonial Service perhaps, that was his guess. Desk wallah. But then how did he know his name? Who had been talking?

'Found a spot of shade just round the corner. Hope she doesn't pick up any scratches.' The man glanced back as if to reassure himself. 'Only took delivery of her yesterday. There's a two-year waiting list usually.'

'Pulled a few strings?' Ross asked conversationally, trying to sound relaxed.

'Oh, nothing like that!' A flush spread under his dark

midday stubble. 'Not in Singapore, you know. We run a tight ship here. That sort o' thing's very much frowned upon. D'you mind if we go up to your office? I'd like a word in private, if that's possible.'

Up to your office, Ross noticed. No pretence about not knowing it was on the first floor. So just who was he?

They crossed the road behind a gang of four Chinese coolies who were struggling with a heavy-laden handcart, blocking the lane of traffic. Then Ross led the way up the cement staircase and unlocked the door.

'My name's Browne,' the man said once they were inside. 'Alun Browne. Department of Internal Security.'

'You obviously know my name.'

'Of course.'

As they went through the outer office Browne's eyes lingered on the display of staid black typewriters.

'No staff?'

'Mr Peng. He's gone to chase up the phone company – yet again. Moody's the manager, but he's off sick.' As if you didn't know, he thought. He gestured towards the rattan armchair in Moody's office, inviting Browne to sit down. 'Now how can I help you, Mr Browne? Sell you a typewriter?'

'I've been checking through your immigration form, Ross. Wondered how long you intend staying here.'

'A few days. Weeks. Who can tell?'

'You can't be more specific?'

'My territory's the whole of the Far East. What's the problem?'

He almost hoped there was one. To be deported by the civilian authorities would really spike the Section's guns. Serve the bastards right if they *were* playing games with him. And the longer Peking man kept him waiting, the more convinced he became.

'No, no – there's no problem. No.' Browne produced a

black-stemmed pipe, already filled, and began to light it, puffing out clouds of pungent smoke which hung on the still air. 'I notice you're described by your company as a sales representative. You'll need to base yourself somewhere.'

'That's not yet decided.' Ross spoke curtly, trying to imply it was none of Browne's concern. The man had an elephant-thick hide.

'You could do worse than Singapore.' The tobacco cloud spread, mushroom-shaped, beneath the motionless fan blades. Browne leaned forward, emphasizing his words with his pipe stem. 'Ross, I'll put my cards on the table. We need you here.'

'Why?' The blunt statement caught him unprepared. Was Browne part of their set-up? Was this what they had planned?

'I think you can guess why.'

'You tell me.'

'Very well, if that's what you want. Your name is Peter Ross, aged thirty-three, previously Sergeant Ross of Force 136, Special Operations Executive. You were here in Malaya during the Japanese occupation working in a liaison capacity with the Malayan People's Anti-Japanese Army, mostly run by Chinese Communists. At the end of the war you were with a British Army intelligence unit in Berlin, at least for a year or so until you were invalided out.' Browne had it all pat, reciting the details from memory. He must have a mind like a card index, Ross thought. 'Do I need to go on? There is nothing about you I don't know. Well, now we need you again.'

'To do what?'

The statement that he had been invalided out of the Army offered the only glimmer of light. It was a fiction that Section had invented in Berlin to help him disappear convincingly from Army records, a convenient full-stop to prevent some inquisitive clerk stumbling on the truth. In Browne's case the ruse had obviously worked. That meant, too, that he had gone through Army channels for his information; it had not come from the admiral, or anyone else in the Section.

Or had it, he wondered suspiciously. Since his return from Russia he was no longer certain of anything.

'To do what?' he repeated.

On the low table between them lay a copy of the *Straits Times*. Browne picked it up, tapping it to draw his attention to the lead story. Communist bandits had abused a troop train, choosing a place where the line passed through thick jungle. A textbook SOE-style operation: well-placed plastic explosive; a pressure switch beneath each rail; then rake the wreckage with Sten guns. Only this time the crowded train had been carrying not Nips but young British conscripts. The casualty toll was high.

'Kids,' said Browne angrily. 'And you sit there quibbling. What's bloody got into you? You've lived with these terrorists in their jungle camps. You know them. You speak Chinese, even. I'll tell you one thing, Ross. We do need your help desperately, but if you refuse we can make things very uncomfortable for you.'

Christ, he's trying to recruit me. Hadn't he warned the admiral against Singapore?

Browne was waiting for an answer, but what the hell could he say? He couldn't risk even being seen talking to Internal Security. The moment he heard of it, Peking man would abort the entire operation, leaving him even deeper in the shit with the Section.

'I've been ill,' he said weakly. 'This job is the first break I've had. I can't afford to throw it up.'

Browne relaxed again. 'Not asking you to, nothing like that. Carry on selling typewriters if that's what you want.

In fact it suits us better that way, so long as you use Singapore as your base. It wouldn't involve much time. Our big problem is intelligence assessment. We'd wish to consult you, about personnel mainly, and occasionally to sit in on interrogations which would involve some travel up-country, though you could always claim that was typewriter business. We'd put you behind a screen where you'd be invisible to the suspect. Not too much to ask, is it?'

'I'd have to consult head office.'

'If you must – but no details, mind. Call it translation work or something.'

'As for Moody, I've not even met him yet. Till he gets out of hospital I've no idea what the plan of campaign might be. You haven't exactly chosen the right moment.'

'I don't understand you, Ross. A man with your background. Not a Commie yourself, are you? Because if you are, speak up now. We'll have you out of Singapore before you know what's hit you.'

Ross laughed at him without bothering to answer. 'How d'you think I could fit it in? Not even the phones work in this place. Do something about the phones and I might feel more sympathetic.'

'So it boils down to that. Kids being killed and all you worry about is getting the telephone fixed. I thought you might have more moral fibre. Seems I was wrong.'

'Will you see to it? It would help.'

'Nothing else on your shopping list while I'm at it?'

'Not yet. I don't know about Moody.'

'Moody had a bad time in the war. Interned by the Japs who sent him to work on the Burma railway. Lost a leg. You'll like him.' Browne stood up, heading for the door. 'But don't get him involved in this, Ross. Keep it to yourself.'

'I've agreed to nothing yet.'

'You will.' Browne paused, on the point of leaving. 'Oh, and just a tip, Ross. If I were you I'd not make a habit of eating from these hawker chappies. Hygiene's not a strong point with them. I'll put you up for the Cricket Club when you're settled in. They do quite a decent lunch.'

Ross felt hot, thirsty, and furious. He needed to get out of that office to do some straight thinking. In those jungle camps they'd helped keep each other alive – did that mean nothing any longer? Let alone Peking man, and the Section.

Leaving a note for Mr Peng, he locked up and went in search of a taxi. The sun was at its hottest and he stuck to the covered five-foot way along the front of the buildings, dodging between the piled-up, empty packing cases. Behind him he spotted a coolie he'd previously noticed lounging near his office. No point in trying to shake him off. They knew well enough which hotel he was staying at.

Almost immediately he reached the main road a taxi came along and the coolie fell back, giving up the race. Maybe the taxi driver himself – a sullen-looking, bullet-headed Chinese – was next in the relay. No shortage of manpower on their side, that was obvious.

In the hotel reception a ceiling fan was spinning zanily like some World War One fighter preparing for take-off, though it did nothing to cool the baking heat. Behind the desk the Indian clerk reached for his key without bothering to stand up.

'Any messages?'

'No messages, Mr Ross.'

That didn't surprise him. There never were any messages, not since Moody's letter.

Though the place was equipped with a lift of sorts, Ross

preferred the stairs. By the time he reached his second floor room the sweat was dripping off him.

The door was unlocked, slightly ajar.

He realized he was trembling as he stood pressed back against the wall considering what to do. Since the interrogation he'd tried to build up his muscles again, get back into condition, but he wasn't ready. The bastards must have known it.

Reflected on the chipped edge of the wardrobe mirror he glimpsed a slight movement. Then a woman's voice addressed him in educated Chinese. It sounded coldly neutral, like an airport announcement.

'Please come in, Mr Ross. And close the door.'

She sat on the hard upright chair by his writing table, scrutinizing him coolly as he entered, and saying nothing as he rapidly checked the room and bathroom to make sure she was alone.

'Do relax, Mr Ross.'

Back in China before the Jap invasion he had seen dozens like her. She was a fashion-plate example of Shanghai sophistication: pale, sensitive features with a touch of make-up for emphasis, big dark eyes, and an expression of total self-control calculated to freeze any approach. She wore a *cheongsam* of deep-green silk brocade, sleek and expensive; through its side-slit she displayed more of her black stockings than he felt able to cope with on a hot afternoon. Within her reach lay a small bulging handbag; perhaps a pistol, he guessed from the shape.

'Identities first.' She accepted his gaze with indifference. 'I have to ask you where you intend to celebrate your birthday.'

'Jakarta,' he answered, as instructed.

'I prefer Tonbridge,' she responded mechanically.

Do you, he thought. Why the hell had the Section chosen Tonbridge?

'The time of your meeting,' she continued, betraying no more interest than the Speaking Clock, 'is nine this evening. The place is Lien Jee Bar. Buy yourself a drink and wait until you are contacted. You must be alone, you understand? If not, our representative will cancel the arrangement.'

'So you are not the one?'

'Did you imagine I was? I'm afraid not, Mr Ross. I do not even know who you are, nor what the meeting is about.'

'Where do I find this Lien Jee Bar?'

'You are familiar with Lavender Street?'

'Familiar, no.'

'It's a street many European men like to visit anonymously. Ask your taxi driver to drop you at the corner with Serangoon Road. Tell him you will walk from there; he will not be surprised. Look out for the second turning on your right, and you will find Lien Jee Bar.'

Did he detect a sense of humour in that twist of her lips? Perhaps not, he decided reluctantly. She seemed as cold as unquarried marble, quite unlike the fresh-faced peasant girls of the New China newsreels.

Before leaving she paused in front of the wardrobe mirror to check her appearance. It was an automatic gesture, and unnecessary. Not so much as an eyelash was out of place. He passed her the handbag, but it was soft to the touch; he was mistaken about the pistol. New stockings, probably. She'd been shopping, which figured.

'Nine o'clock,' she repeated.

He nodded and opened the door for her, briefly inspecting the corridor first before standing aside to let her out.

After a moment he heard the metallic clatter of the ancient lift gates, followed by the characteristic whine as she went down. One floor only. He went along to check and the arrow on the old-style indicator pointed to the first floor, so was she staying in the same hotel? But probably not, he decided; at the far end of that floor was a staircase leading down to the bar, and she needed then only to slip out into the garden to reach the street without passing the reception desk.

He went back into his room, locking and bolting the door before taking his shower. As usual when he turned on the cold tap there was a rush of scalding hot water. It took a few minutes for it to cool down sufficiently for him to stand under it to let it wash the heat out of his skin. He found himself thinking not of her but of Browne, the idiot Browne who had yelled out his name from the car window. That was where the real danger lay, he felt instinctively, with people like Browne.

But then who was he to point the finger, he thought bitterly. The ambush which had haunted him for months after . . . himself hiding in the undergrowth, watching helplessly as the Jap officer's sword did its work of execution – hadn't his own wrong decision been the cause of it?

His, and no one else's.

3

It was already dark when Ross set out on foot to report to the admiral at Raffles Hotel. He ignored the clamouring taxi drivers hooting their horns to attract his custom, and did not worry either about being followed. No doubt someone was slinking along behind him to report on his movements. Good luck to them! There was no way he could keep a visit to Raffles secret.

Ross was in a good humour. The cicadas were shrill and the clear night had a humid, hot-house smell which reminded him of some of the better days in those jungle camps when they had sat around in the evening discussing ideas, their dreams of the future, everyone optimistic.

Crossing the Padang he glanced up at the silhouette of St Andrew's Cathedral spire, incongruously English against the star-rich tropical sky. What would be its fate, he wondered, when the Empire had finally gone? Would Singapore's new masters order its demolition? But would it even matter when in the long run only the cicadas would survive – hadn't he read somewhere that insects were unaffected by the atom bomb's radiation? They were the first and last inhabitants of the earth, were insects; humans were merely a passing phase. It was a reassuring thought.

Raffles Hotel, brightly lit, suddenly disappeared into the darkness as he approached. He was arriving in time for yet another power cut. As he went up the steps he could see the staff padding about in the gloom armed with emergency oil lamps which cast giant moving shadows against the walls.

The head waiter intercepted him.

'Jacket and tie for restaurant, tuan.'

'You're joking.'

'No, tuan. Hotel rule.'

At one time Ross might have offered him a terse description of what he could do with his jacket and tie. Outside it was 95° Fahrenheit at least; inside, with the heat from those pressure lamps, it was like a steel furnace. But he'd trained himself over the years not to stick his neck out unnecessarily, which was why he was still alive.

'You have cold beer in ice-box?'

'Yes, tuan.'

'That's all I want. Which way's the bar?'

'Ver' good menu tonight,' the man wheedled, changing his tune.

Ross shook his head and pushed past him.

He chose a table in the shadows as far as possible from the nearest pressure lamp. The admiral was there already, he noticed, togged up in a white tuxedo like he'd just stepped out of some Noël Coward movie. With him were two other people, a husband and wife if the woman's scathing remarks were anything to judge by. Her protruding teeth flashed menacingly as she spoke; her voice carried above the general murmur of conversation. They were obviously in for a pleasant evening.

'Tiger beer,' Ross ordered when the boy came over. 'Make sure it's cold.'

There was plenty of time. It was barely seven-thirty. The admiral had seen him, though he gave no sign.

He scooped up a handful of peanuts from the saucer on the low table in front of him and chewed them absent-mindedly as he surveyed the other customers. Whites, all of them; for the most part probably British. Apart from himself only two were without jackets, both brawny red-necked men perched on bar stools. They carried revolvers carelessly thrust into their belts. Planters, he guessed; that must be their car he'd noticed outside, a saloon from which all the glass had been removed and replaced by solid armour with flapped eye-slits for driving.

The sight of them brought back Browne's visit. Only one answer to that, he knew. The question was, would the admiral agree?

The 'boy' brought his beer, filling the tall glass with froth, then leaving the bottle on the table. He'd be – how old? Forty perhaps? No doubt the patriarch of a large family, if they had been lucky enough to survive the Japs.

'More peanuts,' he requested.

'More peanuts, tuan.'

Twenty minutes, Ross decided as he raised his glass to his lips, silently toasting the admiral. Twenty minutes, and then he'd make his move.

It was like turning the pages of an old photograph album, being back in Singapore. Souvenirs of imperial days. In the thirties, when he'd first come here, the colonial expatriates in their long, light dresses and white dinner jackets – Browne and his like – had seemed like gods, little dreaming that slant-eyed Japs were even then preparing to destroy their paradise. At that time the Japs were already jackbooting Shanghai and he was vaguely heading for the UK, working his passage on an Aussie freighter which was holed up here for three weeks waiting for cargo. But now those snapshots had turned brown with age. He stared around the room. Had they really no idea what was happening in the world? No one could turn back the clock, however many coins they threw into the wishing well.

'Boy! *Dua stingah!*' an imperious voice shrilled out from across the room. 'Boy!'

Time to move.

Ross took one last cool pull at his beer, then dropped

some money beside his glass – more than enough – and stood up. No heads turned as he threaded his way between the tables in the direction of the washroom. No one was interested in a man on his own. Plenty of those in Singapore.

The water gushing into the washbowl was lukewarm. He leaned over it to splash his face and the back of his neck. The WC cabins were unoccupied, their doors ajar. He was alone, with only the pressure lamp's hiss and a persistent mosquito for company.

It was several minutes before the admiral appeared. He glanced briskly around, then went over to the urinal stalls. 'You've heard something, I imagine,' he enquired with his back to Ross.

'I want a plane out. First flight tomorrow.'

'Why?'

Ross told him about Browne. 'It's inviting trouble, staying here. I think he's having me watched. Every move I make he'll record on his file. He's that kind.'

'You're sure? You could be imagining things. Nerves.'

'Someone's keeping tabs on me, I'm sure of that much – either his people or the comrades. My money's on him. They're too obvious.'

It could still be the Section's doing; Ross had thought of that too. He trusted none of the bastards, and this smooth-mannered admiral least of all.

'They'll know you've been here tonight?' the admiral asked.

'Naturally. D'you think they don't have people here on their payroll?'

Frowning, the admiral crossed to the washbowls and turned on a tap. 'No plug,' he commented disapprovingly as the water swirled and gurgled into the outlet pipe. 'You'd think they'd have plugs by now.'

'You're not bloody listening, are you?' With difficulty

Ross kept his voice low. 'I want out. I don't give a damn where. Anywhere. Bangkok.'

The admiral appeared doubtful. 'I could get someone to drop a word in his ear. Browne, you said?'

'Jesus Christ, why don't you broadcast it on the tannoy?' Ross exploded at him.

'No detail. Just hands off.'

'Shit!'

'It's the simplest solution. However, I can see you're against it. Can't you at least stay on till our friends have made contact?'

'They have. It's tonight.'

'Ah. What time and where?'

'That doesn't concern you.' Observing the admiral's eyes narrow, he added, 'Sir.'

No need to make an enemy of him unnecessarily. Why, though, had he risked coming to Singapore in person? If he was genuinely as important as Richards had claimed, he'd be a prize catch for the other side. And pumped full of drugs, how long would *he* hold out under interrogation?

Voices from the corridor warned them they were about to have company. The admiral reached for a towel.

'Good luck,' he said quietly.

Ross stepped into the nearest cabin and closed the door. It was the two planters from the bar. He briefly glimpsed their reflection in the mirror before ducking down out of sight. He heard the admiral say Evening to them as he left.

They took their time, quietly discussing whether to look for somewhere to stay in Singapore for the night or risk the drive back along Johore's jungle roads, notorious for their bandit ambushes. Then, suddenly, silence. A mosquito whined in his ear like a Jap dive bomber. Instinctively he slapped his neck. Blood from its crushed body smeared his fingers; his own blood, mingled with his sweat.

He pulled the chain before unbolting the door, just to sound convincing. Unnecessarily as it turned out. Apart from himself the washroom was empty. He considered leaving the hotel by the rear entrance, but changed his mind. Instead, he waited openly on the front steps and allowed the Malay porter to signal to the first taxi in line.

'Cathay cinema,' he instructed the Chinese driver.

The problem was how to make certain he was not being followed. Eight out of ten people in Singapore were Chinese; they could merge into the background. He glanced back through the rear window but could not be certain if anyone was on his tail or not.

The Cathay building was several storeys high, the tallest in the city, and crowned with a large Hennessy advertisement which stood out as a landmark. They were showing a Rita Hayworth movie. The first house was emptying out and the second already crowding in as he arrived. Mostly Europeans. He paid off his taxi which was immediately grabbed by a boisterous group of Royal Navy able seamen on shore leave.

He felt tense and uncertain, no longer trusting his own instincts, those deep-seated reflexes which had brought him alive through the Soviet Union, always keeping him that vital one step ahead. Somewhere on the way they had died on him. He was vulnerable. The chattering cinemagoers brushing past him offered some temporary cover, but sooner or later the crush would thin out.

Then he saw a Sikh-driven taxi and headed for it. The two previous passengers were Englishwomen, missionaries by the look of them, and they fussed over paying the fare, counting out their coins to present the driver with the exact amount. Ross got in, hiding his impatience with difficulty.

'Tanglin Club,' he grunted once they had gone. Then, waiting till the taxi had turned into Orchard Road and was picking up speed, he ordered the Sikh to go to Lavender Street instead.

'Lavender Street? OK tuan!'

With a squeal of tyres he performed a rapid U-turn which sent Ross sprawling across the back seat. A protesting fanfare of horns blared out from the other cars, but none imitated his move. Perhaps he'd been wrong, Ross thought; this time he had no shadow.

'These drivers no traffic sense, tuan,' the Sikh glanced back, grinning. 'But I get you there double quick. Lavender Street very nice girls. You want good house?'

'Just drop me on the corner.'

'What girl you want? Chinese girl? Malay? Try Malay girl, like ripe mango. All kind of girl you find, only no Sikh girl. Sikh girl stay home, wait for marriage.'

'That right?'

The taxi slowed down. 'Where you want stop? Lavender Street start here.'

The street was in darkness save for soft pools of light from oil lamps in the windows of several bars. He got rid of the taxi, thrusting a couple of notes at the Sikh without waiting for change, then began to pick his way over the uneven ground. A foul stench rose from the open drains; the air was still, and suffocatingly hot. His head ached. The ear-piercing stridulation of the cicadas jarred on his nerves. As he passed one bar an obese Chinese in thick glasses waddled out to greet him, promising untold delights if only he would step inside.

'Push off,' Ross answered briefly.

He found the side road the woman in the hotel had described. The Lien Jee Bar was not on the corner but about a hundred yards down.

Holding back the bead curtain, he surveyed the place

suspiciously before going in. He assumed the name Lien Jee must mean 'Lotus Seed', which sounded romantic enough to Western ears; in reality, the bar was just as down-at-heel as the others he'd passed. The pale blue paint was flaking off the walls. Much of the counter's panelling, once ornate, was now broken. Above it hung an over-populated fly paper; behind, the large mirror next to the shelving was tarnished and cracked.

No electricity, of course. This whole area seemed to be affected by the same power cut that had hit Raffles Hotel. The coloured light bulbs, dulled, only emphasized the general air of drabness, though the management had provided two oil lamps. Streams of thin black smoke rose from the funnel of each, further darkening the ceiling.

The only customer was a Royal Navy stoker with two long-service stripes on his arm. He sat morosely over his beer, ignoring the Chinese hostess next to him. A second girl, also Chinese, slouched over to Ross as he sat down. Her cheap cotton *cheongsam*, some sizes too small, cut into her bulging flesh.

'Hallo, Johnnie,' her lips pouted, thick lips set in a full moon face. 'You wan' buy me a drink?'

She leaned closer to him, trying out an expression of sultry passion which she'd probably rehearsed in front of that stained mirror. It convinced no one, least of all herself. He saw the mockery in her dark eyes, and it reminded him of another Chinese girl he had once known, a girl in a jungle-green uniform, a Sten gun in her hands. A girl whose ghost had lived on with him till Russia had jammed all memories.

'Me Susie. You?'

'Johnnie will do fine,' he told her. 'Where the hell's that drink?'

A man appeared from behind the bar, a cigarette stuck

in the corner of his mouth. He gave the table a perfunctory wipe with a grey rag. As he straightened up again, a length of ash dropped on to the damp smear, but he left it there.

'Whisky-soda?'

'Beer,' said Ross.

'No col' beer. No curren' for ice-box.'

'OK, then warm beer.' He turned to the girl. 'And you?'

'He know my drink.'

'And chop-chop, eh? Compris?'

'OK.' The man shuffled away.

Ross felt irritated. The sweat was soaking through his shirt again. His throat was dry. A mosquito – the place was alive with them – landed on his wrist. He tried to kill it with a hard slap from his other hand, but missed. It flew lazily away, leaving a reddening, itchy spot on his skin. The girl laughed and made some remark about it, but he didn't listen.

When the man reappeared it was without the drinks. He leaned forward confidentially. 'I get you col' beer, tuan. Upstairs. Ver' good room upstairs.'

Something was wrong, he could sense it. He wiped the sweat from the back of his neck, trying to think straight.

'You can bring the beer down here, can't you?' He stared hard into the man's eyes, but saw nothing, only an uncomprehending sullenness. 'Well? What's wrong?'

'Johnnie,' – the girl put her hand on his arm, pleading – 'Come with Susie, yes? You first man tonight, I promise. You come? For birthday?'

Christ, Susie must be the contact! She stood up, holding out her hand to him. Reluctantly he got to his feet, sick in his stomach at the thought of it. At the moment he'd have paid his last penny to be anywhere other than in that bar. Those ducks in St James's Park didn't know just how

67

lucky they were. They had asked for him by name and here he was – obediently walking into their man-trap. Yet he couldn't turn back, not now.

He slipped his arm about her well-fleshed shoulders and allowed her to lead him to the doorway behind the bar. The stoker winked pointedly and guffawed, but Ross ignored him.

At the foot of the narrow stairs he disentangled himself to let her go up first. He followed, staying a few paces behind, out of range in case she took it into her head to lash out at him with her heel. The barman disappeared into a back room.

'Here,' she pointed, pausing when she reached the landing to show him the right door.

'You first.'

When she shook her head, hanging back, he gripped her elbow and pushed her into the room ahead of him.

It was sparsely furnished – just a bed, a chair, a table and a bowl of soapy water on a crudely carpentered washstand. A faded magazine picture of the royal family was pinned to the wall. Princess Elizabeth and Princess Margaret Rose would be silent witnesses of whatever was about to happen.

Peking's envoy – if that's what he really was – was alone in the room. He stood up the moment Ross entered. With a quick word in Chinese, he dismissed the girl who left immediately, without question, closing the door behind her.

'I hope you will excuse me, Mr Ross, for addressing you in my own tongue,' he apologized once the girl had gone. 'I unfortunately have no command of English.'

Ross stumbled over his reply and had to apologize in turn for the fact that it was some years since he had last had an opportunity to speak Chinese. Then he paused, offering the envoy the chance to make the next move.

It was easy enough to guess he must be some kind of official. His lined face seemed at once authoritative and distinguished, like that of some old war lord – though no older than sixty, Ross estimated. He spoke quietly in the polished Mandarin of the classically educated. His clothes were discreet but costly: a white shirt with a sober tie, and a light blue tailored suit, too well-fitting to conceal a weapon. He would not have been out of place in Raffles Hotel; nor in Buckingham Palace, come to that. In this brothel he stood out like a nun at an orgy. How he managed to survive in the New China was not easy to fathom.

'I propose we dispense with the rigmarole of birthdays in Jakarta,' he said with a faint smile. 'I have no doubt about your identity, Mr Ross, and the information I bring will vouch for mine. That is your beer on the table, by the way. Won't you sit down?'

'I'll sit on the bed.' There was only one chair.

For a few moments the envoy seemed lost in thought as if wondering how to begin. Only an occasional *click* broke the silence as an insect collided against the spluttering oil lamp.

'Mr Ross, what do you know about Manchuria?'

'I have never been there.'

'Then you'll forgive me if I indulge in a brief history lesson. The Chinese name is the Three Eastern Provinces, as I'm sure you remember from your schooldays, and it was of course the home of the Manchu emperors. The Japanese invaded in the early thirties in a major act of aggression against a weakened China and they established their own puppet state. They built up industrial capacity, roads, and port facilities, all for their own use. Also military installations. But in 1945, after the defeat of Hitler, our Russian allies came to our aid by sending the Red Army to liberate the occupied areas and handing back control to the then government in Peking.' The envoy paused again, this time for emphasis. 'Mr Ross, this is the point to note. By the terms of the agreement, our Soviet friends retained certain military bases in Manchuria which were previously Japanese.'

'And Manchuria borders on North Korea,' Ross commented. 'What kind of installations are they?'

The Soviets still held a naval base at Port Arthur, that much was well known. And airfields. But instead of replying directly, the envoy appeared to change the subject.

'Have you heard of Khabarovsk in the Soviet Union?'

'A show trial was held there, wasn't it?' He vaguely remembered a short paragraph or two in a recent newspaper. No one had taken much notice of it.

'The Khabarovsk War Crimes Trial. I believe the West dismissed it as merely Soviet propaganda.'

'But you think differently?'

'Twelve Japanese officers – one being the former Commander of the Japanese Kwantung Army – were found guilty of organizing experimentation on Chinese and Soviet prisoners-of-war in Manchuria. Their aim was to test the effect of various bacteria on living persons in order to identify the best strains for bacteriological warfare. According to evidence at the trial, they had several research centres for this work, though they managed to destroy most during their retreat.'

'But not all, I take it.'

'At least one was captured intact. We believe that work there still continues.'

'On humans?'

'No, we do not suspect our Russian allies of that. That would constitute a crime against humanity. But there have been whispers of field tests in Korea if the fortunes of the

70

Korean People's Army should change and the Americans drive them back.'

'A germ warfare attack on United Nations troops?'

'It is only a whisper.'

'And that would not be a crime against humanity?'

'American bombing has already killed or maimed many innocent people. But germ warfare is different, I agree, hence this meeting, Mr Ross. If a large-scale epidemic should start, who knows where it would end.'

The envoy's manner was dry, almost academic, with no hint of drama. It was the old mandarin style, Ross recognized well enough, and he found himself imitating it. They might have been discussing a minor point of administration rather than human suffering.

'Do we know which disease?' he enquired, matching his dispassionate manner.

'Plague, typhus, typhoid, cholera, smallpox, anthrax, tuberculosis, dysentry, salmonella – the experiments covered a wide range.' He made them sound like dishes served at some diplomatic banquet. 'Which one was chosen for development I have no idea. Of course you realize I am no specialist, merely a messenger.'

'How are the bacteria to be dispersed? What delivery system?'

'The information is outside my competence.'

'One research centre, you said? D'you know the location?'

'I know only what I've told you.' The envoy smiled, but it was a private smile which revealed nothing. 'You must understand, Mr Ross, that your side insisted on this preliminary meeting on British soil. I was selected to convey this information precisely because of my ignorance of these matters. If your British colonial police should choose to arrest me, what will they learn? Nothing that you have not already been told. If you are interested in

71

more, and agree to help us, another meeting will be arranged. Not in Singapore.'

'In China?'

'If that is your wish.'

'Is it yours?'

'Again that is outside my brief.' He stood up and replaced the chair neatly by the table. 'In a few days you will be contacted for your reply – a simple yes or no. If the answer is yes, there will be a further short delay before details of time and place reach you. Unless you wish to decide now, in which case time will be saved.'

'What kind of help?' Two quick paces and he stood between the envoy and the closed door, blocking his way.

'A link, Mr Ross. A channel of communication. Wasn't that understood?'

It was too smooth, he thought; too bloody smooth to be credible. If Peking wished to talk to Whitehall they didn't need him as a go-between.

Princess Elizabeth and Princess Margaret Rose looked down at him from the wall, waiting for his next move.

'The Soviet Union is your ally, a fellow socialist state, sharing the same philosophy.'

'Mr Ross, when you have a good friend you do not question his motives, yet there are times when you may be curious about what he is doing in your country. In those circumstances we must gather our information by the most discreet means possible.'

'And pass it on to Britain?'

'As one ancient nation to another.'

It stank. It stank so obviously he felt an urge to laugh in the man's face. Yet he didn't. Someone had requested him by name and he needed to discover who.

'This research centre – I want exact map references beforehand, otherwise there's no deal.' Princess Elizabeth seemed to approve, though Princess Margaret Rose was more indifferent.

'I shall pass on your message. You will have to trust us, Mr Ross. We are on opposing sides in this conflict, and neither of us, I think, pretends differently, but there are certain disasters, world disasters, which a little discreet collaboration between us might help avoid.'

At Peking man's request, Ross waited alone in the room to give him time to get clear. He tried a mouthful of beer, but by now it tasted warm and flat. The air was stuffy despite there being no glass in the windows. Princess Elizabeth was preoccupied with her own thoughts and ignored him. From outside, through the steady, screeching pulse of cicadas, came the sound of passing cars mingled with occasional voices. Nothing was to be seen, only thick patches of darkness and a scattering of stars. The electricity was still off.

He pondered the envoy's last cryptic words. Discreet collaboration. He could already guess how the admiral would react – a one-way ticket to Manchuria and no argument. Back through the quicksands. After the Hampshire interrogation centre, he had found a kind of life for himself, begun to take pleasure in it even – feeding the ducks, making a sketch or two, spending the wet days in the public library reading back issues of newspapers to bring himself up to date, with no more uncertainties, no unwished-for incidents to threaten him. It was all he wanted. Not the Section though; for them it had not been enough.

Out in the darkness a car horn sounded – one long note, followed by a very short one, no more than a quick jab on the button. An obvious signal.

He moved rapidly, with no evidence, no logical reason to suspect anything, only a sudden hunch forcing him to go outside and check. At the foot of the stairs he shoved the bar owner aside. 'This way out?' he demanded, making for the back door. It was unlocked, opening on to a dark yard.

'Way out, tuan,' the man confirmed. Producing a torch, he shot the beam across the yard to reveal a solid wooden gate.

'I'll take this!' Ross grabbed the rubber-sheathed torch from his grip. To counter the protests he added: 'Don't worry, you'll get it back for Chrissake!'

Wrenching open the gate, he peered out, playing the torchlight along the rough alleyway. It illuminated heaps of rotting garbage left abandoned on either side of the stinking, open drain. For a moment he was uncertain which way to turn; then he heard voices from the far end of the alley, and sounds of scuffling. He ran lightly to the corner, taking cover behind a section of protruding wall while he checked what was going on.

As he did so, the power cut ended. The effect was dramatic. Lights flickered on in the buildings around and he saw now how the alley opened into a narrow side-road lit by a single lamp high on one end wall. Piled beneath it were some broken wooden crates. A dog scavenging among them looked round at him, then raised a leg and relieved itself.

No other sign of anyone. The voices, wherever they had come from, had now ceased. He turned to go. Perhaps he'd been mistaken.

It was not until he was almost past the crates that he noticed the half-concealed body. He shone the torch on the dead man's face. The envoy's eyes were open, staring at him accusingly. On his pale blue jacket was a small patch of blood, and more spread across his shirt front. The tear where the knife had entered was directly over the heart.

Ross was permitted no time to mourn him. Even as he was straightening up he was aware of someone's breath wheezing behind him, much too close. Swinging round, he caught the glint of the blade before, razor-sharp, it sliced through his shirt, burning over his ribs.

He twisted away and planted his shoe hard into his attacker's abdomen. The man doubled up, winded. Chinese, Ross saw, with the look of a tough, practised bruiser. He had not dropped the knife and suddenly he lunged upward.

Clumsily Ross side-stepped – any slower and he'd have joined Peking man among the discarded crates – but he succeeded in getting a grip on the thug's wrist and forced his arm back, muscle against muscle, into a lock which gave him no alternative but to drop the knife.

But he did not drop it, not soon enough. To the last second he held out, till the bone cracked and his arm went limp.

Sickened, Ross kicked the knife away, then pushed the thug hard against the wall to question him. Not even then did his antagonist give up, though his right arm hung uselessly at his side. He brought his knee up sharply, but Ross sensed his intention and dodged back. Then he charged, his head down like a bull, catching Ross in the solar plexus, leaving him clutching his stomach.

Coughing and retching, gulping in the stale warm air by the lungful, Ross cursed his own stupidity at letting himself be caught like that. He was too slow, too bloody slow to be in this business any longer. Meanwhile the thug had made off in the direction of the main road. Moments later came the sound of a car driving away rapidly and a door slamming as it accelerated.

Still struggling to recover his breath, Ross searched the ground for his torch. Finding it, he began to go through the dead envoy's pockets. It was a futile exercise. No wallet, no identification of any kind, even the tailor's tab had been cut away from the jacket pocket.

His eyes misted dizzily as he leaned over the corpse. His hand was sticky with blood. More blood dripped on to the dead man's light blue suit and it puzzled him. Only slowly did he realize it came from his own wound; his shirt was saturated with the stuff. He was forcing himself to think clearly, each step slow and deliberate, as he struggled against the waves of faintness washing over him.

He had to get away from the place, he knew that much. He couldn't risk being found with the dead man, stooping over him, their blood mingling. Never do. Had to . . . get . . . away . . .

An unsteady walk it was along that dark, narrow street, and much farther than he'd imagined to the bright lights at the far end. To stem the bleeding, he pressed his forearm across the wound while groping for the wall with his other hand to keep himself from falling. The dizziness came, and went, and came again; he longed to rest, but that was not allowed. It was against the rules. The rules of their bloody game.

Find a taxi.

Though no taxi would take him in that state, with all the blood. Yet somehow he had to contact the admiral. He had to confess . . . that was it . . . fucking confess that the line to Peking was severed before it could even be tested. His fault. Too slow. Too late to help Peking man. Reflexes useless. That thug, hired muscle probably; no more to be squeezed out of him even if they picked him up. That was his guess.

Jesus, he felt lousy!

He stopped, breathing deeply to get some oxygen to his brain. The cut across his ribs ached agonizingly. He had to lie down somewhere. That room over the bar perhaps, if he could make it up the stairs. Yes, that was it.

'Johnnie! You come with Susie now?'

She was an answer to his unspoken prayer, looming up on him as he neared the corner, flashing her teeth in a warm professional smile.

'Sure Susie.' For support he placed his arm across her comfortable, plump shoulders. 'Sure I'll come with you.'

The way he leaned on her, she probably thought he'd drunk too much; deliberately, he slurred his speech to encourage the impression. She hadn't noticed the blood, not yet. If she made a fuss he'd have to deal with her. He hoped she wouldn't.

'No, Johnnie! No!' He was about to steer her up the road towards the Lien Jee Bar when she stopped him. 'No go there, Johnnie. We go my room, yes?'

'How far?'

'No ver' far.' Then: a sharp whistle of breath through her teeth as they passed near one of the few street lamps. 'Oh, Johnnie, you hurt!'

'I need a clean shirt.' He kept his forearm tightly over the wound. 'Nothing to worry about.'

'You hurt bad!' she protested.

Any other cheap whore would have left him standing there in the street to avoid getting involved, but Susie stayed with him. Not only because of his grip on her shoulder, he reflected; she obviously had some other motive too. Or maybe the traditional heart of gold, who could tell? But he doubted it.

The place where she lived had a flight of concrete steps up the side of the house to a separate front door serving the first storey. She had to help him up, more than once waiting for him to fight down his nausea and fatigue. But at last she got him inside, along the short corridor and into her room.

Gradually he slumped to the floor at her feet. He was aware it was happening but could do nothing to stop it.

His legs gave way; his thoughts became hazy and distant. The room itself refused to stay still. Its cloud-like walls dissolved and Susie's voice receded down a long, narrow cavern.

'*Aeeyah!* Johnnie, you hurt bad!'

Vaguely he was aware of her opening his shirt, leaning over him as she struggled with the buttons, too careful simply to tear them off. He was lying flat on the cement floor and staring up at the dazzling splurge of light set in the ceiling.

'I wash you,' he heard the cavern announce. 'Wash away blood.'

The splash of water on his skin was soothing, trickling over his burning sides. His head was splitting; his mouth parched. He mumbled something about water to drink; she held a cup to his lips but it didn't help.

Once she had cleaned him up a bit, she wanted to get him on to the bed. 'Johnnie, lift up! You too heavy for me!' she insisted, trying to pull him upright with her hands under his arms, but the room refused to hold steady and he sank back again. Every limb ached. His throbbing brain felt bruised and raw inside his skull. He was still bleeding.

'I give you bandage to put on it,' she said, the worry evident in her voice. After a moment's hesitation, she rummaged in the wardrobe, then held out something white, he couldn't be certain what. 'Here, you take panty. Fresh from dhobi. Ver' clean. How much you pay?'

Despite the way he felt, he managed to extract a couple of ten dollar notes from his back pocket. She snatched at them, thrusting the cotton pants into his hand with the instruction that he should hold them tight over the wound while she fetched a doctor.

'No, no doctor,' he began to protest, but the slamming of the door cut him short.

Left alone, he succeeded in propping himself up against the bed, though he was still too giddy to risk standing. The wound was a clean cut across his ribs, not too deep despite the steady bleeding which had not yet stopped. He needed some sort of dressing on it, and stitches perhaps, and he had to prevent it from becoming infected. But he was also feverish. His skin was hot and dry; his eyes burned.

Bloody hell, he swore, what a time to fall ill! Unless the wound was already infected?

He removed the bloodstained panties and examined it as best he could, trying to get his eyes in focus, though they hazed over again immediately. Yes, the flesh was still a vigorous red and the cut seemed clean. He pressed the cloth back over it to stem the bleeding.

Time to get on the bed, he thought determinedly. Couldn't remain lying on that cement floor. It was a miracle he wasn't already crawling with ants. Gripping the bedpost, he twisted himself round on to his knees, then slowly attempted to stand up, but his legs still refused to take his weight and he fell, this time landing sprawled across the mattress. Another couple of heaves and he lay straight, breathing heavily.

He was in the process of kicking off his shoes when the door was flung open again and Susie hurried back in.

'So you move, huh? You don' wan' I help you? OK, Johnnie, so we go again!' But she stayed, glaring at the bloodstains on her worn bedsheets, her face betraying her anxiety. 'My cousin,' she introduced the young, spruce Chinese who had entered the room with her. 'Doctor.'

Her 'cousin' – if that was what he really was – had a clinical, ascetic look about him. He wore metal-framed glasses and a long-sleeved white shirt which seemed freshly starched and ironed. His sober tie was neatly anchored. Despite the stifling heat, he betrayed no hint of perspiration. When he spoke, his voice was cool and precise.

'Not a bullet wound, I hope? In case of bullet wounds a report to the police is required.'

'It was a knife.'

'You were robbed?'

'No.'

'Good. In that case I will look at the wound. My fee is one hundred dollars, payable in advance.'

'Get fucked,' Ross told him.

Perhaps the family honour was at stake, because Susie intervened, taking the doctor aside to argue with him urgently. At first he refused to listen. When he did reply, he seemed to give the impression that he could lose face by charging too little. But finally he gave in.

'Fifty dollars then,' he conceded.

'Forty.'

Ross took the notes from his pocket and spread them on the bedsheet beside him. The wound throbbed uncomfortably and the intense pain in his head shifted again as if searching for the most sensitive spot.

The doctor collected up the money, placing it carefully in his wallet. His fingers were deft as he cleaned the wound; a few stitches would be necessary. He had no anaesthetic.

'Also you have a high fever,' he said. 'For treatment of fever there is extra charge.'

Once he had gone, Ross lay back on Susie's soiled pillow and closed his eyes, unwilling even to think yet about getting back to the hotel. He was not even certain if that would be the best move. His instinct was to lie low for a few days; perhaps not in Susie's room – her link with the Lien Jee Bar would be too suspect – but maybe she knew somewhere better nearby.

He also had to get information to the admiral.

The thoughts rushed through his head chaotically, going off at sudden tangents, no pattern to them. What if the envoy's murder were merely coincidence: a thug comes across him in an alleyway, well-dressed, obviously well-heeled, so out comes the knife? It would explain why the wallet was missing. But even as Ross pieced it together he knew it would not stand up. What about the car he'd heard driving off? And the signal on the horn? One long, one short – obviously pre-arranged.

'Drink.'

'What?'

'Johnnie – *drink!*'

Opening his eyes, he found Susie leaning over him, a chipped enamel cup in her hand. He pushed himself up on the bed and his aching head immediately punished him for it. The pain was across the back of his eyes, like a saw-toothed skewer. Heat exhaustion, her doctor-cousin had diagnosed, and advised him to drink plenty of water. Obediently Susie had stirred in a spoonful of salt. It tasted foul and he managed to swallow no more than a few mouthfuls.

'More,' she insisted, but he waved the cup away.

She was right, though. He should have guessed it without needing to dish out that extra ten dollars. In his jungle days he'd experienced it often enough. At times they had been without salt for weeks; he'd had to lick up his own perspiration even. Or each other's, he and . . . Susie's eyes had reminded him of her, the girl whose name he refused to even think, bringing back the memories he'd tried so hard to suppress, quick pictures of her smiling with a sudden flash of teeth, and her torn Three Star uniform, her . . .

Oh shit!

A taxi, that would be his best course, he decided,

letting himself sink back on to the bed again. Get away from this place. If he sent Susie out for a taxi to take him to the hotel . . . Not immediately, perhaps, but as soon as it was light. A night with a whore, no one was going to ask any questions about that, but he must not put her at risk by staying longer. Pick a driver you know, he'd tell her. They all knew plenty of taxi drivers, these girls. Must do. Had to pay them their cut, didn't they?

'Sleep,' she said, switching off the light.

She stretched out on the bed beside him, but he was only vaguely aware of her. Perhaps he slept; perhaps he didn't. Either way, his thoughts flowed on in an inconsequential stream, never ceasing.

He'd know that thug again if he saw him. The pock marks around his mouth would give him away: oh yes, he'd know him without any doubt. He'd been lying in wait for the envoy, he was convinced of it now; his other theory about it maybe being a casual robbery just didn't wash. That meant someone else must have known about the meeting, didn't it? He tried puzzling it out, but instead of logical thoughts his brain produced only a jumble of disconnected impressions – the envoy's discreet, underplayed manner, self-deprecating, while blithely betraying his country's allies with this germ warfare story; the admiral's white dinner jacket; Potts feeding the ducks while Mrs Smith stood by with her knitting; the Sikh driver pursuing him into the Lien Jee Bar and demanding fifty dollars for an introduction to Susie . . .

Susie.

Oh Jesus!

Ross sat up on the edge of the bed, his throbbing head on his hands, struggling to fight down his nausea. In his disturbed sleep he had suddenly realized what he'd been overlooking about Susie. His mind must have been affected by the heat exhaustion, he'd been so stupid to miss it. All along he had simply accepted that she'd been set up to make the first contact with him in the bar because that was her regular pitch. What could be more natural than to slip her a few dollars to help with the introduction while the envoy remained out of sight?

Except: that was not the way they worked.

They would use one of their own people, wouldn't they? Someone they could trust not to talk.

Someone like Susie.

It tied up.

A heavy booted kick smashed the door open. The light came on as a squat Chinese burst into the room. He made directly for the barred window opening, glanced out, then took up his position in front of it. In his hand was an automatic pistol.

Two uniformed constables followed him in, with a very young red-faced British police officer bringing up the rear. Straight off the boat, Ross judged; not a day older than twenty-two. He seemed nervous.

'On your feet!' he barked. 'Quick now! Not got all night!'

Susie obeyed immediately, trembling. Ross remained seated on the side of the bed. It took an effort not to vomit over the young officer's boots.

'Both of you!' He pointed his swagger stick at Ross. 'That means you. Understand English, don't you?'

'He sick!' Susie declared, finding her courage once more. 'You no see that man sick?'

'Sick, is he? Don't look sick to me.'

In two strides he stood in front of Ross, forcibly turning his face to the light with the tip of the swagger stick. Ross grasped it, twisting it out of his hand. The move took the officer by surprise.

'No need for that,' Ross said. 'The girl's telling the truth. I am sick. Here, you'd better have this back.'

83

Politely he held out the swagger stick. The officer snatched it from him, then glared at him angrily, tapping the stick against the palm of his hand as if trying to decide what to do next. He had lost face in front of his men.

'Technically,' Ross continued without pity, 'touching me with that stick constitutes an assault. I should report it.'

'Get the girl outside!' the officer yelled at the two bemused constables, bullying them into action. He repeated the order in Malay, stumbling over the words. 'Handcuff her, d'you hear me? And you, Tan . . .' He turned to the plain-clothes man. 'Search the room. This bloodstained clothing we'll take with us for a start.'

He ordered Ross to get off the bed, kicking the hard chair away from the table and telling him contemptuously he could sit there if he must. Then he stripped off the bedclothes, tugging the mattress aside to reveal the sagging wire netting. Nothing else there; nothing hidden. Within a few seconds he and the man he called Tan had between them made Susie's tidy little room look as though a typhoon had hit it.

Picking up Ross's discarded shirt from the floor, he held it out on the end of his swagger stick.

'Yours?'

'It's hardly Susie's.'

'How d'you explain the blood?'

'It's a rough neighbourhood.'

'Involved in a fight, were you? Well that can be easily checked. We found the knife.'

'What knife?'

'You're not going to pretend you don't know.' The young lieutenant's confidence had returned. Clearly he felt he now had the upper hand. He indicated the dressing on Ross's chest. 'What happened there?'

'An accident.'

'Let's see if the police surgeon agrees with you, shall we? Your name?'

Ross told him, adding no explanations of any kind. They'd discovered the body, he worked that much out. More likely someone had reported it, someone who knew Susie's address. Christ, his head was giving him hell. If only he could think straight. Obviously he and Susie had been seen together in the street, perhaps even in the bar . . .

'Peter Ross, I am arresting you on the charge of obstructing a police officer in the execution of his duty,' the kid copper was intoning, his mouth twisted into a grin, clearly enjoying this bit. 'It is my duty to warn you that . . .'

'Forget it!' Ross stopped him. He stood up, pushing his chair back. 'Let's get to the station where I can speak to someone with authority.'

But his dizziness flooded back, spoiling the effect even before the kid copper could react. To prevent himself from falling he had to grab the bedpost again.

'Tan – handcuffs.'

Professionally his arms were twisted back one at a time and the metal bracelets snapped over his wrists. Tan marched him through the door, but then released him again at the top of the steps to make his way down as best he could. He had to support himself against the rough wall, concentrating hard as he descended one tread after another, stumbling, almost falling as his head spun and his eyes refused to focus.

He was aware that Tan had returned to Susie's room where, left alone, he would no doubt 'find' whatever evidence they needed. As for the kid copper, he was just a step or two above, goading him to hurry.

Perhaps he actually felt the touch of a hand on the small of his back, pushing him, or perhaps it was merely his imagination, but suddenly he pitched forward. By instinct he threw himself sideways, landing painfully on his arm before rolling down the remaining steps, and somersaulting to a halt at the bottom.

'Get up, man.' It was a tone of bored insolence, aided by a quick shove with the side of a shoe. 'Constable, get him up on his feet, will you? I've half a mind to book him on a drunk-and-disorderly as well.'

Ross had a close view of the Malay constable's stocky legs clad in thick woollen knee-socks and drill shorts, that absurd boy scout uniform which was standard issue for the colonial police. Then his arms were gripped and he was unceremoniously dragged upright.

They almost threw him into the back of the police jeep. The constable joined him there to make sure he stayed put. Kid copper sat in front next to the driver, twisting back from time to time during the short trip to check on his prisoner. No doubt what he was thinking. Arresting a murderer was a feather in his cap. A plus-point for his annual report. It might even earn him an extra increment.

'Your first arrest?' Ross enquired sarcastically.

'Just keep your mouth shut.'

'Oh, I was forgetting. There's the girl too. You've done well.'

No reply this time. What had they done with Susie, Ross wondered. He'd seen no sign of her when he came out; probably they already had her locked up somewhere. Jesus, what a mess. He could imagine the Section's reaction when the full story got back to them, if it ever did.

With a shock he realized that he no longer suspected the Section of setting it up as some kind of perverse test for him. Not even HOS was capable of a shambles of these dimensions. This had to be unforeseen. It was the first law of covert operations, whoever your masters were: the more detailed your planning, the bigger the balls-up.

Hell, how did he ever get into this business? That itself was something he had never intended. His shoulder was bleeding, his arms grazed, aches and pains all over his body – and for what? To help some desk-bound type back in London to a knighthood? HOS, perhaps? Shit!

Hardly slowing down at all, the jeep turned into the police compound, narrowly missed scraping against the high security-mesh gates, then swung round the curving track to the rear of the building where the driver kicked down on the brake. The wheels spun on the loose surface as the vehicle came to a halt.

'Out!'

Only five years before it would have been a Jap officer yelling the order. Same tone of voice; same unerring instinct for brutality. Ross brooded on it angrily as he jumped down from the jeep with his hands still shackled behind him.

He landed awkwardly and might have fallen on his face if a Malay constable hadn't put out a hand to steady him.

Inside the police station his handcuffs were removed and he was taken into a high, bare interview room to await questioning. The Malay constable who had helped him remained inside guarding the door.

Ross sat on the hard bench and tried to massage some circulation into his wrists. It was self-evident that the only way out was going to be through the door. The unglazed windows were heavily barred. The walls stopped short a couple of feet beneath the sagging ceiling panels but solid-looking wire mesh filled the gaps. Besides, any attempt to escape would only bring the entire police force out hunting for him. And he had to protect his cover story; that was vital.

He squashed a fully gorged mosquito on his arm, leaving a smear of blood.

A senior officer with a cluster of pips on his epaulettes entered briskly and sat down at the table, opening a folder he had brought with him. His bronzed, balding head and bleached eyebrows suggested long hours spent at the Swimming Club or on the beach. Kid copper followed him in, pausing at the door to switch on the ceiling fan.

'Stand!' he snapped.

'No, no . . .' The older officer indicated with a wave of his hand that Ross should remain where he was. 'If you're comfortable there. I believe you're not too well.'

'No.' The room was like an assembly point for mosquitoes and several were hungrily feeding on him. 'I'd like to know what the hell's going on? How much longer am I going to be kept here?'

'Ah now, that depends. I am Assistant Superintendent Winterton, by the way. Lieutenant Morris you have already met. We have reason to believe that you were present when a certain Chinese gentleman was murdered earlier this evening. Suppose you tell us what happened.'

Ross slapped at a mosquito on his bare stomach. It dodged away. Where it had fed, it left an itchy swelling as its trade mark.

'I'd like to have a wash,' he said. 'And the loan of a shirt. How come you have so many insects here? D'you breed them, or what?'

Kid copper Morris flushed with anger and thumped his hand on the table. 'Answer the question!' he yelled.

'Superintendent,' Ross replied patiently, determined to squeeze every ounce out of the situation, 'I am considering making a formal complaint against this young officer. May I speak with you alone for a second?'

The assistant superintendent sighed. 'Is that necessary?'

'It could help clarify the situation.'

If he was to avoid blowing the whole operation this was his only chance. Whatever the risks, he grasped at it like a non-swimmer out of his depth. He felt helpless, despite the confident front he was putting up.

'Very well.' Again the officer sighed, not disguising his disapproval. 'Morris, wait outside a moment, there's a good chap.'

Kid copper straightened to attention, turned on his heel, and marched out parade-ground style.

'And the constable,' Ross insisted.

The constable was ordered out too, leaving the two of them alone in the room.

'Before you start,' the assistant superintendent warned him coldly, 'I have this to say. Any complaint against any of my officers must be written down in a formal statement signed by you and supported by witnesses. If it is later proved that you have lied in any respect I shall personally ensure that you receive the maximum penalty allowed by law. Is that clear?'

'I think so,' Ross replied patiently. 'Now Superintendent, in order to save time I suggest you get in touch right away with Alun Browne of the Department of Internal Security. We don't want any unnecessary complications, do we?'

Then he fainted again. The mists filled his head, blurring his eyes. The superintendent's voice was saying something, he couldn't make out what it was. And he felt himself slowly subsiding on to the hard floor.

4

'Twenty-three . . . twenty-four . . . twenty-five . . .'

At the twenty-fifth press-up Ross collapsed, the perspiration dripping from him, his head aching, and the wound in his chest protesting beneath its dressing. His eyes felt hot and inflamed; his whole body shook. Holding on to the edge of the bed, he managed to get to his feet, then staggered to the bathroom and turned on the shower.

Everything swam around him. The bathroom fittings floated in the air . . . shifted away as he reached out for them . . . but after groping almost blindly he succeeded in gripping the tap to moderate the flow of water. Once he was under the shower things stabilized a little though he still had a vague sensation of movement . . . constant movement . . .

He picked at the dressing and ripped it off. His sweat had soaked through it anyway; it needed changing. The wound was tiny, just an angry red line about an inch and a quarter in length with two stitches to hold the edges together; not much to write home about, though it nagged and throbbed incessantly. Once Browne had arrived at the police station, he'd insisted on carrying him off to hospital to be checked out, and they had pumped their bloody penicillin into his backside. Just in case.

While drying himself his dizziness returned and he almost fell. Somehow he got back to the bed and stretched out, closing his eyes and letting his mind wander. Christ, what a balls-up, he thought. He should have insisted he was not up to it, not any more.

'Oh, there you are, old man! It is Ross, isn't it?'

Ross must have falled asleep because he had only been vaguely aware of the light knock and the sound of the door opening. The man who entered was heavily built, though running to flabbiness; his stomach bulged over his waistband, giving him – together with his receding, wavy hair and benign face – the appearance of a middle-aged scoutmaster.

'Tim Moody,' he explained, thrusting out his hand. 'Heard you'd been in the wars. Must apologize for not being around when you arrived in Singapore, but every so often I have to let the quacks drain this damned stump. Usually doesn't take that long. No, don't get up, old man. I'll bring a chair over.'

Though he used a walking stick in his left hand, he seemed quite capable of getting around without it. He placed it on the dressing table and swung an upright chair across to the bed.

'Think you could pass me that water jug?' Ross requested, his throat parched.

'Of course, old man. Didn't eat your breakfast either, I see. Not up to it, eh?' He hovered over the tray the room boy had brought in a couple of hours earlier. Before picking up the jug, he helped himself to a piece of papaya. 'Didn't they give you a thermos? They should have given you a thermos with some ice to keep the water cold. I'll organize it.'

'Bell's not working,' Ross told him. 'Power's off.'

'As usual. Well, I'll go and hunt for your room boy in a minute. You need looking after.'

'I'm OK.'

'Taking salt, are you?' Moody eyed the salt pills the Chinese doctor had supplied. 'Good lad. Browne came hunting me out this morning. Didn't tell me much, just the essentials. Says he'll do his best to keep the keystones

91

off your back. Don't ask me why. You must have made an impression on him.'

'What d'you know about Browne?'

'Queer as a coot. Not pansy, mind you. Straight queer, if you take my meaning. He intends calling on you later, so you'd better put some clothes on. You don't want to get him excited, or he'll start spouting Latin at you, or some such lingo.'

'You don't think much of him then?'

'Bloody amateur, if you ask me. Internal Security? Colonial Service, that's all he is. Not your district officer type either. Strictly a desk wallah.'

'Dangerous?'

'Very. Doesn't know a fart from a fanfare. Innocent abroad, if you like. I'd warn you against him, only you're obviously in cahoots already.' Ross began to say how Browne had called at the office, but Moody interrupted. 'If it's not my concern, don't tell me, old man. Need to know basis, that's the rule. Remember I've still got to live here after you firemen have moved on.'

Ross began to warm to the man.

'Now, about you. It's my opinion you'll be a lot more comfortable staying at my house till you feel better. No argument, Ross. That's the way it's going to be. We have our reasons.'

'We?'

'The old Sea Dog wants a word, but not here. Humour him, will you? OK?' He stood up and fetched his walking stick from the dressing table. 'Right, I'll get that iced water organized for you, then I'll go back to the office. Collect you this afternoon.'

'OK,' Ross agreed unenthusiastically. He dropped back on to his pillow, his head throbbing. 'If that's the way it's got to be.'

Moody paused, his hand on the door-handle. 'Meant to

92

tell you, old man, they're fixing the phone this morning. That's one thing you've achieved. Mr Peng's over the moon. Can't speak too highly of you.'

He went out and a few seconds later Ross heard him in the corridor haranguing the room boy in a fluent mixture of English and Malay.

With a tap on the door the boy came in, flip-flopping across the floor to the breakfast tray. He was a thin, wasted Chinese in his late thirties; his face was pock-marked, his eyes sad.

'Tuan ta' makan breakfas?' he enquired reproachfully. 'Tuan sakit?'

'Yeah, ill,' Ross told him. 'You bring water.'

'Thermos, tuan.'

As he moved to go, taking the tray, the electric ceiling fan began to turn slowly. He made some remark about the current being on once again and for once Ross saw him smile. But though he had picked up quite a bit of Malay during his jungle days, Ross replied in English; as with his cradle Chinese, he preferred to keep it to himself. He was not out of the maze yet.

Browne parked his new Riley in the shadow of the Padang Hotel feeling pleased with himself. The gentle purring of its finely turned engine delighted him. Only a week before he had still been driving that wheezing, rattling Ford left behind by the Japs. But in particular he patted himself on the back over this business with Ross.

The man was an odd fish, no doubt about that. Fortunately Winterton had agreed on that point, if not on anything else. It had made the matter of extracting him from the clutches of the police that much easier, though he had certainly succeeded in putting young Lieutenant Morris's back up, which was a pity. Browne sat for a

93

moment in the car, sucking on his unlit pipe and thinking it over. Yes, that was definitely a pity.

His story too that he'd found himself in that district by chance after an aimless stroll through the streets – well, was that likely? More probably he'd gone to the Lien Jee Bar for a girl, though at the police station he'd denied it. The place was no more than a low-down whorehouse, so naturally he denied it. According to Morris – he'd inspected the room above the bar – the sheets must have been on that bed for a couple of weeks at least. With the Navy in town and the army camps full to bursting, God alone knew how many sordid encounters had taken place on them in that time.

Afterwards the girl had even taken him home. Blood dripping from his wound had left a trail anyone could follow.

There could only be one explanation. Ross was a fantasist with a pathological desire to make mysteries where none actually existed. Yet why? Some psychological problem perhaps? Was he afraid the simple truth would leave him exposed and vulnerable? He'd been invalided out of the Army of course, Browne recalled. Had that some bearing? Had he cracked up?

Browne wound up the windows and locked the Riley, resting his hand briefly on its gleaming maroon roof, reluctant to leave it. *Et nos cedamus amori*, he thought; last night's reading of Virgil had brought the passage back to mind. 'And we also yield to love': in itself a form of madness.

In the hotel the desk clerk did not even look up from his newspaper as Browne passed. On the lift gates was the inevitable 'Out of Order' sign. He took the stairs, cursing Ross for living on the second floor.

He knocked once, then opened the door without waiting for a reply, expecting to find Ross stretched out on

94

the bed. Instead, he was sitting out on the rattan chaise-longue on the veranda, dressed. It was marginally cooler outside, he supposed, though noisy with strident car horns and trishaw riders' bicycle bells from the streets below.

'May I come in? Sorry I couldn't get here earlier, old chap. How d'you feel today?'

'Fucked up.'

'You don't look too good. You should take things easy.'

Ross didn't bother to reply. On his lap was a sketch pad. He tore off the top sheet, offering it to him. 'That's the man you want. The killer. Not an exact likeness maybe because the light wasn't too good, but the main features are OK.'

Browne took it, more to humour the man than anything. To his surprise he found it was a highly competent sketch using only very few lines, more in the Chinese style than European. Good enough for the Singapore Art Society's exhibition, and he said as much, tapping it with the stem of his pipe.

'As I pointed out, it has the main features,' Ross commented, 'so the police might find a use for it. I imagine they're still searching for him.'

'Every hospital has been checked. You're quite sure about that broken arm?'

'No question about that.'

'He came at you with a knife and you broke his arm?'

'It's a trick they teach you in the commandos.' He had started drawing again. 'You wouldn't like a demonstration?'

'I'll take your word for it,' Browne said drily. Was that intended as a threat, he wondered. He no longer felt comfortable in Ross's presence. There *was* something strange about him. 'He must be holed up somewhere, and in considerable pain I should think.'

'Nothing a pipe of opium couldn't make bearable.'

'You're a callous bastard, Ross. You surprise me.'

'I'm alive.'

'The police have doubts about whether you've told us the truth.'

'Why should I lie? I've nothing to gain.' Ross glanced up at him, then went on drawing. 'So what's worrying them?'

'The girl denies that there was a doctor.'

'Not very wise of her. Somebody gave me the stitches.'

'A *Chinese* doctor, you said? Short and fat?'

'Tubby,' Ross confirmed, untruthfully.

'They've interviewed every fat Chinese doctor in the Colony. There's not one who can't account for his movements. She told them something else too.' Browne spoke reproachfully. 'You weren't merely wandering round the streets, Ross. You met the girl in the Lien Jee Bar and went upstairs with her. Why spin such yarns if they're not true?'

Ross actually grinned. 'Gentlemanly thing to do, Browne, wasn't it? Protect the girl's reputation?'

'A whore?' Browne exploded in fury. Was the man trying to make a fool of him or what? 'Christ Almighty, Ross! If we're going to get anywhere, we've got to keep the police on our side. I thought you were agreeing to help?'

There was a moment of awkward silence. Browne turned his back on him and stared down at the tangle of traffic in North Bridge Road, regretting he had ever become involved with Ross. It might be best if he found some discreet way to get him out of the Colony.

'Browne, she's a nice kid,' Ross was trying to say apologetically. 'When she saw the blood on my clothes she'd no need to get involved. Any other girl would've left me there in the street.'

'OK,' Browne conceded. He had to humour the man.

96

'You've a soft spot for her. Don't let it get you into trouble, that's all.'

'What's going to happen to her?'

'For the time being she's still at the police station. Hidden in her room they found a couple of pages torn from a Chinese Communist magazine. Under the Colony's emergency regulations possession of such material is an offence.'

'Jesus, are the police so desperate, they have to plant that on her? So I suppose she'll be charged and tried?'

'I doubt if there'll be a trial.' Browne waited for the usual instinctive reaction of people straight out from the UK, but Ross said nothing. Instead, he merely concentrated on his drawing. He decided to try and save the situation; after all, the man *could* be useful. 'Look, when you get over to Moody's house, why don't you try to relax? Forget about her.'

'You know about that too?' Ross sounded sarcastic. 'Congratulations.'

He handed over the sketch pad, then leaned back against the cushionless rattan of his chair, still flushed from the fever.

It was a picture of himself, Browne discovered. Not a caricature, though the pencil-drawn eyes held an air of mockery which was also present in the twist of the lips. Accurate though, he had to admit grudgingly: that was the face which gazed back at him every morning from the shaving mirror.

'Show it to the police if they've any doubts about that first drawing I gave you. Should prove a point.'

'If you're an artist, what the hell are you doing selling typewriters?' Browne demanded, feeling out of his depth and irritated.

Ross laughed. 'Picked up the trick of it when I was a kid. I'm no artist, don't get that idea.'

'I'm not sure what you are, but I do know this. You're causing me one hell of a lot of trouble, Ross. If we're to get on together, I want no ambiguity where your loyalties lie. People are dying, some of them rather horrible deaths. Women and children as well as men.'

'Have you ever killed anyone, Browne?'

He shook his head. What the hell was *that* question supposed to mean?

'Thought not. I know which side I'm on, don't worry. Now fuck off. I've got a headache.'

'Before I do, I've a snapshot for you to look at.'

'*Oh Jesus!*'

'Thought you liked pictures.' Browne opened his brief-case and took out a glossy black and white print. It was a full-face portrait blown up from a passport or identity card photo, taken with the light directly on the subject, flattening the features. 'Recognize him?'

'Vaguely. Can't be sure.' Ross's reaction was guarded. 'It's the man who was killed, isn't it? I couldn't see him too well in that alleyway.'

'Ong Chou-fei,' Browne explained, his eyes never leaving Ross's face. 'He was legally resident in Singapore since mainland China fell to the reds. A colonel in the Nationalist Army during the war, fought against the Japs, and afterwards he took over running the family business. Quite a flourishing business too, by all accounts. Head office in Shanghai originally. I'm told the Singapore branch was established back in the nineteen-twenties. Dealt in most things – importers, exporters, wholesalers . . . Rubber and tin interests . . . tea . . . silks . . .'

'They'll probably give him quite a funeral,' said Ross.

'Pity you didn't save his life. It might have been worth something to you.'

'Might have been.'

'What was he like to talk to? You did meet him, didn't

98

you? When you went upstairs in the Lien Jee Bar?' Ong had been seen there earlier in the evening, that much the police had clearly established. Browne waited for Ross's answer.

'In the alleyway,' Ross corrected him gently. 'And he didn't stop for a chat, either. He was too busy dying.'

Browne sighed and got up. It had been a long shot, and not even an important one at that. No doubt it would turn out that Ong Chou-fei's company had a stake in the girlie bars too.

'Get yourself fit again, then we'll talk,' he said as he put the photograph and drawings into his briefcase. 'Oh, and if you want to leave Singapore, for Chrissake let me know first. Our friends in the police are likely to be very tiresome if you don't.'

Tim Moody came for him at two o'clock. He organized two room boys to help him down the stairs. The lift was still out of order and in any case the power was off again. Probably he could have managed just as well by himself, but Moody meant well, so Ross let it all happen, concealing his irritation. The car – a black, dented saloon – was parked by the front steps where there was no shade; to balance himself, Ross rested his hand briefly on the roof, only to jerk it away again immediately before the heat stripped the skin off his fingers.

'I've told them they must keep the room. You'll be back in three or four days.' Moody manoeuvred himself into the driving seat, shifting his leg into the right position by hand before slamming the door. 'Had to pay in advance, but we can settle up later on.'

For the sake of saying something Ross asked: 'You're able to drive with that leg?' But he wasn't really interested; his head ached, and the car was a sweat box.

'You'd be amazed. It's a metal alloy. Lightweight

metal. Beautifully engineered.' He started the car and edged it out into the line of traffic, ignoring the irate horn-blasts from the drivers behind him. 'You may as well relax, old man. It's a trip of twenty minutes to half an hour. Time to work out what you're going to say to the old Sea Dog. Seems he's in a hell of a mood.'

With good reason, Ross reflected sourly.

If Browne was right about the dead envoy having been one of Chiang Kai-shek's officers, that changed the whole game. Not suprising either; to his nostrils it stank from square one. For a start, the admiral's London contact must be suspect. His message had obviously not originated, as they thought, from the new Communist government in Peking, but from the discredited Nationalists, in which case that entire story about the Soviet Union's preparations for germ warfare was probably a hoax. But for what purpose? To persuade Britain or the USA to launch a pre-emptive attack on Manchuria? At least that made more sense. It would force them into China's civil war on the Nationalist side. According to the newspapers that was just what Chiang Kai-shek and Washington's China Lobby were demanding.

'You OK, old man?' Moody enquired after some fifteen minutes. They were driving past a row of expensive villas whose spacious gardens were fringed with coconut palms and banana plants. 'Not far now.'

Ross grunted. He no longer minded how long it took. The admiral could wait. The old Sea Dog, as Moody called him.

'You must have come across Richards in the Section,' said Moody after another couple of miles' silence.

'Richards?'

'London. We were at Cambridge together. He's acting HOS now, they tell me. HOS is in hospital. Heart attack.'

100

God rot him, thought Ross. Unforgiving. 'How long have you been out here, Moody?'

'Me? Oh, I'm the resident. I don't move around. Thirty-eight I came out. Been here ever since, 'cept when the Japs took over. I'm a permanent fixture.'

'Selling typewriters?'

'What else?'

The car slowed down and soon they turned off the main road, taking a track which had once been tarred – traces of the old surface still remained – though now it was pitted and needed careful driving to manoeuvre. Ross glanced back once more but nothing followed them.

'What'd be the point?' Moody demanded when he mentioned it. 'Everyone knows I live here. Singapore isn't the jungle, Ross. There's no way a European can hide in Singapore. He'd stick out like a nudist in a nunnery. That's the house, by the way – through the trees. From the first floor there's a view of the sea.'

It was an old, colonial style structure, two storeys, with wide verandas and a roof designed with a generous overhang to provide plenty of shade. The drive approaching it, skirting a large garden which already showed signs of losing the battle against the rapid luxuriance of the tropics, was in no better condition than the track along which they had just come. As the car drew up at the front steps, a Malay girl appeared on the veranda. Moody called out to her as he opened the car door and she disappeared into the house again.

Ross raised an eyebrow, glancing ironically at Moody. 'Obviously you do all right for yourself.'

Quite a beauty, she was: bare-shouldered, her ink-black hair tied back from her face, wearing only a batik sarong whose top hem bit into her pale tan skin just above her breasts. Her smile when she recognized Moody's car had been unmistakably genuine. 'I'm the resident,' he said. 'A permanent fixture.' No bloody wonder.

'You'll meet Asiah later on,' Moody was explaining. 'She's gone to fetch Suleiman, my Malay cook. He'll help you up to your room.'

'Oh shit!' Ross swore, protesting. 'Just point me in the right direction, Moody. I'll get there. And when I do I'd like a cold beer. D'you have such a thing in this palace?'

He got out of the car, stood up and strode to the steps, reaching them only a second before the first wave of dizziness dissolved everything and he found himself unexpectedly sitting down. 'Shit!' he said again.

Moody, taking the steps one at a time and using a walking stick to steady himself, looked down and laughed at him. 'Come on, old man, let Suleiman help you. No point trying to fight it. You're ill, so take to your bed and enjoy it. The Section can't quarrel with that.'

'Fuck the Section,' Ross said, hauling himself to his feet again.

Suleiman turned out to be a squat, over-weight Malay casually dressed in a singlet, with a faded sarong round his bulging waist. Beaming, he placed a hand under Ross's arm to steady him; he had a wrestler's muscles.

Patiently he assisted Ross up the stairs to a large first-floor room, cooled by a pleasant breeze blowing in from the veranda; through its unglazed windows he caught a glimpse of the distant sea beyond the clusters of palm trees. Gratefully he stretched out on the bed. Moody was right, he thought: he was ill, wasn't he? What more could they expect of him? From a timber frame suspended beneath the high ceiling, the folds of a mosquito net billowed and waltzed before his eyes, constantly – it seemed – changing shape. He found it an oddly reassuring sight, like wind-blown white clouds against a tropical sky; he sensed his tensions gradually slipping away. Far away.

* * *

The Malay girl, Asiah, brought the tea. He opened his eyes as she set the little tray down on his bedside table. She poured the first cup, then turned and noiselessly went out of the room again.

'A bit under the weather, I hear,' the admiral's upper-crust voice floated at him from the foot of the bed. 'And wounded. You'd better report what happened.'

Ross pushed himself up on one elbow, his head clearer, but his mouth dry. It was China tea, God bless the girl, weak and without milk. He sipped it till the cup was empty, then poured another. His hand was steady.

'They've not told you?' It was a stupid question which he regretted immediately. He tried to concentrate his thoughts.

'Even if you are on your deathbed, Ross, I still expect a concise and accurate account.' The admiral's tone sharpened like a honed razor, though he spoke no louder than before. Ross recognized that quiet arrogance which the British officer class call authority. He was no picture-book sea dog either, this admiral in his well-cut navy shorts and white shirt. 'Right, laddie. Get on with it.'

'Yes, sir.' Ross felt he was flung back in uniform again. Three stripes on his arm and shit flung at him from all directions at once. He drank some more tea.

'Come on, laddie. You can't be that ill. You met the man.'

Laddie: he had not heard that example of Royal Navy upper deck impertinence since he was landed on the Malayan coast by submarine during the war. In their earlier interviews he had not actively disliked the admiral, but now he was beginning to.

But he delivered his report, that whole germ warfare yarn which the envoy had spun, though he no longer believed it, if he ever had. Then, more briefly, he described how the envoy had left first by the rear door, and the obvious signal on the car horn, and how he met his death in that dark alleyway.

'He's been identified, but you may know that already,' he concluded. 'Ong Chou-fei, held a commission in Chiang Kai-shek's army, now a Singapore businessman – or he was till they killed him. Throws a new light on the whole thing, doesn't it?'

'Tell me the rest. Why did you follow him?'

'Curiosity about that signal. I wasn't satisfied. Just as well, in the event.'

'Your orders were clear enough. You already had the message. Your duty was simply to report back, not to play bodyguard.'

'He was already dead when I found him. I was checking his pockets when the killer came at me.'

'You're sure you didn't kill him yourself?' the admiral asked drily.

'Oh sweet Jesus!' Ross let his head fall back on the pillow and gazed at the bunched-up mosquito net again. He was in the interrogation centre once more; they never gave up, did they? Now it was murder they wanted to pin on him. 'It's too convenient, my friend.' He corrected himself: 'Sir.'

'What about the girl, this whore with a heart of gold? Christ, Ross, I'd imagined you to be more professional than that.'

'Nobody's professional, not in this business. It's all chance. The throw of a dice. We call it professional when there hasn't been the usual cock-up.'

'Quite the philosopher, Ross. I hadn't realized. So tell me now about the heart of gold.'

'What heart of gold? She earns her money, same as the rest of us – or she did till our upright colonial police planted that evidence on her.'

'You're sure it was them?'

'Who else?'

The admiral's cross-examining continued. He probed into Ross's exact relationship with Browne, a blow by blow account of what Browne had said, then back to Susie, wanting to know how long she'd been absent fetching the Chinese doctor. Ross stuck to the fictional description he had given the police. Finally he returned to the interview with Ong Chou-fei in that room above the tawdry, mosquito-infested bar. He seemed to accept the germ warfare story at face value and Ross commented on the fact.

'If I were you I'd not dismiss it out of hand, Ross. Loyalties are not always as simple as they appear on the surface.' It was the admiral's turn to be philosophical. 'China's Revolution has been going on for a generation or more. You know that better than anyone. Our press, British and American, see it as two-sided – Communism versus the rest. That's too simple. Ong could be a Vicar of Bray type, a trimmer, serving whichever creed is on top. Like Talleyrand – a first-rate example. Or maybe he's a patriot, doing what he thinks best for his country. No, I'm not taking it at face value; not rejecting it either.'

He got to his feet.

'As for you, Ross. I want you to take things easy for a couple of days. That's an order. Do nothing, understand? If Browne comes out here bothering you, tell him you're sick. Any problems, Moody knows how to contact me. Need a doctor?'

'I've seen two already.'

'Quite. One last thing, Ross. No more hearts of gold. Got that?'

'If you say so. Sir.'

Ross closed his eyes. Faintly he heard the admiral's footsteps as he went out of the room, and then the distant sound of voices from downstairs. Moody's laugh was

105

unmistakable. Not professional? He recalled the training courses they had put him through: how to garrotte a man with a length of wire; how to set up a radio transmitter, or manufacture a micro-dot. None of it had ever prepared him for the uncertainty, the fear of what might be lurking around the next corner, the sudden tensing of the nerves, the quick, surging exhilaration of taking life with his bare hands man to man, nor the inevitable plunge into the blackest disgust with himself which always followed. Unprofessional? That might have some meaning for high-ranking officers planning to send men into action and estimating how many casualties they might find 'acceptable' – how many dead, how many wounded. For him it had none.

The darkness came rapidly and with it the high-pitched call of the cicadas. From somewhere in the room he could hear a gecko's kissing-clicking call. He imitated it; it fell silent, then replied. Many a conversation he'd held with geckos during one period in his jungle days when he had lived in a kampong hut. They had kept him sane.

'Awake, are you?' It was Moody.

'Sea Dog left?'

'An hour back, old man. Asiah looked in for the tray. You were sleeping. But just to set the record straight, she's not a servant.'

'No?'

'Just thought I'd put you right, old man.'

The admiral drove back alone to the naval base on the far side of Singapore island. He remembered the Khabarovsk War Crimes Trial only too well. The first Moscow Radio reports had come on Christmas Day the previous year, and he'd been called away from his plum pudding and brandy sauce when the despatch rider arrived with the Foreign Office signal. General MacArthur had issued an immediate denial from Tokyo that any American POWs had been used as guinea pigs, or any other nationality come to that. 'No evidence that the Japanese used human beings for experimentation' – that had been the official line and His Majesty's Government had gone along with it.

Yet there had been stories back in 1945 among Allied prisoners-of-war that the Japs had been up to something. Somewhere in the bowels of the War Office their debriefing reports probably still existed. It could turn out that the Peking envoy had spoken the truth.

Though he prayed to the Almighty that the civilians were wrong about the dead man's identity. He had first read it that morning in the brief summary report shown him by the Royal Navy intelligence officer responsible for liaison with civilian internal security. If the man Ross had met genuinely turned out to have been a colonel in Generalissimo Chiang Kai-shek's army, they could no longer trust any of their source's information.

Pray God that was not the case.

Darkness fell rapidly in Singapore. He switched on his headlamps. Their twin beams picked out the ordered groves of banana plants on either side of the narrow road.

In another couple of hours his son's ship would be in position off the Korean coast, blacked out and standing by for the opening bombardment to begin. The admiral felt sick in his stomach, that old familiar nervousness before going into action, though this time he'd be waiting safely in the naval base for the signals to come through while Nigel was in the firing line. To make matters worse, General MacArthur's planned landing at Inchon, far to the rear of the existing front line, must be the most ill-kept secret in all military history. The North Koreans would be waiting for them. A Royal Navy frogman had done a detailed recce of the shoreline, reporting it strongly fortified; casualties were bound to be high.

All the same, MacArthur might well succeed – the man had the luck of the devil – and if he did, it could relieve the pressure on the Pusan perimeter. The North Koreans could find themselves retreating as rapidly as they had originally advanced.

And then?

What if MacArthur pushed north, crossing the 38th parallel into North Korea itself? Would Red China come in to help? Or the Soviet Union?

Uncomfortably, the admiral realized they might have a third card up their sleeves. Bacteria. And if Ong Chou-fei was right, that was the card they would choose to play.

He arrived at the main gate of the naval base and acknowledged the salutes of the ratings on duty as he drove through, parking outside the naval intelligence hut. Though only a visitor – to most of the officers he was merely a has-been put out to grass in an Admiralty desk job – the old-boy network had proved its value in obtaining the facilities he needed.

'Anything new?' he asked.

A very young sub-lieutenant, hardly more than a boy, glanced up from the clutch of signals he was entering by hand into the duty log. 'They're observing radio silence, sir. But the weather reports are encouraging.'

He sounded eager and excited; probably he was regretting not being there himself.

'Be grateful if you'd let me know when anything comes through.'

'Aye-aye, sir!'

The admiral went into the duty cubby hole where they had allotted him a desk. On top of the filing cabinet stood a small electric fan. He switched it on and sat down. At moments like these he itched for a more openly active role again; these hole-and-corner cloak-and-dagger games might be very necessary, but they were not why he had chosen to join the Navy. Ross now . . . , well, Ross was different. Ross was one of a special breed. Disruptive. Sending Ross into a situation was like dropping grit into well-oiled machinery; oh yes, if it came to the crunch and this germ warfare story turned out to be true, he'd have no hesitation about despatching Ross into China. No chance of him coming out alive of course, or precious little, but every action had its cost.

He drew a signal pad towards him and jotted down several precise questions to which he needed urgent answers. It was a heavy responsibility; ideally he'd have preferred to fly back to London for consultations, but the flight alone would take almost three days. Slowly, he translated the questions into the Section's top restriction code, then took the result to the Royal Navy's cipher clerk for second generation coding and transmission. The plain language original he burned, powdering the charred cinder between his fingers.

Of course it was still possible, he mused as he made his way back, that Ross had been turned during those months in Russia. One must never lose sight of that. He could easily have killed Ong Chou-fei himself as that police lieutenant suspected, and the prostitute might have helped him to get rid of the wallet which had not yet been found. The admiral's hunch was against that interpretation. Men of Ross's background – from one of the old trading families of the Shanghai Bund – were the least likely to fall for Communism. But he could not rid his mind of that nagging doubt: Ross might be just as effective as the grit in their own finely balanced works.

'No news?' he challenged the sub-lieutenant who must have finished entering up the signals, being now engrossed with the crossword in an out-of-date copy of the *Daily Telegraph*.

'Nothing, sir. A character in Dickens, six letters beginning with P, sir?'

'Can't stand the man,' the admiral replied. He glanced at the clock. It was the waiting, he knew; it made him nervous. 'I'll get over to the wardroom then for a spot of dinner. Keep me up to date, will you? Don't forget.'

'Soon as anything comes in,' the sub-lieutenant promised. 'Sir.'

As acting HOS Jack Richards had sight of all incoming signals at the Section's London office. Over the years he had built for himself a solid reputation for reliability in administrative matters; it went without saying that he forwarded the admiral's questions to their various destinations without delay, though for the rest of the day he pondered deeply over their possible significance. Both Ross – who was certainly suspect, and perhaps tainted – and the admiral were in Singapore, and he had not been able to discover the reason. Perhaps HOS – good old HOS whose shoes he had temporarily inherited – had known before he died, but he had left no notes and there was nothing on the files.

The questions themselves intrigued him. A Chinese Nationalist called Ong Chou-fei . . . Japanese war crimes investigations . . . Soviet installations in Manchuria . . .

Whatever lay behind them, it certainly did not resemble Tim Moody's handiwork. Hardly Moody's fault of course that his information was so routine: he was little more than a post office, able to send only what his string of agents gave him. Troop movements, shipping intelligence, armaments, some good political stuff, and the occasional titbit about the covert activities of certain US officials. All very useful, but unsurprising.

But this stuff from the admiral had real potential. Towards the end of the afternoon, Richards opened his briefcase and took out the cheap Woolworth's stationery he had bought earlier in the week. For once he felt he had something interesting to report, something to make them sit up. He wrote it out in detail, then added a few notes concerning Ross and the admiral. When he had finished he checked it through twice and folded it till it was small enough to slip inside the cigarette packet. Capstan this time, never the brand he usually smoked himself.

'Goodnight!' Mrs Smith called out to him as he passed the switchboard on his way out.

'You're late!' He was surprised to see her still there. 'Catching up on something?'

'Going to the theatre with my sister.'

'Good. Take you out of yourself. Goodnight!'

At Charing Cross he bought a *Standard*, then stood at a bus-stop reading the latest news from Korea. Heavy fighting at Inchon. It was still touch-and-go whether the mainly American UN troops would be able to consolidate their toe-hold. Of course, he remembered, the admiral's son was serving with the naval task force; that would explain his special interest.

The bus was packed solid, but the conductor accepted the first two in the queue, himself and a tired-looking woman in a headscarf. Richards politely stood aside to let her get on ahead of him. It seemed unlikely that she was tailing him; nevertheless he stuck to the rule and left the bus at a request stop half-way along Bayswater Road. He was the only passenger to alight, which was reassuring, nor were there any suspicious cars lurking at the kerb.

Along the railings the usual bored prostitutes were already spaced out at roughly ten-yard intervals, waiting for customers. Seeing him approach, one stepped half-heartedly forward, but then retreated again when she found herself ignored. The first taxi to come along he hailed, ordering the driver to drop him at Euston station, where he paid the man off. A Northern Line tube took him to Hampstead.

It seemed so childish, this whole procedure, having to tramp across Hampstead Heath simply to place a used cigarette packet into a hole in a tree, but they insisted on it, he couldn't understand why. There must be simpler methods, he always thought; certainly more convenient ones.

But with the packet delivered he felt a lot easier in his mind. He headed back into Central London, making for the Reform Club where he was expected for his usual bridge evening.

5

The day Pereira came out to see him Ross decided to return to the Padang Hotel. Not that he had any reason to move. Nothing had come from the admiral, not for a week now, and he felt well cared for at Moody's house.

For the first twenty-four hours he'd done little but lie on his bed letting the fever take its course. He hadn't eaten, nor drunk anything stronger than the tea which Asiah brought him from time to time. After a day or two Moody must have noticed his involuntary glance as – with her back towards him – she bent down to retrieve his tray. 'Soon as you feel up to it, Ross old chap,' he'd announced cheerfully, 'I'll ask her to invite one of her friends to keep you company. Won't cost you too much.'

'Spare me,' Ross had answered, meaning it. These days he preferred being alone.

Once the fever went, he sat out on the veranda sketching the palm trees or simply gazing at the wild growth of hibiscus and bougainvillea. Moody was not a tidy gardener but there was a quietness about the place which pleased Ross. Gradually his tensions dissolved and he felt more at peace than for many years. He was not disturbed even by the news that a Chinese food hawker had set up a stall at the end of the lane. He speculated on going down to buy something just to look him over, but he never did.

Perhaps it was the lush jungle foliage which brought Yen-hua back to him – the others too, but above all Yen-hua. Gently this time, without distress. Faces, voices, snippets of conversation, it was like meeting them again still alive. No accusations either, though the guilt was his alone. He had led that Three Star Army commando into the Jap ambush which killed more than half of them. Yen-hua had died four yards from where he lay hidden; he'd been helpless, unable to save her.

For his sake she had put up with the vicious criticism at the group confessions the communists went in for. Unjustly too, for she'd always remained passionately loyal to their creed, despite falling in love with this awkward British sergeant; and he with her, a fierce overwhelming love which had distorted his judgement. He should never have sent them down that particular track which he'd only chosen because he'd thought it safer. Till too late he'd not even realized the risk he was taking.

Yet it was all distant now; not the same war. To get his mind off it he asked Moody to buy him an atlas in Singapore. What he turned up was a pre-war edition showing Korea as part of the Japanese Empire, with Manchuria to the north printed as 'Manchukuo', but it was good enough for Ross to follow the BBC's news broadcasts. Fighting had been heavy following the landings at Inchon and he suspected the American casualty figures were being deliberately understated as they pushed on towards Seoul.

Whoever Peking man might be, his story was beginning to feel very convincing. Once Seoul was back in UN hands the temptation would be to cross the 38th parallel into North Korea and roll the enemy back as far as the Yalu river. A germ attack from bases in Manchuria might stop them if nothing else would.

But it was his job merely to await orders, the admiral had made that clear enough. So why should he worry?

That night, asleep under his mosquito net, he dreamed Asiah approached his bed, smiling at him as she retied her sarong to leave her breasts bare. They swung gently

114

against his face as she bent over him. His hands touched her shoulders, drawing her towards him till she twisted away, laughing. As she straightened up his fingers caught in the top of her sarong, tugging it loose again. It dropped to her feet and she stook naked before him, reaching up with both hands to untie her dark hair. Then suddenly she was astride him, her soft naked buttocks pressing on his thighs as she sat bolt upright, tossing her hair back from her face. He ran his hands over her waist . . . her hips . . .

When he woke up he was bathed in sweat; between his legs he clutched the thick bolster. A Dutch wife, the old planters called them. With reason. The mosquito net was still in place, pale and luminescent in the moonlight which flooded into the room.

Perhaps he should take up Moody's offer after all, he thought ruefully as he tried settling to sleep again. Perhaps if Asiah did know of a girl who'd suit him . . .

But the following morning he slept long. Moody left for the office before he woke up, so he'd no opportunity to mention it. That was the day when Pereira arrived.

From the veranda outside his first-floor room he spotted the trishaw turning into the drive. Its rider – a thin, wiry Chinese wearing a khaki pith helmet – stood on the cycle pedals, committing his whole weight into coaxing the machine up the slight incline. In the sidecar his passenger sat straightbacked, swaying with every bump encountered by the wheels.

Once the trishaw reached the house steps he could no longer see it, but he heard Asiah's voice, then the man's reply asking for him by name. Pulling on a shirt, Ross went down to see what he wanted.

'OK, Asiah, I know,' he said, meeting her on the stairs, and with a sudden flash of teeth she smiled at him, a teasing, quick smile, simultaneously inviting yet reserved, as if she too was remembering what had happened in his dream – impossible though that was, he thought regretfully.

His visitor, he found, was a Eurasian whose pale face was pitted with tiny holes: smallpox, chickenpox, some childhood disease. He wore horn-rimmed glasses which gave him a learned appearance but his dress was formal: long brown trousers, an obviously starched shirt with frayed cuffs, and a nondescript tie anchored by a gilt tie-clip. Civil service clerk was Ross's guess. Not smart enough for a job in business.

'I'm Ross,' he said. 'What can I do for you?'

'Pereira.' The man stuck out his hand. 'Thomas Pereira, from the Department of Internal Security. I am to deliver a message on behalf of Mr Browne. In person.'

'Well?' He was right about the civil service.

'Strictly speaking I should request to see your identity papers before I hand this over, but of course I recognize you from your file.' He began fumbling with the button of his shirt pocket.

'You've come all this way by trishaw?'

'By bus, then trishaw. A clerk has no entitlement to petty cash for a taxi.' From the pocket he extracted a crumpled envelope. He smoothed it out before handing it over. 'Mr Browne said this would interest you.'

Ross tore the envelope open. In it was a Chinese newspaper clipping pinned to a roughly typed translation on unheaded civil service paper. It was a simple announcement of the death of the prominent businessman Ong Chou-fei, giving the time and place of the funeral.

'Yes, it does interest me, Mr Pereira,' he responded after taking in the main gist. 'Thank you. Now, can I get you a cool drink? Beer, perhaps?'

'Very kind, but no. I am expected to return to the office right away.' He sounded tense, though maybe his high-pitched, sing-song voice gave a misleading impression.

'Perhaps I'm not in order telling you this, but that bar girl who helped you when you were wounded . . . Susie? Was that her name? The police have released her.'

'Browne implied they'd enough evidence to put her away for life. A torn bit of Commie newspaper.'

Pereira did not react. 'They have changed their minds. Why, I don't know.'

'Seen sense perhaps.'

'Whatever the reason, they freed her at dawn this morning.'

Again he refused Ross's offer of a drink. He backed down the steps, still talking, and the trishaw rider unfolded himself from the passenger seat where he had settled down to doze. Pereira climbed in.

Ross watched them go and the questions crowded through his mind. As they were speaking, he'd noticed how Pereira's eyes had darted around the living room, taking it all in. Perhaps Browne expected a report when he got back. He certainly hadn't sent his clerk out this far only to deliver a press cutting, nor out of the goodness of his heart. And the information about Susie being released – what was he fishing for there? Pereira's little deception about it not coming from Browne was just so much hogwash. They would be watching him, expecting a reaction.

For the first time, he began to suspect that Browne might be more than a fool and a nuisance. This bedtime reader of Virgil in classical Latin had hidden depths.

Ross studied the press clipping and its translation once again, puzzling over the Chinese characters. His amah – so proud that she could teach him Peking Chinese rather than the local Shanghai patois – had been lost when it came to reading. She was illiterate. Not until the age of fourteen had he developed a longing to understand the written language as well and used his own pocket money to pay for private lessons, secretly. But they were of little help to him now, though he picked out Ong Chou-fei's name printed beneath a smudged photograph. No mistaking him; without any doubt that was the man he had met in the room above the bar.

Ross knew he had to attend that funeral.

Later that same day he announced his intention to move back to the hotel. He chose the most difficult moment, when they were sitting out on the veranda eating satay and drinking beer as they watched the darkening sky. The sun had just dropped below the horizon, but there was still a faint shimmer of light, enough to outline the jagged, breeze-blown palms.

'What's the hurry?' Moody asked him lazily. 'Stay as long as you like. I've organized a car for you, so you won't be stuck in the house. A bit of an old wreck, but it goes.'

Asiah, who had been sitting on the straw mat in the doorway, got to her feet and took the empty satay dish, saying she would fetch more when they were ready. Moody waited until she had gone.

'Like me to have a word with her? She'd find you someone attractive.'

'So you said.'

'Just what you need now you're well again and your wound's healing. It'd set you up.' He lay back on the low rattan chair, stretching his arms. 'This is Shangri-La, old man – know that? A cool, roomy house, the sea not a mile away, and the only noise comes from insects and bull-frogs. No yelling voices, no traffic. Peace. Plus plenty of food and cold beer, not forgetting the other: all any man could want! Don't you agree?'

'You've heard nothing from the admiral?'

'Relax, old man. He'll be in touch with you when he's

ready, expecting you to jump to it. If I were you I'd be grateful he's been quiet this long.'

'Maybe.'

'You know, a year or two back I had a spot of leave in London. That was an experience I'll never forget. Poor sods queuing for food. Coupons for everything. Even bread was rationed. Ross, I can assure you this is Shangri-La out here. How long it'll last I can't say, with Korea blowing up. By the end of this year we could all be sitting on a mushroom cloud. You'd be an idiot not to grab this while we've still got it. Eat, drink, and fuck – what else is there?'

They were an odd match, the two of them, Ross reflected in the silence which followed. Both had survived the Japs, of course: Moody at first in Changi prison, then working in a Jap slave gang building the Burma railway where he was one of a handful who escaped death; and Ross himself in the jungle where at most times sickness and malnutrition posed a greater threat than enemy bullets. No glory either way, but they had both come through.

At most times? He seemed to see Yen-hua's face again . . . the expression of surprise . . . the startled eyes . . .

'I'm sure you're right, Moody,' he admitted, trying to fight the memory down. 'One day I'll take your advice.'

Asiah returned with more satay. He took a stick, dipping the meat into the bowl of sauce before conveying it to his mouth.

'More beer, old man?'

They drove into Singapore together early the next morning before the heat became too fierce. Moody dropped him off at his hotel. He had half expected to discover his room had been let during his absence but they had kept it for him, though he had to send the room

119

boy scurrying around changing the sheets and refilling the thermos with cold water. Nothing was ready.

Leaving him to get on with it, Ross went out to buy more clothes. God alone knew how long he'd have to stay in this stinking climate now. The Section's miserly kit allowance had been spent before he left London. From a shop a couple of streets away he picked up half a dozen American-style shirts and then sought out a tailor who measured him for a couple of pairs of trousers, promising they would be ready that evening.

By the time he arrived at the office, his head was aching again and the wound in his chest had started to throb. He'd been a fool to reject Moody's advice, he thought as he climbed the stairs. At that very moment he might have been padding around that cool, spacious house, bare-footed, clad only in a sarong, waiting to see what kind of girl Asiah had chosen for him.

But at least the current was on. The ceiling fan in the outer office was turning slowly, fluttering the papers on the desk. A smiling Mr Peng stood up to greet him and delivered a brief welcoming speech in that over-correct, clipped accent of his, punctuating his remarks with a series of little bows.

'That you, Ross?' called Moody's voice from the next office. 'Everything OK at the hotel?'

Ross pushed open the half-doors. 'No problems.'

'Move you to Raffles if you prefer, though there's a waiting list, I'm told.' Moody held up a long white envelope as he spoke, indicating with a gesture that he did not wish to say anything Mr Peng might overhear. 'Noël Coward stayed there once. They've never forgotten it.'

'Oh?'

Ross took the envelope and sat down with his back to the door. It was unaddressed and the flap was stuck down.

He eased it open with his thumbnail. Inside was a typed list of places and dates headed: *Ong Chou-fei – Itinerary*. No signature. No other information. The dates covered the past three months; if they were correct, Ong Chou-fei had seldom stopped anywhere for more than three or four days at a time. There was nothing suspicious about the places he had visited, not in themselves. Hongkong, Macao, Bangkok, Formosa, Penang, Malacca, Jakarta, Saigon . . . That was a route any businessman might follow.

'From Sea Dog,' Moody filled him in quietly. 'Read and destroy.'

In the outer office the telphone rang and they heard Mr Peng answering it.

Ross went over the list again. Hongkong and Macao turned up frequently; of course they were close neighbours, which might be significant. The time spent there, taking both together, amounted to a week or more each visit. Enough leeway for him to slip over the border into China with no one any the wiser. As for his links with Chiang Kai-shek, his three trips to Formosa would have given him all the opportunity he needed. So was he playing a double game?

Borrowing a box of matches from Moody he burned the paper, holding it till the heat licked at his fingers. As he ground the curling black cinder to fragments between his hands he became aware of Mr Peng lingering in the doorway, looking on with curiosity; he asked him to fetch the telephone book.

The name Ong occupied several columns, but Ong Chou-fei himself was not listed. That hardly surprised him. Running his finger down the page he found the import-export company mentioned in the funeral announcement and noted the address.

'Moody, any sign of that car you promised?'

'I'd hardly call it a car, but it's wheels. Parked outside.'

He reckoned it could do no harm to look at the place, regardless of the admiral's instructions. His only chance now to pick up broken threads was to become visible again. He'd lost a week. Before going he double-checked the list of Moody's client companies. Ong's was not among them. Perhaps if he called with promotional literature for the new typewriters and adding machines it might get him through the door. He stuffed a few copies into a folder and requisitioned Moody's street map.

The car was worse than he'd feared, jumping out of gear whenever he braked too hard, too much play on the steering, and as stubborn as a mule when he asked it to do something it didn't like. But in its own time it got him to the bustling, down-at-heel street on the far side of Singapore river where – according to the telephone book – the Ong family business had its offices.

Parking in the first available space, he walked along between the bales and crates crowding the five-foot way in search of number 22. He found its high shutters closed and padlocked. On them was a note in handwritten Chinese with a few words of clumsy English beneath the scrawl saying simply 'death in family'.

'No open.' A thick-set Chinese, probably in his forties, waddled up to him from the next building. He had one of those moon-like Cantonese faces, constantly smiling. 'Ol' man dead. *Mati*. OK?'

'Ong Chou-fei?'

The man nodded, still beaming. 'Ong Chou-fei. Dead. You wan' buy? China silk brocade? Ver' top quality. I give good price.'

'I want to see young Mr Ong. Is he there?'

'No Ong here. Live far 'way.' He gestured vaguely in no particular direction. 'Ong villa. You look-see, tuan. Silk brocade. Ver' good trade. For you big profit.'

'Where's the villa?' Ross was tempted to question the man in Chinese but decided against it. That card was best kept face down for the moment. 'Address? You know the address?'

'Dress?' In his enthusiasm the man gripped his arm. 'Silk brocade ver' good ladies dress.'

He shook the man's hand away and started back up the street to where he had left the mule to roast under the direct sun. Getting in, he had to slam the rickety door three times before it clicked shut. Sweat dripped from his face; his shirt stuck to him like a second skin.

About a hundred yards behind was a parked taxi which had not been there before. As he drove off it pulled out to follow him. No passenger as far as he could judge through his rear mirror, nor was the driver touting for any. Very well, this time he'd give the shadow something to report. He turned the mule towards Lavender Street, following the route he'd picked out on Moody's map. The taxi stuck with him.

Again he chose to park some distance away, this time finding a patch of shade. In daylight Lien Jee Bar looked still more sordid than after dark when at least the soft light of the oil lamps had lent it a certain romanticism. Now its pale blue walls seemed to be in an even worse condition than he had noticed at the time. From the ceiling above the bar hung the same fly paper covered with dead insects; no one had bothered to renew it.

'Beer,' he said to the man behind the bar – not the same man he'd seen before, either. Someone new.

'Tiger beer. Ver' cold.'

Ross watched him as he levered off the crown top and poured some into a tall glass. The foam rose rapidly till it reached the rim.

'Where are the girls?' he demanded, looking around. Apart from the barman the place was empty.

'This evening girl come, plenty good girl. You like.'

'And Susie?'

'Please?'

'Last time I was here I met two girls.'

'Las' time?' He was pretending to be puzzled, putting it on for Ross's benefit but not making too good a job of it. 'I no see you before.'

'Too right, chum,' Ross said, taking his glass and the bottle across to the table where he'd sat with Susie. 'Too bloody right. Because it wasn't you serving, was it?'

'This is my bar. I see all customer,' the man protested, but a little too eagerly. 'You wan' I send for girl? Bes' girl in Singapore I send for. All ver' clean. Good jig-jig.'

'I can wait.'

Ross drank his beer slowly. They had made a clean sweep, he understood that much. Changed the barman, brought in fresh girls; no one who knew anything of his meeting with Ong Chou-fei existed any longer. Of course, whoever owned the bar would want to stay on the right side of those powerful enough to close the place down, whether colonial police or some Chinese secret society to which they no doubt paid protection money. It did no business any good to be openly linked with murder.

The man fiddled with a rediffusion box high up on one wall till it produced the usual wail of Cantonese popular music. Perhaps he was trying to liven things up, though only the two of them were there, no one else.

'Turn the bloody thing down!' he protested, blustering as though he'd drunk too much. 'It's too loud, d'you hear?'

'OK, Tommy. OK.'

The man reached up for the volume control and the music became softer. Then he looked towards Ross for some sign of approval.

Ross drained his glass without even taking the trouble

to glance at him. He stood up and pulled out a handful of loose notes. 'How much?' He threw some money down on the table, a dog-eared note. 'You can fuck your girls yourself!' he informed him before striding out into the street.

His visit would be remembered, he felt confident.

The taxi was still with him, waiting a few yards away; to reach the spot where the mule was parked he would need to pass it. Briefly he hesitated before deciding he might as well nose around a little while still in the district. Take a closer look perhaps at the side road where Ong Chou-fei had been stabbed.

It was difficult to recognize. The last time he'd seen them those buildings had been dark and locked up; now the heavy wooden doors stood open and half a dozen coolies were manhandling soapboxes and packing cases on to a couple of handcarts. They stopped and stared at him as he passed.

But he identified the alley leading to the back of the Lien Jee Bar, and the single lamp set high on the warehouse wall. Nothing else – and Christ, what else was there to find? He'd been trained as a saboteur, a guerrilla fighter, and in the techniques of survival, not as a bloody detective. 'Ross, you're a romantic, a fuckin' dreamer!' an instructor had bawled him out one day; he could still recall the bastard's vicious face. 'You'd better snap out of it double quick if you count on stayin' alive!'

He hadn't snapped out of it, not ever. Couldn't. And he *was* still alive.

Just.

So far.

He turned back towards the road, hoping to find the way to Susie's room though not too sure of himself. When she had taken him there his main worry had been staying conscious and on his feet. But the house was nearer than he thought – on a corner, with the frontage chipped and scarred, and a flight of concrete steps leading up the side to her door. He still had his bruises from the time he'd been shoved down them.

The door was closed when he got to it. He tried the handle but with no success. Even as he knocked some instinct told him she was not there. He felt a pang of disappointment and told himself he'd come to thank her, nothing more; she'd had a rough time of it because of him.

He knocked again, louder.

'What you wan'?'

The man had come up silently behind him, a tough-looking Chinese with a bulge beneath his loose shirt which could easily have been a pistol. At the foot of the steps stood two other Chinese, watching them. Play it cool now, Ross told himself; they're just waiting for you to make a move. He put on his tipsy act again.

'Come to see Susie.' He slurred the words. 'You know Susie? This the place she lives?'

'No Susie here. You go now. *Tuan*.' The sarcastic stress of that word *tuan* was obviously intended to warn him off.

Ross banged on the door, drunkenly. 'Susie? You there, Susie?'

Then the man's hand grasped his arm and swung him round. 'You wan' girl, you go bar. No make trouble here, OK?'

'OK . . . OK . . .' Ross raised his open hands before him in a gesture of peace. This narrow landing was no place for a rough-house, least of all with a gun-toting Chinese pimp. He eyed the other two as well, still at the foot of the steps, still waiting for him to make a wrong move. He became conciliatory. 'You're right, she'll be in some bar knocking it back. That's where I'll go.'

The man gestured to him to go down first, which Ross

126

did, taking his time about it and expecting at any moment to feel a sudden push between his shoulder blades. But it never came. Maybe the pimp was also anxious to avoid trouble; or maybe he just couldn't be bothered in that heat.

Then, at the bottom, one of his sidekicks thrust out a foot, catching Ross unawares. He tripped . . . stumbled . . . but somehow managed to avoid falling. Steadying himself, he turned and took a long look at the joker who had done it. They were ready for him, all three, their grinning faces daring him to make one move. Farther along the road he could see the parked taxi, its driver still at the wheel, his head protruding from the open window expectantly.

Ross disappointed them all. He turned on his heel and walked off, heading back towards Lavender Street with the sound of the three Chinese thugs' laughter trailing behind him.

'Show's over,' he said as he passed the taxi. The driver had a gap in his teeth, he saw. No answer, of course.

He reached the mule again and got in, conscious that he had really achieved nothing. The taxi stayed on his tail as he drove back to the office, quite openly now, almost bumper to bumper where the traffic was heavy. When he went in, he noticed how the driver had found a spot to park immediately opposite the entrance.

'I was on the point of going,' Moody announced, closing the folder on which he was working. He asked no questions, showed no curiosity, but suggested a bite to eat.

Ross grunted his consent.

Looking down from Moody's window he caught a last glimpse of the taxi as it pulled away again. No doubt within an hour a report on his movements would be on Browne's desk. Meanwhile, beneath the tree on the far side of the road the food hawker was in his usual place.

'Cricket Club, I thought.' Moody cut cheerfully across his musings. 'Haven't been there yet, have you? We're a bit late but they might still be serving.'

The Cricket Club was on the Padang almost directly facing his hotel. It was a cool building in the open colonial manner. A smiling Chinese steward in a white drill tunic greeted Moody the moment they entered and conducted them to the dining room where the lazy murmur of conversation blended with the busy sound of whirring ceiling fans. In the centre of the room one table had already been vacated though not yet cleared; in seconds the dishes had been removed and a clean cloth laid.

'Ross, my dear fellow!' He had just picked up the menu when Browne appeared at his elbow, his face flushed from his lunchtime beer. 'Noticed you coming in. Fit again? Quack signed you off? I imagine Tim here's been looking after you properly? Still, we must have a chat. Finish your meal first, then come and join me for coffee. I'll hang on till you're ready.'

Ross watched him weave his way back to his friends at a corner table and wondered irritably what the hell he could want this time.

'Colonial Service, that lot with him,' Moody observed as he studied the menu. His words were tinged with rancour. 'Treat the business community like we're some kind of *Untermenschen*.'

'Is that what we are. Business community?'

'Don't ever forget it.'

They took their time over the meal, but at last Moody made some diplomatic excuse and left Ross to seek out Browne in the bar. By then the place was practically empty. The few members still around were dozing on the shaded veranda. Browne sat inside, alone at one of the tables, leafing through a dog-eared copy of *Esquire*. Ross dropped into the armchair next to him.

'Boy!' Browne called across to the bar. 'Coffee!'

'Coffee, tuan,' the boy agreed, and he wandered off to organize it.

Browne turned to Ross, keeping his voice low. 'The funeral takes place tomorrow. Pereira brought you the cutting?'

'Yes.'

'We'd like you to be there. Moody told me he'd fixed up a car for you.'

'Of a kind.'

'It'll have to do. Now I've sent details to your hotel giving the time and the route the procession will take. Park the car somewhere where you can get a good view as they pass, but make sure you're not too conspicuous. Watch their faces. I want to know if there's anyone you recognize.'

'Who do you expect – Mao Tse-tung?'

'It doesn't do to be frivolous, Ross. You're not out of the jungle yet. Anybody you've come across before, whether in that bar or any other place, we need to know. Savvy?'

Back at the hotel Ross found an envelope resting in the pigeon-hole with his key. The Indian clerk even managed a smile as he handed it over, but then perhaps he was the one who had tampered with it. It contained one sheet of folded paper. The funeral details. He cursed Browne for leaving it there.

Moody was quite right to describe Browne as a dangerous amateur, he thought grimly. It was the sort of risk he could do without.

Twice Ross drove up and down the long road which led to the Chinese cemetery before he settled on a suitable spot to park. The richly endowed spreading trees offered plenty of shade from the sun and that helped. He wore the dark sunglasses he had bought that morning, though without any thought of disguise. There was no way he could hide in Singapore, as Moody had once reminded him.

He heard the loud clashing of cymbals some minutes before the head of the procession appeared round the curve. All that clatter was intended to drive off the evil spirits. It was probably effective too, he thought. He couldn't imagine any devil wanted to stick around with that row going on.

The other musicians were not unpleasant to hear. As they came into view he estimated at least forty were playing flutes and fiddles, and that was in addition to percussion. Behind them walked the usual paid mourners in their white head-bands, many bearing banners and scrolls honouring the deceased, and then the friends and lesser relatives who held the long rope with which they symbolically 'drew' the flower-bedecked lorry doing duty as a hearse.

Ong Chou-fei was being buried in style as a man of great standing and Ross felt glad about that. During their talk in that upstairs room beneath the portraits of Princess Elizabeth and Princess Margaret Rose he had taken a liking to him.

A life-size photograph of the dead man was mounted above the driver's cab; as the hearse approached the eyes in the picture seemed to stare directly at him, acknowledging his presence. Seconds later the effect was lost, but Ross watched the coffin, half-buried under the flowers, even removing his sunglasses as he paid his respects.

She was walking immediately behind the hearse, not alone but with a small group of mourners.

Her coarse white linen mourning hood had slipped back from her face a little, otherwise he might not have recognized her. No Shanghai make-up this time; no green silk brocade or black stockings. Her legs were bare, her lips pale, and her *cheongsam* was plain and white.

Their eyes met, then she drew the hood closer over her face as she walked on, passing his parked car.

After she had left his hotel room that day, he had assumed she was one of those wealthy women who find it chic to run little errands for the revolution, a salve for the conscience mingled with the thrill of illegality, but her place in the procession was that of one of the family. The dead man's wife? Or his daughter? It was something he would have to find out.

Again the big question nagged at him. Mao Tse-tung or Chiang Kai-shek – which China had Ong been speaking for?

6

Fang Mei-lin, walking behind the hearse in the afternoon heat, her neck damp with perspiration, had not been pleased at the sight of Ross parked beneath the trees to spy on the funeral procession. His presence was an intrusion.

To her surprise Chou-fei's death had shaken her, leaving her with a haunting sense of desolation which she had not expected. She had stayed with him because the Party had ordered it, not for any emotional reason, or so she'd always reminded herself. None of the cadres would understand her grief; in fact she could almost hear their voices condemning her, demanding that she should correct her mistakes. Yet what mistakes? Liking him? Having enjoyed his company and failing to harden herself against his affection?

They would disapprove of the funeral of course. In the New China all such traditional ceremonies were disappearing along with the superstitions which for generations had been used to oppress the people. Yet Chou-fei himself would have regarded this long procession as an honour – the groups of musicians, the mourners, the members of his business association following the coffin with their colourful umbrellas, even the paper scatterers distributing fistfuls of printed 'hell money' along the route. But there had always been a touch of the mandarin about him. He had loved the old forms.

'Forgive me,' she whispered, remembering his face before they nailed down the coffin. She had been shocked at how cold he felt after all those days of refrigeration in the police mortuary.

Had she killed him?

She had arranged the meeting not knowing why, following the Party's instructions to the letter. Who this Chinese-speaking Englishman was she had not been told, but he had been observed talking to an Internal Security official they called Browne, and only yesterday he had returned to Lien Jee Bar, asking questions. Now he had turned up again.

If only she could discuss it with someone she might feel more confident, but who was there? No one in the Ong family. In their eyes she was merely the concubine Chou-fei had inconsiderately brought with him from China. The mistress, these Singapore people called her, to stress that she did not even possess the traditional status of concubine. She was temporary. She was no one. Once the funeral was over she was expected to leave.

No fresh orders had come from the Party either, no word at all since the night Chou-fei had died. Lee San, the gardener at the villa who was her contact, had been unable to advise her. 'Wait,' he had said. But then he was no more than a mouthpiece.

Now her job was over she had been forgotten, she thought as the funeral procession reached the cemetery. Among those half-moon graves tucked into the hillside was the plot where Chou-fei's body would be laid to rest. They needed no more reports from her, no more accounts of whom he met or what they said. That was all over.

She felt a tremor of apprehension like a chill breeze in that tropical heat. Sooner or later they would decide what to do with her next. Send her back to teaching infants in that slum school in Tientsin perhaps. Did they really understand how different a person she had become since knowing Chou-fei?

Could they ever understand?

The Taoist priests were intoning their prayers near the graveside. Soon it would be over and they would all return to the villa; by evening she would be packing her belongings, ready to move out the following day. Perhaps she should go to a hotel if no instructions came.

Or take the emergency route back to China – by air to British-occupied Hongkong and then on by ferry to Macao where the resident agent could make the necessary arrangements.

She just didn't know.

Ross had followed them into the cemetery and now stood among the mourners on the other side of the grave. He'd had the good manners not to push himself forward to the front row, she noticed, but stayed with those at the back. She kept her face covered, though he was bound to pick her out. Probably other police agents were there too, perhaps among the musicians or the undertakers' men. Renegade Chinese working for the imperialist regime.

The gongs and cymbals started up again as they eased the coffin into the ground and the mourners stepped back to make sure their shadows did not fall across it. If only she could hear his voice again, one of his ironic comments; it would lighten her tensions.

One by one the family came forward to sprinkle soil on the coffin. Then the younger Mr Ong was at her side, urging her to do likewise. 'M-mei-lin?'

She hesitated. Since Chou-fei's death he had gone out of his way to speak kindly to her with secret sidelong glances which caused her to suspect that he planned to take his uncle's place in her bed. Somewhere away from the villa, of course; somewhere not too expensive. She imagined he had already worked out the cost, totting up the figures to the nearest cent; he was that kind of man. For both brothers Uncle Chou-fei had been simply a businessman; they had known nothing of his other concerns; they had never really shown any genuine interest in him.

She glanced at the older brother but he raised no objection. Slowly she moved to the graveside and scooped up a handful of wet soil. Breaking it between her fingers, she dropped the crumbs gently on to the coffin while silently bidding her lover goodbye for the last time. When she stepped back, she stood apart from the family as an acknowledgement that she knew her place.

Ross, she saw, had already gone.

That evening, in the brief Singapore twilight, a storm blew up. Short gusts of fierce wind engulfed the villa, banging the shutters and sending papers flying. A brilliant lightning flash was directly succeeded by an explosion of tearing thunder immediately over the roof.

While the maids rushed around securing everything, Mei-lin deliberately left her shutters open. Throughout these days she had remained deadly calm, not daring to lose control unless she betrayed herself; the storm was a release, a mirror of her pain. She paused in her packing to look out. The palms were tossing and bending against the darkening sky, with the wind howling around them.

The rain came suddenly, first a few large drops, then a rush of water lashing against the house till she felt the refreshing spray against her face as she stood at the window, although it did not open towards the wind.

Maybe it was the funeral which set her dreaming, or maybe the low, howling undulation of the wind recalled that Tientsin winter – the worst in living memory, according to the older people. Even indoors her fingers had been numb and useless; no one ventured out willingly, but she had been given no choice. The Party needed her to deliver a message after curfew to a comrade in hiding on the far side of town, and of course she could not refuse.

By then the Japanese war was over but no one felt safe, not with Chiang Kai-shek's Nationalist Kuomintang in control. In Tientsin that night the soldiers had seemed unusually jittery, she remembered; to avoid their road blocks she'd had to take a long, roundabout route and more than once she heard the sound of shooting in the distance. Everyone was convinced that it could only be a matter of days before the People's Liberation Army broke through to free the town from the Kuomintang yoke, so absurdly optimistic had they all been.

She had delivered her message and was on her way back when the Kuomintang police arrested her. In the police station she discovered they had been rounding up everyone they could lay their hands on. Prisoners of all ages were crowded in there, stamping their feet and rubbing their wrists as they tried to keep warm. She had stood among them, frightened and shivering, fearful that she was about to be shot, until two peasant women took pity on her, making room for her to sit between them on the only bench.

'Heard the news?' one whispered encouragingly. 'It's said the line to Peking has been cut and they can't get their ammunition trains through. That's why they're arresting everybody. Ssh, here he comes, the officer. Keep your eyes down. Don't draw attention to yourself.'

Mei-lin had stared at the floor and prayed she would not be noticed, but the sight of the officer's expensive, highly polished boots made her curious. She risked a quick glance up, just long enough to take in the elegant but obviously warm greatcoat, the muffler, the fur hat and the gloves. How cosy he looks, she had thought enviously; and she had hated him for standing there in his finery while everyone else was in threadbare rags.

Suddenly she realized he was observing her thoughtfully. He tapped her on the shoulder with his stick. 'This one,' he ordered. 'Take her through to the back room.'

This, though she did not know it at the time, was her first encounter with Colonel Ong Chou-fei.

Her arms were seized. The other prisoners were elbowed roughly out of the way as she was dragged across the room and into the rear corridor. Once in the interrogation room they searched her again, poking their cold stubby fingers into her most intimate parts in their hunt for anything, even the tiniest scrap of paper, which might link her with the Party; and they questioned her and tried to browbeat her into a confession, banging the table and yelling at her, though the louder they yelled the more stubborn she became. Perhaps even the extreme cold helped her, making it easier for her to sink into herself, deadening her mind to the point when she found she was merely repeating the same denials, identical words, whatever question they asked.

Then the colonel entered, ordering the others out of the room. He removed his fur hat, placing it on the bare table in front of him, and sat down.

'No need to stand.' He indicated a chair and waited until she was seated before picking up the interrogation sheet and glancing at it. 'Fang Mei-lin – you're a teacher? Arrested out-of-doors at ten o'clock in the evening . . . Hm. Hm. In contravention of the curfew order. We live in strange times, don't you think, Miss Fang Mei-lin?'

She heard his words, her mind still numb, and neither answered them nor even raised her eyes to his face. If she had any thoughts at all at the moment they amounted only to the conviction that he was playing with her as a cat toys with a trapped mouse prior to killing it.

'Strange times,' he repeated. His voice sounded gentle

and civilized, but that was one of their techniques for softening up a victim. The Party had warned her of it.

He went on: 'For almost a decade we Chinese struggled against the Japanese invader. Yet now we have control of our own country again, what do we do? We fight against each other. You and I, Miss Fang. Chinese against Chinese.'

That had roused her to protest that she was fighting nobody. 'I teach small children how to read and write,' she informed him sullenly.

But he hardly seemed to take in her words.

'This is heresy, I know, but I sometimes think our China needs another emperor to hold us all together. Not your Mao Tse-tung, needless to say, nor the Generalissimo. But an emperor.'

She met his eyes. What a snake, she thought; he was a poisonous snake.

Then he had started to boast about how he had once met Mao when they were both young men, and how he judged him to be a good poet in spite of his political errors. Did she know Mao's poems perhaps? Did she teach them to her children?

'I don't know them.'

In his own way, his questioning had been worse than the bullying interrogation which had preceded it. She recalled it as she stood at the open window enjoying the cool rain-spray against her skin. If only he had yelled at her, or hit her even, she would have understood better; instead, he had tried to insinuate himself into her friendship by talking of poetry, and smiling at her, and teasing her. Laying traps for her. No, she had not studied Marxist-Leninism, she had lied; nor had she read the Russian authors he mentioned. Eventually, feigning shyness to hide the fear in her trembling voice, she had

138

countered by quoting a line from a Yüan dynasty poem: 'The brook lingers where the willow weeps.'

He had beamed his approval. Thirty minutes later he issued her with a pass and ordered her release.

So relieved had she been that she had hardly noticed the cold any longer as she hurried home through the dark, unlit streets. That night, though, she had been unable to sleep. Had she made a slip in one of her answers? Perhaps he had freed her in order to have her watched wherever she went, though she felt quite certain no one had followed her home. She had to remind herself that she was only small fry in the Party after all. But it was so easy to betray a comrade through a moment's carelessness. Without intending to.

The next morning she was taking a reading lesson when his car drew up in the muddy lane outside their unheated schoolhouse. From the window she observed a soldier getting out from behind the driving wheel and stepping gingerly across the mud to hold open the rear door for him. The children continued chanting the lines from their primer, but then began to falter as they noticed she was no longer listening to them. When he entered the class-room they all stood up as one – forty-five peaked, shivering, ill-fed children standing to show respect to Colonel Ong Chou-fei, warmly clad and probably with an excellent meal in his belly.

She knew nothing about him then, of course; not as she learned to know him later. Yet she caught the essence of his character even as he glanced around her classroom. Not cruelty; no, far from that. But distance. A sense that he was something apart.

His driver followed him in with a basket of food which he began to distribute among the children and she remem-bered it had taken all her will-power to conceal the fury building up inside her at the sight of it. This food he and his like had first stolen from the peasants to fill their own bloated stomachs, so how dare he now expect those infants to smile and thank him for it? Had they been old enough to understand, they'd have thrown it in his face.

That same afternoon, a squad of Kuomintang soldiers – building workers they had been, conscripted into the army against their will – had turned up to repair the dripping roof; and in the morning Colonel Ong Chou-fei reappeared to inspect their work and gave out slabs of American chocolate to the children.

And so it had gone on. Day after day he had arrived at the school, always with gifts, always trying to engage her in conversation, and with each visit her anger had grown. She talked it over in a painful interview with the leader of her team who told her bluntly she no longer had a place in the class struggle, not as long as this went on. Her comrades mistrusted her.

Then the time came when Ong Chou-fei spelled out what he had in mind and she had been so taken aback, she almost laughed in his face. He was leaving Tientsin, he said, and he invited her to go with him as his mistress. Perhaps for the first time she had realized she found him not unattractive, although he was old enough to be her father. She had stalled, uncertain how to refuse, and requested a few days to think it over. One wrong move, and she could find herself back in that police station; others could be endangered too. She consulted the cadres; they listened to her in silence, then kept her waiting for almost a whole week before pronouncing their decision. Agree, they said. The Party could make good use of informants in the Kuomintang camp. They would arrange for contacts to whom she could report wherever she went.

The rain was already easing and Mei-lin turned away from the open window to carry on with her packing. She had been so shocked at the Party's decision, she recalled as she folded her silk *cheongsam* dresses, laying them carefully in the suitcase. It amused her now to think of it. Of course she had not been entirely innocent. While training as a teacher she had fallen deeply in love with a fellow student and they had spent long hours together discussing the role of education in the class struggle; then his team had joined the active fight against the Japanese and for months she had heard nothing from him until at last news came that he had been killed in a skirmish. No, not entirely innocent, but still a simple, serious girl who had felt in her heart that the Party should be above the deception they were asking of her.

If she now regretted anything, it was the loss of that simplicity, she felt. She closed the first case and began to pack the second. Chou-fei had bought her so many things, squandered money on her. She caught sight of his framed photograph on the bedside table, and it seemed he was smiling at her. Almost three years she had been with him: was it any wonder she had changed? Old mandarin, she thought. It was ridiculous even to imagine the younger Mr Ong could take his place. Out of the question.

'Eh . . .'

A man's voice. Very soft, hardly audible above the rush of rainwater in the gutters. She moved quietly to the window and saw him standing pressed against the wall in the shadows, a loose waterproof sheet over his shoulders. His face was not visible but she guessed it must be the gardener, Lee San.

'I'm listening,' she breathed. She felt ill at ease. Usually they communicated well away from the house. This was too risky.

'New China Hotel, Bras Basah Road. A room has been booked for you.'

'When?'

'Go tomorrow in the forenoon. Ask me to fetch a taxi for you. It is all arranged. Not their car.'

'Wait,' she whispered urgently. 'What if they . . .?'

But he was no longer there. He had stepped back quickly among the rain-sodden shrubs and was lost in the darkness. What if the younger Mr Ong insisted on driving her, she had been about to ask; but that was a problem she would have to handle when the time came. At least the Party had made up its mind, she thought apprehensively. They would return her to China perhaps; the New China Hotel would be a transit address. From there she'd . . .

She caught a glimpse of herself in the dressing-table mirror as she emptied more of her things out of the drawers. Her eyes had a haunted look, tired and drawn; only then did she begin to realize how nervous she really felt. Like the day she left the Tientsin school and stepped into the colonel's staff car for the first time. Symbolically stepping into a new life, she had told herself then, and wasn't that what she was about to do again?

As she placed her last few things in the case the maid came into the bedroom, opening the door without knocking as though she already realized Mei-lin no longer had any status in the villa. Her manner was sullen as she announced that the family was about to eat. 'I am to say you are invited to join them because this is your last evening here.'

Mei-lin nodded, surprised. Perhaps the younger Mr Ong had put his foot down; she had fully expected to eat alone in her room again, as she had every evening since Chou-fei's death.

In order not to provoke trouble she remained dressed as she was in the discreet cotton *samfu* she had put on for the packing, though the temptation to flaunt herself in silks and pearls was strong. It was her last meal with them.

She had been right about the younger Mr Ong planning to set her up in a place of her own. He came to her room in the morning, nervous that his wife might overhear him, and blurted it all out. She could have laughed in his face but what was the point of making an enemy of him? Instead, she listened carefully to his confused explanations, then politely refused him, also declining his offer to drive her to the hotel.

The rest of the family remained discreetly out of sight that morning. The previous evening they had taken formal leave of her, enquiring with well-mannered non-interest where she intended staying, while making it quite plain once again that she was no longer welcome at the villa. She had casually named a hotel several miles out of Singapore, not the New China of course, and didn't conceal her indifference to their remarks.

Lee San left his work in the garden to stand in the roadway as if attempting to stop a cruising taxi – a fiction intended to deceive the family, she suspected, though none of them was around to witness it. The rattling black car he found must have been parked beyond the bend awaiting his signal. It was Lee San who had to carry out her cases too; the house servants were staying well clear of her.

She sat on the back seat, discovering as they drove off that several springs were broken. Every unevenness in the road meant a painful jolt. 'New China Hotel,' she ordered the driver once they were well away from the villa.

'No, that has been changed. Your room is now in the Peking Hotel.'

'Why?' She felt uneasy, not liking the look of him. His face was hard, like some street thug. His lips parted in a

143

brief, threatening smile; a front tooth was missing. 'Who changed it?'

'Comrade, what do I know?' he protested. 'This is the message for you. Your room is booked in the Peking Hotel where we are going now. Do not go out – understand? If you need food, room service will bring you something. Then this evening after dark you go to the Great Wall cinema which is close to the hotel, in the same road. Sit upstairs. At 8.30 you visit the ladies' room. OK?'

'What then?'

For the rest of the drive he was silent. She had had three years now of cryptic messages and secret meetings with unknown contacts, but always in the knowledge that she would be returning to Ong Chou-fei. This time she felt everything was uncertain; her mouth was dry, her stomach queasy. They were now going along South Bridge Road, she saw. Looking down the narrow side streets shaded by rows of washing strung out on bamboo poles protruding from the upper windows, she experienced a weird sensation that they were unreal, like a dissolving dream. She would blink and never see them again.

Stay out of sight till dark, then proceed to the rendezvous: nothing more. She did not even know if she would be returning to the hotel afterwards. They might smuggle her on board a China-bound junk. Or post her to some jungle commando out of reach of the colonial police.

Or kill her. With Chou-fei dead her usefulness was over, her knowledge an embarrassment.

The taxi drew up before the Peking Hotel, a four-storey white building advertising its name in both Chinese and romanized script above the first-floor windows.

'Do I pay you?'

The driver leered at her. 'Trying to say you've never been in a taxi before, is that it? Of course you pay.'

144

She reached over to give him a ten-dollar note, waving away the change. 'I think you need it, comrade,' she told him sarcastically. It was a last gesture before her readjustment to poverty. 'You can bring the cases in.'

The girl at the reception desk handed her a key, asking no questions, not so much as her name. 'Third floor, straight up the stairs. Anything you want, the floor maid will fetch. Electricity is off this morning.'

A man was called to relieve the taxi driver of her suitcases; carrying one in either hand, he followed her silently up the bare staircase, even unlocking the door and standing aside to let her enter first as though she were an ordinary hotel guest. But then ordinary guests have names, complete registration forms, give tips. She offered him a tip but he refused it, still not uttering a word.

The bedroom itself was simple but clean, with white walls and a small bathroom – nothing elaborate, just a squat-lavatory set in the floor, plus a shower. In this cell she was to spend the whole day, she thought bleakly.

Kicking off her shoes she sprawled across the hard bed and no longer attempted to inhibit the memories from tumbling through her mind unrestrained, one incident merging illogically with the next, all so vivid, till the sobs shook her, catching her off-guard: her first real tears since it had happened.

She wept uncontrollably – for the end of everything which had been her life since she left Tientsin, for this new sense of desolation and loneliness, and for Chou-fei himself, and the realization that part of her had died with him. How the Party would have despised her for it!

The Great Wall cinema was showing a Hongkong-made historical romance in Cantonese. As instructed, she paid and went upstairs to the balcony, groping her way to a seat near the central aisle. If the illuminated clock-face

145

next to the screen was accurate she had just half an hour to wait.

It was an unending half-hour and a slow-moving film. Beneath a full moon the love-lorn heroine stood singing on an arched bridge over a river. Its supposedly flowing water was motionless, and so too were the trees, permanently bent under a slight breeze. The hands of the clock crept forward; the song still continued.

But at last it was time. She stood up and headed for the exit, her mouth dry, her hand trembling as she pushed the door open and walked along the empty corridor towards the 'Toilets' sign at the far end. From the auditorium she could hear actors' voices. The music had stopped.

The ladies' room was deserted, though she found a tap had been left running. She turned it off. There were four cubicles, doors standing ajar, unoccupied. She was quite alone.

No other way out, not that she could see – so what was she supposed to do? Stand and wait?

The place was stiflingly hot and plagued with mosquitoes. The air-conditioning system serving the auditorimum clearly did not extend to the toilets. There was also a smell of badly maintained drains. Reluctantly she hunted around in the cubicles in case a note had been left, a message, some kind of hint at least. Nothing.

Puzzled, she decided to go back into the corridor. It would be more pleasant to wait out there, she thought – though for how long? And what would she do if no one came?

She pulled open the door and suddenly there he was, framed in the doorway, blocking her path. Tall for a Chinese, that was her immediate reaction; well-built and muscular, like an athlete. Dark glasses hid his eyes but his lips were oddly twisted as if in a permanent grin, yet he was not grinning at all, but grave. His face was long rather than round, she noted, and very smooth.

For a moment they stared at each other.

'The comrade from Tientsin.' It was a statement, not a question. He spoke standard Mandarin but with an accent she could not place. 'Come with me, please.'

With a gesture he pointed towards a low door set in the blocked-off end of the corridor and stood aside to let her go first. It was not a display of bourgeois politeness, she understood, but simply a means of keeping an eye on her. Several times he glanced back towards the auditorium entrance to make sure they were not observed.

The low door led into a large cupboard where brooms and cleaning materials were kept. She hesitated, uncertain what to do until he put a hand on her shoulder and steered her forward. Only when she was inside, stooping, did she discover how the side panel was in fact another door which opened on to a narrow passage. He followed her through, then swung the panel back into place. Metal bars at the top and bottom held it firm.

'Straight along, Comrade Fang,' he said quietly.

A single bare electric bulb provided the only light. Around it a cloud of insects circled, while a foot way, flattened against the wall, a fat brown gecko fed on any that came within reach of its tongue. Another lizard darted across the floor at her feet, startling her; she almost trod on it.

'In here,' he directed her.

They were in a store room; nothing sinister about it. It contained a number of small wooden boxes piled up against one wall, a couple of chairs and a folding table.

'The Party is pleased with you, Comrade Fang.' He drew forward a chair for her, quickly dusting the seat with the side of his hand. 'I could not get here sooner, but I want to say you have done a good job. Your reports on Ong Chou-fei were a model of their kind.'

'Why did you have to kill him?' she burst out in a quick spurt of anger she could not suppress. She stopped instantly, dismayed at what she had said.

'What's your explanation?' He had removed his dark glasses and she could now see his eyes examining her face. 'Come on, comrade. I'd like to hear how you analyse the situation.'

'With my help he made arrangements to meet the Englishman Ross. I reported that.' She was stumbling, not knowing how far she could go. 'Ross was seen to be in contact with the imperialist Internal Security man, Browne. There was a possibility he was betraying the struggle.'

'Do *you* think so?'

His gaze made her feel even more uncertain of herself. Who was he? What authority did he have? She had followed the rules, not asking his name until he offered it – but he didn't offer it. He volunteered nothing.

'What could he betray? I don't know.'

'His death upset you, of course. The circumstances of your work caused you to become emotionally attached to him. The Party understands that.'

'I . . .' Her clothes were sticking to her skin, it was so hot in that room.

'Don't let it lead you into error, comrade. Whoever killed him, the Party did not give the order. In fact his death leaves us with a problem.'

'I shall obey any orders the Party has for me.'

'I do not refer to your personal position, comrade.'

'My wish is to return home to assist in the work of reconstruction.' That was the correct line to take; somehow she had to demonstrate how uncorrupted she had

148

remained despite her years of luxury living with Chou-fei. But was it true? She was no longer sure.

'When you have finished your work here you will be informed what decision has been reached, comrade.' His face remained inscrutable. 'But your first duty is to renew contact with Ross. Colonel Ong died before he could report on their meeting.'

'And Browne? He has seen Ross several times.'

'If Browne proves to be a difficulty he can be handled. You seem surprised, comrade. The Party uses whichever instruments best suit its purpose. Colonel Ong, for example.'

'Ong was working for the Party?' she was shocked. The thought that Chou-fei might have been a clandestine Party member had never occurred to her. It seemed totally out of character. If it were true, then she had never really known him after all.

'Come now, you were fully informed of our business dealings with him.'

'Business dealings, yes.' Was that all he meant? Chou-fei himself had been the first to tell her, half-amused, how he was supplying scientific and medical equipment to the new Communist regime. But then he had always claimed to be merely a trader with no interest in political theories; no respect for them either. Besides, the New China needed everything he could sell them. Profit and patriotism – he never saw anything incongruous in the link. And she had smiled when he spoke of it, encouraging him to confide in her, though in her heart she had disapproved – not of what he was doing of course, no one had expected an amoral capitalist to have great ideals, but of the Party for allowing it to happen.

'On this occasion Colonel Ong had agreed to carry a message for us.'

'To Ross?'

'In the People's interest. Comrade Fang, if you genuinely wish to serve the class struggle you will now listen carefully. Get in touch with Ross again – but discreetly, I want no bungling – and instruct him to be at Soon Thian Keng Temple at twelve noon on Sunday. There will be the usual crowd of onlookers. He will wait with them until contacted.'

'Ross,' she said again. Would he too be killed?

'Have you understood?'

Briefly she repeated her instructions. It was Friday. She would have to reach Ross quickly in case he planned to return to Moody's house for the weekend. This Party agent from Peking would not excuse any failure; talking to her, not once had he softened.

'May I ask something?' She plunged in without pausing. 'Why was Ong Chou-fei entrusted with this message? He was not politically reliable. His background was well known to the Party.'

'It does not concern you, comrade. There are reasons of course why the decision was taken. The matters you raise were all considered, you can be sure. Now one more thing – remember you have not seen me. I am not here. You do not know what I look like, nor who I am. I do not exist. Is that clear?'

'It is clear, comrade. But after I've spoken to Ross, what then?'

'You wait till you are contacted. If all goes well, arrangements will be made for your return to China. Now I shall take you back.'

This time he went first along the narrow passage. She followed him closely, then stood watching when he removed the bars holding the secret door in place. As he bent forward she was aware of how powerfully built he was, solid bone and muscle; and the bulge at his waist must be a gun. With Chou-fei she had seldom given a

150

thought to the danger she might be in; it had seemed so improbable, yet now he was dead.

He went through the broom cupboard ahead of her to check the corridor outside. A second later he beckoned her out. 'Go back to your seat and stay till the film ends,' he ordered. 'Then leave with the rest of the audience. Stay with the crowd.'

At the door back into the auditorium she glanced over her shoulder, but the corridor was already empty and the broom cupboard door was shut.

7

Ross ate alone that evening despite a pressing invitation from Browne to join him at the Tanglin Club. Cornered, he excused himself by pleading a prior engagement without specifying what it might be and was relieved when Browne at last drove off in that damned Riley he was always boasting about.

For Ross's taste Singapore was too bloody chummy. What he needed was anonymity, which didn't seem possible. He'd warned the Section before he left London.

At random he chose a Chinese restaurant offering Shanghai food. It was a down-at-heel place on the first floor above some shops and the waiter was surprised to see a European there. His English was halting but Ross cut across his efforts impatiently and spoke to him in Chinese. No point in making a secret of it any longer, not with Browne on the loose.

He was on a fool's errand, he was convinced. It seemed the whole operation was blown; if, in fact, there had ever been one. Whichever way he tried to work it out he found blocked, like one of those old Chinese puzzles.

While waiting for his meal he sat cracking melon seeds between his teeth and sipping beer. The bottle was too cold, straight out of the ice-box, and the condensation on his glass ran down the sides to form a little pool on the table.

After the funeral he had tagged along behind the Ong family limousines as far as the villa. His woman contact from the hotel was the only mourner to seem genuinely upset; he glimpsed her again as they arrived but he didn't stop, not wishing to draw attention to himself.

Then that morning he had gone back to the villa hoping to find someone he could question about her, perhaps a neighbour's servant, or a gardener, but she was standing outside inspecting the shrubs and might have spotted him if he hadn't dodged back in time. It was wasted effort. He returned to the mule having learned nothing, not even her name.

Glumly he watched the waiter setting out his bowls of food on the table before him. Probably Browne could supply a whole file on her if he asked but he'd want to know the reason. That man was too inquisitive about him as it was. In his verbal report on the funeral he hadn't mentioned her at all, though he pointed out that one of the thugs he'd encountered at Susie's place had been in the procession. No reaction at that news; maybe Browne himself had ordered him to be there.

He wiped his chopsticks on a paper napkin before picking up a piece of duck and tasting it. Eating, his mood mellowed a little; living in Singapore might have some advantages after all, though Browne was no guide to them.

But after his meal he still felt restless. He considered driving out to the villa again but decided against it. In that mood he was liable to make mistakes. Perhaps also he was being over-hasty. The admiral had started this business rolling, so let him sort it out. He could imagine the War Office types in Whitehall peeing their pants at the thought of their battlefields being sprayed with germs instead of bullets.

And towns packed with civilians? Children? Which death was preferable – phosphorus bombs or anthrax? Was there really any difference? The defence of civilization, wasn't that what they used to say? People had believed them.

153

His anger smouldered as he strode along the road, not heading anywhere in particular, aware only of the futility of the whole operation. Outside a cinema were posters announcing the latest newsreel pictures of the battle for Seoul and General MacArthur's triumphant ride through the streets while fighting was still in progress on the outskirts; another few weeks and the war would be over. He hesitated, tempted to see it, but thought better of it. Showing with the newsreel was a Hollywood Western. The sight of those pansy actors blasting away at each other in some phony gun fight would only infuriate him even more. He walked on.

He came to the New World amusement park and went in, more out of curiosity than anything else. The wizened elderly woman guarding the coconut shy near the entrance cackled an invitation at him to try his luck. He put some money down on the ledge in front of her and picked up the wooden balls. The first one hit . . . and the second . . . and the third . . . He paid for another three.

With every ball he worked off a fraction of his rage. An audience gathered to watch him, mostly Chinese family groups with children, while the old woman muttered curses as his prizes piled up. He had no idea how long he kept it up, how long it took to rid himself of that blind fury, but at last he stopped, sweat-soaked, calm, and in control of himself again. Vaguely he was conscious of his nagging wound.

Despite deprecating refusals and protests from a few of the men, he distributed most of his prizes among the onlookers and told the old crone to return the rest to her shelves, all but one coconut which he took back with him to the hotel. It had hardly been the best way to avoid notice, he told himself grimly. But what the fuck did it matter?

Usually the Indian desk clerk at the Padang Hotel

would reach behind him for the room key before Ross even requested it, but this time he didn't. He announced with studied indifference that a police officer was waiting for tuan in the bar, adding: 'Half hour he sit there.'

Hell, what now, Ross thought.

He went through and found kid copper Lieutenant Morris, smart in his well-pressed khaki uniform, perched on a bar stool with a half-finished beer before him.

'Been picking coconuts, *Mr* Ross?' Someone must have been talking to him, Ross guessed. Giving him a few lessons in good manners. 'Shinning up the old palm tree?'

'Something like that. Another beer?'

Morris drained his glass, then shook his head. 'I don't drink on duty, *Mr* Ross.'

'Just being sociable,' Ross shrugged. 'So you're on duty, *Mr* Morris?'

'Lieutenant Morris,' kid copper corrected him, flushing. 'Now you've arrived – yes, I'm on duty. You're to come with me. The station wagon's outside.'

'Could do with a beer myself first.'

'Don't push your luck, Ross. Let's go. Don't want to keep important people waiting, do we?'

That was more like the old kid copper, Ross noted with approval. Pity he was born too late; the Japs could have used him in their camps. He'd have enjoyed that.

With a raised finger Ross summoned the barman.

'Here.' He put the coconut down in front of him. 'Present for the family. You got a family?'

'Yes, tuan.'

'OK. Tell 'em it's from me.'

The police station wagon was driven by a Malay constable. Kid copper sat beside him facing front, cap on, very official. Ross, relegated to the back seat, had an unimpeded view of his closely shaven neck.

'Am I not to be told what this is about?'

155

'Orders are simply to fetch you, Mr Ross,' the shaven neck said.

'Whose orders?'

'You'll find out.'

At least, Ross reflected, he was not under arrest; no handcuffs this time. That was an improvement. He leaned back, gazing out at the night streets – the shuttered shop fronts, the nightwatchmen wrapped in their blankets, mummy-like, asleep on their string beds. The air was heavy and humid.

Minutes later the station wagon turned into a well-guarded police compound – a different one this time – stopping beneath the covered porch of a large two-storey building.

'Out!' Kid copper's old charm had returned. '*Mr* Ross.'

It was not the usual police station, that was obvious the moment they stepped inside. No sergeant's desk, no visible telephone, no wire mesh or bars. Kid copper pointed laconically to the wide staircase.

'Up there!'

Nervous, Ross noticed. Afraid of that bad annual report perhaps. They went up to a first-floor corner room big enough for a five-star general. Assistant Superintendent Winterton sat sorting through police report sheets. For paperweights he used miniature soapstone carvings.

'With you in a second, Ross.'

No invitation to sit down, but Ross selected an armchair and stretched out in it just the same. Kid copper flushed angrily but seemed uncertain whether to bawl him out for taking this liberty or not; he hesitated too long and then it was too late.

'Told him?'

'No, sir.' Kid copper was standing to attention, Ross noticed; he really was in the shit about something.

'Why the hell not?' The papers in Winterton's hands

were flapping like sails at a regatta as the breeze from the ceiling fan caught them. 'All right, Morris, you can cut along. I'm sure you've something more useful to do.'

'Sir!'

Morris saluted and marched out of the room without a glance at Ross.

'Not a very pleasant business this, Ross. Hope you've been blessed with a strong stomach. We've the body of a young Chinese woman in the mortuary. Fished out of Singapore river. We'd like you to take a look. She may be someone you know.' He returned the papers to a box file on his desk, checking that the various bundles were in the right order before locking it in the metal cupboard behind him. 'Let's go over there now, shall we? It's just at the back of this building.'

Ross's first reaction was a surge of renewed anger and frustration. Even without waiting to see the body he felt certain he knew who it must be. He cursed his own stupidity for having let himself be spotted at the funeral; at the villa too, probably. That same morning when he had ducked behind the hedge . . .

Struck by a thought, he asked: 'How long was the body in the water?'

'Only briefly, I'd judge.' Winterton paused on the stairs, surprised. Then a look of understanding appeared on his face. 'Oh, she's not bloated or anything of that kind. No decomposition either. Bloody unpleasant all the same. Force 136, weren't you?'

'That's right.'

'The old 136 lot. Spent most of the war in Jap prison camps myself. First Changi, then elsewhere. Not much can turn my stomach after that little experience. Ask me, they didn't hang enough of 'em.'

The mortuary was a small windowless building at the rear of the car park. A couple of air-conditioning units

157

protruded from the walls; pale fragments of old cobweb swung from the power cable spanned between the eaves and the nearby generator shed. Winterton unlocked the door and switched on the light. It was like a butcher's refrigerator inside. Ross shivered as the arctic chill gripped him. There were two stone ledges, one either side, with runnels scored into them to permit unwanted fluids to drain off. When he saw her body his shock must have been obvious because Winterton said: 'Steady now, Ross. Take your time. Know her?'

'You fuckin' know I do!' Ross answered with a quiet intensity, seething at the stupidity of the question. Luckily it wasn't Morris standing there or he might not have been able to control himself. 'You could've prevented this. You guessed it would happen.'

Winterton said nothing.

Uncovered, the body lay on that slab obviously in much the same state as when they had recovered it. Her hair was still wet, he noticed. Red gashes on her cheek and across her throat still gleamed as if the blood had not yet had time to congeal. Her *samfu* tunic and underwear had been cut away, perhaps by the police surgeon as there were no corresponding marks on her body. The entry points for the stab wounds to her chest and stomach were unmistakable and one exposed breast, white, small, bore across it a dried-up trickle of blood.

'Don't you even have a sheet to cover her with?' Ross demanded in disgust.

'The body is about to be removed for post mortem. Killed some two hours ago, our surgeon reckons. Of course decomposition sets in quickly in this climate.'

'Poor Susie,' Ross said, but he felt relieved it was not the grieving woman from the villa, Ong's messenger, as he'd feared. 'Poor bloody Susie.'

'Perhaps if you've seen enough we could return to my office. I think we need to have a little chat.'

'Very well.'

The warm air outside was vibrant with insects. It was so assertively alive, the concept of death seemed hardly possible. Change, yes. Continuous change, one life form translating into another. It was the refrigeration which made her appear so horrifyingly dead, arresting the cycle.

He let Winterton lead the way back into the main building and up the stairs to his spacious office. The room where he had met Ong could have been slotted into this space several times over. There, on a more usual evening, Susie would probably have taken her customers to sweat out their aggressions on that narrow bed while the two princesses smiled benignly down on them.

'If your loony lieutenant hadn't come jackbooting in, that girl might still be alive.' Ross's bitterness was genuine, though he realized that the balls-up, if anyone's fault, was his. 'Or are you charging me with both murders.'

'I've checked on your 136 days, Ross. Such records as still exist. Had a nickname, didn't you? Hantu – the ghost. With a reputation for killing. Always a neat job, I'm told. Not this butchery. Besides, we've a good idea of your movements over the past few days. At the estimated time of death you were just about to enjoy Shanghai roast duck. My detective-inspector says the restaurant you chose can be recommended.'

'So why am I here? Not to identify the body, that's for sure. You kept her locked up long enough.'

'You're here, Ross, because I ordered it. Don't get any stupid ideas about the police being bloody idiots. We're not. I accept you didn't murder Ong Chou-fei – that was another messy job which possibly you'd have handled better, and the fingerprints on the knife weren't yours – but you still haven't told us the truth. However, you have friends in high places so we'll not press the matter. I assured Alun Browne we'd co-operate. He thinks highly of you.'

Friends in high places? Could he really have meant Browne, Ross pondered, or had the admiral been too talkative after all? Come to that, who the hell was his informant about 136? They were spinning webs around him. Tying him down.

Winterton went over to the metal cupboard behind his desk, unlocked it again, and took out a file. 'You'll be interested to have a look at this, no doubt,' he said, bringing it across to where Ross sat. 'When you've read it, perhaps you'll believe us.'

Lim Chun-shu, also known as Susie Lim, Ross saw neatly printed on the cover by some clerical hand. He opened it. One sheet of personal details – date of birth, place (Singapore), distinguishing marks, height, date and circumstances of arrest . . . of release . . . Photographs, full-face plus left and right profiles. Fingerprints, both hands, all fingers. Family background – mother and two sisters alive, living in Penang; father and one brother executed by Japanese Kempeitai secret police, second brother died under interrogation, third brother killed in action with the Malayan People's Anti-Japanese Army (MPAJA).

'Obvious Communist link-up there,' Winterton commented, looking over Ross's shoulder.

He turned to the remaining two papers in the file analysing the information he had gleaned from her. It was not much. One interrogator commented that more than once he'd sensed he was on the point of pinning her down, but each time she had managed to avoid betraying herself. But circumstantial evidence was there in plenty. Places were listed where she had been spotted at the same time as other suspects who were now in custody. They

160

included at least two possible meetings with a courier at Lien Jee Bar.

'No Marxist literature? Found in possession of?' Ross asked sarcastically.

Winterton stonewalled. 'What gave you that idea?'

'Never was any, I suppose?'

'No more than there was an obese Chinese doctor,' Winterton reported but without rancour. 'Either that was an obvious lie to protect the girl, in which case it backfired . . .'

'Or else there was an obese Chinese doctor and I told the truth.'

'If he exists he certainly wasn't registered to practise in Singapore. Maybe someone with shaky qualifications from one of those mainland Chinese places; maybe not even that. A bit of elementary medical training, enough to sew up a wound or administer an abortion. That's the most likely when you think of it. She must have known a few, a girl like Susie Lim.'

'Why did you let her go?'

'To see where she'd lead us.'

'And?'

'Led us to you, didn't she? You *were* at her room, weren't you? Creating a row because she wouldn't open the door?'

'So those three thugs were your men?' He'd suspected Browne might have planted them there; he'd not been far wrong.

'Come on, Ross. You know better than to jump to conclusions.' Winterton removed the file from him, re-tied the tape, then took it back to the cupboard. 'Tell me why you went there.'

'The girl saved my life, for Chrissake. I might have bled to death. Has saying "Thank you" gone out of fashion, or what?'

Winterton shook his head, obviously not believing his explanation. 'In due course Browne will come with the true story, I suppose. I imagine you cooked up something together.'

What yarn had Browne been spinning, Ross wondered. They made mysteries when none existed, and all to disguise how little they knew. Then, fleetingly, he speculated once more about the admiral's role. Drop Browne a hint – hadn't he said that? In which case . . .

'I could be the next victim.'

Winterton beamed at him, unexpectedly jovial. 'Always possible, Ross. You saw for yourself we've room for one more in there.'

The same Malay constable drove him back to the hotel in the police station wagon, this time without kid copper in attendance. There was a man who would be glad to find him dead, he mused. If no message came through in the next twenty-four hours, he should get out of Singapore; he'd asked Moody to put the idea to the admiral in the morning. Colombo perhaps, or Bangkok – some place where no one knew him. The more he thought it over, the more convinced he became. He had to get away.

It was past midnight and the traffic had thinned out. For a time they were held up behind one erratic car which stuck obstinately to the middle of the road until the constable gave it a blast on his siren. A tipsy European steering one-handed, Ross saw as they roared past. With the other hand he was busy exploring his woman passenger.

The Malay constable grinned and the tip of his tongue appeared, wetting his lips. He was still grinning when they arrived at the Padang Hotel where he honoured Ross with VIP treatment, going round to open the car door for him, then straightening up and saluting him. For that gesture alone kid copper would have bawled him out.

The reception desk was unattended. Ross punched the bell and waited but no one came. The whole place had a late-night, deserted atmosphere. Apart from whirring fans and the inevitable cicadas the only sound was an occasional woman's laugh from the direction of the bar.

He went behind the counter to collect his own key, then headed for the lift, only to find it was out of order again. He took the stairs slowly. His wound was bothering him and the salt-sweat trickling down his skin didn't help. If it hadn't been for that tipsy woman in the bar he might have gone for a drink. What he needed was a moment's quiet to think things over – Susie lying on her cold slab, for one.

She must have screamed. Those savage stab-wounds indicated quite a struggle and people probably heard her, though no doubt they hurried off, not wanting to get involved, leaving her to a lonely, helpless death.

In that mortuary he'd had difficulty holding back his tears. What in God's name had she done to deserve that kind of end? She had lent him her clean underwear to help staunch his wound, no thought for herself, full of concern; a tougher girl would have left him to bleed dry in the street.

So were both deaths his fault, hers and Ong Chou-fei's? Strangers to each other until that evening, perhaps, when she had been paid to pick up this Englishman in the bar, just like any ordinary customer, and coax him upstairs? And for that service she'd ended up in the police morgue.

He reached the second floor. The corridor was empty save for some shoes outside the doors to be cleaned. A rumble of snoring came from one room as he passed it. A drinker's snore. Some red-necked pillar of the Empire sleeping off a skinful.

Outside his own door he listened for a second before easing the key quietly into the lock and turning it. No visitors this time. He flicked on the light before going in and glanced instinctively around the room. Everything was in order. Dropping the key on the bed he stripped off his shirt with a sense of relief. A cold shower first, he decided.

It was then, just as he was about to toss the shirt into his laundry basket, that he became aware of a faint breathing. The sound shocked through his nervous system though anything might have caused it – the movement of a bathroom curtain (but there was no curtain), or a couple of lizards moving. It need not be human.

He heard it again, this time louder. From the bathroom – definitely an intruder. For a second he paused before the door, then kicked it open violently.

'Out of there!'

No one appeared. He could see the shower fitment and WC, nothing else. Susie . . . Ong Chou-fei . . . now his turn. If the killer was lurking behind the door this cramped bathroom was no place to tackle him.

'Come on – outside!' he repeated. 'Unless you want a bullet through your guts.'

He said it again in Chinese, just to make sure, but it was pure bluff. He'd refused the Section's offer of a gun.

'You caught me at an awkward moment, Mr Ross.'

She stood there, a superior smile on her face, with one shoe held in her hand and the other possibly still behind the door. Once again she wore that dark-green silk *cheongsam* in which he had first seen her. He took the shoe away from her, tearing it out of her hand; her face quivered slightly as if afraid and she retreated a half-step towards the shower.

'Pick up the other shoe,' he ordered, pulling the door back to reveal it lying on the hard cement floor. At the side of the washbasin was her small handbag; he relieved her of that as well. 'Now – slowly – go into the bedroom and stop by the foot of the bed.'

Following her through, he dropped the shoes and handbag on his bed and then told her to face the wall, raise her arms and place her hands against it, well spread out. He frisked her thoroughly, checking her armpits, spreading his fingers over her small, soft breasts beneath the thin silk, then over her ribs, her abdomen, her hips, anywhere she might conceal a knife.

'I'm not armed, Mr Ross,' she remonstrated. 'Nor are you, I think.'

Ignoring the rebuke, he kicked her legs apart and plunged his hand beneath her split skirt. His fingers encountered the bare flesh as the top of her stockings but no knife. With the skirt bunched up he tested the hem. Nothing there either, nor in the high collar.

'Now sit down over there.' He pointed to a low arm-chair. 'And stay there.'

Flushed and angry, she obeyed. 'I hope you enjoyed yourself, Mr Ross!' She spat the words out at him furiously.

'I didn't.' He tipped out the contents of her handbag. Powder compact, lipstick, mirror, money, handkerchief, and a headscarf which he shook out. 'Count yourself lucky you're a woman. If you'd been a man I'd've had you stripped naked.'

'Don't let that stop you!' Her eyes blazed at him darkly, but he noted she still had enough self-control to keep her voice low. She began to get up.

'No you don't.' He pushed her back into the chair. 'I've not finished yet.'

Among the scarf's folds was a small identity card of the type everyone in Singapore was expected to carry. He opened it and read the details. Fang Mei-lin, nationality

165

Chinese, race Chinese, religion Christian. Her thumb-print's vortex-whorl was even attractive, though the full-face photograph was harshly lit and unflattering.

'Fang Mei-lin,' he read aloud, and nodded.

He replaced the card in her handbag and turned to the shoes. By now he expected to find nothing, but he might as well be thorough. They were elegant court shoes with moderately high heels which could be hollowed out to contain a weapon but they seemed firm enough . . . or were they? A troubled look in her eyes warned him not to give up too easily.

It was in the left shoe, the one she had been holding in the bathroom. Concealed in the leather sole was a thin blade some three inches long.

'Not armed?' He tested the edge with his thumb; not too sharp but still a vicious instrument in the right hands.

She said nothing.

'Did you really think you could kill me with this?' He tossed it contemptuously on to the dressing table. It was not impossible though, and he was only too aware of it. A quick thrust in the right place.

'I've never in my life killed anybody, Mr Ross.' She was calmer again, though less self-possessed than before. 'I don't think I could.'

'Then why did you come here?'

'Not to be assaulted by you. But I suppose this is how you treat women in England. In China we were always taught that your race were uncouth barbarians. It was obviously true.'

'You murdered Susie,' he accused her.

'Susie?'

It couldn't have been the same blade, he realized; those wounds were from a much heftier knife. But he pursued the attack, wanting to hurt her. 'Died badly, didn't she? Messy business. Lot of blood.'

'I know no one called Susie.'

'At Lien Jee Bar?' He spoke contemptuously, standing over her. 'The good-time girl you told me to meet there? Was it really necessary for you bastards to kill her? Wasn't Ong's death enough?'

'That girl?' She became tense again as if shocked by the news, although she could have been putting it on. 'But when was she killed? It can't have been that same evening when . . .' She bit her lip.

'You don't expect me to believe you didn't know, Miss Fang Mei-lin? Not even her name?'

'I didn't arrange that part.'

'What part?' She was getting confused, he thought. Lying.

'The meeting. *Your* meeting. I never even met her.'

'Who else killed her if not your people? Who else had any reason?'

'When did it happen?'

'Does that matter any more? She's dead.'

She stared at him, leaning back in the chair, all the fight seemingly having drained out of her. Then her eyes moved down his chest till they rested on the pinkish scar left by the stab wound.

'Mr Ross, I carry messages, I don't kill people. As for your meeting, I know only that it went wrong and they want to try again.'

'Who are we talking about?'

'You must know that better than I do. I was to say the arrangements will be different this time, so please listen carefully.'

Gradually her poise returned as she recited her lesson, describing how he was to mingle with a crowd of onlookers watching the monkey god ritual at Soon Thian Keng Temple. Someone would contact him there. Different? It sounded much like the same rigmarole as before.

'Plenty of blood,' she added sarcastically. 'The priest goes into a trance and cuts his tongue with a sword. You will enjoy it.'

He ignored the jibe. 'The first man they sent was murdered, so who is it this time?'

'I know nothing.'

'They must have told you his name.'

'No. Don't you understand, Mr Ross? Your police could arrest me, but what could I tell them? Even if I'm tortured they'll get nothing out of me.'

(Hadn't Ong used almost the same words?)

'And that's why your people had Susie put down? You imagined she'd talked to the police?'

'You're making a mistake.' She got to her feet and this time he did nothing to prevent her. At the dressing-table mirror she began tidying her hair. 'Her death was none of our doing. As for the blade in my shoe, its purpose is self-defence, that's all. I've never yet had to use it.'

'I'll walk down with you. See you into a taxi.'

'Oh, I'm free to leave, am I?' She leaned forward to check her make-up.

'You live in the Ong family villa?'

'Do I?' She neither confirmed nor denied it. 'Keep your appointment, Mr Ross. That's all. I'll make my own way out. May I have my shoe?'

'Perhaps you'll need this too.' He retrieved the blade.

It was good quality steel and supple. He eased it into the groove in the leather sole and it snapped into place with a metallic click. A nice piece of workmanship, he thought with approval; invisible at first glance. It took Chinese inventiveness to produce equipment of this quality. The girl hadn't found this footwear in some average downtown shoe-shop.

Her lips twisted into a mocking smile as she slipped the

168

shoe on. 'Are you quite sure I can be trusted with it, Mr Ross? Or would you like to search me once more?'

'That won't be necessary.'

'I advise you to watch what you do with your hands in future. They could land you in trouble.'

Opening the door, he checked the corridor and then stood aside to let her pass. She glanced at him with unconcealed scorn. Her heels clacked noisily on the hard floor as she walked away from him, making no attempt to be discreet. He heard them on the staircase too till suddenly, quite abruptly, they stopped. She must have taken the shoes off somewhere half-way between the two floors and continued in her stockinged feet.

It had all been bravado for his benefit. A gesture to put him in his place.

8

As usual at Saturday lunchtime the swimming pool at the naval base's wardroom club was as crowded as a fishpond. The admiral made his way over to a group of officers at the bar and hooked out the young surgeon-lieutenant who had introduced himself earlier in the week as one of his son's friends.

'News from Nigel,' he said simply, heading for a quieter spot in the shade. 'Can hardly hear myself think in this crush.'

'He's OK, is he?'

'Came through without a scratch.' He explained the little he knew, adding that the destroyer his son commanded was still patrolling off Inchon, escorting supply ships. It was hardly classified information, not at that stage. 'What about you – any plans for later this afternoon? I'd like to introduce you to a civilian I ran into. Interesting chap, represents a British company, been out here for years. Invited me to his house. I'd like to take you along.'

The surgeon-lieutenant flushed; it was obvious he would try to wriggle out of it if he could.

'We'll be back in good time for anything you've got on in the evening,' the admiral promised him. Then he dropped his voice. 'Bring your medical kit along, will you? Your little black bag or whatever. I don't want to make this official, so keep it discreet.'

The surgeon-lieutenant flushed an even deeper red, the admiral saw with amusement. No doubt he was envisaging some secret mistress with a dose of clap, maybe; or in need of a quick abortion.

'It's all above board, young man, whatever might be going through your mind,' he added drily. 'Be ready by four o'clock. And discreetly, remember. Civilian clothes. Informal.'

At the car pool he waived aside the duty petty officer's suggestion of an official car with a driver, picking out in its place an ordinary plain saloon with one of the usual RN markings. He drove it across to the cluster of tall palms behind the sick bay and found the young lieutenant already waiting there clutching a zip-up grip from which the handle of a tennis racket protruded.

'Thought this would be less conspicuous, sir,' the young man commented cheerfully as he placed it on the back seat before getting in. 'I say, I hope this really isn't something illegal.'

He had an absurdly boyish manner, the admiral reflected. With his sandy hair, freckles and innocent blue eyes, why was he wasting his talent on mere matelots? He could be making a fortune with all the richest matrons in London queuing up along the entire length of Harley Street to pour their troubles into his ear.

'The place isn't far,' he said once they were clear of the gates. 'Chap's name is Moody. You'll like him.'

'Is he the patient?'

'I take it you're aware of the provisions of the Official Secrets Act?'

'Yes, sir.'

'Very well. If anybody asks, this is simply a friendly neighbourhood call on Tim Moody and a colleague. Stick to that story – savvy? The rest – anything you see or hear – is hush-hush. I'll tell you his name because you're bound to hear it. Ross. I want Ross to have a complete medical check-up, as thorough as you can make it under the

171

circumstances. He's not been well and I need to know just what condition he's in. Just how fit is he, that's the question. Physically and mentally.'

'Why not bring him into the base if it's that important? Lend him a uniform. Nobody would spot him. New faces come through every day.'

'Can't risk it, more's the pity. He's too finely tuned, this man, as you may find out when you meet him.'

'Tense?'

'Finely tuned, doctor,' he repeated.

And resentful too, he might have added. Justifiably so, in his opinion. He had not forgotten those distastefully matter-of-fact reports on Ross's treatment at their own interrogation centre; there was an obvious danger that being ordered into the sick bay would drag all his natural hostility up to the surface again. It was too big a chance to take. He could not afford to have Ross going sour on him.

Ong Chou-fei's murder had been like a door slammed in their faces and so far their attempts to re-establish contact through the London–Warsaw link had met only with a great wall of silence. Moody's urgent message that morning was the only glimmer of light they had had. If it genuinely meant that they were in touch again, then at least the ball was back in play. And through Ross – that was significant.

He swung into the drive, slowing down as the car bucked at the rough, pot-holed surface. Tim Moody limped out to greet them and waited at the top of the steps as he parked in the shade of a group of high, spreading trees. It was more like a patch of jungle than a garden, he thought as he switched off and got out. A waste, when he considered what could be made out of it with a bit of effort.

'Alone?' he greeted Moody. 'Where's Ross?'

'Upstairs having a shower. We had curry tiffin today, a Suleiman special, and till now he's been sleeping it off. Oh, Suleiman's my Malay cook,' he explained to the surgeon-lieutenant who joined them after retrieving his grip from the car. 'He thinks Tuan Ross needs feeding up.'

'I'll go straight up. This is Ian, by the way. Friend of my son.' He felt relieved he remembered the young man's first name. 'Offer him a drink or something, would you?'

The bedroom was empty. Ross's clothes lay carelessly thrown over an armchair; on the bed's crumpled sheets was a discarded sarong. From the bathroom came the steady sound of rushing water. He opened the door and peered in. That Malay cook was dead right, he felt, seeing Ross standing there under the shower. A skinny devil. Plenty of muscle, though.

'You going to stay under that shower all day, Ross? You'll have the tank running empty.' It was meant to be a light friendly remark to help get the interview off on the right footing, but Ross simply frowned. None of the younger men seemed to have much sense of humour these days. 'I'll wait in the bedroom, but I haven't got for ever, laddie.'

Then, of course, Ross was no longer quite so young, was he? That was another reason for not taking too many chances with him. He was not the man the Section would have chosen for a mission of this sensitivity, not if they'd had a free hand, but now with the prime minister breathing down their necks demanding results and the Chinese apparently refusing to talk to anyone else . . .

'It's fixed for tomorrow,' Ross announced. He emerged from the bathroom with one large towel around his waist while he dried his hair with another. 'Same set-up as before, except this time it's not a bar but a Buddhist temple. I go there and wait for someone to approach me

173

again. No description. No means of recognition. They know me, I don't know them.'

'Very well. Let's have the details.'

Before beginning, Ross slipped the coloured sarong over his head then down to his waist, folding it over expertly and tucking the end in to secure it. Then he sat sprawled in a cane armchair, tapping his fingers as he spoke. The admiral was conscious that the man's eyes never left him as he briefly recounted the events of the previous evening. The prostitute's death was not a development he'd expected, though the Chinese woman messenger interested him more.

'Fang Mei-lin – how d'you spell that name, Ross? How did it appear on the identity card?' As Ross told him he wrote it down. 'Something may be known about her. I'll run a trace.'

'Not through Browne,' Ross warned him. 'Not unless you plan to see me stretched out in that morgue.'

'He nags at you, this man Browne. I wonder why.'

'I've just told you why.'

'Tell me more about Fang Mei-lin. How good is her English?'

'My guess is that she speaks no English at all. She's mainland Chinese, I'm sure of that. It's also what the identity card says, which implies she must have other papers to support it. A Chinese passport maybe. With Malayan Chinese you always hear a scattering of English words; not with her, though. She lives in the Ong family villa – did I tell you that?'

'Go through everything you know about her.' The admiral listened carefully as Ross listed all he had discovered, which was not a great deal. Then he asked: 'D'you think we've underestimated this lady? Let's say she's the one in charge. She came to your room to set up the meeting with Ong. That's what we're meant to think. It could be she wanted to look you over. And from what you say, that meeting was carefully stage-managed. Perhaps the murder was too.'

'Oh, I agree. It's certainly possible there's no research station, no threat of germ warfare, no Soviet secrets. Simply a plot to bring Colonel Ong together with a known British agent as a prelude to leaving him dead in the streets. Discredited – whoever he worked for. But I don't believe it.'

'A *known* agent, that's the point. Who knew you, Ross?'

'In Singapore, practically everybody. Browne, certainly. Force 136 at least. I warned you this wasn't the best place.'

'They insisted. You wouldn't have wanted mainland China, not for this kind of blind date, not without a preliminary meeting. I seem to remember you laid down that condition yourself.'

'OK. So what about this meeting tomorrow? Do I go?'

'You'll be at the rendezvous on time.' It felt like a sentence of death he was pronouncing, yet he had nothing like that same pit-of-the-stomach sensation he'd always experienced on sending armed, uniformed men into action. This was a cold-blooded decision; if it went wrong, Ross's chance of survival were nil. He repeated the order. 'You'll go there alone, without back-up, nothing to scare them off. Now hear this, laddie – and remember it.'

Briefly he summarized the little he had been able to learn via the Admiralty's coded signals. Both London and Washington had confirmed the wartime existence of Japanese germ warfare research centres in Manchuria, all run by Unit 731 of the Kwantung Army under the command of General Yamada, but only London indicated experiments on POWs. Washington's signal drew attention – somewhat blandly – to the statement the previous

December from General MacArthur's HQ denying human experimentation.

'They've pulled the blinds down,' he told Ross. 'Our evidence suggests trials on humans were extensive, specially in Manchurian centres. Mukden was mentioned, but others too. When the Red Army went in there, Soviet communiqués always claimed these places had been found derelict. Jap scorched earth policy.'

'Till the show trials. They were an admission that something was still there.'

'How much – well, that's guesswork. Whitehall would like to know.' He did not add that his first signal to London had really set the alarm bells ringing; they were demanding answers, and quickly. Probably the Americans too, if the truth were known. 'The scenario as I see it is this, Ross. Our Soviet allies overrun a Jap research centre intact, Japanese scientists still hard at work on the premises, test-tubes bubbling away or whatever these things do. I can't imagine the Russians simply closing it down.'

'Which country would? I can't see any power closing such a place down, not before they found out all there was to learn.' Ross spoke lazily, as if this were no more than a casual chat. 'We all play the same game. We round up the enemy's boffins – his rocket engineers, atomic scientists, chemists, biologists, whoever we can lay our hands on. Set them working for our side for a change.'

'I'm glad you said *our* side, Ross.' He felt increasingly irritated; why was it that interviews with Ross always took an unforeseen turn. 'You do identify with the United Kingdom?'

'Of course, what else? Sir.'

He controlled his anger. 'You've spent the best part of your life in other countries. It would be understandable if you didn't,' he commented in as neutral atone as he could muster. 'Right, now what has to be done? First, I've

176

brought a quack with me, a young naval surgeon. He'll check you over to make sure you're fit for duty.'

'Yes, sir.' Ross merely looked bored: the protest which the admiral had expected did not materialize.

'Second, at tomorrow's meeting – assuming that's what it turns out to be – get them to go over the story again. Make sure it all tallies, detail for detail. Remember they've no means of knowing exactly what passed between you and Ong Chou-fei.'

'Aye-aye, sir.' Still that lazy tone of voice.

Impertinent bastard, the admiral thought. But he ignored it.

'Third, press them for more hard facts – location, types of disease, method of delivery of the weapon. And the time of year – the season it's likely to be most effective. Our people say that's important. Now, fourth: tell them you want to see this research station for yourself.'

'Do I?' Ross spoke softly, more alert this time, the admiral noticed with some satisfaction.

'Call their bluff. Take them up on their offer to get you into China. They can do it.'

'But can you get me out again?'

'If they're serious, now is the time to prove it. So far they've told us nothing they couldn't have passed on through normal diplomatic channels, so why choose this method of contact? And why specify you by name? Insist on going there, Ross. It's what they wanted – your own conditions of course.'

The admiral stood up. Though Ross's face betrayed no visible signs, it was obvious that the man was nervous. Not from fear though, he judged, nor cowardice; after a lifetime of commanding men at sea he'd experienced enough of both to feel quite certain about that. No, it was more the type of nervousness he'd observed in that expensive, highly strung hunter his wife was so fond of

177

riding; it would pass once he was given his head. But if it didn't . . . if he cracked . . .

That didn't bear thinking about. It was not the simple fact of bacteriological research which had sent shivers through Whitehall, but the threat of an actual germ attack in battle. That could only mean that Stalin and his Jap slave-scientists were way ahead of the field in solving the problems which had so far held up British researchers. In the 1940s, tests in the use of small bombs to scatter anthrax spores over the Scottish island of Gruinard had proved deadly but left the entire island uninhabitable, a degree of overkill which would be unacceptable to most military commanders. Current experiments – insofar as he had been briefed on them at all – involved aerosol spraying of plague bacteria, but trial runs off the Scottish coast earlier in the year had been unsatisfactory for different reasons. As a weapon it was most effective when concentrated at short range, but only then when weather conditions were ideal. Yet Whitehall was only too aware that the first power to master the techniques needed to target living bacteria against an enemy accurately and reliably would have in their hands a weapon far deadlier than the West's present small stock of atomic bombs.

'Ross, they're too damned close to Korea,' he said abruptly. 'If they have attack capability, and they decide to use it, we can expect UN casualties to be in the thousands. Tens of thousands if the strike is widespread. They won't go for the front line. They'll hit well to the rear, either by aerial bombing or some other means, perhaps anti-personnel devices. Hard facts, Ross – that's what we need, and quickly.'

'The silent death, isn't that what they call it?' Ross said.

'If it's successful in Korea, Europe'll be next.' He paused at the bedroom door, still uncertain about Ross. The way the man continued to lounge in that armchair wearing only a flowered sarong did nothing to reassure him. Though it seemed from all he'd heard that sarongs were the normal nightwear among the old hands out here. 'Well, good luck tomorrow,' he said. Nothing better occurred to him. 'I'll find a moment to come over to hear how it goes. Meanwhile I'll send the quack up.'

Not very satisfactory, he thought as he opened the door.

'An answer to your question, Admiral.' Ross got to his feet and stretched himself. 'I've been recalling when I was a kid in Shanghai – three years old maybe, or four. Early every morning I was taken out to see the Union Jack being hauled up in front of the British Consulate. A little ceremony it was. With a bugler. And the marine, I think he was a marine, used to salute it and I'd do the same. Salute the flag.'

'Your father took you there?' The admiral was non-plussed. 'Did he?'

'No, it was my Chinese amah who took me. She couldn't speak a word of English of course. In fact, I don't think she ever set foot outside China.'

The Pereira family usually regarded Sunday as the one day in the week which was wholly theirs. In the early morning while it was still cool they would dress in their best clothes – the little girls in clean white frocks with wide sashes and wearing their pink hats, the ones with the artificial primroses sewn on the band; Mrs Pereira in stockings, high-heeled shoes, white gloves and hat; and Pereira himself in his light suit and dark tie – and they would all go together to attend seven-thirty mass. Afterwards they might visit some other member of the family, or plan an outing to see the Haw Par Villa, or the monkeys in the Botanic Gardens, or even spend a quiet day at home – but always together.

On Sundays he could forget Browne and the irritations of the office.

On Sundays Pereira himself was the only king-emperor, his wife was queen, and they had their own two princesses. Or so he often said.

But this Sunday was different. As he explained to his two daughters, an old schoolfriend – one Francis Jones, a fellow Eurasian – had been rushed into the General Hospital for an operation, so naturally he was under an obligation to visit him. They did understand, didn't they? Reluctantly they admitted that they did. As usual the family went to mass, returning home for breakfast together. Half-way through the morning Pereira went out to wait at the bus-stop, saying he'd be back in time for Sunday dinner.

Cross my heart, he promised them – and meant it too.

The first bus to come along was not one which stopped at the General Hospital. Had it done so he would almost certainly have been able to keep his promise. But it went close enough – a mere five-minute stroll away – and so he boarded it. Not many passengers. He sat sideways on the hard bench-seat which ran the full length of the bus, one leg partly tucked under him as he looked out. That was another factor: had the bus been crowded he would never have been able to observe the passing traffic.

He would never have spotted the tall figure of Peter Ross, also known as Hantu, extracting himself with difficulty from behind the wheel of a dilapidated black car parked at the roadside. The bus was moving quite slowly at that point so he was able to watch Ross locking the car door, then setting off on foot down a side road.

Pereira sprang abruptly to his feet, rang the bell and lurched along the bus to alight at the next stop. Of all the information he regularly passed through his brother-in-law to those mysterious Russians at the end of the line, only his report on Ross had stung them into offering double the usual money for anything more he could find out. It was not an easy task. Browne held the sole key to the cabinet where Ross's file was kept; the most he ever managed was a brief glimpse at its contents while the great man was phoning. The day he had been ordered to deliver that press cutting announcing the dead *taipan's* funeral he had still known no more than Browne had chosen to tell him, which was very little. After the long trishaw ride back from Moody's house he had gone directly to speak to his brother-in-law, but his information was hardly worth double the money. He needed far more than he knew so far.

By the time he reached the side road, Ross had disappeared from view. He could have gone into any of the shops or houses, though some instinct told Pereira that he hadn't. The road curved sharply and the brisk manner in which Ross had set out suggested that he was going farther than these first few blocks. As Pereira passed the open-fronted shops he glanced in just the same, but there was no sign of him. Though why had Ross chosen to leave his car on the main road, he wondered.

Rain was threatening. Dark grey clouds were sweeping across the sky and the shopkeepers began to rescue their goods from the sudden gusts of wind. Pereira hesitated. He still wore the trousers of his new suit, his *only* suit, though at least he had left his jacket at home; if he had any sense he would give up this nonsense of chasing Ross and take a trishaw or taxi to the hospital before the rain started. He could imagine what his wife would say if he arrived home drenched to the skin. But . . .

Double the money, he thought. And he might discover more about Ross than even Browne knew. That would be one up over bloody *Mr* Browne with his pipe and his breezy patronizing manner. One up over fucking Mr Browne.

He would go as far as the three-storey building where the road turned right, no farther, he decided; if he couldn't see Ross from there, he would give up. Besides, those clouds were still moving rapidly and behind them came a patch of blue sky. It might not rain at all, not here.

Around the curve, though still some yards ahead, was a Chinese temple: could he be there? Something was certainly going on, judging from the people standing about and that raucous, clashing percussion which seemed to come from the courtyard. A disturbing, heathen sound it was; a sound he had always hated, feeling menaced by it, as by all the secret beliefs and practices of these non-Christian Chinese. In his heart he scorned them with the same intensity as they despised him for his mixed Eurasian blood, though he always took care to keep his hidden fear of them to himself.

He was convinced that was where Ross must be, this man known by the Malay word Hantu – the ghost – whose mere presence in Singapore had made everyone jittery: Browne, Winterton, the Russians . . . Born and brought up in China, wasn't he? Did it mean he had connections with one of the triad secret societies which had their tentacles throughout the Far East, reaching – if he could believe the rumours – as far as Liverpool and San Francisco?

The urge to turn and hurry away as unobtrusively as he could was strong – not run, because then they might come after him – but instead he forced himself to go closer. Damn! Oh damn, Pereira thought nervously, wished he had listened to his family and stayed at home that morning. No one in his right mind tangled with Chinese secret society gangsters. If Ross were somehow one of them – and odder things had happened, he knew from the office files – then he would be best left alone.

Ross was there. Pereira spotted him deep in the court-yard standing with his back to the temple wall. His height made him easily visible despite the press of shorter Chinese around him.

Crowded though the courtyard was, a space had been left clear at the rear of the temple for the priest to perform his ritual gyrations in time with the feverish drums and cymbals. Pereira insinuated his way through the crowd for a better view of what was going on. This must be the temple of the Buddhist monkey god, he realized. The priest, dressed in a monkey robe, his face painted red and white, was dancing himself into a trance; later, Pereira had heard, he would draw a sword-blade across his tongue and allow the blood to drip on to scraps of paper which he would sell as charms. A pagan practice.

Pereira laughed aloud, his sense of relief was so great. This was no secret triad meeting after all. Ross had been led here by curiosity, nothing more sinister than that. To observe the quaint customs. Those women in the crowd were just local grannies ready to believe any superstition; he could see it in the expressions on their lined, worn faces. The men – squat, rough-looking coolies whose tight singlets emphasized their muscles – were simply enjoying their day off.

He noticed that Ross was moving, edging along the temple wall, but thought nothing of it. After all, where could he go in this crush? Although . . . that Chinese in front of Ross . . . was he actually leading him somewhere? Pereira began to manoeuvre himself into a position where he could see better. Perhaps he was mistaken but . . .

In that moment a charge of lightning cut across the sky, dazzling everybody in the crowd. It was followed immedi-ately by a ferocious crash of thunder, then – almost simultaneously – the rain started, first in thick heavy drops like gobs of spittle, but soon becoming a downpour so intense, it might have been a rush of water from a standpipe.

The people fled from the courtyard with cries and squeals and laughter, almost knocking Pereira down as they went. When he recovered his breath Ross had disappeared again. He hesitated, already soaked through, uncertain what to do next, but then his arms were seized from behind, twisted, gripped by fingers as unyielding as metal clamps.

'What . . . wha' . . .?'

Those fingers were expert in selecting the most sensitive points to dig into his muscles and the pain caused him to burble rather than speak.

Two men were there, holding him up and forcing him towards a doorway. He'd tell them anything they wanted, he tried to say. If only they'd ease that terrible agony searing through him. Was Ross responsible for it? But what harm had he ever done to Ross?

The question hovered in his mind as – inside a bare, dark room – he felt another hand fasten over the back of his neck. More fingers seeking the right spot. It was not painful but numbing, bringing waves of darkness . . . of mist . . . In its way it was a relief which he . . .

Dora . . . his wife Dora . . . their two little princesses, *real* princesses when they dressed up for mass on a Sunday morning . . . of the royal Pereira blood, they always joked . . . how would they manage if he never got home?

Dinner would be ready . . . sitting around the neatly laid table . . . Sunday dinner . . . without him . . .

Ross caught the first few drops of rain as he dodged into the temple, ducking his head as he went through the low doorway. He had immediately recognized the man who had contacted him in the crowd as the taxi driver who had tailed him to the Lien Jee Bar a couple of days earlier, the one with the gap in his upper front teeth.

'This way, tuan,' he urged him on along the dark passage in which they found themselves.

The full force of the storm began to hammer on the roof tiles above him; drips of water penetrated the gaps; he felt the slight spray against his face as they hit the walls.

'Through here.'

Another door, this time leading into a practically bare room with closed shutters; just enough light filtered in around their edges for him to see a patch of wall and the vague shape of a chair in the centre of the floor. He paused on the threshold, sensing danger, then swung round defensively as he heard the taxi driver move back.

'Straight in – don't stop!' The automatic pistol in the man's fist was small, but it could put a bullet through his stomach all the same. 'Move.'

So that's what it was about; a simple snatch after all. He might have guessed. He spread his hands, palms upwards, in a gesture of submission. The passage was too narrow and the automatic aimed too professionally for him to risk anything. He stepped into the room as ordered.

'Good to see you, Hantu,' a voice greeted him out of the room.

A Chinese voice he recognized – and speaking English. He turned to peer into the shadows, not believing what he had heard. Obviously he was mistaken. People can sound alike; often do. Or it was a trick to confuse him. Temple priests through the ages have developed a whole armoury of techniques to mystify the faithful. In the darkness, though, someone *was* watching him as if waiting for a reply.

'Thought you were dead,' Ross said cautiously. 'If you're who I think you are.'

The voice spoke sharply in Chinese to the taxi driver, ordering him to shut the door and stay in the passage outside to make sure they were not disturbed. 'Wait!' he added as the man was about to obey. 'What about the Eurasian?'

'That is arranged.'

Once the door was closed, the figure in the corner stepped forward to allow the pale, diffused light from the gap in the shutters to fall on his face. He had not changed since Ross had last seen him, save for an unusual twist to his lips which could have been a smile. No obvious wounds or disablement either; he stood tall, as he always had, every muscle alert. Yet after that hail of Jap bullets in the ambush Ross had found no further trace of him.

'Well, Hantu? Would you prefer me dead?'

'Chuan! My God, Chuan – you might be a ghost, the way you're standing there! I went back. I searched the whole area thinking you might be wounded and need help. I found nothing there but spent cartridges, plenty of those.' Dried patches of blood too he might have mentioned but refrained. 'Later I found the grave the Japs dug.'

'I dug it. They looked on.'

'You were taken prisoner? I could have sworn you'd bought it right at the start. Saw you fall. We were all too busy diving for cover the moment they opened up. No one knew what happened next. When I realized how many Japs were there, I was even relieved you were dead. Best way out, I thought.'

'Not like Yen-hua. Captured alive.'

'I was helpless to do anything.' He was defending himself, even after so long. Seeing Chuan – and *alive* – all

186

he had tried to suppress came flooding back. 'We withdrew. Lay low for a while. Then I went forward alone to reconnoitre. They'd moved the bodies, I thought that odd – yours too. Only Yen-hua was there with a group of Japs who were knocking her around. One was an officer.'

'I witnessed it, Hantu. No need to go over it now.'

But once Ross had started he had to go on. 'They were yelling at her, and I saw one man hit her across the face with the back of his hand. He was in my sights, Chuan. I had it all planned out. One bullet for him; one for her. Then someone blocked the way – the officer – shouting orders. When he moved she was on her knees, a Jap soldier holding each arm. The officer raised his sword. It was so quick, I don't think I understood what they were doing. Then her head was on the ground rolling over a soldier's foot. He laughed – I've never forgotten that laugh – and then he kicked her head out of the way. Like a football.'

'I was there,' Chuan repeated soberly. 'I buried her. And the others.'

Outside, the rain kept up its hard, steady drumming against the building. The rush of water in the deep drains sounded like one of those Welsh mountain streams near the training camp where he had received his first lessons in how to kill, lessons which he later passed on to the volunteer anti-Japanese fighters in the Malayan jungle. Among them Yen-hua. At last he had told someone how she died, though he felt no better for it. Back at their jungle base, to those who had managed to make their way back, he had reported merely that Comrade Yen-hua had been killed, no more than that. No details. For most of that group involved in the ambush it was their first time under fire; it was a miracle so many had survived.

Chuan, too, he had reported as dead. A flash of lightning briefly illuminated the room and he saw the

Chinese more clearly, looking at him quizzically. Beneath that loose shirt he was armed, Ross guessed.

'My wound was no more than a graze over the ribs,' he was explaining. 'Brought me down – you were right about that – but that may have been shock. You used to warn us about shock in the training sessions.'

The thunder rumbled across the sky at last, but some distance away. What now, he wondered. Those same jungle fighters with whom he had lived day in, day out – including Chuan who more than once had saved his life, they had relied on each other, been each other's eyes and ears – they were the enemies now. Was he expected to betray them? To hand them over? But he remembered the message which had brought him to this temple.

'Still in the jungle, Chuan?' he asked incautiously.

'No. You? Let's be frank, Hantu. You've been seen with a man called Browne, Internal Security. And Browne's clerk followed you here.'

'Nobody followed me. I'd have noticed. He turned up in the temple yard. One of the crowd. It's a public place.'

'Unless somone tipped him off where you'd be.'

'One of your people then. Isn't that what happened before? The Lien Jee Bar? Poor old Ong Chou-fei! They must have been lying in wait for him. It was no ordinary street crime.'

Chuan grinned broadly and Ross could now make out the scar which affected the shape of his lips. 'Not changed, have you, Hantu? You always were a suspicious bastard. It's how you survived. Know why you're here?'

'Tell me.'

'Because I sent for you. The world is different now, comrade. These days I sit at a desk in Peking and issue orders. And here you are. Welcome!'

'Ong Chou-fei was no red. He was a Nationalist officer.'

'In charge of stores and making a fortune on the side. He did what we paid him for. He's not important. He's dead.'

'Meeting in Singapore was a stupid idea.'

'He lived here. He could travel legally. Forget him.'

'Why did you have to kill him?' It was a long shot, and it went wide.

'Perhaps you know something I don't,' Chuan said. 'We didn't kill him. His death is inconvenient. At one time we trusted each other, Hantu.'

In the jungle, Ross thought. They had been as close as two men can ever be with all the tensions of guerrilla warfare gnawing at their nerves. Chuan had been younger then, an earnest, idealistic party theorist who enjoyed practising his English and was a tough fighter into the bargain, but something had changed him. Success perhaps. Since those wartime days he had gained sophistication; his tone held more irony.

'Chuan, prompt my memory,' he said. 'What was the message Ong Chou-fei was supposed to deliver?'

'It was an appetizer, Hantu. You remember it as well as I do or you wouldn't be here. However . . .'

Chuan repeated the key details with no significant variations, passing the test with top grades. He grinned when Ross told him so.

'Naturally I knew the message since it was I who instructed Ong to contact you. Who else could have told him your name – a British agent who speaks Chinese like a Peking amah? Don't you remember all those stories you told me? We had time to talk in those jungle camps, you and I. The long dark evenings, with only the fireflies and mosquitoes for company . . . Didn't you tell me all about your Peking amah who lived in Shanghai? And some Russian friends? A Shanghai bar girl, one of them – isn't that right?'

189

'A singer. They were like family to me. Her father taught me to play chess.'

'You all spoke Russian together. Hantu, I'll put it to you straight. I want to get into this research centre and take a peek at what's going on. I can't disguise my Chinese face, that's clear, but you – wearing a Russian uniform, speaking the language? Together we'd have a chance.'

'We'd need documents. In Russia you can't breathe without the right papers.'

Ross cursed the lack of light in that temple room. When a man was conning him into laying his life on the line he preferred to see his face. He had only Chuan's word for any of it.

'Documentation is no problem.' Chuan had lapsed into Chinese. 'Tell me which country produces better craftsmen than China. Forgery is one of our most ancient arts.'

'If it were anyone but you, Chuan, I'd say it stinks,' he informed him grudgingly. 'OK – convince me. I suppose I owe you a life.'

He felt he was re-entering a long-forgotten dream world. In the old days they had argued this way. The same old banter as they discussed each operation, knowing neither of them had much chance of coming out alive.

'Try it on your people, Hantu. Evidence suggests – I'll not put it any stronger – that our Russian allies plan a test strike against Korea. From *our* territory, you understand? An area where our people will suffer any backlash. For political reasons our leaders are not able to confront the Russians over it.'

'You'd rather pin it on the West.'

'The casualties on your side could be greater than Hiroshima and Nagasaki together. It's in your own interest. You should stress that in your report.'

'My masters will want hard fact, not guesswork.' Despite the admiral's orders Ross was prepared to refuse

190

the offer. It was all too pat. There had to be more than he'd been told. 'Where is this research place? What means of delivery will be used? Military attack? Air raids? Infiltration? How? And I need to know what disease, or will there be more than one?'

'The location I can tell you. It's a small mountain town called Paikow, named they say after some sacred caves in the mountainside. White rock. The actual research centre was built close to them, outside the town, together with an army barracks. There's a rumour that the Jap commander liked painting landscapes. There's a deep gorge, rocky hillsides, plenty of snow in the winter months. I took some pictures of the place itself – watch towers, approaches, fortifications. If your people are thinking of aerial reconnaissance these might help them identify what they're seeing.'

Ross accepted the small roll of micro-film which Chuan passed him and dropped it into a pocket. A token of good faith, he thought with amusement; Chuan might almost have been eavesdropping on his briefing session with the admiral. That had been the admiral's own expression.

For the rest, though, Chuan had little hard fact to offer. A lot of hardware had been moved up to Paikow, it seemed, mostly concealed beneath large tarpaulins. Artillery had been his guess, big stuff, Big Bertha all over again, but Ross was doubtful. As for which bacteria they intended to use, again Chuan could only offer guesswork, though mainly based on a local prostitute's account of how many inoculations her clients had been forced to suffer. Quite a few.

The only satisfactory part of the story was Chuan's scheme enabling the two of them to travel across revolutionary China without arousing too much suspicion. It was open and simple; for a moment his hesitation died away. He almost felt proud of his ex-pupil.

'I'll have to clear it with those on high,' he explained before they parted. Outside the rain had stopped and two bright shafts of sunlight came in through the gaps in the shutters. He could now see Chuan's eyes but found no deceit in them. On the wall, motionless, was a gecko lizard, its eyes bulging, perhaps at all it had overheard. 'How do I get the message to you?'

'You will be contacted in one week. Till then – Hantu!'

Chuan slipped out, leaving Ross alone in that hot, stifling room. The sweat was pouring off him; he took off his shirt and attempted to dry himself with it. Thirty minutes he'd agreed to stay there, allowing Chuan plenty of time to get away unseen. He did not even think of cutting it short, convinced that the taxi driver would still be waiting outside the door with his little 9 mm automatic.

And if not him, then another.

No one took much notice of two coolies pushing a handcart past the shops at the end of the road. It was lightly laden, the long round object in it having the appearance of a rolled-up carpet or mat; impossible to say definitely, for it was sewn into sacking as if about to be shipped overseas. Once the coolies reached the main road they broke into a trot which sent the package slithering and bouncing about on the cart as the wheels rode over the rough surface.

Forty-eight hours passed before Pereira's body was recovered from the deep drain behind some godowns. Neck broken. Skin mottled. Decomposition already started. A number of small, coarse fibres were found on the clothing and hair, though the police never managed to explain how they got there.

* * *

By that time several coded cables had already been exchanged between the admiral and 10 Downing Street. With the slow reluctance characteristic of all administrations, London finally signalled approval for a tentative course of action.

9

The RAF flew the admiral to Okinawa, landing en route in Hongkong and Manila for refuelling. General Corby of the USAF was on the tarmac to welcome him. He whisked him off by jeep to his own quarters for a hot shower and a generous American-style breakfast of ham and eggs before they got down to business. On the way any attempts at conversation were drowned by the roar of engines as several heavily laden B29 bombers took off, one after another.

'Pyongyang!' General Corby yelled, stabbing a finger at the sky in their general direction. He was a muscular man become stout with age; above a face sagging into flabbiness his crew-cut seemed like a desperate attempt to hold on to youth. 'Aircraft and munitions factories. Marshalling yards. Show the bastards we mean business.'

Clearly he was one of those enthusiastic Americans who put their heart and soul into whatever they touch, whether bombing the shit out of the enemy or driving a jeep through a busy air base. Or eating, as the admiral discovered when they sat down to breakfast.

'Take plenty now!' he recommended through a mouthful of cornflakes. 'No food shortages here, Admiral. I guess you've had a rough time over in Europe.'

The admiral, newly emerged from the bathroom, pink-faced, freshly shaven, wearing the general's bathrobe, had a stale taste in his mouth. He had slept only fitfully during the flight and the smell of ham and eggs made him feel queasy. He took some fruit juice.

'You've been informed of the new directive from Joint

Chiefs of Staff? We have authorization to push on north of the 38th parallel. Objective – destruction of North Korean Armed Forces. Well, Admiral, as we sit here at this moment – go on, help yourself to cornflakes – that push has started. Here's good luck to our boys! There's still plenty of fight in those gooks.'

'More than we expected.'

'I'll tell you honestly, Admiral, if those North Korean gooks had US equipment and our air superiority, they'd have deposited us right out into the sea, and that's no lie. They knew the terrain, they had the numbers, and reds or no fucking reds, they've got balls. Eighteen major strategic targets we've hit. Thirty thousand tons of bombs thrown at them by the best air force in the world. Their five largest cities practically burned to the ground – and the gooks still go on fighting. I guess we'll reach the Yalu all right, perhaps quicker than we think, but if our politicians back home imagine that'll be the end of the matter they're bigger fools than I took 'em for.'

'Not over by Christmas then?' After the cornflakes the admiral began to feel he might try the ham and eggs after all. The general's enjoyment of food was infectious.

'Christ, over by Christmas!' Corby waved his fork and splashed egg yolk on to the table. 'Don't they say that in every war? It's estimated sixty thousand Chinese troops are sitting there north of the Yalu. My hunch is those reports are phony. I'd reckon double that number. So what's the scenario – war with China? And the Soviets sit there and let it happen? No way, that's my view. Look – they push too far, so Uncle Sam gets restless and intervenes, then *we* push too far and Uncle Joe Stalin wakes up. World War Three, here I come! Only this time we've got the atom, and not even Nostradamus himself could tell us where that'll finish.'

'What word on Paikow?'

'You get my drift, Admiral. If your Paikow information is verified – I don't know how reliable your source may be – but, Jesus, let's postulate that it is. Bacteriological warfare is the ultimate nightmare. Know what killed off more North American Indians than any other weapon? Not the Winchester, no sir! It was measles.' He reached across the table. 'Try some honey with that.'

'You must have some results by now,' the admiral said, declining the honey.

'Sure. RB29s of the 31st Strategic Reconnaissance Squadron overflew Paikow yesterday. The pictures are still being analysed but I reckon we may have identified the research establishment. One more cup of coffee and we'll go over to take a look.'

Reading aerial photographs was a specialized job and the admiral's previous experience had been limited to interpreting the possible functions of port installations or changes in a ship's silhouette. The pictures he was shown in the aerial intelligence section foxed him at first. All he could see was wisps of white cloud and snow-covered hillsides dotted with odd shapes which could be anything.

'Notice that pipeline down the mountainside leading to that group of buildings in the valley?' the crisp WAC officer instructed him; not a wrinkle in her perfectly ironed shirt, not a millimetre's inaccuracy in her lipstick or eye-shadow, not a single hair out of place. 'Now compare that picture with this one from a different angle. These two structures here – higher than the surrounding buildings but triangular in shape. I'd say they're pyramids.'

'Like in Egypt?'

She ignored the question. 'Now compare with this third picture . . .'

'I see what you mean. Definitely pyramids, and built

196

right up against that slope . . . no, it isn't a slope, is it? It's a sheer cliff.'

'With dark patches near the bottom which could possibly be cave openings.'

'And these two lines here . . . and here . . . Walls?'

'I guess they're defensive walls, one controlling access to the buildings closest to the rock face, and the other farther out encloses what appears to be an army camp, probably there to guard that inner installation. All the buildings are stone, and you can see vehicles – quite a few in that section. Trucks, a couple of armoured cars, and ordinary limousines. These marks in the snow here we estimate could be a railroad, though nothing has been through since the snowfall.'

The admiral produced a folder of blow-ups made by the RN photographic intelligence unit from the roll of film which Ross had obtained. They were blurred, snatched pictures, some taken from ground level and others seemingly from the top of that cliff, but at least they confirmed that 31st Strategic had photographed the correct target.

'We requested two sets for our own use,' he reminded Corby when they were back in his office for a final word before he boarded the USAF plane for the next leg of his journey. 'One is to go to Singapore for our analysts to examine. Among them is a woman who once lived in Manchuria. It could be useful to hear her views.'

'Both sets are ready for you. I guess you agree there's nothing in that lot to suggest germ warfare.'

'Whatever's going on there, it must be something worth guarding.'

'Admiral, what we've seen so far could be no more than a prison camp. If we go ahead an' blast it . . .?' Corby spread his arms in a big question mark. 'One mistake an' all hell'd break loose. I guess you appreciate our dilemma. How far *can* you guys trust your informant? Truthfully?'

'We don't trust him. And there's no question of bombing till we've taken steps to verify.'

'OK, now grab hold o' this. This is what a certain high-ranking US officer popularly known as God Almighty said to me when your first signals came through. One, last winter the Soviets staged a show trial about Jap bacteriological experiments on human guinea pigs. Two, we've officially denied they ever happened. Three, in June a Soviet-trained army invades South Korea. Four, in September British Intelligence is fed this phony story – it's what he said! – of germs on the warpath. And for why? Deliberate misinformation, that's his view. We're permitted to overfly an' take snapshots; otherwise no action.'

'D'you share his view?'

'Now I guess that's hard to say. What bothers me is our official denial of those experiments. Back in 1945 most of us thought differently.' General Corby stood up, ground out the butt of his cigar into the ashtray, and accompanied the admiral out to the jeep. 'First, we need hard evidence. That's vital. Then we might get somewhere. As some guy or other said, if we can't move Mahomet then we'll have to shift the goddam mountain. I guess we have the fire power to do that. Have a good flight now! I've instructed our boys to take care of you real good!'

It was two-thirty in the afternoon, but so dark that the lights had been switched on. The autumn rain lashed against the window panes of that rear upstairs room in 10 Downing Street where the admiral was completing his brief verbal report for the prime minister's ears only. The folder of photographs, both those Ross had obtained and the US aerial reconnaissance pictures, lay on the desk between them.

The prime minister hardly glanced at them. He sat thinking it over for several minutes. When at last he spoke, it was to make a more general remark than the admiral had expected.

'I'm not convinced our American friends fully grasp the essence of the Far Eastern situation,' he commented mildly as though he had been turning the thought over in his mind for a long time. 'I often wish they were more open to listening to advice. We are allies after all, not subordinates.'

'They do have some very good people.'

'Of course. So do we. If our information turns out to be true and it becomes urgent to destroy this installation, I suppose we do have to rely on the United States to do it for us? We couldn't use our own carrier-based aircraft?'

'For what reason?'

'Obviously to maintain a degree of control in British hands. I'm thinking primarily of the political implications.'

'It's not yet clear what the Americans plan to do. At the moment they doubt the reliability of our information.'

'So you say. Though I imagine they're making some kind of preparation.' He started to clean his reading glasses as he talked. 'Our man, I remember, you once described as burnt out. What d'you feel now?'

'He's . . . Well, I'd not place him in command of a corvette, but I think he'll do. Stubborn – that's one thing on his side, I suppose.'

'And kicking his heels waiting for a decision?'

The admiral smiled wrily. 'We've got him tucked away where no one can get at him.'

'No details, please.' The prime minister held up a hand. 'But you do understand I'd prefer not to have to sanction aerial bombing of what is now Chinese territory. We have to think globally. The European front. I don't want to wake up one morning to hear of Russian troop movements in Germany because of something that has been happening in Manchuria.'

Captain Robert J. Schroder of the United States Air Force strode through the light drizzle towards the hangar where the briefing was to be held. His pale, high-cheeked face was set and expressionless; that in itself betrayed his fury and his hurt. Burning a hole in his breast pocket was his wife's untidily scrawled confession that for the past twelve months she'd been hopping regularly into the sack with some limey lawyer and now wanted to marry the bastard.

Confession was the wrong word. He sensed her gloating mockery between every line. Like she was boasting about it all. Like she was proud of it.

Twelve lousy months and he'd known nothing, not suspected it even. Her letter had been his only mail that week. He'd experienced his usual surge of pleasure at the sight of her handwriting on the envelope, and King George's head on that British stamp, only to tear it open and find this shit inside. The bitch. He cursed the day he first ran into her in that English country lane, high hedges on either side blocking the view as she'd manoeuvred her tractor into a field, and he'd stood by and watched, and applauded.

He cursed himself for plunging head over heels in love with her, and the goddam Air Force for keeping them apart so long. Though –

Could be they had been at it more that twelve months. He thought back to the time he was stationed in England, the days she said she was going to visit her mother, or else her sister. She might have been with that limey lawyer then, sprawled on her back while they sorted out her father's will, her legs twining round him the way she always –

Oh shit!

'ID, Captain?'

The security lieutenant's crisp voice sliced into his thoughts like a surgeon's scalpel. He produced his special ID card, issued to B29 Task Group T only and waited while the lieutenant checked his name and number against the list on his clipboard.

'OK, Captain. Proceed.'

'Tight as a monkey's ass, security round this hangar,' Al Rossi, his navigator, grumbled as he joined him. 'Saw you had mail. Elaine OK?'

'Never better,' he lied. Al meant well.

One end of the hangar had been curtained off using heavy tarpaulins. Beyond them some fifty men squatted uncomfortably on narrow benches, keeping up a low buzz of conversation. Bob Schroder and Al joined them, pushing their way along the centre row to sit with their own crew. With the colonel at the table in front was a long-haired civilian who must be new on the base.

'Right, if we're all here we'll get started,' the colonel announced mildly, clearing this throat.

His manner was deceptive; perhaps he was laying it on for the civilian's benefit. Rumour was that beneath this immaculate tunic and rows of medal ribbons beat a heart of pressed steel, though when a drunken medic had issued a certificate to this effect he had found himself given an immediate posting to the Pusan front line. Which proved the colonel had a sense of humour.

'Where's Baby Jane?' a voice called out.

'If you're patient you'll soon meet her,' the colonel responded drily. 'First I want to introduce the professor here. He will brief you on her more intimate details.'

The inevitable whistle shrilled around the hangar's high roof.

The long-haired civilian professor could have auditioned successfully to take over from Boris Karloff. He was a tall gangly man with an elongated, cavernous face. When he spoke, his Ivy League voice rasped like a file against timber.

'I shall begin, gentlemen, by distinguishing between Hiroshima and Nagasaki,' he stated undramatically. He gave the names no special stress, as if any others might have served the purpose just as easily – New York and Washington, London and Paris, Athens and Sparta, Sodom and Gomorrah.

'Some of you may have visited Hiroshima, only a short drive from Iwakuni Air Base. You will have observed the type and extent of damage resulting from the first bomb we dropped. That bomb we named Little Boy in reference to President Roosevelt. It had a long compact appearance, seven-eighths of a metre in diameter, and its punch came from uranium 235. A successful weapon of its kind, I think you'll agree.

'However, various factors lead us to regard our second bomb as more effective for its purpose, namely to cause widespread devastation of buildings and personnel. It was dropped three days after Hiroshima, to be exact on August the 9th, 1945. We called it Fat Man in honour of Winston Churchill whose contours were not dissimilar.'

A hush had fallen over the assembled aircrews. Every man there had at least overflown both devastated cities. Perhaps every man too had shared Bob Schroder's reaction at what he had seen. After experiencing Germany where every city had been bombed almost out of existence using high explosives and incendiaries, he had been surprised at the apparently small amount of rubble in Nagasaki and Hiroshima. Everything had been reduced to ash, or powder, disintegrated, all except, here and there, stark twisted girders of what once had been war factories or public buildings. A single bomb on each city – that was all it had taken.

'With both bombs the burst point was some five hundred metres above the target,' the professor continued as unemotionally as if describing the destruction of a wasps' nest. 'But there the resemblance ends. In Fat Man the fissionable material was plutonium 239 which is itself a product of radioactive uranium and very unstable. When triggered – that is, when it is bombarded with thermal neutrons – fission takes place with the resultant chain reaction. This releases a vast amount of energy, roughly equivalent to twenty kilotons of TNT.

'A word of warning, gentlemen. Such comparisons give only part of the picture. Within a fraction of a second after the burst, temperatures are reached of several million degrees centigrade and a fireball is formed. In addition, the explosion produces a shock wave. To give you some idea, at Nagasaki there was considerable blast damage up to fifteen kilometres away and beyond. Burns on the skin occurred up to four kilometres from hypo-centre. And then of course radiation, specifically gamma rays and neutrons. This is something we at present know very little about, save that radiation can kill, injure or cause long-term health problems varying according to the dose to which the victim has been exposed. The effects on humans or animals, on the soil, on the whole environment, are still under study.

'Gentlemen, these first two atomic bombs were power-ful weapons, but in the five years since they were used to put an end to the most terrifying war in history things have not been standing still. One result is Baby Jane – daughter, if you like, of Fat Man. It is about Baby Jane that I wish to speak next. Any questions so far?'

Thoughts of her rolling on the bed with that tubby British lawyer nagged at Schroder throughout the professor's talk, attacking him like swarming, ill-humoured mosquitoes. Fighting them down, trying to concentrate on his job – Christ, he'd be responsible when it came to dropping the bitch bomb, wouldn't he? – he raised his hand to ask a question.

'Captain Schroder, officer commanding *Elaine*,' the colonel identified him for the professor's benefit.

The sound of her name in the colonel's mouth hit him like a kick in the balls. Officer commanding Elaine . . . Oh shit, that was a tack he'd never attempted. Command her? He'd not even wanted to try. Perhaps secretly she'd despised him for that. It would explain the gloating tone of her letter.

Al Rossi was the genius who had suggested calling their B29 after his beloved wife, rot her fucking guts. No way could he change it now.

They were waiting for his question. Were there any projections available, he asked, of the likely area of damage Fat Man might have caused if the explosion had been on ground impact as compared with the air-burst at 1,600 feet? For the past few weeks all five B29 Task Group T crews had been flying daily practice runs over an offshore Jap island, aiming their 10,000-pound concrete-filled 'punkins' at the ruined Samurai fortifications. So far the highest marks for accuracy had been picked up by his own crew, which put them all right out there in the front line.

The professor was already launched into his answer. '. . . air-burst ideal for disposing of large troop concentrations on the understanding that . . .' He raised a bony forefinger to emphasize the point. 'The weather, gentlemen. Radioactive debris may be carried on the wind over an area of anything up to fifty or a hundred kilometres away. It has been known to come down as black rain. We have to be doubly certain there is no danger of blow-back over territory held by our own boys.'

'It's on then?' came a question from another crew. 'We're gonna hit those Chinese reds with the A-bomb?'

The colonel intervened crisply. 'Negative. Now hear this. Nothing – repeat nothing – we say today implies the use of any atomic weapon in the present conflict. Our task – I've told you before – is to be ready *if and when* the order comes. Fully trained, capable of delivering Baby Jane rapidly and efficiently over the correct target. The decision to A-bomb or not to A-bomb is for the politicians in Washington. OK, any more questions you can save till later. Now let's get the technical data on Baby Jane. Professor?'

I am not a whore, Mei-lin repeated silently to herself as she lay back in the steaming bath under the watchful eyes of her two women attendants. Whenever she glanced up at them they smiled and nodded encouragingly, though they pointedly shied away from any attempt at conversation, even the plump one who was her masseuse and would later on pummel and knead her soft body again, leaving every muscle aching. Obviously they distrusted her as much as she did them.

The Chairman of Intelligence Surveillance had agreed immediately when she had insisted to him that she was not a whore. No one in the department, he said, would ever accuse her of decadent, capitalist motives. But then he had gone on to congratulate her on the excellent work while reporting on Colonel Ong Chou-fei. Having thus proved her value to the Revolution she could surely not object to undertaking a similar task with this English spy, Ross? For a week or two . . . perhaps at the most three . . .? Once it was over they promised to see about allocating her to something more congenial.

I'm not a whore whatever they assume, she thought yet again as she gazed down through the water at her pale body – her long slim legs, the tiny patch of dark hair, the flat stomach, and her swelling nipples just breaking the surface. It might easily have been someone else's body she was seeing, not belonging to her at all.

Except – it was still the same body Chou-fei had savoured. And that same body – *her* body – had taken such intense, unbelievable pleasure in his while they were together.

No, she experienced no disgust at the prospect of the Englishman's hands caressing her, stranger though he was. It was in her mind that her objections were strongest; her fury was aroused that they should even dream of abusing her in this way. They had been so sure she'd consent, yet what indication had she ever given?

She *had* consented. Weakly. Stifling her anger.

The Party could demand any sacrifice, that was what she had always been taught. Hardly a week back in China, she had not wished to appear stubborn or rebellious. Had she been right, though? Should she have shown herself to be outraged when at heart she wasn't?

She'd admit – to herself at least – that she had found the Englishman disturbing, but it didn't mean she was ready to fall into his bed the second he raised an eyebrow in her direction. Nor that she welcomed this assignment. She didn't.

They despised her, it was only too clear. Why else would they have expected her to do it? 'The fewer people who meet him, the better,' they had tried to explain, but unconvincingly. 'You already know him from Singapore.' Was that their only reason?

This house in Shanghai was the test. A high-class

brothel it had been during the occupation. Courtesans for Nippon staff officers, hence the vast mirrors in the bedrooms and this luxurious marble bath large enough for three or four people to share. Outside, the neon lights had been switched off and party slogans were now painted on the walls. The rich were now poor, and the poor were at least fed. That was where she really longed to be – out there with the people building the New China, part of the great proletarian Revolution. Instead, using the excuse that all accommodation was full, they allocated her a room here where she could be fed, pampered, massaged, and kept fit for a man's bed. She might as well have been living in the age of the old emperors, and one hour's daily training in light unarmed combat, with time out at a firing range, did nothing to contradict that impression.

All the Shanghai prostitutes had been rounded up, every one of them sent off to re-education camp or to work on the farms. Was she the only whore left, spared their humiliation because she was a Party member and they needed her?

'But I'm not a whore.'

This time she spoke the words aloud as she pulled herself out of her bath. The masseuse, pretending she hadn't heard, stepped forward to wrap a large towel round her as she must have done so often when other high-priced girls had used this apartment in earlier days.

In a high, sparsely furnished room in Moscow the four-man Military Intelligence Assessment Committee was questioning Colonel Borkin about his most recent report. That day Marshal Shigalyov took the chair and as Borkin's voice droned on he found it difficult to concentrate.

'I see no point, Comrade Colonel,' he interrupted, 'in subjecting this committee to a repetition of your analysis. We have all studied the paper you prepared. Your views have been noted. Now come to this British agent, Ross. What progress have you made on his activities?'

The marshal's belly rumbled. As usual the meeting had gone on far too long. What a dreary man this Borkin was, he thought with distaste; not the sort he could imagine indulging himself with a skinful of vodka or a plump secretary in his bed, though the experience might improve him. No doubt behind that hangdog air was quite a sharp brain; he had made a good reputation for himself in Berlin, and later in Peking. But he was a bore nevertheless.

'Our source in London can tell us nothing,' the bore was intoning. 'Our only pointer is the security blanket over the whole operation. His whole Section is kept in ignorance.'

'Perhaps your man is distrusted.'

'He thinks not. It's something different. The presence of their top man in Singapore indicates something big.'

'Code-named Sea Dog?'

'He has quarters in the naval base but we've been unable to discover why, though our London source managed to read one of his signals. That is in my report, you'll remember. General enquiries, including one about germ warfare experiments. Not linking directly with Paikow. My impression is that he had information from the Chinese merchant Ong – a Kuomintang agent – and was running a check on it.'

'Ong was killed. By Ross?'

'Uncertain. Our informant in Singapore has not been in touch. But I'm fairly sure of one thing, Comrade Marshal. If we look for a shape it's only too obvious. A triangle. Sea Dog – Ross – Browne. Browne's the Internal Security man, and he's the key. Our partisan comrades in Malaya have shaken the British, who don't know what to expect next. Hence the germ warfare enquiry. Anti-personnel devices. From other reports we know the imperialist police are recruiting triad secret society and Kuomintang members to fight against the inevitable Revolution. Now Ross is there, and Sea Dog. The pattern is quite clear.'

Marshal Shigalyov's belly rumbled for the second time, loudly. He shifted on his chair and leaned forward. 'No connection with Korea then? In your estimate?'

'Nothing in my *evidence* points to Korea.'

'Thank you, Colonel Borkin. That's all.'

He waited till Borkin had left the room before raising the question of Okinawa again, asking each member of the committee in turn for his opinion. Reports from locally recruited agents working on the American base left no doubt that they were planning an A-bomb attack. Borkin had no knowledge of these reports; his judgement was based strictly on the facts available to him, which made it that much more reliable.

'I think we are all agreed then,' he concluded when everyone had spoken. He gathered up his papers. 'The likely target for an A-bomb attack is troop concentrations massing in Manchuria, thereby removing the only major threat facing the Americans on the Korean front. I shall report accordingly.'

Hylas, he thought to himself as he strode along the corridor in the direction of his office. He would put in a phone call right away to request an interview and then go for his meal. But the decision couldn't take any other course. Once Comrade Stalin had indulged the North Korean's dream of military adventure, a wider conflict became inevitable. It followed as night follows day. *Hylas* was the bishop on the chess board. Not a solution; simply a reply.

* * *

When the MV *Hylas*, 5,000 tons, Greek-registered if the lettering on her stern could be believed, had first dropped anchor off Las Palmas, the usual swarm of small boats had appeared bearing traders clamouring to come on board, standing perilously to display their fine lace and other wares, but by the third day they left the inhospitable ship in peace. None of the crew had shown any interest; not so much as waved a greeting.

Captain Tukachevsky of the Soviet Navy, holder of the Order of Lenin, remained out of sight. He spoke no Greek, though three members of his crew were sufficiently fluent in the language to keep up the deception if necessary, and the role of commanding a general purpose cargo ship sat as uneasily on the shoulders of a man of his seniority as the ill-fitting uniform he was forced to wear. To pass the time, he moodily lost one game of chess after another to the crazy scientist they carried on board. Bad chess; neither of them took any pleasure in it.

Whichever way it turned out this was the last voyage for both of them. Daily he awaited the signal ordering his next move. Moscow could still call the operation off; in that case, those who knew too much could expect exile and house arrest at least. Or Moscow could order engagement. A few days' sailing to the target. The crazy scientist would descend to the ship's bowels to fiddle with the trigger mechanism of his prize baby, and then death for all of them. Their escape plan was a fairy story, all four officers realized that much, and the crew knew nothing.

'Check,' said the crazy scientist for the fifth time that day.

Captain Tukachevsky shook his head, staring at the board unable to comprehend how he could have missed so obvious a tactic. His mind wasn't on the game. The problem was, Comrade Stalin might well be mad, but he still held the power. Every man on board the *Hylas* had a family at risk back home in the Soviet Union. What choice had they other than to obey?

'Signal, Comrade Captain.'

The radio operator handed him the sheet of rough paper on which the brief message was written out. Three cipher groups only, identifying the target and ordering the *Hylas* to proceed immediately. He double-checked against his cipher books before dismissing the man with the instruction to send a 'received and understood' acknowledgement at the next pre-arranged time.

'You've won again,' he told the crazy scientist once they were alone. He reached into his pocket for a bank-note which he reluctantly passed over. 'The target's New York.'

It had been a standing bet between them. The US Air Force stationed in Western Europe could mount an A-bomb attack against Moscow, Leningrad, Kiev, any target they chose. Retaliation against the American mainland was more difficult. The distances involved put their cities beyond the range of the Soviet Air Force, yet if their aggression was to be halted it was essential to bring the war home to them on their own territory where it would hurt most. The MV *Hylas*, sailing under Greek colours with a Soviet-made A-bomb on board, was their only chance. From the start the crazy scientist had insisted that the target would be New York – 'For maximum psychological effect,' he'd said – while his own choice, thinking of strategic needs in a long-drawn-out conflict, had been the destruction of the Panama Canal.

New York it was.

He moved his knight. The scientific wizard was blind after all. 'Checkmate!' he said.

And with that victory under his belt he went to the bridge.

10

Knife! his mind screamed as, turning, he glimpsed the blade flashing towards him. Chubby, a vicious look on his face, seemed to have run amok and was intent on killing him.

Ross could do nothing to stop him. He had been caught while pulling off his shirt. His arms still struggled uselessly in its folds. In desperation he threw himself backwards, rolling over the Nissen hut floor till he was in a position to kick hard with both feet into the fat sergeant's belly.

But they made no impact. Chubby, dangerously light on his feet for a man of his weight, sidestepped the kick and came at him again, his eyes intense with hatred.

Somehow Ross somersaulted clear, no fancy tricks this time, no skill either, only an urgent need to stay alive. He struggled to free his arms, ripping the shirt apart. Backing away crab-like he managed to get to his feet, his back against the wall, and waited for Chubby to lunge at him again.

He let it happen, willing the man to close with him. It was a matter of nanoseconds only that he avoided the blade, a stupid risk, but it worked. Gripping his arm he applied a lock from which the fat man could not struggle free. The knife clattered to the cement floor and he kicked it away.

Suddenly – how it happened he'd never discover – Ross found himself thrown violently against the wall. Chubby went for the knife again. Oh sweet Jesus, this was serious. He launched himself after him, bringing him down heavily. It became a bar-room brawl with no finesse, using

212

knees and elbows wherever it hurt most. Rolling and squirming, dripping with sweat, Chubby was like a slimy, fat slug; it was impossible to get a grip on him.

Then – unexpectedly – Ross had the man at his mercy. One quick blow on the right spot would kill him.

He knew it too. With his hand flat against the floor, Chubby signalled surrender.

Distrusting him, Ross did not release his hold. The two men lay there intertwined, trying to recover their breath, till Chubby spoke first.

'Still a bit out o' practice, aren't you, sir? I'd several chances o' killin' you this time. That wouldn't have pleased 'em. I'd have had to put in a report. They don't like extra paper work. Still, accidents do happen in trainin'. Occupational hazard.'

'What if I'd killed you?'

Chubby, still pinned to the floor, looked shocked. 'Kill an instructor, sir? You'd swing for that. Now ease up, will you? We both need a shower.'

It had been at Ross's own request that the admiral had arranged for him to hide out at this jungle training school till the Chinese were ready. He had left Singapore quite openly on the early morning BOAC Argonaut flight to Hongkong and his ticket showed onward connections to Manila and Tokyo – connections he would never make. It was a routine business trip, Tim Moody was to explain if anyone bothered to ask.

His disappearance in Hongkong was a piece of cake. A young, blond Englishman collected him from the airport and drove him to a down-at-heel hotel, chattering non-stop about cricket on the way. The room was adequate for the few hours he stayed there; he did not need to register. At two o'clock when the night was darkest, the young man returned to convey him to the RAF transport plane which was waiting, blacked out, on the tarmac.

During the flight to Borneo he had been unable to sleep. Giving up the attempt, he went over all the details again in his mind, convinced there must be a missing factor which he had overlooked. There was Browne of course. This disappearing trick was as much for his benefit as anyone's. Bloody Browne. Colonial Service every inch of him. His unquestioning faith in the righteousness of it all – this British Empire on which the sun never set, *civis Britannicus sum*, all that crap.

Browne – now convinced he would collaborate once he'd settled in – had helped clear this trip with the Singapore police. 'As a favour, old man. Save you bothering.' He'd been less benevolent, though, towards his murdered clerk. Puffing out clouds of that filthy tobacco smoke, his only comment had been, 'Rum sort o' chap, Pereira. Never quite knew where you stood with him. Something was going on in that head of his. Couldn't fathom what it was though.' That was typical of Browne.

On landing in Borneo, this red-faced, chubby instructor had come on board the DC4 to meet him, explaining he was not to disembark till the helicopter arrived. Almost twenty minutes passed before they spotted it through the windows as it skimmed across the airfield.

'Bristol type 171,' Chubby informed him. 'British designed an' built. Makes you proud, don't it?'

Briefly it hovered, then set down on the blind side of the DC4. They scrambled down the metal ladder and sprinted across to it, ducking instinctively as they neared its giant blades which were still turning.

For barely a quarter of an hour they flew over thick jungle before dropping down on the parade ground of an almost deserted army camp. A Union Jack drooped from the flagpost. A few yards away an officer in knee-shorts stood observing their arrival. No one else in sight, and no one came over to welcome them.

The jungle warfare training camp was between courses and it was understood among those permanently stationed there that these two strangers were to be left alone. Other than Chubby who seldom left him, Ross met only the armourer, a bronzed warrant officer with years of service under his belt. He ruled over his own kingdom with pride, introducing Ross to his extensive collection of weapons from all countries, many having been handed in by the Three Star Army freedom fighters at the victory parade in 1945, though some had been captured more recently in jungle skirmishes. Ross tried them at the range – the Chinese Hanyang 7.92 rifle, a Soviet Stechkin machine pistol, a Canadian-made 9 mm Parabellum Browning HP to remind him of his own life in the jungle, and others too. Even a Chinese Generalissimo, hardly fired before.

In a tight corner he'd prefer the Stechkin, but he prayed it wouldn't come to that, not this time. He'd simply go there, snoop around, and report back. What could be more peaceful?

The helicopter flew in almost daily. His first visitor was an RN surgeon-lieutenant he had met before who came bearing syringes and refrigerated containers. He initiated a series of additional inoculations. With him was a pale, pinch-mouthed civilian who stayed behind to brief him while the jabs took effect, expecting him to memorize lists of the most likely diseases, showing him drawings, cross-sections and micro-photographs of the damage they could cause, while with every hour his fever mounted and his arm swelled, itching like hell.

It was three weeks before the admiral turned up.

Three weeks of jabs, unarmed combat every day he felt up to it, weapons instruction, morse practice – Chubby ran the refresher session on the B2 'suitcase' transceiver –

endless drip-feeding of data from the civilian bacteriological warfare specialist, and jungle sweat. Not forgetting the mosquitoes which nightly thirsted for his blood.

Three weeks during which – according to Radio Malaya news – United Nations forces advanced through North Korea against only token resistance. Perhaps the war would be over before the Chinese were ready for him. But the admiral disillusioned him.

'It's on. You leave tomorrow.' Gold braid gleamed against his spotless white uniform. He was on his way to a shindig in Brunei, Ross gathered. 'No illegal entry involved, no parachute drops. They're sending a special plane for you. Red carpet treatment, if you can trust them. Can you, Ross?'

'Chuan, yes. I still like to think so.'

In the jungle it had been the David-and-Jonathan touch – but trust? Did he ever trust anyone?

'We're not sending you in light-heartedly, you realize that. They're playing a double game. You've heard they're infiltrating troops into North Korea?'

'Rumours, yes.'

'More than rumours. The Americans have taken some prisoners. They're coming over the Yalu river bridges after dark. Silent routine. The latest intelligence estimate – it's only a guess – puts the number at over a hundred thousand troops so far. It's rough country, difficult to make an accurate assessment it seems, but the situation doesn't look good. Some units are operating way to the rear of what we took to be the front line.'

'So now we're at war with China? Considerate of you to mention it.'

'There's no question of full-scale war, not yet. Peking claims the troops are volunteers. Compares them with the Americans who came to help out on our side in 1940. Either way, Ross, we need all the intelligence you can pick up. Paikow isn't two hundred miles from the Antung bridges and it could be those volunteer troops include bacteriological warfare units. We must find out how they propose to disperse the bacteria – sprays, booby traps, or how? And what diseases. Paikow could be the key supply depot.'

With him the admiral had brought a new batch of aerial pictures of Paikow and the valley. They studied them together but they revealed nothing new save for a transmitter mast on a hillside opposite the cliff. On the previous photograph it had been obscured by cloud. The two pyramid shapes were also clearly visible, but there was no evidence as to their purpose.

'I'll wish you luck then.' A quick handclasp. 'You're taking your own transceiver, you've been told that? God knows why they agreed, but they did. Chinese motives has always been a mystery since the dawn of time.'

The admiral replaced the photographs in their case and strode across the parade ground towards the waiting helicopter. Ross watched it take off. Luck? In a country where even the fleas were now Party informers? He could have puked.

Next day he discovered Chubby was to accompany him part of the way, perhaps to make certain he was handed over safely to the Chinese. The admiral wanted no hitches. The helicopter flew them both over the dark jungle to the airfield where he immediately boarded the DC4. It headed north across the South China Sea. His old tensions revived. Christ, what was he doing going back to China? As an official visitor – that was the cover this time. An admirer of their Revolution, for God's sake! A fellow traveller! Hell!

After a while the flight lieutenant came back to offer stale cheese sandwiches and a thermos of coffee. He forced himself to eat though Chubby hardly touched his,

217

preferring to sleep. His snores competed with the drone of the engines.

It was dusk when they came in to land at Hongkong. On the far side of the airport the terminal building was brightly lit but they taxied away from it and eventually stopped on an isolated stretch close to some large oil tanks. Parked close by was one other plane, its dull grey paintwork chipped and scarred. It bore no markings.

'Dakota,' Chubby grunted, heaving himself out of his seat. 'An old Flying Tigers plane, I'd guess.'

The two aircraft were parked so close together that his transfer would go unnoticed. All cabin and navigation lights had been switched off. A stocky figure in a Mao Tse-tung cap stood waiting for them by the Dakota. Chubby handed him Ross's grip and the attaché case transceiver which he passed up into the dark cabin. No words were exchanged.

'OK, your turn now, sir.' Chubby sounded solicitous. 'Have a good trip. Come back in one piece.'

Ross climbed the metal ladder. He felt a hand steadying him in the darkness as he entered the cabin, and someone led him to a seat. There were at least two other passengers, he reckoned, though it was too gloomy to see their faces. Then he heard the engines start up and the plane began to move towards its take-off position. From the cockpit he could hear the clipped voices talking to the control tower. At last, accelerating, they rumbled forward, bumping a little, rocking, till finally they lifted off, climbing into the black sky.

How long they were in the air he had no means of knowing. The cabin lights were never switched on and from the window he could see only stars. He guessed that they must have crossed the Chinese coast long ago. At last, after what seemed like an hour or more, they began to lose height. Suddenly, ahead, two rows of flares sprang into life, marking out a landing strip. His stomach tightened again, cramping into knots of nervousness. He had flown unerringly into a trap, he told himself. Chuan had sold him out to the Russians.

The wheels hit the ground, bouncing two or three times before settling down to a steady deceleration. Once the plane had stopped his suspicions were confirmed. His two Chinese fellow-passengers took charge, gripping his arms and marching him over the rough grass towards a low building which might once have been a farmhouse. Both were armed. A third man followed a few paces behind with the luggage.

Reaching the farmhouse Ross hesitated, not knowing what was expected of him, but they pushed him roughly through the door.

'Welcome to the Chinese People's Republic!' Chuan stood there with his twisted grin, no longer in civilian clothes but wearing a quilted blue uniform of the People's Liberation Army, tunic buttoned to the throat, no insignia other than the five-pointed red star on his cap. 'Good flight?'

'Good enough.'

Chuan ordered the other men to wait outside, then he asked for his passport. It was the genuine article, supplied from London and suitably scuffed to give the impression it had been used a few times. Peter Bentley, place of birth Birmingham, profession lecturer. With him he had letters and other documents to support his story that he was a British Marxist, a member of the Labour Party and trade union activist on an invited visit to China to assess the achievements of the Revolution.

'Peter Bentley is in China for the first time in his life. An interpreter will therefore be supplied and he will be expected never to go anywhere unaccompanied.' Chuan stamped the passport twice, then filled in a permit to travel. 'Naturally these documents are adequate to fool any minor officials who ask to see them, but remember our Foreign Visitors Section will not be able to verify them. They know nothing about you.'

'In other words, keep out of trouble.'

'We still have many subversive elements at work in China. Until they are eliminated people will remain suspicious of strangers.'

'Who is the interpreter? You?'

'That would be unwise. An interpreter will join us in Shanghai.'

'Can we trust him?'

'This interpreter can be trusted, but many can't.' He grouped the passport and other papers together on the table. 'Are you armed?'

'No.' They had offered him a choice from the training camp's armoury but he had decided against, correctly as it turned out. Chuan would have confiscated any weapon.

As it was, tapping his clothes skilfully, he discovered the commando knife and the time incendiary Churchill cigar in its aluminium tube and took charge of them.

'Out of character for Peter Bentley,' he commented, turning to the grip whose contents he tipped out on to the table. 'I'll return them later.'

Ross flushed with annoyance as Chuan went through his clothes, checking the pockets and seams, as well as the safety razor handle and toothpaste, but he said nothing.

Chuan seemed to sense his reaction. 'Have to make sure our police find nothing if they decide to search your luggage, with or without your consent,' he explained. 'Or my head could roll as well as yours. But everything seems OK. The radio I'll take care of. So welcome to the People's Republic of China, Hantu tuan. Shanghai first stop.'

Dawn was already whitening the sky as they tramped

across the grass towards the Dakota with the three security men falling in behind them. Once airborne, one of these men brought them a pot of pale lukewarm tea and some oil strips. As a child he used to buy such strips of pastry cooked in oil from the street hawkers. He was back in China. Home, the admiral had once said. How little he understood.

It was a long flight and during most of it he tried to sleep. Whenever he opened his eyes he could see nothing below but agricultural land with very few houses. Then – he had lost all count of time but they must have been in the air for two hours already – he spotted a railway line and several clusters of buildings. The plane circled and began its descent.

'Shanghai,' Chuan announced.

But they could be anywhere; he still could not see the city. A river, yes – but he'd only Chuan's word that it was Shanghai. That was a problem which would stay with him, he realized. Trust – he had to trust Chuan – can be tricky; one wrong move and it disintegrates. In some ways it was easier to deal with open enemies.

It was Shanghai Airport after all.

In the shabby terminal building an official demanded to see his papers. Ross played dumb, pretending not to understand, and turned to Chuan for help. 'A British trade unionist,' he heard him explain as the permits were rubber-stamped once again. 'Official visit, one day only. Then he goes on to Peking.' Before allowing them through, the official reminded Chuan that they would need passes to re-enter the airport even as passengers.

'We Chinese invented paper and printing, both,' Chuan commented with a touch of self-mockery as they were driven into the city. 'Our gift to mankind, now in the service of the Revolution.'

Ross grunted. He was too busy trying to identify the

221

streets they were passing through. Was this where he had once lived? The masses of people hadn't changed, mostly on foot, and there too were the handcarts, pedicabs, bicycles, even an occasional bus, overcrowded as always. A tram clattered along Nanking Road and he recognized some pre-Revolution advertisements on the high buildings – Ovaltine, Pepsi-Cola, Singer, Aspro, Clover Beer. Tattered now, and competing with bright new red banners bearing Maoist slogans.

'Mr Bentley, every visitor from the West asks to see the famous Bund.' Chuan glanced warningly at the back of the driver's head. 'We can go that way, then walk for a few minutes if you like. The car can follow us.'

'Good idea,' Ross played along. 'Stretch our legs.'

They stopped on the Bund and all eyes were drawn to him. Probably not many Europeans still remained in Shanghai. The river was a bleak stretch of cold water where once cargo ships of every nation on earth had anchored. Nothing of all that was left save for the clusters of sampans around the jetties.

'We have to be careful,' Chuan said as they strolled along ahead of their wheezing old Mercedes. 'Our driver is not the man I expected, though that might mean nothing. Anyone watching could be a police informer. All foreigners are kept under surveillance.'

'How long do we stay here?'

'Too soon to say. Play the tourist, that's your only job for the moment. Or stay indoors. You should feel at home here in Shanghai – don't you?'

'Do *you*?' he retorted.

There was resentment behind the question, he knew. The mere existence of international concession areas had been regarded by all Chinese as a personal humiliation.

They paused to allow the Mercedes to draw up beside them and got in. All hotels were occupied, he explained, so he had arranged accommodation in an apartment block in Bubbling Well Road.

It was a road Ross remembered as the Latin quarter of Shanghai though now it seemed drab and neglected. Several of the old hotels and cabarets had become government offices guarded by armed soldiers. The apartment block itself had an uncared-for air; in the hallway the paint was flaking off the plaster and the doorman was no longer a uniformed flunkey with gilt buttons and gold braid, but wore a faded boiler suit plus a Sam Browne belt and pistol. From the way he greeted them Ross guessed he must be one of Chuan's men.

'Second floor,' he told them. 'Lift's out of order.'

He must have phoned up to announce their arrival. When they reached the second landing the apartment door was already open and Fang Mei-lin stood waiting for them, unsmiling.

'Your interpreter, Mr Bentley,' Chuan said.

Had Ross met her on the street he might not have recognized her. This was no longer the fashionable, wealthy woman who had hidden in his hotel room with a razor-sharp blade in her shoe. Her face bore no trace of make-up. She wore no jewellery, no stockings, and her grey cotton *cheongsam* was cheap and shapeless. Her shoes were flat-heeled, her hair simply combed back into a knot. After Singapore, it smacked of sackcloth and ashes.

'Welcome to China, Mr Ross,' she greeted him once they were inside the apartment. Her tone was formal.

'Mr Peter Bentley,' Chuan put her right, carrying Ross's grip into the living room. 'Don't take risks, comrade.'

'Where's the small case?' Ross asked.

'It's in good hands. You won't need it here. Now I'll have to leave Mei-lin to look after you. Something

223

unusual is happening in Shanghai but I don't yet know what. Mei-lin, can you feed him? We've been travelling all night and most of today.'

'I was issued rations for two.'

'Good. I'll try to get back in two or three hours, I hope with some news. Meanwhile it's safer for you not to go out, either of you.'

Mei-lin went with Chuan to the door and Ross heard her bolting it after him. 'What's going on?' he asked when she returned.

'Would I know?'

'You probably do.'

He checked over the apartment. Its large living room had windows overlooking the race course; in addition there were three bedrooms, two bathrooms and a kitchen, all obviously unoccupied for some time. Twenties-built, he imagined, with furniture which must have been the height of fashion when it was bought, though now it was chipped and scratched, its upholstery torn. No one else there. He was alone with Mei-lin.

'So you're my interpreter?' Deliberately needling her, he tried out her English. 'Think you're good enough?'

With a toss of her head she accepted his challenge. 'I study. Chuan speak better. I study short time.'

'Very pretty! How far d'you think we'd get with that?'

'How . . . far . . .?' She puzzled over it. 'I go with you all way. Chuan, you, I. We go all-all.'

'Together,' he corrected her. He went on in Chinese, wanting to discover how much she had been told. 'Where d'you think we're heading? The Ming tombs? Some tourist outing?'

She flushed. 'I may not speak good English, Mr Ross, but I'm not a fool. An interpreter is provided for all foreign visitors. If you travelled alone you'd be arrested

224

immediately. Where you move in public I go with you, even to Paikow.'

So she did know, he gathered – though perhaps not everything. 'Don't get in my way, that's all. I can't stand being crowded.'

'You have the typically bad manners of an imperialist barbarian,' she snapped. Her spoken Chinese was balanced and elegant, not least when she was furious. 'Or else it's hunger. I'll get the food ready, but don't expect much. It's a few years since I last had to cook. Have a bath while you're waiting. I think you need it. Your room's at the far end of the corridor.'

'If you say so.'

'Mr Ross, if you drown I shan't miss you.'

The plumbing worked and the water was surprisingly hot. He might easily drown, he thought as he lay back drowsily. His tiredness crept up on him and he found himself nodding. Despite her lack of cosmetics she smelled very fresh and sweet . . . and her skin was still soft . . . Not one of the labouring poor. He wondered how she'd fit in with life in the New China. No easy ride, that seemed obvious.

He dried himself, shaved, and put on clean clothes from his grip before following the smell of cooking. They ate at the kitchen table, stir-fried fragments of chicken with bean curd and boiled rice, and for a long time he was too busy with his chopsticks to say anything other than give an occasional grunt of appreciation. It was his first real meal since leaving the jungle warfare training camp in Borneo more than twenty-four hours earlier.

'Christ, I was hungry,' he announced at last, leaning back, having retrieved the last rice grain from his bowl.

'I hope you realize, Mr Ross, not many peasants know the privilege of eating meat, whether chicken or any other kind.' Before he could return an unwise answer, she

225

added: 'I'm sorry, I'm not to call you Mr Ross, am I? What shall I say?'

'Bentley.'

'Not that.' She shook her head impatiently. 'A more . . . a more *intimate* name. I am ordered to, you understand.'

'Not if you don't want to, Miss Fang. Though I find Mei-lin very attractive – as a name. Comrade.'

'Shall I call you Peter or Pete? What do your friends call you?'

'Friends?' He thought of Moody; then – naturally – of Chuan. 'Some call me Ross, but that's not allowed, is it? Perhaps you'd better call me Hantu when we're alone.'

'Hantu? Is that a name?'

'Ah, you've been inadequately briefed. Very well, I'll explain.'

No harm in her learning about Force 136, he thought. The main outline, not the details. Not the final Jap ambush, the sudden slaughter from that stream of bullets through the leaves, nor Yen-hua whose death had been his death. The gleaming sword. Her head rolling over the rough ground. Yen-hua's head. Yen-hua herself. No, none of that. He stayed with the less unpleasant events, mentioning them briefly, the Robin Hood adventure as some drunken idiot on the troopship afterwards had once called it.

'Hantu,' Mei-lin repeated when he had finished. 'It's unusual.'

With a quick, harsh buzz the house telephone rang and she went into the corridor to answer it. It was the doorman, warning that Chuan was on his way up earlier than expected. A few seconds later he was with them.

'A hitch,' he announced, coming inside. 'A delay. I see you've eaten. Good. Enough food?'

'I think Mr Bentley might still be hungry.'

'I'll try to organize more for your next few meals.'

'Next few?' Ross woke up to what Chuan was saying. 'How long do we expect to be here, for Chrissake?'

'It's unpredictable. The airport is closed.'

'Till when? What's gone wrong?'

Chuan looked at his watch, holding up his wrist to squint at it in the increasing gloom. 'You'll see for yourself in a minute. No, don't put the light on. Come over to the window.'

'See what?'

He joined Chuan at the window overlooking the race course, itself as commonplace a symbol of the dying British Empire as the Union Jack and HP sauce. All three invariably went together and the Chinese undoubtedly realized it. They had already started demolishing the spectator stands.

'There!' Chuan exclaimed, pointing.

Swooping down out of the clouds came a formation of jet fighters, first five together, then another five, streaking across the evening sky in the direction of the Bund.

For a few moments they had gone, though their screaming engines could still be heard. Climbing again, Ross thought, hearing the change of pitch. When they returned it was in a single formation flying high over the city till, one by one, each plane peeled away, went into a dive, then flattened out to pass low over the race course and recreation ground.

'MiG-15s,' he identified them.

'The Air Force of the People's Republic of China.' Chuan's voice betrayed his pride. 'You see now why the airport is temporarily closed. Those pilots have volunteered for service in Korea. They are in Shanghai to demonstrate their support for our Korean comrades and their loyalty to the Revolution.'

Loyalty to my arse, thought Ross. He said: 'The longer

we wait, the tougher this job's going to be, you realize that? Paikow has already had heavy snow.'

'The prime minister is expected to arrive for the passing out parade,' Chuan responded placidly. 'Our volunteers include ground troops as well as air force. Such parades help the masses understand the sacrifices they are asked to make.'

'Fuck the masses!' Ross swore, mixing English and Chinese.

Chuan raised an eyebrow. It was as though he had blasphemed.

'How long then, d'you reckon? Stuck on the ground, I mean?'

'Impossible to foretell, but I'll arrange a programme of activities for you tomorrow. We must not forget your duties as an official visitor.'

He left. Ross and Mei-lin were alone again. She refused his help in the kitchen and bade him a firm goodnight as she began to rinse their few dishes. She had not welcomed Chuan's news any more than he had.

'Get some sleep,' she said. 'You're worn out. You'll have to make up your own bed.'

No arguing with that. He went to his room, irritated.

It was a double bed. On it the bare mattress was rolled up, tied with a length of frayed rope which disintegrated into separate strands when he picked at the knot. He cut through it then looked around for blankets. A search through the wardrobe yielded three, all stained and torn, but no sheets and no pillow. He tried the chest of drawers – all empty save one which contained some Shanghai Club notepaper, several broken pencils and a few paper clips.

He made up the bed as best he could, switched off the light and lay down, using a folded sweater for his head and trying to forget the stains on the blankets. He was so tired it was like a drug sending his mind swimming off vaguely, unable to grasp anything any longer.

Shanghai, he thought as he drifted off into a distant sleep. Why was he back in Shanghai?

Three planes, not five. Not MiG-15s either, where had he picked up that idea? They crossed the sky like dark birds of prey, three Jap bombers and behind them a trail of tiny puffs of smoke from the anti-aircraft shells which never came close enough to do any damage. He was fifteen, struggling with his maths homework, and he ran out on the veranda to watch. The planes turned, flying in line, and he heard the *thud-thud-thud* of the bombs hitting home.

No, it was later they told him about the bombs – wasn't it? Two hours later, an arm round his shoulder, a man's voice unnaturally sympathetic. Direct hit on the house . . . everyone inside dead . . . Yes, but *who* was inside? *Who?*

By the time he reached that little house in the Shanghai suburb all that remained was rubble and blackened timber. Killed instantly, they said. His father. Auntie Tanya – his father's 'concubine', he'd overheard the Chinese call her – and Great-Uncle Andrei Nikolayovich who taught him chess, and most of that White Russian family whose home he had loved more than the emptiness of his own.

Numbed, he walked through the artillery bombardment as the Imperial Japanese Army closed in, not bothering to take cover, almost challenging the whistling shells and shrapnel to do away with him on the spot. Houses crumbled before his eyes . . . roof tiles crashed inches from his face . . . a woman writhed on the ground, screaming, her belly a shapeless red mass, one of her legs a couple of yards away, torn off . . .

Then his amah was there, crying, staring into his face, repeatedly asking where he had been, gone for a whole week, thought he was dead, killed, and what a state he was in, covered with dirt and blood, his clothes in tatters . . . She dragged and pushed him into the house, shouting to the servants for hot water, insisting on bathing him herself, cleaning those wounds, picking out the fragments, clucking over him like any mother would have done. He must never leave the International Concession again, not while the fighting went on.

He tried to tell her about his father, about Auntie Tanya and the little house in the suburbs, but she knew all about that, he was not to talk about it, they had been given a proper funeral and now he must make an effort to forget it.

The guns still fired over the city, the planes still came, machine-gunning, bombing, but for weeks he never left the big house, feeling secure there with her.

Secure.

He opened his eyes. This was Shanghai, though he could see nothing in that darkness. He was in Shanghai again.

Adjusting the folded sweater under his head, he lay there awake, thinking. It had been part-dream, part-memory, but no less real for all that. His father had rented that little house for the White Russian family whose daughter Tanya had earned a sordid living hiring herself out in dance halls, one ticket a dance, till he had fallen in love with her and rescued her. As a boy Ross had loved staying there, hardly aware of the gossip-mongers among the British community. To him it had been quite normal, too, that he could switch easily from English to Chinese or to Russian, according to whoever he happened to be with at the time. Couldn't everyone?

Great-Uncle Andrei Nikolayovich had once beaten

Count Tolstoy at chess – long before the Bolshevik Revolution, while still a boy – and he always laughed when he talked of it as though it were the funniest joke on earth.

It was some weeks after his father's death before he ventured into the study, opening cabinets which had previously remained closed to him, examining the drawers of the heavy mahogany desk and going through the old sea-chest with the name ROSS still visible on the lid. It had belonged to his great-grandfather who had founded the business in Shanghai. As he went through the things he could not shake off the conviction that at any moment his father might walk in through the door to take his usual seat, and then everything would be just the way it had been before. But it never happened of course. Instead, Mr Tan came over from the godown, a lugubrious man who never smiled. He had managed the business for as long as Ross could remember. There were debts, he explained; the banks were refusing to extend their credit, and what with wages to be paid and the shipping company agitating for the balance of the dues owing to them . . . From the expression on his face it was obvious what he felt about having to take orders from a mere fifteen-year-old boy, next in line or not.

'Pay the wages, as much as we can afford.' It was the best he could think of. 'And let the shipping company wait.'

Mr Tan had looked at him pityingly, then gathered up his papers and left without another word. Ross never saw him again.

Then the day came when his amah didn't return from a visit to her sister in another part of the city. He set out in search of her, unwilling to believe she had deserted him. She had been attacked in the street by marauding Jap soldiers, he discovered. They had dragged her into a yard where they had raped and killed her. Neighbours had found her body and informed her sister.

They had laid her out in a dark narrow room which he recalled only too well. The bruises and cuts on her body were only too plain to see and he had stood there trembling, his eyes blurred, the entire world dissolving around him. Someone took his arm and led him out. In the alleyway he was sick, retching violently.

That same night it had been when he set out after curfew vowing to kill the first Jap soldier he met. With him he had his father's revolver from the desk drawer, loaded and with spare rounds crammed into his pocket. He had it all worked out. He would shoot them down from the shadows, giving them no chance to challenge him or attract attention. He was declaring a one-man war on the Imperial Army. But when the first three came along, staggering drunkenly out of a bar, his hand shook and his forefinger refused to tighten on the trigger. They passed him unharmed.

Another two came, striding along very smartly this time, so close he couldn't possibly have missed them, but his nerve broke. He turned and ran for his life down the dark alley, making so much noice he was convinced they were chasing after him. Perhaps they weren't, but he'd never know. Reaching the river he hid in the deep shadows beneath one of the jetties till he felt sufficiently confident to untie a sampan and push off into mid-stream. The current carried him towards a New Zealand freighter which had been anchored there for some days already and was soon due to sail. The crew must have been asleep or ashore, all but four who were playing cards under the awning. They didn't hear him as he climbed over the rail, nor when he crept below to find a hiding place among the crates and bales in the dark hold.

More than three weeks he lay hidden there till the day

when a violent storm convinced him they must be well clear of the China coast. He might have starved to death before then if the ship's cook – a Goanese – hadn't surreptitiously fed him scraps from the galley in exchange for the revolver and all his ammunition.

He checked his watch. Three o'clock in the morning and hardly a sound to be heard. Despite his tiredness he couldn't get back to sleep.

Pulling on his sweater, he fetched the broken pencils from the chest of drawers and padded down the corridor to the kitchen to sharpen them with the vegetable knife. Mei-lin's door was closed. Before sitting down to sketch – his usual way of dealing with sleeplessness – he took the chance of Mei-lin being out of the way to examine the apartment more thoroughly but found nothing out of the ordinary. Standard domestic locks on the doors, nothing an amateur couldn't have picked blindfold. No hidden microphones, nor two-way mirrors. The sideboard cupboards were empty, so were the drawers. No glasses, no drink, and the only dishes were the bowls and chopsticks they had used for their supper. If Chuan's department or section or whatever they called his intelligence outfit really did run this apartment block – as he suspected – it was impossible to guess what purpose they had in mind. Save for its general shabbiness it looked much as its original European occupants must have left it when the Nips came to round them up after Pearl Harbor catapulted Britain and the US into the Sino-Japanese war.

He started sketching with several light pencil strokes on the Shanghai Club notepaper from the bedroom. Mei-lin, semi-profile. It took a couple of attempts to get the right balance in the face – the arch of her eyebrow, how her lips curved, and her nose. But then he quickly filled in her hair, with a few additional lines to suggest the gentle swelling of her breasts beneath the *cheongsam*, and the softness of her arms. He was just finishing the drawing when she came into the room.

'Not asleep yet?' Quickly he turned the paper face downwards on the table.

'I heard a noise, then saw the light under the door.' She was wrapped in a long blue bathrobe which left her shoulders bare; as if aware of his interest she pulled it closer around her. 'I thought it must be Chuan.'

'He has a key?'

'The doorman could have let him in.' She shivered. 'It's colder in Shanghai than Singapore. I can't get used to it.'

'Are you warm enough in bed? Enough blankets?'

'Yes.' She hesitated. 'People sleep early here these days. If they see this light on too late they'll get suspicious.' Another pause. 'I am held responsible for you, Hantu. If you need anything, my door is next to yours.'

'I'll remember that.' He was not sure what she was trying to say. In pre-war Shanghai her meaning would have been obvious enough, but by all accounts the new Communist regime outrivalled even Oliver Cromwell when it came to puritanism. Besides, one immodest move from him and she'd be at his throat with that blade she carried in her shoe, he was in no doubt about that. 'Best get back to bed,' he said. 'I'll put the light out.'

He waited till her door had closed before returning to his own room, still speculating about her. She had been ordered to . . . instructed to . . . told to . . . how many times had she used those words? Of course it was not unknown for a girl to donate her virtue to a cause, he realized that well enough. Left-wing revolution was usually high on the list.

Was that what she had meant?

As he dropped into half-sleep his mind jumped unpredictably away from this problem to the question of those

234

MiG-15s. They could cause havoc over Korea if they went into action without warning. Somehow he should get word of them back to the admiral.

Mei-lin, sitting in her bathrobe on the edge of the bed, heard him pass her door and go into his own room. She could have cried with relief, only tears never came easily to her.

She had obeyed instructions. If asked, she could describe the steps taken to tempt him, deliberately letting the bathrobe slip from her naked shoulders to whet his appetite, going to him bare-footed – she was proud of her feet – and with her hair loose, practically inviting him to her bedroom. But she might have been stone for all the interest he had taken. He had looked at her, yes – with that odd, disapproving frown. That was all he had done.

Perhaps he didn't like her. Perhaps he didn't find women attractive, not any woman. A man's man, like those self-admiring athletes photographed in the magazines in Singapore, displaying sleek muscles to each other. Though admittedly it was hard to imagine Mr Ross in that role.

Hantu.

Strange name. Nothing ghostly about him in her experience. She forced herself to analyse her real feelings about him. Despite her sense of relief, one part of her was sore at him for rejecting her. Illogically she was annoyed that he had not found her too attractive to resist, like the courtesans in those famous risqué novels Chou-fei had given her to read, though she would have hated him to take advantage of her, not so soon. She was not a whore, whatever they thought.

Restlessly she turned over in her uncomfortable bed, unable to sleep. What had he been doing alone in that living room, and so late? She had not checked, and that

235

too was one of her duties. She had been so embarrassed at the role she was playing, she had hardly taken in the fact that he had been writing something. There could still be British agents hiding in Shanghai, and perhaps he intended to get in touch with them.

She got up again, slipped on the bathrobe and went to investigate. The pencils were still on the table together with several sheets of headed notepaper, one lying face down. Turning it over, Mei-lin gasped with surprise.

The portrait caught her likeness as she sometimes imagined herself to be: the Mei-lin of Singapore, very sophisticated, with her hair up, ear-rings, and the silk, patterned *cheongsam* she had often worn there. It flattered her, making her seem both independent and desirable, as if the artist had been wooing her as he drew. It told her all she needed to know about him.

She left the pencils and spare sheets of notepaper on the table for him to find in the morning. The sketch she took back to her room. He would not mistake that signal. The bathrobe incident had not even been necessary.

At first light Chuan turned up at the apartment with his 'programme of official visits' as he referred to it, insisting yet again that too many questions would be asked if Ross were not seen out and about admiring the achievements of the Revolution. He would find it more interesting than he imagined, Chuan assured him.

A guide had been provided, a smiling bespectacled girl who welcomed him yet again to the People's Republic of China, this time in lilting Shanghai English which sent his mind reeling back through the years. Chuan did not accompany them.

They had been allocated the same driver and the guide sat next to him, twisting round to face Ross and Mei-lin while giving her running commentary on the various

236

buildings they passed. Consulates and clubs, the great business houses, the banks, even the shop in Nanking Road which had first introduced ice cream soda into Shanghai – he could have retailed more stories about them than the guide herself.

He glanced at Mei-lin beside him, but her face remained strictly neutral, not once betraying her feelings. He wondered how much longer they would have to keep up this farce.

'We go now to visit model school,' the guide announced brightly. 'With young people of today lies future of tomorrow.'

Bravo, he thought.

Behind the Mercedes trailed a second black car, Soviet-made he guessed. Perhaps someone keeping an eye on him. For a moment he imagined he was mistaken – they reached a stretch of clear road where it pulled out to shoot ahead – but then he recognized the man in the rear seat as the PLA soldier who had taken charge of his luggage on the plane. He realized he was probably not wrong after all; he was going to be under surveillance every inch of the way.

The road approaching the model school was lined with armed soldiers. From every post and every window banners fluttered bearing some sacred text from the Communist creed. Near the school gate a small reception committee – teachers and officials, the guide said – stood patiently waiting, though not for him. The driver produced a pass and showed it to the soldier on duty who waved them on, pointing out where they could park.

'We're late,' the guide fussed. 'By now we must sit in place.'

Clearly it was going to be a big event and Ross cursed Chuan for involving him in it. In the extensive compound behind the school, rows of chairs had been set out for visitors, most of them already occupied. Three women came forward, welcomed him – inevitably – to the People's Republic of China and led him to his seat, with Mei-lin and the guide on either side of him. He felt he was on show; every Chinese there – a couple of hundred at least – would recognize him again easily.

A hush fell on the already subdued conversation and everyone stood up. Then the clapping started, like polite applause at a British cricket match, and the eminent guests filed in to take up the front row. All were dressed in the standard plain uniform, though cut by more skilful tailors from better quality material than average. Ross scanned their faces but recognized only one: Chou En-lai, prime minister, veteran of the Long March, close associate of Chairman Mao Tse-tung himself. Chuan had mentioned he was in Shanghai.

But was it mere coincidence that they were both there at the same time? Ross sat worrying at the question like a dog with an old slipper while the children crowded into the compound with their red flags and banners to dance and sing the praises of the Revolution. From the start they had assumed that someone very high up in Peking government circles must be behind this operation. If it were Chou En-lai they were much closer to the centre of power than he had imagined.

The dancing gave way to a drama performed by the older children, a tale of two young peasants oppressed by a wicked landlord and how they joined a covert cell of the People's Liberation Army, eventually returning to free their families and the village from his clutches. (Throughout the action the guide whispered inaccurate translations into Ross's ear.) To cap it, a more warlike dance spelled out the lesson: when the people unite, exploiters and their running dogs can be overcome.

No doubt the reappearance of the MiG-15s at that point

was unplanned, but a mixed gasp of wonder and pride came from audience and children alike as they shot across the sky with a triumphant roar of pure power, leaving widening vapour trails like long slashes across the pale blue.

Everyone applauded, standing, and Ross felt obliged to join in to avoid seeming boorish. Was he not after all Peter Bentley, Marxist sympathizer and fellow-traveller?

It was as Peter Bentley – some ten minutes later, after the children had brought hot towels for the guests and served small sweet cakes and fruit juice – that he was summoned to be introduced to the prime minister. A great honour, the guide twittered earnestly, and Mei-lin seemed impressed. The conversation was stilted and left him with no clear answers.

'I hope you find your visit to our country interesting, Mr Bentley?' Chou En-lai's English was careful, perhaps seldom exercised.

'Inspiring,' Ross said diplomatically.

'You can see how healthy these children are, and full of hope for the future. Yet war threatens the world, Mr Bentley. Imagine what will happen to these children if we experience another war. With perhaps bombs falling on Shanghai. How many killed or injured would that bring? People burned, or starved, or dying of some terrible disease. That is the danger which faces us.'

'We must work for peace,' Ross responded cautiously, feeling his way. Was he implying the Paikow operation, or were his words simple generalities?

'Give the workers of Britain this message, Mr Bentley. Through solidarity find strength; through strength find victory.'

Chou En-lai, the sly old fighter who had survived so many campaigns, moved away to talk to the other guests leaving Ross uncertain whether his mission had just received the papal blessing or not.

'Can we go?' he asked the guide abruptly.

'Oh no, not before Comrade Chou leaves!' She was visibly shocked at such *lèse-majesté*.

She was right of course; that was bound to be the protocol. And Chuan too was right to insist that travelling as an official visitor was the safest way to cross China at that moment; without guides, interpreters and the correct documentation no one could move anywhere.

Among the crowd he again spotted the PLA man who had handled his luggage. He stood alone, a narrow-faced morose type with a haunted expression; probably he had been one of the men already on board the Dakota when he had joined it in Hongkong, Ross thought. And would stay with him, no doubt, even as far as Paikow.

11

In 10 Downing Street the prime minister had let it be known that he was not to be disturbed. He had already decided what he would say in his statement to the House of Commons later that day but he needed half an hour of peace and quiet to go through the relevant papers once again. The attack would come from both sides of the House and he had to be ready for it. As he opened the file he could not help wondering how many of those vocal members of parliament would even have known where to find Korea on the map twelve months ago.

But now Korea could well turn out to be the Sarajevo of 1950, triggering off a third world war. After President Truman's notorious press conference it seemed more likely rather than less; he couldn't have chosen a worse time for that kind of blunder. The House had been debating foreign affairs when the tapes chattered out the news, offering the government's critics the chance of a lifetime.

He rustled through the papers, deciding to start with the transcript. The questions were bound to refer to it. Truman had been on home ground in the White House, that was what surprised him. He shouldn't have been caught off guard on home ground. It was lucky he made no mention of Paikow and germ warfare.

The press conference had started with a read statement which seemed innocuous enough, though he checked it over once more. 'Recent developments in Korea confront the world with a serious crisis. The Chinese Communist leaders have sent their troops from Manchuria to launch a strong and well-organized attack against the United Nations force in North Korea. This has been done despite prolonged and earnest efforts to bring home to the Communist leaders of China the plain fact that neither the United Nations nor the United States has any aggressive intentions towards China . . .' He skimmed through the rest . . . an assertion that there was no intention to abandon the UN mission in Korea . . . then a restatement of political and military aims . . .

No problems there, though one of his own backbenchers was bound to remind the House of the US Seventh Fleet's presence off Formosa to protect Chiang Kai-shek. But the sting in the tail came in the journalists' questions, picking up General MacArthur's demands for authorization to bomb Manchuria.

Question: If the UN resolution should authorize General MacArthur to go further than he has –

Truman: All necessary steps to meet the military situation will be taken just as they always have.

Question: Will that include the atomic bomb?

Truman: That would include every weapon we have.

Question: Mr President, you said every weapon we have. Does that mean there is active consideration of the use of the atomic bomb?

Truman: There has always been active consideration but I do not want to see it used. It is a terrible weapon that should not be used on innocent men, women and children who have nothing whatever to do with military aggression.

Question: Did we understand you clearly that the use of the atomic bomb is under active consideration?

Truman: It always has been. It is one of our weapons.

The prime minister read the words two or three times before putting the paper to one side. The storm of protest in the British press and among MPs had been predictable. Indeed, had he been Leader of the Opposition at that moment, ignorant of the Paikow threat, he'd have had a field day in the Commons himself. Yet he did know about Paikow, there was the rub, and so too did President Truman.

After the press conference a snowstorm of paper had poured into Downing Street, most of it along the same lines. One letter objecting to any use of atomic weapons, whatever the circumstances, had been signed by over a hundred of his own backbenchers. In their position he might have been tempted to add his own name. If only politics were as simple as backbenchers sometimes assumed! The note which touched his most sensitive nerve was his colonial secretary's memorandum warning him of the effect on public opinion throughout Asia if A-bombs – never yet used against whites – were again dropped on an Asian country.

He was quite certain there was no question in the president's mind of launching the A-bomb against civilian populations, or even troop concentrations or industrial targets, not at this stage in the conflict. But the Paikow bacteriological warfare installations were in a different category.

He turned to the admiral's latest signal. All the evidence so far – both photographs from the air and interrogation of ex-POWs held in the area during the Japanese war – indicated a network of caves in the mountainside probably housing the main production units. They were served directly by a single-track railway and movement in and out of other cave openings had been spotted. Aerial bombardment with conventional weapons, military experts advised, would cause little more than superficial damage. Only an accurately placed A-bomb could produce the degree of heat and blast to destroy the installation effectively.

That raised quite a number of questions, not least the

possibility of Russian retaliation in kind. Reports had already come in from Moscow that they would respond in strength to any bombing of Manchuria. On the other hand, it would be foolhardy to risk germs ever being used against United Nations forces. In the Burma campaign, he recalled, more troops had died from disease than from enemy bullets; according to the government's scientific advisers a deliberate, concentrated attack – perhaps with anthrax spores – could wipe out an entire army within days. And after Korea, then Japan, or Europe.

He was in a cleft stick, the prime minister brooded as he reassembled the papers and closed the file. He headed the government of a world power which had lost its strength, its muscles atrophied. It felt much like trying to drive a double-decker bus across a skid-pan.

The germs might not exist, that was the other possibility. Until the admiral's man succeeded in getting through to Paikow they could not be certain how far Chinese information could be trusted, but would Truman wait?

Persuading an American president to hold his fire until a British intelligence officer gave the word – that was going to be the major difficulty during his trip to Washington. He rang the bell and his private secretary immediately appeared at the door.

'Er . . . a cup of tea perhaps? Before I go over to the House?' he suggested tentatively.

'Of course, Prime Minister. And the foreign secretary is waiting for a quick word.'

'Give me one more minute.'

His statement in the House would be short and to the point, briefly informing them that he would be flying to Washington for immediate discussions with the President of the United States. He would stonewall any questions, he decided. Let them hang fire till he knew where he stood.

The Chinese question too needed more thought. Chinese intrigues could resemble their famous boxes: prise open one and you find another inside. What if their plan were to draw the West – and the United States in particular – into a full-scale Far Eastern war, leaving Europe wide open to Soviet encroachment?

Intelligence reports of Soviet troop movements indicated that something was on the move, as Truman must be well aware.

He sipped his tea as he mulled over the idea. There was another factor. An important one. America's weak spot was their insistence on regarding Communist China as no more than a Soviet satellite. In Joe Stalin's pocket, so to speak. And to his mind that interpretation seriously underestimated China's traditional skill at making those trick boxes of theirs.

From where Ross stood partly hidden by the pillars of the tiny Taoist temple perched high on the rock face he had an uninterrupted view of the entire valley. Paikow Research Centre was more extensive than he had assumed from the aerial reconnaissance photographs. Through his field glasses he scanned its solid walls topped with tangles of snow-heavy barbed wire to discourage intruders and overlooked by two watchtowers. On the hillside opposite he spotted the slim wireless mast and traced its black cables down to a squat building inside the base. Outside the main gate was a meandering road, obviously in regular use for the snow had been cleared, which led across the valley and eventually disappeared round the hill.

The base itself was a typical Red Army set-up. He identified the transport yard, two-storey barracks blocks, what could be officers' quarters, and a parade ground where a platoon was being drilled in the snow. Near another building a couple of trucks were being unloaded.

'Can you see what's going on?' Mei-lin was beside him, shivering despite her thick, quilted coat and ear-muffs.

'Stocking up Ivan's rations.' He handed her the field glasses. 'Black bread and lentils.'

'Caviar more likely.' Behind her puritan disapproval he sensed nostalgia for the good times with Colonel Ong Chou-fei.

'Caviar's for officers,' he grunted.

She was not one of the strait-laced Chinese Communists, that was something to be grateful for. Strict and unyielding, every one of them. At least *Homo Sovieticus* still knew how to get drunk.

They had flown through the night, their Dakota landing only once to refuel and taking off again immediately. In the plane his radio and other belongings were returned to him and he changed into the uniform of a GRU colonel, the Intelligence Service of the Soviet General Staff. It was Chinese-made, by Chuan's people, but every tiny detail was correct including greatcoat, fur hat and boots. He had only to run into trouble once in this get-up and he'd be immediately shot as a spy.

It was daylight when they reached the small airstrip near Mukden where a car was provided for them, a hybrid Chinese effort built on an old jeep chassis. Siew, the morose PLA man, drove, first through a sprawling industrial complex, then up into the hills over snow-covered rough roads. When they stopped there was not a building in sight.

'This place should appeal to your poetic soul, Hantu!' Chuan announced cheerfully. 'Know that, Mei-lin? Chinese are realists; British are poets. Why else is he here?'

Perhaps he was right, Ross thought wearily as he

tramped through the thick snow. No rational person would do it.

Paikow was down in the valley, Chuan explained. They were following a cart track up the mountainside. It twisted and dipped even as it climbed; with snow-laden trees on either side they might have been anywhere. It was fifteen minutes' hard trudge before, rounding an outcrop of rock, they saw the temple.

It was tucked into a cleft in the mountain and to either side were monastery buildings which – as they came nearer – they saw were grouped around little courtyards. Above, the steep white hillside soared, partly wooded, partly snow-bedecked rock. Ross stopped appreciatively. He might have been standing before some classical Chinese painting.

'Taoist,' Chuan explained briskly. 'It'll be our base. You'll see its advantages when you've had a sniff round.'

A thin, elderly monk wrapped in a blanket-like robe conducted them to one of the courtyards, explaining that this was their guest area. It offered two rooms only; in both fires had been lit, and both were equipped with a long, brick-built shelf, or *kang*, for sleeping. Before anyone else spoke, Mei-lin voiced her decision on the sleeping arrangements.

'Chuan and Siew can share this room,' she said firmly. 'Hantu and I will take the other.'

Ross remained silent. The old monk had obviously expected them, so it was probably pre-arranged; nor was he shocked, though perhaps that was not surprising. At some point in history Taoism had originated a whole philosophy of sexual techniques.

'You will wish to eat,' he was saying. His shaven head gave him a sculpted, ascetic appearance. 'Food has been prepared. Also, the steps leading to the rock shrine have been cleared of snow, as requested.'

With that he bowed and withdrew.

After they had washed and eaten, Chuan and Siew announced that they had business in the town of Paikow but would be back by nightfall. A young monk was sent to take Ross and Mei-lin down the long, twisting flight of steps to the minute temple dizzily perched on the rock face overlooking the valley; it was the only part of the entire monastery, Chuan explained before he left, which would be visible from the research centre.

Ross retrieved the field glasses from Mei-lin and began a systematic observation of the research centre compound. Heights didn't usually bother him, but nevertheless he wedged his shoulder against a pillar to steady himself. That huddled gathering of low stone buildings against the rock face must be where the scientific stuff went on, he guessed; a high security fence separated them from the rest, no doubt to exclude the blundering soldiery. It was yet another obstacle he would have to deal with.

'Strikes me we've a wee problem,' he said, more to himself than to Mei-lin.

'How to get in,' she agreed practically.

'Getting in won't be easy, but not impossible. The catch is how to get out again. Too many military, not to mention watchtowers and the rest. Not even Ivan goes in and out without being challenged.'

He fell silent, trying to think it through, but no ideas came.

'What are those pyramids for?' she asked inconsequentially.

'Wish I knew.' The two giant pyramids he had first seen in the photograph dwarfed everything around, though from that angle he could not estimate their height. Nor their purpose either. He focused his glasses on them.

Sides mostly snow-covered, yet – 'Could they be made of timber? What d'you think?'

Mei-lin took the glasses. 'Planks?' she suggested after a while. 'Like a wooden house?'

'Let me see again.'

'Look at the ground near them where the snow has been cleared. Every side is the same, can you see? And those lines – could they be tracks? Perhaps tanks?'

'Caterpillar tracks?' He shook his head. 'Can't be that definite. Not from this distance. I'd have to get a lot closer to be able to say that.'

'What else could they be?' She flared up at him defensively. 'It's obvious they're caterpillar tracks!'

The lovely Mei-lin disliked being contradicted, he noted with amusement; he wondered how long she would survive in the conformist New China she supported so fervently.

'Could be anything,' he admitted to mollify her. 'We're both guessing.'

He was about to suggest that they should return indoors to the warmth of a fire, when he spotted some movement at the far end of the valley. To begin with it was little more than changes in the pattern of hazy light but it came slowly closer, moving at a snail's speed through the white landscape. A train, he suspected – though a couple more minutes passed before he felt certain.

Bringing more supplies, perhaps. This branch line serving the research centre joined the main Antung–Mukden rail link, originally constructed by the Japs to carry troops during the 1904–5 Russo-Japanese war; and from Mukden the line eventually arrived in the Soviet Union. But it was not until the train approached the centre's fortified perimeter wall that he realized it must be carrying something very unusual.

Guards hurried out of the blockhouses to tug back the

obviously heavy metal gates barring the way at the point where the track passed through the wall. The muffled sound of shouted orders carried faintly on the air. Once the gates were open, the train itself – which had slowed down almost to a stop – eased its way through: first the massive steam locomotive and tender; then a sleeping car and passenger carriage with men in Russian uniform at the windows; a long freight wagon; another passenger carriage full of military; and finally a second locomotive to bring up the rear.

'Must be something important,' Mei-lin breathed. She held out a hand for the field glasses.

Ross held on to them long enough to count the three four-wheel bogies on the freight wagon, then passed them over. That wagon must be some fifteen or sixteen metres long, he reckoned, with its superstructure covering most of that length. It looked like an elongated crate, a single large container the size of one of the passenger units but with no visible doors; in fact, a sequence of overlapping tarpaulins protected it both from the weather and from prying eyes. Those coaches fore and aft carrying Soviet troops – what could they mean? It could simply be an ammunition train; after all, coming from the Soviet Union it would need to cross Outer Mongolia before even reaching Manchuria; there could be pockets of unrest anywhere along that route, hence the military. But the explanation didn't satisfy him.

'Hantu, it goes right inside the rock!'

'Stay in the shadow!' he warned, pulling her back. 'We're not invisible up here.'

The late afternoon sun, low in the sky now, had broken briefly through the cloud and shone directly on them. Reflection from the field glasses would be enough to betray their presence.

But she was right about the train. Like a fat, sluggish

caterpillar it crawled past the two mystery pyramids and eventually disappeared into a long, tunnel-like shed jutting out some thirty metres from the rock face.

'You've not seen this place before, Mei-lin?'

'Chuan was here, but until three days ago I did not know it existed.'

'And Ong Chou-fei?'

'He was a merchant.'

'Not a soldier too?'

'Supplies and administration. He was no fighter.' Her voice was sad; her eyes turned away from his critical gaze. 'In another country he might have been called a merchant prince. I don't think he ever came here.'

Her previous, brittle nervousness when she spoke to him had gone, he realized; she had relaxed with him, and now he was uncertain how to interpret the change. Nor was he happy with the fact that she had been chosen to keep tags on him, even to the extent of sharing his room; it smacked of the duplicity of the old China, not the new moral earnestness. Whatever game they were playing, its rules were obscure.

A number of lights came on in the research centre as the sky slowly darkened. The drilling soldiers had been marched off and the supply trucks were now in the transport yard, parked in line with others.

'I've had enough for now,' he said at last. 'Let's go while there's still enough light to see the steps. It's a hell of a long way to fall if we miss our footing.'

They went back through the little temple to begin their climb up the steep narrow steps which curved around the rock face. Beyond the first bend the young monk was waiting for them, motionless, as if sunk in contemplation. Without a word he led them upwards, slowly and steadily; he was so sure of his footing, he might have been walking on level ground.

At the top he took them through the confusing maze of courtyards, each one exactly like the next, and left them at their own door, pausing only to bow politely before going.

'I'd have managed the steps without him,' Mei-lin declared, out of breath after the climb, 'but I'd never have found my way back here. In the old Chinese stories the princess uses a ball of silk to find her way through the maze. She unwinds it as she goes along. We should have done that.'

'Princesses now, is it?' Ross laughed, teasing her. 'First caviar, now princesses and silk. Mei-lin, you're the oddest Communist I've ever met.'

'Why d'you say that?' she challenged him, her voice betraying her sudden anger.

'Sorry.' He had touched a sensitive spot and it left him even more thoughtful about her.

'Don't think I approve of you coming here, Hantu. An imperialist lackey. A saboteur. I'd doing my job, helping you. That's all. My job. Playing my part in the struggle.'

'I was joking,' he admitted humbly.

'If you understood how serious this is for the Chinese people you would not joke.'

'No.' He recognized again the woman he had met in Singapore: sharp, alert, serious. Competent, too. Able to slip in and out of his hotel room without being noticed; ready to slash the face of anyone getting in the way. 'I'll check if Chuan's back,' he said, giving up the attempt to put things right. She would not be wooed, she'd made that clear enough.

He tried Chuan's door but they were not back from their unexplained mission in the town.

The room he shared with Mei-lin was warm enough for them to shed their outdoor coats and boots. He undid the top buttons of his high-collared Russian tunic and settled down to draw a rough sketch map of the research centre, using the headed notepaper he had brought from the Shanghai apartment. Of his pencil portrait of her he had found no trace; no doubt she had torn it up or burned it.

He had only twenty-four hours before his first radio contact was expected. Storms permitting, of course; at this time of year there was always a chance the weather would be too bad for the plane to take off. If anything could go wrong, it would.

That was known as 'old hands' nous' back in the London Section: the weary acceptance that a balls-up was inevitable. Wasn't it?

Mei-lin, who had not spoken since they returned to their room, got up from rummaging through her small wicker case and stood watching over his shoulder as he drew.

'Heavy bombs,' she said unexpectedly. 'On the train. Like poison gas shells. Can bacteria be loaded like that?'

So she knew about the bacteria at least. They had told her bits of the story though not all of it.

'Whether it's bacteria or a virus to be tried out we can't know yet,' he attempted to explain, though he was only repeating the lesson he had learned from the boffin at the training camp. 'The weapon itself will most likely be a liquid sprayed over the target area.'

'From the air?'

'Not like crop-spraying, at any rate. That would involve flying too low and risking the planes being shot down. And the higher a plane's altitude, the less certain they could be of hitting the target. The wind could disperse the bacterial cloud, or the bacteria themselves might not survive to do any harm.'

'Bombs then. There are Soviet bombers at Lu-shun.'

'Lu-shun? Where's that?'

'Europeans call it Port Arthur. The Party has abolished

253

all the treaty ports and concessions, but there is still a Soviet military base at Lu-shun.'

'Using Soviet planes would bring Russia officially into the war against the United Nations. I don't think they want that, though I suppose they could give 'em a lick of paint and disguise them as Chinese or Korean instead. It might be a face-saver, though it wouldn't convince anybody. No, we're guessing again, Mei-lin. Which means you may be right. What puzzles me is those pyramids. Any ideas?'

'The trains bring the bombs in, which is what we saw. Once the germ warheads have been fitted, they are stored in those pyramid sheds until they can be moved to the air base.' She had it all worked out and was daring him to contradict. 'Why outside in the pyramids? Space? Temperature? The need to keep them apart from the others? Any of those reasons.'

Ross stood up. Leaving his paper and pencils on the warm *kang*, he went through to the little adjoining room to light the charcoal stove. 'I'll make some tea,' he said.

For a moment she watched him, resentful that he returned no comment on her theory. Then she offered to make the tea for him. 'It is my duty. You are a guest in our country.' Grudgingly.

'You're the brains,' he retorted. 'Best let me do it.'

A knock on the door and Chuan stood outside, kicking the snow off his boots before bustling in and complaining of the cold. 'A bit different from the Malayan jungle, this place. The wind is bitter coming up here from the road.' He nodded approvingly when he saw the tea being made.

'What news?' Ross asked. Chuan was obviously in a good mood; something must have happened to cheer him up.

'We placed a girl here in Paikow, one of the Shanghai

good-time girls, with orders to get friendly with our Soviet comrades. She has hooked a corporal for us. A driver.'

'That's a start. When do I see her?'

'Tomorrow. It's all arranged.'

'Has she been inside the centre?'

'No civilians go in there, so she says. Not even the officers have civilian guests. But she says most of the troops are Mongolians, with some Koreans. They're never allowed off the base. Only Russian soldiers visit the town.'

'What do they do in Paikow?' Mei-lin intervened.

'Certain bars are set aside for them, one for officers, others for the men. Everywhere else is out of bounds. They have Russian drinks, food, music . . . We like our Soviet guests to feel at home.'

'But not for too long?'

Chuan ignored the opening.

They ate together that evening, all four of them in the room shared by Chuan and Siew. It was the haunted Siew who cooked the rice and pieces of fish, but throughout the meal he sat in silence as if resenting their presence. Chuan, still cheerful after his trip into Paikow, reminisced about how he and Ross had once sabotaged a major railway junction north of Ipoh.

'With help,' Ross commented, taking advantage of a gap in the flow of words. 'As a team.'

Mei-lin's earlier fit of temper had dissipated as rapidly as it had risen; while they were eating she was as charming and friendly as if nothing had happened, even picking out the choice morsels of fish for him with her chopsticks. Much to his surprise, on their way back across the little courtyard she quoted poetry too:

> No footprints on the mountain tracks
> The pale snow reflects the purity of the moon.

255

And once they were in their own room again, alone together, she waited uncertainly as though expecting him to take the initiative. Ross merely smiled, spread out his bedding on the *kang*, and settled down to sleep.

'Goodnight, Mei-lin.'

'Goodnight.' Pointed. Ironic. 'Sleep well, Hantu.'

He lay awake for some time thinking about her. She was no Delilah, whatever her masters thought. Almost certainly they had ordered her to get him into bed, but she was taking her time about it. He chalked that up in her favour.

'I'm cold,' she murmured late in the night. He had slept already, though for how long he didn't know. 'I can't get warm.'

'I'll put more wood on the fire,' he offered, getting up to do it.

The night seemed unnaturally quiet after Shanghai and Singapore. Even in the jungle training camps the darkness had been alive with constant sounds.

The fire flared up and he returned to lie down again, this time sharing his bedding with her, his arm round her, holding her close for body warmth, but his thoughts were with Yen-hua and the attack on that railway junction. Her grenade had put the signal box out of action, he remembered, killing two Jap guards and the Indian signalman. That Indian's life had been on his conscience for days afterwards, though he'd been a known collaborator and on the death list. But Yen-hua hadn't hesitated, realist as she was. She had belly-crawled across the open ground towards the signal box, then lobbed the grenade through the open door.

Even in those days, full of hatred as he was, he had felt sickened at all the killing.

Mei-lin snuggled closer to him. He might have been lying with Yen-hua again, quietly, restfully, belonging to each other. In a *cheongsam* she might have looked very like Mei-lin though he never once saw her wearing one. Expensive silk brocades, perfumes and make-up, high-heeled shoes, all those ancillaries of Singapore sophistication were alien to her, nor were they available to anyone at that time outside the Jap officers' whorehouses.

Since Yen-hua he had not touched another woman. On occasions his body had hungered for someone, nothing wrong with him in that department, no lack of carnal appetite as the army chaplain from Wales used to say, but he had always drawn back from the final step. Fear of complications perhaps. Of disappointment.

Tim Moody had the right attitude. He and Asiah. He could take it all so lightly. One of life's pleasures. Shangri-La. He didn't get involved.

Yen-hua.

He drifted into sleep, fearing the nightmare of seeing her again . . . her severed football head kicked aside by a Jap's jungle boot . . . But this time, dreaming of her, she had – oddly – Mei-lin's face.

Before setting out for Paikow the following day, he and Chuan spent half an hour at the small cliffside temple watching the research centre for any signs of movement. In the military section plenty was going on, though nothing that might not have been seen in any army camp. A convoy of five trucks drove in through the gates. Soldiers jumped down from the tailboards, sorted out their kit, then lined up and were marched off to their accommodation; meanwhile more platoons appeared, loaded one truck with luggage and clambered on board the remaining four, clearly eager to get away now they had been relieved.

'Probably being transferred,' Chuan commented.

'Rumour has it that all leave is cancelled. Hope our man isn't among them.'

According to Chuan the girl they had set up in Paikow was co-operative. Probably glad to be there. She had been rescued from one of the New China re-education camps for prostitutes and promised an exit permit and her fare to Formosa if she did the job well. Though she'd be a fool to believe that story, Ross felt, saying nothing.

Paikow itself was no substitute for Shanghai. When they drove in, their car wheels spinning and skidding over the hard snow, he found it to be a seemingly endless settlement centred on the railway station and marshalling yard. Straight unnamed roads cut callously through untidy clusters of single-storey stone houses and compounds, few of them connected to the snow-laden, overhead power lines festooned along the route. The tallest, most imposing structures were giant hoardings bearing portraits of Chairman Mao Tse-tung and 'Little Father' Stalin.

According to Chuan, the bar towards which they were heading was on the main road to the research centre. When they got there it turned out to be more like a mess hall, big enough for sixty or seventy people to crowd in; from inside came balalaika music from a scratched record, clicking as regularly as a clock.

They left Siew to park the car somewhere out of sight and Chuan led the way to a warren of decrepit living quarters to the rear of the courtyard. The girl, Yu-li, was waiting in her sparsely furnished room which was heated only by a charcoal stove in the middle of the floor. Chuan had chosen her well, Ross noted. She was not a striking beauty, but homely and pleasant-looking: short, on the plump side, and with a round friendly face. Just the girl-next-door type a lonely soldier miles away from home might fall in love with.

'You expect him soon?' Chuan demanded coldly, showing her no sympathy.

'He will be here if he can. Sometimes he sends a message that he can't get away. He has to go where they send him.'

'But they haven't sent a message this time?'

She shrugged. 'It is still early.'

Ross's presence seemed to bother her. Apprehensively she eyed his GRU colonel's uniform. Turning to Chuan, she asked what was going to happen to her soldier. Clearly she assumed that Ross spoke no Chinese.

'Nothing will happen to him. Leave it all to this officer. And don't warn him, remember. We'll be in the next room. Act as normal. Understand? Do it properly, and in two weeks you'll be out of here.'

Again Ross caught a glimpse of fear in her eyes as they went out. He paused, but then contented himself with gazing at her sternly as though he had understood nothing. This interview was going to be tricky enough as it was.

Twenty minutes passed before they heard the soldier arrive, greeting her in soft, lilting Russian, though from the room next door he could only pick out occasional words. Yu-li was laughing, an intimate welcoming laugh full of sexual meaning; from the rhythms when she spoke – again Ross could not identify the words – it was in Chinese. Neither knew the other's language; well, that was not so unusual in this sort of situation.

Ross gave them ten minutes together; then, indicating that Chuan should stay where he was, he went quietly to Yu-li's door and burst it open. They were on the bed, partly undressed, and the soldier swung around, startled and swearing at him.

'On your feet, soldier!' Ross yelled in Russian. 'Hold

259

your mouth! D'you know who you're talking to? And pull your underwear up, you disgust me!'

The corporal had stiffened to attention at the sight of the GRU colonel, but his long johns were keeping only his ankles warm. Shamefacedly he tugged them up. On the bed, Yu-li, not concealing her anger, hastily covered herself.

'Identity book?' Ross snapped. The soldier retrieved it from his tunic pocket, handed it over, then stood to attention again. 'Ivan Yakov, corporal driver. Well, Corporal Driver, are you not on duty?'

'N-no, C-comrade Colonel!' the man stuttered, red in the face. 'I-I am off d-duty when I re-return to b-barracks.'

'But not yet.' Ross examined the identity book again. 'Those your trousers on the floor? Then put them on, man! Is that how you go around in Paikow? Driven here, have you? In an army truck?'

The man had stooped to pick up the trousers but he dropped them again as though they burned his fingers and straightened up to reply. 'O-on my way b-back from railway station! D-duty trip, C-comrade Colonel!'

'Wasting army diesel fuel for your own pleasure, were you? Economic sabotage, know that? Well? Speak up!'

Deliberately Ross gave him a hard time, using every bullying trick he had learned from a generation of sergeant-majors and adding a few refinements acquired as an undercover agent in the POW camps for Red Army officers. He cross-examined him about his length of service, parents in the Soviet Union, their political attitudes, the type of truck he drove, the name of the officer in charge of transport, and finally returned to the back pages of the identity document which recorded his vaccination details. Smallpox, TAB, cholera, anti-tetanus, *Past. pestis* . . .

'You're a valuable man, Yakov. Look at what Soviet medicine has invested in you. Somebody thinks you're worth keeping alive, that's evident.'

The man gawped at him sullenly, not understanding. Not the Communist world's brightest specimen, Ross thought. It could make the job easier.

'How many have died since you've been at Paikow? Among those working on the . . .' He hesitated. This was where he could slip up. He had to convince Yakov he knew everything about the weapon. 'Those on the secret work?'

'Black death, we call it among the men,' Yakov volunteered unexpectedly. Now he was in his uniform again he showed more confidence. 'The Koreans handle that, we don't. Among them – well, they do say eight got the sickness an' died. Don't know how true that is.'

'But you're protected by your vaccination?'

'All of us Russians had our jabs the first week here, Comrade Colonel. Nearly killed me. Laid me out.'

A few more general questions and he could end the interview, Ross considered. Yakov would be none the wiser. Or he could risk the next stage, the tricky one. The man was already trying to ingratiate himself, undisguisedly shit-scared of the uniform.

'I selected you, Yakov, for a special purpose. You have a reputation for being reliable and a good Communist.' Yakov's expression betrayed nothing. 'Word has reached Moscow of class enemies operating in the Paikow garrison. The Party intends to root them out, d'you understand?'

Yakov's heels clicked to attention again as Ross's voice sharpened.

'You can help the Party, or you can hinder our work. The choice is yours. Before you make up your mind, think what your parents back home would want. They

261

wish to be proud of their son. A sergeant, at your age? It's not impossible.'

With a genuine offer like that from the GRU, Corporal Yakov would have no alternative, not if he wished to keep his family out of the labour camps. Ross counted on him reckoning up the odds.

Stiffly, arms pressed to his sides, chin in and his eyes staring blankly at nothing, Yakov stated that the Party's leadership must be followed at all times.

Then he relaxed and a slow grin appeared on his face. 'Make sergeant, did you say, Comrade Colonel? I'd be the first to do it in our family.'

Ross bestowed a word of encouragement, then issued his orders and insisted on Yakov repeating them. They were simple enough: he must not mention to anyone that there was a GRU investigator in the area, least of all to any officers on the base; he was to keep his eyes and ears open for anything concerned with the black death operation in case of a security leak; and finally they arranged a time to rendezvous the next day, again in Yu-li's room.

As they tramped through the snow back to the car neither Ross nor Chuan spoke; both were stern-faced, keeping up the pretence. It was not until they were heading out of Paikow on the mountain road that Chuan grinned across at him. 'You sounded a real bastard,' he commented approvingly in English. 'Didn't understand a word of all that, but – boy, it was convincing! I swore you could do it!'

'Who *are* you working for, Chuan?' Siew's only word of English was 'cigarette' and no one else could overhear them in the car.

Chuan avoided the question. 'Aren't we all on the same side?'

'I doubt it.'

12

This time it could mean his death, as Ross was only too aware. In the past, even in the Soviet Union, he'd had the luck of any feline, but his nine lives had been used up by now. Chambered in some guard's automatic rifle down there in that military base was a bullet with his name on it.

He stood in the cliffside temple, alone, snuggling close to a pillar as much for shelter from the biting wind as from any need to stay out of sight. Occasional vehicles, mainly trucks, entered by the main gate, and each one stopped while the driver handed down a paper from his cab. A pass. Was the stolid Yakov genuinely stupid enough to obey an order to smuggle him through?

Of course, to a Soviet citizen all security operations were as mysterious as acts of God, and unchallengeable; he had that much on his side. Yakov would not ask questions.

Staring down at the research centre his mind again clouded with suspicion. What if Chuan was working *with* the Russians, not against them? Will you step into my parlour, said the spider to the fly – and he, Hantu, was that fly. With his escape from Russia, the MGB and MVD, twin arms of the Soviet security system, had lost face. They needed revenge. Only too clearly he understood the mechanism of their trap: Chuan and his henchman Siew had smuggled him into China, bringing him to Paikow; Mei-lin's task was to spin the silken threads of sex, the oldest method of all; Yakov himself was probably an MGB agent, his stupidity merely an act.

And Chou En-lai? The political head of the intrigue, shrewd, calculating, Moscow-trained, and with every reason to do the Soviets a favour which cost him nothing.

Which explanation was most likely – this, or Chuan's involved story?

Neither made sense of the killings in Singapore. And if the report of a planned germ attack were true, would they put it in jeopardy by warning the West in advance, simply to entrap a British agent who was finished anyway? A man no longer trusted even by his own Section?

'It interests you, that establishment?' The old monk who had welcomed them the previous day stood at his elbow. His close-shaven head was uncovered, his feet bare and in sandals despite the severe cold. 'The valley used to be a place of pilgrimage because of the caves in the rocks. Pai-k'ou – white caves, white mouths. But they can no longer be visited since the camp was built.'

'When was that?'

'Dates are no more than a puny attempt to measure the "immeasurable". But I was still a young man when the Japanese constructed the buildings closest to the caves. Later the Russians arrived. They extended the railway line and enlarged the camp.'

'What goes on in there?'

'I think you know already, which is why you are here.' The old man was mocking him; he could see the gentle laugh in his eyes. 'We have withdrawn from the world for a life of contemplation. You are more inclined to action. So be it. That is your nature.'

'You have not always been a monk,' Ross guessed.

'At a very young age I studied engineering, first in Peking, then in Harbin. The world had to change, I was convinced, and I would be in the forefront. Youth knows everything and nothing; age acknowledges that nothing can be known. At college I learned about electricity – the new science! A positive charge and a negative charge, imagine! For two thousand years philosophers of the Tao have taught the principles of positive and negative, Yin and Yang, in all things. Now Western science with its electrons and neutrons has begun at last to share our understanding.'

To escape from the cold wind Ross left his vantage point by the pillar and retreated into the shrine itself. Through the gloom he felt the presence of its symbolic brass ornaments and wood carvings; they reached back through the centuries.

'You monks opt out of the world, so it's easy for you to be philosophical.' It was an accusation; even an expression of envy. 'Is it meaningless to you, what is going on down there? They're planning to wipe out people's lives. Is that nothing?'

'Disease is also life in one of its many manifestations,' the old monk answered simply. 'By its very nature, whatever is born must one day die. The only permanence is constant change.'

'Easy to say.'

'Not so easy to accept,' the monk retorted, but then he fell silent, seemingly lost in thought. 'You speak our tongue so well,' he said at last, 'it is a pleasure to talk to you. I shall tell you about the caves.'

'Pai-k'ou?'

'Pai-k'ou,' he nodded. 'The first monks lived in them many centuries ago. Then during the time of civil war they were forced to retreat farther and farther into the cave complex. Many died, of hunger mostly, but a small nucleus survived and eventually, in commemoration, this little temple here was built into the cliff face itself.'

'And the pilgrims when they came . . .?'

'Until very recently. I can remember them.'

'And there were monks still in the caves then?'

265

'On important days. Until the Japanese came and sealed the caves. They kept their prisoners there, at first from town – men, women and even children, those people who had not been transported to Harbin to work in the factories. In later years captives were brought from many other places. Some were your own countrymen.'

'What happened to them?'

'Most prisoners died from the various diseases they were investigating here. Paikow Medical Institute, the installation was called in those days. I am told that several professors from important universities worked here. The prisoners were experimental animals, little more. They lived in steel cages inside the caves. When they died – as most did – their bones were stored in some of the more remote tunnels in the heart of the mountain. They are still there.'

'Are people imprisoned there now?'

'I have heard nothing of that. Men are seen going in – marching, as they do, in small groups. But they emerge again. Now the caves – once visited in humility – seem more like a factory. Though of course from the outside we witness very little.'

It was getting dark and time for them to return up the winding steps to the monastery. But Ross was not satisfied.

'The monks who built this temple must have found a direct route here through the caves.'

'That is possible,' the old man agreed.

'And you have used that route yourself?'

'Did I give you that impression? In that case I am sorry. Perhaps we could talk on another occasion about the principles of choice between contemplation and action.'

'Contemplation told you about the bones stored in the tunnels?'

'The nature of knowledge – that is another subject we might discuss one day.'

The old monk refused to say more. A deep gong-like bell sounded from the monastery above, obviously a summons; his pace quickened as he climbed the steps. Despite his age he soon drew ahead and was lost to sight.

Thoughtfully Ross went back to his room, glad of its warmth. During his absence someone, perhaps the young monk, had stoked up the fire with fresh logs which crackled loudly as the flames licked them. Mei-lin had still not returned – according to Chuan she had asked Siew to drive her into town – but that was just as well. He needed to be undisturbed to code his signal.

He unpacked his civilian clothes from his grip and examined the hard base inside. The stitches around the edges were still intact and he began to pick them out carefully, just sufficiently to allow him to slide out a slim wallet about a tenth of an inch thick. It contained ten octavo sheets of ultra-thin Bible paper with rows of jumbled letters printed on each. They were so flimsy, it was difficult to peel the top one away and he had to place it on a white surface to read it. The rest he returned to their hiding place.

The table needed for use with this 'one-time key' was printed on a square of very light silk which he carried, folded down to practically nothing, in a concealed pouch in the back of his belt. Some Section operatives hid it in a hairbrush or the handle of a safety razor, which were the first places anyone would search, and one woman agent usually tucked it into the waistband of her panties, and more than once had lost both.

His message was simple and short, confirming his arrival and adding: PROPOSE ENTER WITHIN TWENTY-FOUR HOURS TO IDENTIFY WEAPON. But then it occurred to him that this might be the only signal they ever had from him. Once inside the research centre, who could say what would happen?

He considered adding the information gleaned from the contemplative old monk – in reality itching for action, Ross suspected – but decided against. A long transmission was too great a risk. On the other hand, he had learned something vital from Yakov's documents. Those inoculations, including *Past. pestis*.

Pasteurella pestis, bubonic plague, the black death. He remembered that well enough from the boffin's list.

Scrapping part of his signal, he re-wrote the text to read: PROPOSE ENTER TO IDENTIFY WEAPON BUT SIGNS INDICATE PASTEURELLA PESTIS STOP ALSO EVIDENCE CHINESE MIG-15 FLIGHTS OVER KOREA ENDS.

He watched the fire dispose of the one-time sheet and his first draft message, then folded up the silk and tucked it into his belt again. The enciphered signal he slipped into his pocket; transmission time was not for another three hours. Anyone listening on that wavelength might hear his brief burst of morse, but it needed the twin of the one-time sheet – the only other copy in existence – to make sense of it, and that twin would be in the hands of an anonymous cipher clerk he would never meet.

Again he ate an evening meal with Chuan and Siew, but Mei-lin had not yet reappeared, nor did they volunteer any information about her. After eating, he sat talking to Chuan and told him about the possible route through the rocks down into the caves. Chuan dismissed the idea, giving Ross the impression he had already explored it. 'A non-starter,' he said.

Siew remained silent as they talked; then, morose as ever, he suddenly stood up, pulled on his shabby, quilted coat, and went out.

A few minutes later Ross left, saying it was time to set up his aerial. He made no secret of the transmission; radio contact had been one of the articles of the agreement. Chuan did not even ask what was in the message.

Outside the snow was crisp and hard, eerily luminescent in the bright moonlight. From the valley came raucous shouts, no doubt from drunken Russian soldiers weaving their way back to the base, but they quickly quietened down. No other sound. He listened carefully for a while. Nothing.

He ran the aerial outside, using the exterior roof posts, and leaving the room door slightly ajar for the lead. The little suitcase transceiver itself he set up on the *kang*. During that night in Shanghai when the comrades had 'taken care' of it for him they had probably stripped it down to its last inch of copper wire, but there was no sign of damage. Everything seemed to function well enough.

The drone of the plane's engines came dead on time, approaching from due south, he estimated. God bless America! A B29 it would be, possibly from Okinawa, with a limey passenger on board, a Section radio operator who knew his 'handwriting'. His hand hovered over the morse key for a second, then he tapped out his identification code.

N-T . . . N-T . . . N-T . . . Three times. A pause. Then he repeated it. N-T . . . N-T . . . N-T . . .

He turned the switch to 'Receive'. Through his handset the response came, surprisingly loud, acknowledging his identity and giving him the go-ahead to transmit his message. A couple of minutes later he had confirmation that the message had been clearly received, then the airborne radio operator signed off.

Within seconds, it seemed, not even the plane's engines were audible any longer, only the soughing of the wind over the mountainside. It would be another twenty-four hours before their next contact, assuming he'd managed to stay alive. If the radio's 6-volt dry cell battery lasted, he might even be able to give them the information to justify him getting away from this place.

Find out and report – that had been the order. Nothing else. And the moment he did find out he'd be on his way.

'Transmission complete, sir,' the prissy voice of that limey radio operator came over his intercom. A civilian, too; a dried-up civilian shrimp who had spent the outward leg of the trip being airsick. Only God and the President of the United States of America knew why they were ferrying a shrimp radio ham over the target area.

'Let's get the hell outa here!' Captain Bob Schroder yelled, wanting every man in the crew to hear the good news.

The B29 *Elaine* responded immediately, gaining height with no effort at all. Through the plexiglass he glimpsed the sheen of moonlight on the plane's wings which took him back to when he had been flying B17s over Germany, except then the flak had been in earnest and the only markers on the ground to help them were the fires their own incendiaries had started. That was what he found so strange about this mission. Every light in the valley was switched on as if they didn't give a damn who saw them. It was all laid out for the taking – the railway marshalling yard, the pathetic little town and the walled military base a couple of miles away with those unexplained Egyptian pyramids near the cliff face, everything recognizable from the reconnaissance snapshots the RB29 boys had brought back. It might have been peacetime, it was so lit up.

And flak? Two or three guns they had counted, firing half-heartedly. Shell-bursts well over on the port side, too far off to be dangerous. They might have been aiming at the moon for all the damage they caused. It puzzled him that such an installation – if it was really important – was not better protected. Maybe now the intelligence agencies had their own man on the ground, they might discover they were mistaken; he'd be transferred back to ordinary duties.

Schroder had volunteered the *Elaine* for this mission, spinning the pressed-steel colonel some shit about needing to get the feel of the target, a claim the colonel saw through without difficulty but he agreed all the same. By now every aircrew on the base knew his marriage had gone up in flames. No bastard was to blame for that but himself. He needed a shrink, he'd been so stupid – sending her a cable, trying to fight it out long-distance. The cable clerk must have spread it around.

The bitch hadn't shifted either. Like some prim British schoolmarm she had wired back lecturing him on self-control and having to accept 'her sincere and genuine love' for her fat lawyer bed-mate. More hot merchandise for that fucking cable clerk who had not needed to pay for his own drinks for the past month.

Genuine love, for Chrissake! Hadn't she said the same to *him* not a year ago?

Maybe that shit-bound colonel understood something after all when he okayed the request, though two days later he announced that all five B29 Task Group T crews were to take their turn at these R/T runs over Paikow as an element – his choice of word – in their familiarization routine. Came the day, any one of the crews might find itself flying weather scout or delivery man, whichever way it crumbled. Meanwhile precision bombing practice runs proceeded as per schedule, depositing yet more concrete-filled 'punkins' on the ruins of Samurai history.

Jesus Christ, when he remembered it was for Elaine's sake that he'd turned down the chance of a well-paid job in civil aviation back in the States! Having him stationed

271

in Europe suited her, to be close to her family she said. Then Korea blew up.

'Bob – starboard side. Ten o'clock.' Al Rossi reported laconically over his shoulder. 'Those fires must be Antung. The guys from 19th Bombardment have been having a party.'

Ross was coiling the aerial when Mei-lin got back, shivering. She tossed her worn fur hat and mittens on to the *kang* and stood by the fire for a moment to get warm before taking off her coat.

'Did you have any success in making contact with your friends?' she asked. It was a question addressed by one stranger to another, polite rather than friendly.

'They send their love,' he told her, tucking the aerial into its compartment, then closing the case, snapping the locks shut.

'Thank you.' British flippancy seldom translated well into Chinese. But then, from her coat pocket, she produced a small bottle. 'Rice wine, Hantu. We both need something to warm us up, I think.'

'The room's chilly, I'm sorry. I had to leave the door open because . . .' He stopped, feeling foolish.

'My first colonel introduced me to rice wine which I'd never tasted before. As my second colonel you have a duty to drink with me.'

From her other pocket she took three small sticky cakes wrapped in a handkerchief which she opened out on the *kang.* Then she slipped the coat off; under it she was dressed in an elegant brocade *cheongsam* which succeeded in looking both warm and sleek.

'Paikow must be more exciting than I thought,' he remarked. The sarcasm surfaced despite himself.

But she merely laughed and shook her head. 'I'm afraid it isn't!'

272

She emptied the small kettle and tipped in the rice wine, the whole bottle, to warm it over the fire. When it was ready she took two teacups, poured a small amount into each and handed one to him.

'It mustn't get cool, so we only take a little at a time,' she explained, looking into his eyes as she held up her cup. 'Now, Hantu – bottoms up!'

The second drink followed immediately; then she offered him a sticky cake. As he had expected, they were sickeningly sweet, but the frugal meal had left him hungry and he was glad to eat it. This operation was turning out to be a nostalgia trip, he thought; those sweet cakes and the sherry-like taste of the rice wine took him back in memory to when he was fourteen, one day in Shanghai, when, daringly, he and another boy had drunk it for the first time.

'Mm, that's warming!' she exclaimed, putting her cup down. 'Let me help you out of your jacket. No, stay still – I'll undo the buttons.'

She had already bolted the door and piled more logs on the fire. Taking charge of him, just as Yen-hua had liked to do on those few occasions when they had managed to be alone together; and he relaxed, letting it happen. When he tried to force the pace, slipping his arm around her, wanting to kiss her, she twisted away from him with a laugh.

'Not yet!' she teased, giving them more of the rice wine. 'More haste, less fun! Tell me about yourself. Where did you learn to draw?'

'In Shanghai, from one of my father's friends. A very beautiful White Russian girl. Her name was Tanya.'

'Were you in love with her?'

'My father was. I was only a kid.'

'You could still be in love with her. I think you were.' She took a little bite out of the remaining sticky cake,

273

then held it to his mouth to share it. 'I was lucky getting three. A lot of people in Paikow are going hungry.'

'Where did you find them?'

Again she laughed, and a pink tip of tongue appeared tantalizingly between her teeth. 'I'll tell you afterwards. Mm, it really is warming up. Your turn, Ghost! Can you help me with these hooks?'

The hooks and eyes of her *cheongsam* turned out to be stubborn under his clumsy fingers which brought more laughter gurgling from her; she offered him no help, but let him struggle on till the last one was undone. Her clinging black silk slip and stockings were not exactly conventional special forces wear for this kind of mission and, drawing her to him and running his hands gently over her bare arms and shoulders, he told her so.

'Expert are you?' she murmured as she snuggled close to him. One by one, deliberately, she fitted her soft fingertips into the little hollows between his ribs. 'Then you'd better help me get rid of them.'

But, instead, he kissed her eyes, the tip of her nose, her puckered lips, tasting the sweetness of the wine on her tongue, until at last she broke away from him for breath, her eyes mocking and vivacious, her mouth still slightly open, her lips pouting their invitation for more.

Drawing up her slip, she unfastened her suspenders and peeled down the black silk stockings, aware he was watching her; with his help the rest of her undressing took much longer – lingering . . . exploring . . . caressing . . .

The hard, brick *kang* on which they made their love was warm to the touch as if baked by the Singapore sun. She gently moved her fingers down the full length of his spine, around the curve of his haunches, lightly investigating every fold of flesh, torturing him with her feather-touch; then she arched back from him with a gasp of total abandon, pressing her hips against his, squirming, becoming one with him.

Afterwards they sat together, still naked, though with blankets round them, drinking the last of the rice wine, and they talked over their first meetings in his Singapore hotel room, those initial impressions.

Which had not been very far wrong, Ross considered silently. He stood up and the blanket slipped from him as he went over to feed the voracious fire with yet more logs. Mei-lin dropped her blanket on the *kang* and came towards him, her alert, teasing breasts red-tinged in the light of the flames. Even naked she looked sophisticated and expensive.

He took her in his arms and they kissed, each conscious of desire already stirring. 'What if I were not a colonel?' he probed, tempted to provoke her.

'Of course you're not, I know that. But you look good in the uniform.'

'I was in the Army once. Sergeant.'

'A long time ago,' she retorted, punctuating her words with hungry kisses. 'And I – ,' kiss, 'was – ,' kiss, 'a teacher.'

'You still are.' With an open palm he brushed the tips of her breasts one after the other, from hilltop to hilltop. 'A brilliant teacher.'

13

Mei-lin was good for him. The best medicine.

Not in all the months since his escape from Vladivostok had Ross felt so fit and confident, as if a burden had fallen away from him at last. The intense cold no longer bothered him; his skin glowed, the warm blood pumped through his arteries like new, he was on top of the world.

The Gogol factor was his best bet, he decided as Chuan drove him down into Paikow. It had already worked with Yakov. Old Andrei Nikolayovich had taught him the expression back in his youth in Shanghai while telling him those endless stories of Tsarist Russia. 'In every Russian soul is a deep-rooted fear of authority,' he would say. 'I call it the Gogol factor because Gogol recognized it and wrote about it. Faced with a foreign enemy, a Russian is as brave as the next man; but confronted by an official – *any* official in a uniform, and he is capable of the very worst stupidity. You should read Gogol, young Pyotr. You can learn from him.'

He would order Yakov to drive him openly to the research centre after all. He would bluff his way past the guards on the gate. Praise them for their attention to duty if they tried to stop him. Demand to see their commanding officer. Insist on an inspection tour of the whole set-up.

Once in Paikow and nearing the other ranks' bar where Yu-li worked, he changed his mind again. Twice he saw platoons of Russian soldiers tramping purposefully through the snow-covered streets and his doubts grew; he would never get away with it. He must have been drunk to think of it. Perhaps he was. Mei-lin had intoxicated him more potently than any alcohol; he was no longer rational. Getting through the gate was the problem. Once inside and in uniform, few would challenge his right to be there. Though . . . in his experience, hadn't it been often the crazy, *instinctive* plans that succeeded best?

Yakov, waiting for him in Yu-li's room, sprang to attention when he entered. His expression was eager and conspiratorial; obviously he was enjoying this special, secret assignment which set him apart from the crowd. Sooner or later, Ross guessed, he would start boasting about it, if he had not done so already.

'You and I, Yakov, are going to test security,' he said crisply. 'We are going to break into the base.'

'Yes, Comrade Colonel.' The smile faded from Yakov's face.

'Into the inner security area where the secret work is done. Understand?'

'No, Comrade Colonel. How do we do it?'

'We drive in, blockhead!' Ross snapped. Was it stupidity or was the man making fun of him? 'In the truck. Now, tell me what happens when you take the truck through. Step by step.'

Yakov's slow smile returned. 'Oh, no problem about that. Got a load on board now that's going to that place. Came in on the through train. Not an hour since I loaded up at the depot. Here's the paper.'

It was a printed form filled in by hand. Ross had difficulty deciphering the Russian scrawl. Respirators, it looked like. Thirty cases. He returned it to Yakov and repeated his question.

'Well now, at the main gate I stop. Show 'em this plus my ID book. Then they wave me through.'

'Do they check the load?'

'Times they do, times they don't. Depends what mood

they happen to be in. Usually don't bother me too much. They all know me. I fetch 'em things from town.'

'And the inner security area?'

'Same, only . . .' He changed his mind. 'A dozen times a week I'm in an' out of there. An' we're all Russians. They don't bother. Mind you, they're a lot tougher on the others – Koreans, Mongolians, that lot. Have to be, don't they?'

Ross didn't answer. When he came in he had seen three parked trucks outside with no guard on them, though Chuan had pointed out a Chinese People's police post a few yards along the road. He asked about them.

'The truck drivers always stop here, do they?'

'On their way back. Just for a quick drink, and to get warm again. There's a lot of waiting around down at the railway depot. Can be a cold job.'

'They all have girl friends here?' He glanced at Yu-li sitting patiently on the bed, preferring to be ignored.

'Some do, some don't.'

He and Yakov were two of a pair, he thought. The Venus fly-trap – one and the same method for both of them – though Mei-lin was no Shanghai bar girl, to that he could testify.

Briskly he issued his orders and forced Yakov to repeat them. He would ride on the back of the truck under the tarpaulin. Yakov was to drive back to the base where he would go through any usual procedures; once inside the security area, he would find a place to stop where Ross could jump down before he parked for unloading.

'What if they search the truck an' find you? What do I say?'

'Say nothing, Corporal. You will stand to attention and remain silent until ordered to speak. By me – understand? This is an important exercise to test the security of the base. Heads will fall if things are as bad as I hear they are. Make sure yours is not one of them.'

'Yes, Comrade Colonel.'

Instructing the now humbled Yakov to wait ten minutes before returning to his truck, Ross strode out. It was a role that suited him, he felt; bawling out some poor peasant in an ill-fitting uniform helped to clear out his hang-ups. In comparison, intelligence work had to be self-effacing simply to survive.

Chuan appeared as he rounded the corner after leaving the courtyard. Briefly Ross outlined what he intended, saying that the car should rendezvous with him in five hours' time. If he arrived too soon he would wait in Yu-li's room.

'She won't be there,' Chuan said – was that a hint of amusement in his voice? 'We'll move her out as soon as it's dark.'

'And Siew? Is he in place? Thirty minutes after I've left here I want those telephone wires down, no earlier. Once I'm inside, the research centre must be cut off for the rest of the evening.'

'They have radio communication too.'

'Probably for longer distances. That's a risk I'll take. The telephone breakdown will be enough to keep them busy, but it must not look like sabotage. They must blame the snow.'

'Trust Siew,' said Chuan. 'He knows what he's doing.'

Chuan had not insisted on coming with him, he noticed; in their jungle days he would have nagged ceaselessly to be included because that was how close their friendship had been. Chuan had been the left hand to Ross's right; or vice-versa, depending on what mess they found themselves in. But now they were more distant, like strangers.

* * *

Yakov's truck was last in the line of three parked near the bar where Yu-li worked, a bleak uninviting place. Its lights had already been switched on; as on the previous day a record player was blaring out crackling Russian music. Placing Yu-li there had involved no more than obtaining an official's chop on a piece of paper, Chuan had explained. All entertainment facilities for foreign troops in China were directly controlled by the Chinese People's Intelligence Bureau.

First checking to make sure he was not observed, Ross went to the rear of Yakov's truck, loosened one corner of the tarpaulin, then climbed quickly over the tailboard and crawled beneath it. The respirators were packed in light wooden cases and he prised two of them apart to make a space for himself. It was going to be a rough, cold ride, sitting on the hard boards with his legs drawn up in that foetal position.

He shifted his holster around a little to get at it more easily. His Stechkin automatic pistol was a precaution he prayed not to have to use, but he carried two spare 20-round magazines just in case. Few handguns boasted the Stechkin's punch.

It was late afternoon and already getting dark. With the tarpaulin over him he was as good as blind. Impatiently he cursed Yakov for taking so long. Ten minutes he had given the man, but with Yu-li waiting so submissively on the bed it was not difficult to guess what he must be doing. That set him thinking again about Mei-lin. Had all her joy and affection been no more than acting?

Someone came to the truck, he couldn't see who it was. A hand grasped the tarpaulin's loosened guy-rope and tied it down in place again. 'Now we leave, Comrade Colonel,' came a hoarse whisper.

Once again Ross silently cursed Yakov for his stupidity. What if someone had heard the fool?

He tested the tarpaulin above him, wondering if he should not jump down and abort the whole operation before the truck reached the base, but Yakov had lashed it so tightly it was impossible to move. He was virtually a prisoner.

The truck throbbed as the engine noisily revved up. Diesel fumes met his nostrils, sickening him; then he heard the rear wheels spinning on the snow before they gripped and the truck lurched forward. Without those wooden cases penning him in on either side the journey over the rough roads would have been much worse; as it was, he felt them bruising him each time they shifted.

Eventually – some fifteen or twenty minutes must have gone by – the truck slowed down and stopped. Voices, one of them Yakov's, calling to each other. Shouting. The main gate, Ross thought though he saw nothing. It was here the guards should check what load was being carried. If they were on their toes.

Heavy boots crunched over the snow, coming closer. Something hit the tarpaulin; a guard's hand, maybe.

'On your way, Yakov!' a bullying voice shouted in Russian. 'But next time don't forget our vodka!'

'No, comrade.'

'Speak to the bar manager. It should've been sitting there waiting for you.'

'He didn't go to the bar, more likely!' came a second voice. 'Too busy screwing that girl.'

Laughter, in which other men joined.

'They wear out after a time, these Chinese whores – know that, Yakov? Not like Russian girls, they're tough! Chinese biddies are delicate. One day you'll be at it an' she'll die underneath you from over use. Worn out like an old slipper. Only once that's gotta happen, you'll never fuck again.'

More laughter. Raucous.

Yakov yelled some reply which Ross failed to catch against the gunning of the truck's engine and clumsily they shot forward, the rear wheels skidding crazily sideways as they took a curve. A second later Yakov regained control and the truck drove on as sedately as a London bus. They were inside the military base. Ross had a mental picture of the roads. If Yakov obeyed his instructions they should turn left in another few moments and that would bring them to the inner security fence.

Yes – this was it. The truck had stopped. Voices again – though only a quick greeting this time and they moved on inside. The guard had not even bothered to check Yakov's papers.

At their next stop he heard Yakov jump down into the snow, leaving the engine ticking over. Then the tarpaulin was freed and tugged back. They were between two dark buildings, one with a light bracketed to the wall a few yards away on the corner. No one else about, only the two of them. Ross pushed his Stechkin back into the holster, secured the flap and extricated himself awkwardly from between the cases. His legs were stiff from the cold.

Joining Yakov on the snow he congratulated him on his good work. 'Those men on the gate – you can identify them when the time comes?'

'I know that lot all right. Regulars, they are.'

'Till then, keep your mouth shut. I want no tip-off. Right? Now, where d'you take this stuff?' He indicated the cases on the truck.

'Two more blocks. They'll be waiting to unload. Gate will have told 'em.'

'On your way then. I'll follow.'

Yakov shuffled uneasily. 'You'll not forget about promotion to sergeant, Comrade Colonel?'

'The recommendation is already written, Yakov. I've only to sign it when I get back tonight.' Poor sod, he thought; his reward will be ten years in a labour camp; if they don't shoot him.

Stamping his feet and flexing his knees to bully his circulation back into life, Ross waited for the truck's tail lights to disappear round the corner of the second block before he set out after it. He marched as briskly as the snow permitted, making no attempt to conceal his presence. His nerves were taut. His life depended on putting up an appearance of self-confidence, but beneath it gnawed the fear that he might fail. It was like a high-dive act in a circus; one mistake and he was dead.

No moon yet, though the sky was already quite dark, blacker still in the direction taken by the truck. He realized he was looking at the towering cliff which dominated the whole base; in daylight the small temple would be seen perched precariously on its rock ledge. No lights were visible anywhere on the cliff; no evidence that the main temple even existed.

Reaching the spot where the truck had turned left, Ross paused to check what lay ahead of him. He wanted the unloading to be already under way before he made his appearance.

No sign of truck or men.

Had Yakov deceived him? Left him there while he went to report to the guards? He had certainly driven along this way; the tyre marks were fresh on almost untrodden snow.

With difficulty, his boots sinking into the snow practically up to his ankles, Ross followed them. A gusty wind blew powdered ice against his face and he pulled his fur hat closer over his head.

At the next corner his anger drained away. He had reached what was obviously the main roadway through the research centre. Lighted windows and entrances on either side illuminated the grey snow with rectangles of crisp white. In front of one building, parked alongside a covered platform beneath harshly glaring lamps, he saw the truck. A team of five soldiers were busy unloading it, two standing on the truck itself passing the cases to the others while an officer stood by supervising them.

Spotting Yakov, Ross strode over to him.

'Yakov!' he ordered loudly. 'Come with me. Leave the truck and let them get on without you.'

The officer, a young lieutenant, brought his men smartly to attention and saluted. Ross acknowledged it; so far so good. The real test would come when he encountered a Russian officer. These men, from their appearance, must be from one of the Mongolian units Chuan had mentioned.

'Well, Yakov?'

Yakov stood there stammering with the delivery chit in his hand. He needed a signature. Of course.

'Then get it, Corporal! Hurry, man!'

Briefly the lieutenant hesitated, no doubt wondering if he should sign the chit right away to avoid keeping this GRU officer waiting. Clearly deciding he would be on safer ground sticking by the book, he carefully counted the remaining cases on the truck before taking the paper and scribbling a signature on it.

'Lieutenant, what's in these cases?' Ross demanded.

'Respirators, Comrade Colonel.' The lieutenant's Russian was heavily accented. 'Ten in each case.'

'Good! You can tell the men they can carry on!' Ross dismissed him. 'Yakov! How much longer must I wait?'

Thirty cases . . . That would total 300 respirators delivered here to Paikow. Not the first delivery either, Yakov assured him. Were they equipping men to go into action? Germ warfare assault troops – was that possible? The railway through Paikow was the main line to Antung on the Yalu river; over the bridge they were in Korea.

Or were they planning a large-scale experiment here in the Paikow Research Centre itself, perhaps to test the respirators' effectiveness by deliberately exposing their wearers to droplet infection?

At the end of the roadway was a large squat building snugly constructed against the cliff wall. 'That's where it all goes on, that place,' Yakov volunteered as they approached it. But even had he said nothing, the massive warning signs at either side of the well-lit entrance would have informed Ross that this was the top security zone.

By the steps he paused to scrape the caked snow from under his boots. 'Yakov, go in and hold the door open for me. Go ahead, man!' he snapped irritably.

It had only been a hunch, but it worked. A string of heart-felt Russian curses issued from inside. 'Close that stinking door, you clot! Want to freeze us to death, or what? You born in Siberia, idiot?'

Ross chose his moment, then marched into the guard room and stopped in the middle of the floor to stare contemptuously at the occupants. The two men scrambled to their feet, confused, and stiffened to attention. Both were sergeants of some seniority, one with a Stalin-type moustache. They had been sitting by the stove drinking tea. Their tunics were unbuttoned at the neck and their weapons were out of reach on the far side of the room.

'Sorry, Comrade Colonel,' the man with the moustache apologized. He seemed to be the older of the two. 'Hadn't cottoned on you were there.'

'So I see.' Ross used his premier brand of sarcasm. 'From Moscow, are you?'

'Moscow, yes. An' he's from Kiev.'

'So far from home, you think you can take things easy, is that it?' he barked at them.

'No, Comrade Colonel.'

'The Party has a long arm, don't forget that. Neglect of

285

duty amounts to state sabotage. There are many more uncomfortable postings than Paikow – you take my meaning?'

'Yes, Comrade Colonel.'

'Then learn this. We have reports of security leaks from Paikow Base. Just make sure they don't come from this section. How many men work here?'

The two sergeants glanced at each other uncertainly. One nodded, buttoning up his tunic. Then he plucked up enough courage to request Ross's identification.

'Colonel Gayev, Army Intelligence.'

Ross produced the forged warrant Chuan had supplied, holding it out for the sergeant to see, hardly giving him time to read it before returning it to his tunic pocket again. The second sergeant was strapping on his belt.

'About time, Sergeant,' he said scathingly. 'You should have checked my identity the moment I came in here. I repeat the question. How many men do you have here?'

The sight of his GRU warrant card had obviously satisfied them. The two sergeants now stumbled over themselves in their eagerness to help him. Scientists apart, they explained, only special service units of the Korean People's Army worked in the caves, and no leak could have come through them. They were allowed no contact of any sort with the outside world. There was even a sick bay for them in there with their own doctors and nurses.

'And the officer in charge?'

'Korean.'

'Guards?'

They looked uncomfortable, stiffening once more to attention as if bracing themselves for one more onslaught. By now both were correctly dressed, belts and holsters worn, and standing by the duty desk. Their sub-machine guns were within reach on the wall-rack behind them.

'We're the guards on this entrance, Comrade Colonel,'

the Moscow sergeant confessed. He rapped the words out, arms pressed to his sides, eyes forward.

Ross demanded to see their identity books, glanced at them cursorily and kept them in his hand while he described in unpleasant detail what their futures might be if they didn't smarten up their ideas. God bless Gogol, he thought as he made them suffer. God bless too those bastards Vladimir Ilyich Lenin and Josip Vissarionovich Stalin who struck the fear of hell into every Russian heart and made them capable of any stupidity at the mere sight of a uniform.

He tossed the identity books on to the desk. 'Inform the Korean duty officer I am here,' he ordered. 'Security inspection. I shall need him to show me round.'

The Moscow sergeant with the Stalin moustache picked up a field telephone and wound the handle. He could have been calling for help or instructions: Ross felt his nerves tensing as the man waited for someone to answer. But when at last the receiver at the other end was lifted, his request was repeated almost word for word.

'Alone, Comrade Colonel? Or will the corporal be with you?'

'The corporal does not have security clearance, so of course he won't be with me,' Ross replied with irritation. It was a necessary decision, though he regretted it. Having Yakov in attendance gave him credibility. 'Yakov, get down to "Transport" and organize a car to take me back to Paikow when I've finished. Wait for me there. You're to drive – understand?'

'Yes, Comrade Colonel!'

'Right, is the Korean officer ready, Sergeant?'

To the rear of the guard room was a corridor blocked off at the end by a heavy closed door. The moment the sergeant knocked, an observation hatch slid open and a pair of dark, Asian eyes inspected them both. He heard the sound of a bolt being tugged back, then the door opened to let him through. The moment he was inside it was bolted again behind him.

The Korean officer first greeted him with a parade ground salute and then, relaxing, shook his hand warmly. 'I am Captain Kim, Korean People's Army. You are very welcome, Colonel Gayev. Please step into my office. You are my third visitor from the Soviet Union in three weeks. I am honoured.'

'I'm afraid, Captain, this is an inspection, not a social call.'

'So I understand. But before we go through – perhaps a vodka?'

'Not on duty, Captain. Afterwards, maybe.'

'Quite right. I was trained in the Soviet Union myself, you know. Duty comes before pleasure. Now, I have to explain what happens in the rooms we shall see. Once in there, we'll be wearing respirators, so it is not so easy to talk. First we look at this chart . . .'

Captain Kim had obviously worked out a routine for dealing with official visitors and was not to be deflected from it. He was a small, almost dapper man with a dark clipped moustache; he must have spent some time in front of a mirror to achieve that degree of neatness. His Russian, slightly sing-song, was fluent and easy on the ear as he went through the details step by step.

'We are now in the caves under the rock. No unguarded exits to the world outside. Everything controlled.' He glanced at Ross who merely nodded. Then he continued, turning back to the chart, 'In this first hall you will see the tanks we use for cultivating the bacteria . . .'

The whole situation struck Ross as absurd. It was like a fairy story. One touch of the wand and everything was laid out before him – on this chart. But of course the name 'research centre' had been misleading. The research stage was over, or not conducted here. This was a factory and Captain Kim was its production manager. Such charts were simply one of the tools of management.

A series of caves – 'halls' Captain Kim called them – housed each stage of the production process. Cultivation of the bacteria, a laboratory for quality tests, special tanks for mixing the living bacterial cocktail, canning the fluid in the aerosol containers . . . At first glance they might have been manufacturing soft drinks, it was so routine and low-key.

The area where the final stage took place was labelled 'Charging Bay'. If the chart was accurate, that cave was vastly larger than all the others taken together.

Ross experienced a strong urge to take a short cut and simply ask Captain Kim what went on there, but that was one question which would betray him. Any admission of ignorance on his part would blow this entire game of bluff wide apart.

'I want to examine the walls,' he said brusquely. 'I'm told there's a whole network of caves in these hills. Any rift in the rock, any opening, any possible way through, I have to check it.'

In case I need to get out in a hurry, he might have added but refrained.

'Any such openings have been filled with concrete. A few are closed off by steel doors, though I have never seen them unlocked.' From a cupboard the captain removed two respirators, handing one to Ross. 'We wear these. No one is allowed in without one.'

'I hope that rule is followed strictly.'

'It is.' The Korean was offended.

'Pneumonic plague is not a pleasant way to die.' He checked the respirator, then put it on. 'Let's go,' he said, his voice muffled.

At the end of the passage they went through two sets

of curtains made of overlapping rubber sheets; the device served as a rough-and-ready airlock. It brought them into the first hall where, ranged down the centre, were four rows of open tanks on low benches. He went closer to look into one, catching a glimpse of the unsavoury broth it contained before he felt Captain Kim's hand restraining him. Those working there, creaming off the scum into little metal scoops, were totally enveloped in white 'plague suits' from which only the snouts of their respirators protruded.

Captain Kim followed his instructions meticulously and led him to inspect a steel door set in the rock wall. Ross tried it and found it locked, though given the right charge it could perhaps be blown open. Before going on he glanced back at the tanks and their shrouded attendants, whether male or female he couldn't even guess. This place was a real hell's kitchen.

As they made their slow progress through the caves from one hall to the next his disgust grew. He visualized the devastation a germ attack could cause; the most raging natural epidemic would seem mild in comparison. Within days, entire populations might be lying desperately sick, the lucky ones already dead; hospitals and water and electricity supplies no longer functioning; nothing left but the stench of disease.

His remark about pneumonic plague had been more than a guess. Warnings against the disease were posted on every wall, in the office as well as the production halls, and in both Russian and Korean. They stated clearly that the bacteria being bred and processed were *Pasteurella pestis*. Merely breathing the air could bring death. 'Wear your respirator' was the message.

'Pneumonic plague,' he recalled his pinch-lipped boffin's scholarly voice instructing him. 'Aerosol dispersal. Droplet infection. Victim breathes the bacteria directly into the lungs where they grow fruitful and multiply. Death can follow in as little as two or three days. Cough, spit, sneeze or even breathe out during that time, and the disease has spread to the neighbours. Epidemics? Winter months mainly. The droplets hang about in the atmosphere much longer in cold weather. Of course it's the same bacteria as bubonic plague, but bubonic epidemics are more likely in summer. Transmitted by fleas. Of the two, my money would go on pneumonic as the most likely weapon, though neither can beat anthrax.'

Down here in the caves even the memory of that desiccated government scientist made Ross want to throw up. He might have been discussing a fly spray, he showed so little concern.

'Canning section!' Captain Kim yelled vigorously through his mask as they entered one more hall.

He was another with no inhibitions about his work. It was patently a well-run, efficient production line despite the makeshift nature of some of its equipment and he was undisguisedly proud of it. No hesitations about the mass slaughter this stuff would bring about: the disease-ridden men, women and children; the death agonies; the unburied rotting corpses left lying about like so much street refuse.

In the hall a line of shrouded, ghost-like figures was at work manually pouring the death-bringing plasma into rows of slim metal canisters, each one some eighteen inches high and about three inches in diameter. He watched for a few seconds only, then moved on to the far end of the bench where more white-swathed workers were sealing the canisters, using hand-operated presses; others finally screwed on the complex, finned tail units.

Bombs.

In fact, not dissimilar to standard wartime incendiary bombs.

Some yards away one of the shrouded brigade was cautiously propelling a trolley-load of finished bomblets towards the wide opening which led into the next cave. Ross followed him, irritably waving aside the diminutive Korean captain's attempts to draw his attention to another of those damned steel doors.

At the entrance one glance told him what he had come here to discover. The vast cave was busy with activity. To the rear was a miniature shunting yard served by the branch railway line which entered through a separate tunnel leading off at an oblique angle on the far side. The mysterious freight wagon he and Mei-lin had observed from the cliff-side temple waited, already uncoupled, in a siding; one end of the timber cladding had been removed, sufficient to reveal the front few feet of a rocket.

More rockets lay in the forward area of the cave. Eight, he counted altogether, and each resting on its own wagon. Small groups of men clustered round them, also wearing respirators but no plague suits. Travelling lifting gear drooped down from the overhead gantries; one team, he saw, was preparing to remove the warhead.

V2 type rockets, he thought at first. Getting closer he realized he was wrong. These were not V2s but the later generation designed by the German engineers the Russians took back to the Soviet Union after Hitler's defeat. He swore at himself for not having suspected it earlier. It was this rocket – the R12, the Soviets had dubbed it – whose prototype launch he had witnessed in Kazakhstan. The same design, with only modest alterations.

He examined one closely. The men working on it glanced at him, but his GRU uniform and colonel's insignia killed their curiosity dead.

The warhead – lying separated from the main torso – revealed the most significant modifications. For the Kazakhstan tests – Christ, he'd dossed down for days in that old rubbish-tip shed to see it happen – the payload had been cement bricks to provide weight; now the warhead cone contained a skeleton framework into which the Korean ghost-workers were slotting charged germ canisters. Forty or fifty of them, he estimated.

His guess was that the cone would blow apart over the target to scatter the bomblets, thereby increasing the area affected.

Against such a weapon there was no defence. The long, slow, radar-tracked approach of a manned bomber gave time to warn the civilian population and scramble the fighters. But rockets arrived unannounced, as London knew from experience of the V2s. It made them all the more deadly.

The London Section had refused to believe him. Soviet rockets? Ridiculous – the Russians were technologically backward, and in any case the range was too great. After Kazakhstan, then months on the run, hiding, starving, helped by people he later refused to name for fear of endangering their lives, he had been thrown into an interrogation centre, accused of selling out to the Russians. Would London react any differently this time?

Last time they had written him off and when they discovered him still alive it discomforted them; it meant re-opening a file they had already closed. Untidy administration. Salaries had been very upset about having to resurrect a deceased member of staff and a memo war had broken out over whether or not he was entitled to increments during the period of his 'death'. They even sent him a reminder about unpaid contributions to the Civil Service Widows & Orphans Fund.

So what now? As he inspected the rocket and its germ-carrying warhead – with Captain Kim at his heels, proud and enthusiastic about this technologist's dream – ghosts from his past came floating into his mind, warning him it was all set to happen again. The admiral didn't expect him back alive. That plan for a submarine rendezvous, that was so much London fog. All they wanted was one more signal laying out the full details: then silence. File returned to 'Archives'. *Missing, presumed dead*. Tidier that way.

And if he didn't send the signal? Fuck all the notice they took of any signal. Until the bombs landed, then panic stations.

At the far end of the cave were heavy, locked gates under which twin railway tracks passed. Beside them, standing open, was a steel door leading into a narrow corridor sealed off by overlapping rubber curtains which formed a flexible, swaying membrane. Ross pushed through it, tearing off his respirator.

'You mentioned vodka, Captain.'

'I was about to renew the suggestion,' Captain Kim said politely smiling, anxious to please. He ushered Ross into a nearby room, in reality a partitioned-off section of yet another of these interconnecting caves. 'This is not my office but I'm sure the Russian captain will not object to me entertaining you here.'

As Ross watched the Korean unlocking the filing cabinet to extract a bottle of vodka he felt his sudden mood of depression giving way to rising panic. That corridor was his escape route to the outside, so why was he waiting around to drink vodka? He had to get out while there was still time. In these caves he was like a cornered rat. By now those guards would have figured him out, perhaps called their officer; and Yakov . . . he'd blurt out the truth the moment he was challenged . . .

Lost his nerve. He could hear the admiral's voice. *Man's lost his bloody nerve.*

'Thank you, Comrade Captain.' He accepted the proffered glass, disciplining himself to speak steadily. He raised it. 'Excellent job you're doing here. I must congratulate you. Very impressed.' Then, thinking of the admiral and that stinking interrogation centre where they had almost succeeded in breaking him, he added a toast. 'To world revolution, comrade. And death to imperialism.'

'Death to all imperialists!' Captain Kim declared, standing to attention and emptying the glass in one gulp.

He refilled both glasses.

'Without American interference Korea would already be one country once again,' he went on. 'Please do not misunderstand me, Comrade Colonel. I know it is necessary, but I am not happy that the Americans are forcing us to attack Seoul with this terrible weapon. I was born in Seoul. It is my home town, though I had to leave when I was a young man. I was in trouble with the Japanese Fascist police. Without the Soviet Union to offer me training I would be nothing.'

Ross impatiently lifted his glass once more. 'In that case, to Korea!' he announced. Luckily he remembered the Koreans' own name for their country. 'To Chosen!'

'To Chosen!'

And thank you for Seoul, Ross thought. As a target it was a headline grabber: large civilian population, seat of Syngman Rhee's South Korean government, and ringed with United Nations bases, mostly US manned. That information alone doubled the urgency of getting to the monastery in time to make radio contact that night.

The bottle hovered over the glasses but Ross put a hand over his, saying that his work was not finished, he still had other parts of the base to inspect. Besides, the Korean was no vodka drinker, he judged. One more toast and the man would be in tears.

But at least he had a meticulous sense of duty. He accompanied his important Soviet visitor through the guard room as far as the snow-covered path outside, saluting smartly as he said goodbye. As Ross marched away he had the uncanny feeling that the next moment would bring a bullet in his back. It had all been too easy. As if someone had set it up for him.

From each of the two high pyramids he noted that a single railway track led directly to the gates in the rock face behind which must lie the rocket workshop he had just left. Beyond them, too, was the shadowy form of the long railway shed he had observed from the temple. He was tempted to investigate further but decided against it. Somehow he had to get out of this inner security area; he prayed Yakov would be waiting for him with transport.

A guard ambled out of the blockhouse at the inner gate. Seeing the uniform he merely saluted; not even an ID check. Once through into the main base Ross took the route he had plotted on his sketch map at the monastery. Easy landmarks – the mess hall, the wireless building at the far end of an intersecting road, the high-grade housing which he assumed to be officers' quarters. From one building came the sound of a woman laughing.

Not laughing, screaming.

Screaming protests in Chinese while young male voices guffawed and jeered. Her Chinese gave way to English – a few disjointed words which made them roar all the louder – and then, in Chinese again, a furious stream of abuse.

Ross stepped back into the shadows, uncertain what to do, trying to persuade himself it was not Mei-lin; it could be any bar girl they had smuggled into the base, perhaps one of Chuan's people who had bitten off more than she could manage. Leave her to get on with it, that was the best course. Tucked into the side of the building around the corner he spotted their car, camouflage-painted, a four-wheel drive job which might have started life as an

American jeep, though now with a redesigned superstructure. It would get him back into Paikow if Yakov let him down. He felt tempted to take it anyway while the girl kept them busy.

'You soddin' Russian bastards!' she yelled at them in Chinese, loud and clear.

The party was getting noisy again. From their reaction it was obvious they understood no Chinese, but they picked up that one word 'Russian' and repeated it over and over again, making fun of her.

Another shriek from her, and more abuse – but pathetically mild, not gutter language. Jesus, it *had* to be Mei-lin! That accent . . . noticeable even through the unaccustomed shrillness . . .

Ross strode into the building, directly up to the first floor from where the sounds came, and threw open the door. Mei-lin, partly stripped, was being held down on the bed by two junior lieutenants while a third attempted to prise her kicking legs apart. Keeping them tightly together, she succeeded in landing a blow with her heels just below his ribs, sending him staggering back badly winded.

'Amusing yourselves?' Ross demanded contemptuously. He stood motionless in the doorway, his fury boiling inside him. 'Well? Is this how you choose to serve the Revolution, like drunken peasants? Is this your concept of Soviet-Chinese friendship? To rape the women?'

The two by the bed had released Mei-lin and scrambled to attention. They were hardly older than twenty, blond, and their pale blue eyes showed genuine fear. The third, dark-haired, weasel-faced, was still doubled up in agony from Mei-lin's kick. Ross felt an urge to cripple them for life, taking them one by one or all together, he didn't give a fuck which, let them experience a few of those special techniques he had not been able to practise since the Jap surrender. With difficulty he restrained himself. The only chance of getting the two of them safely back to Paikow was for him to stay in character.

'Names?' he bawled at them, pointing at the nearest first.

'S-sermiov, C-comrade C-colonel,' the young man stuttered.

Once the other two had given their names he questioned them briefly, discovering that the dark-haired boy had picked her up at the Officers' Club and brought her in crouched down in the back of the car.

'On at me all the time to come back here with me,' he protested, still struggling for breath. 'Wouldn't let up.'

'So you invited your fellow officers to join in your collective rape?' Ross's anger burst to the surface. '*Soviet* officers? You'll face disciplinary charges, all three of you. Take her down to the car.'

'Yes, Comrade Colonel.'

Outside the snow had acquired a fresh crispness underfoot. The roads and rooftops gleamed eerily in the moonlight and a caul of steam hovered in front of everyone's nose and mouth as they breathed. He ordered Mei-lin to get into the car, still speaking Russian but reinforcing his words with gestures. In the room she had dressed sullenly, not even glancing at him; he had been unable to judge whether she was playing a part or not. The sooner he could get both of them out through that gate, the better he'd feel.

'Up to driving this thing?' he snapped at the defiant young officer who was glaring at him hostilely.

'The bitch has fractured a couple of my ribs.'

'No more than that? You're lucky she didn't cut your balls off, Comrade Lieutenant. You saw the knife in her bag.'

'Isn't she going to be charged?'

'What happens to her does not concern you. Not where you are likely to be going.' Ross was beginning to feel uneasy again. The kid was calling his bluff.

'Perhaps you don't realize the true position, Comrade Colonel. My father is an MVD General. My uncle serves on the Central Committee.'

'They will not be proud of you for this exploit. You are confined to your quarters, all of you.'

Ross was about to slip into the driving seat beside a subdued Mei-lin, huddled up in her coat because of the cold, when a patrol rounded the corner. Four men, marching briskly; three carried sub-machine guns, and the fourth was Yakov.

'That's the officer!' one shouted, pointing in Ross's direction. It was the older of the two sergeants from the guard room. 'Comrade Colonel, one moment please!'

Ross let in the clutch and felt his wheels throwing up the snow before they gripped and the car shot forward, skidding past the patrol and rocking crazily as he took the next corner into one of the side roads. It had been a quick, unthinking instinct, but the rapid smack of sub-machine gun fire told him he was right. He rounded another corner, heading away from them and then slowed down as he approached the main gate.

'You all right? Why the hell did you get into that mess?' he asked Mei-lin.

'Why the hell did *you*?' she retorted spiritedly. 'But I confess I was glad to see you. They'd have killed me.'

At the main gate a line of armed soldiers was busy forming up across the road. Cursing, he swung the car round to the right towards the transport yard; several shots followed them but went wide. Headlights sprang on in the shadows near the gate, then pulled out in pursuit. He changed direction again. The moment they were beyond the next corner and momentarily out of sight he stopped, switched off the lights and got out.

'Wait here,' he whispered, his Stechkin already out of its holster.

He ran back to the corner, dropped on to one knee in the snow and, holding the Stechkin two-handed, he waited till the pursuing vehicle was within a comfortable range before shooting the driver through the windscreen. It swerved wildly, bouncing off one wall before skidding round on the hard snow and crashing headlong into the building opposite.

Calmly he pressed the selector catch to its top position for full automatic fire and with three quick bursts put the survivors out of their agony.

'Mei-lin, listen,' he said urgently when he got back to the car. 'You must try to get back to Chuan. When these Russians find you here tell them I kidnapped you. You know nothing about me. Have a crying fit, do anything to convince them.'

'I'm staying with you,' she said.

He shook his head impatiently. 'Listen, *please*. It's important you get a message to Chuan.'

Rapidly he gave her a quick summary of what he had discovered – the rockets, the type of disease, the target. She took the information so coolly, he began to suspect she knew it already. And if she did, then so did Chuan. But in that event, why was she in the base at all?

From a block or two away he heard a quick shout of command followed by the crunch of men's boots on the snow as they took up their positions. Coming to investigate the shooting, Ross reckoned, but cautiously, fearing an ambush.

Mei-lin understood the sounds too. She took his ungloved hand and pressed it against her cheek. 'Good luck, Hantu!' she murmured, so quietly he only just caught her words. Then she slipped into the driving seat. 'I'll draw them off. Only . . . I loved you for a night. One night and a day. See you in the next world, my ghost!'

She drove off, gunning the engine noisily to attract attention to herself. In response he heard another shout, then more orders as the car shot off between the buildings, leading the Russians away from him. She had joked about calling him Hantu, this time wrongly. He was Hantu again, and for real.

He took no risks but stayed in the shadows, slinking along warily until he was within reach of the rough stone wall surrounding the transport yard. Hidden from the roadway by a long storage shed he found a spot where he could climb over, landing on the far side under the cover of a line of parked trucks. He began to work his way along them, looking for one which had been used recently and would start without trouble. From the snow encrusting many of the windscreens most had been standing idle for some days.

Ideally he needed heavy armour if he was to crash through the barriers at the main gate. A tank at least. But with the gods on his side – though were they? – he might get away with it in a truck.

Overhead a lone plane droned over the mountains. At first he gave it no thought. Once again it was an unusually clear night, cloudless and cold, ideal for launching their rockets if they had them all primed and ready to go. The attack was bound to be planned to happen soon; wasn't there a problem about the life-span of the bacteria being limited to only a few days in those conditions?

Then he realized he was too late. That plane was his radio link. It would fly over, circle once at high altitude, and pass again above Paikow valley in twenty minutes' time which would be his last chance of transmitting the information for another twenty-four hours. Even if he did succeed in breaking out he could never get back to the monastery and set up his transmitter soon enough to make contact. His only chance lay here in the base itself.

Twenty minutes.

By then Mei-lin would either be in their hands or dead. Killed outright if she was lucky. They would never fall for the sob story that she was no more than an innocent whore intending no harm to anyone, caught up in events she didn't understand; that cover was destroyed the moment she took the driving wheel. Jesus Christ, why did it always have to happen like this? It was Yen-hua all over again.

He needed a diversionary action to keep them occupied. Strapped to the side of each of the smaller trucks was a jerrican of petrol, considerately kept fully topped up. Taking each truck in turn – there were five in the row – he scattered some of the contents on the seating and timber bodywork, leaving a partly filled jerrican in each cab. Then he sacrificed his greatcoat, ripping it into broad strips with the sharp-pointed commando knife he carried in his boot. Each strip he soaked in petrol to cover the weaker links in his fire chain. Finally he fished out the Havana cigar tube from his inside pocket and unscrewed the cap; in it, wrapped in tobacco leaf, was a time incendiary packed – so the training camp armourer had explained – with magnesium powder and other delicacies.

A ten-minute fuse, this one. At the present temperature that probably implied twenty minutes. Hantu scraped away a portion of tobacco, exposing the glass bulb which he crushed with a screwdriver from one of the trucks, then tossed the little bomb into the cab and headed back to the wall.

Without his greatcoat he moved more easily. In a second he was dropping down on the other side, up to his ankles in snow. He crossed swiftly into the shadows, then ran partly crouched along the full length of the storage shed. The wireless building was just ahead of him, a squat stone structure with two boarded-up windows facing this side.

Briefly he glanced back. Everything was quiet in the transport yard. He had plenty of time before that Churchill-style cigar did its work. Five blazing trucks should keep Ivan occupied; maybe a few other vehicles would go up with them. But he hated messing with petrol. The stench lingered however careful he was.

A broad open patch of moonlit snow lay between him and the wireless building. He could still hear orders being shouted in the distance, and engines throbbing far off, but nothing close. Then came a burst of automatic fire. *Meilin* . . . The sound shocked through him, paralysing him as he realized what must have happened. It was like witnessing her execution with his own eyes; he was left only with a numbed feeling of desolation.

He sprinted across the snow to the sliver of shadow cast by the wireless building, then edged quickly towards the entrance. Recklessly even: an instinctive glance round to check his back, but no hesitation. Not any longer.

On the outside at least the building was unguarded. Pausing just long enough to slip the commando knife out of his boot, concealing it in his left hand, he pushed the door open. Inside was a bare vestibule lit by a single unshaded light bulb; beneath it, on a small rough table, was a chess board with a few pieces set out and an instruction book beside it. The sergeant on duty must have heard Hantu's heavy boots on the wooden floor-boards for he returned almost immediately, straightening up as he saw the uniform.

Then his expression changed. No doubt in the brief second before he died he realized he was face to face with the imposter who was being hunted throughout the base, but Hantu gave him no time to shout a warning. The point of the commando knife slashed across his throat. A cough, a lot of blood, and he was dead.

Hantu wiped the blade clean on the man's uniform, then bolted the outside door to make certain he was undisturbed. His only feeling was that it was a job which had to be done, nothing else. Mei-lin's death had left him numbed but not vindictive. Though pneumonic plague victims might envy this Soviet sergeant for his quick and easy exit from the world. They would die much more unpleasantly, by the thousand, unless the attack could be stopped.

The noise of his boots on that floor bothered him. He sat down and took them off before, stepping over the pool of blood, he went silently into the corridor at the rear of the vestibule. On either side were doors, three in all; one standing open led into the washroom. He ignored the others but followed the sound of the morse key seeming to come from the end of the corridor.

He was right. This was the transmitter room: an array of old, heavy equipment, nothing very sophisticated. The signals clerk sat with his back to the door patiently tapping out a lengthy message from a paper beside him. He was a stocky, fair man whose hair curled around his headphones.

Hantu stepped towards him, one pace only, shifting his weight carefully to minimize any creaking from the floor-boards. The clerk carried on transmitting, hearing nothing. A second step . . . then a third . . . still no reaction. Then the transmission ended. The man stretched . . . took off the headphones . . . Hantu's right hand jerked his head back from behind; before he could even gasp the commando knife had plunged into his left side between the ribs, and he died.

Once he had lowered the body to the floor Hantu

304

methodically checked the other rooms. They were unoccupied. No one else had been on duty, only the two dead soldiers. He went back to the vestibule to put on his boots again, then returned to examine the transmitter. It was a wartime model with Japanese inscriptions identifying the controls; above them were stuck handwritten labels giving the Russian equivalents. He experimented for a time to familiarize himself with the set-up before tuning to the frequency he wanted, praying that he had forgotten nothing.

Now all he could do was wait. To hear the aircraft more clearly when it flew over he opened a window. The boards he had noticed from outside were hinged shutters, he discovered. Between them he glimpsed a strip of snow-covered road and a stretch of the transport yard wall. No movement, though plenty seemed to be going on some distance away.

He checked his Stechkin. Nine rounds left. He dropped the partly used magazine into his pocket and fitted another with the full twenty rounds. This time he was not going to get out alive, he knew that; at least he could make sure they paid a high price.

Still no plane. He went back to the transmitter and picked up the message the clerk had been transmitting. It was in code, but there were no cipher books in the place. The enciphering was obviously done in some other building.

A dull roar came from outside – nothing very loud and he saw high flames over the transport yard. Churchill's cigar had done its job, thank God. That should keep them occupied for five minutes at least. Now all he needed was the B29 to come over and he could unburden himself of all he had discovered. Warn them of the germ attack even if he couldn't prevent it.

Through the clamour of men and vehicles arriving at

the transport yard he heard the sound he was waiting for: the steady drone of the plane. He dashed back to the transmitter and gave his identification code.

N-T . . . N-T . . . N-T. A brief pause, then he repeated the sequence: N-T . . . N-T . . . N-T.

He switched to 'Receive'. Something was there and he prayed they would transmit long enough for him to get a fix on it. He juggled with the dial, straining his ears – then suddenly there it was, loud and clear. His identity was acknowledged.

N-L-T . . . N-L-T . . . N-L-T, he transmitted, telling them his circumstances were unusual. PLAIN LANGUAGE OVER.

GO AHEAD IN PLAIN OVER, came the response.

He hoped to God they would believe him. They had only to decide he was transmitting under duress for the whole operation to be negatived. Painstakingly he gave them the details the admiral had demanded of him: pneumonic plague; aerosol dispersal; scatter bomblets; rockets; Seoul probable first target; workshops in cliff caves. OVER.

He selected 'Receive' and leaned back, expecting a straightforward acknowledgement. Instead, a different message came back. FROM SEA DOG URGENT STOP STAND BY 1000 HRS TOMORROW FOR FRESH INSTRUCTIONS ACKNOWLEDGE OVER.

Fresh instructions, he thought contemptuously. The admiral clearly prided himself on his blind-eye technique. The Nelson touch. He tapped out a reply. His last word: N-T TO SEA DOG YOULL BE LUCKY STOP SAY A MASS FOR MY SOUL OUT.

He heard the scramble of boots on the snow outside as he flicked the dials around at random to leave no evidence of the frequency he had been using. This was it, then. He switched off the set and drew his Stechkin, selecting fully automatic fire. If he had to go down he preferred shooting it out to some of the other methods they were capable of devising.

The explosion when they blew off the outer door shook the entire structure, clouding the air in the corridor with thick dust. Through it emerged the first Ivans moving cautiously, shit-scared. With two bursts from the Stechkin he put them out of action but others were coming up behind them. Hantu retreated to the radio room, taking cover beside the doorway, crouching as a stream of bullets splintered the door jambs. He fired back, blindly. 'Come on, you bastards!' he whispered. 'Come on! End it!'

They threw a grenade into the room. Simultaneously the window shutters were smashed down and a second grenade was tossed in. Gas! He swung round, firing at everything in sight till the acrid chemical caught his throat, choking him, burning his eyes, his lungs, and he felt the gun slipping from his fingers.

In the B29 Superfortress, now flying at 20,000 feet overhead, the admiral checked through Ross's report once again before handing the signal pad back to Higgins, the Section's star radio operator.

'Sparks, get this signal properly enciphered before you relay it,' he ordered. 'I'll add a covering tailpiece of my own for you to tack on. I pray to God we've had no eavesdroppers. I suppose he must have had a reason for transmitting in plain text. It's a damned big risk to take.'

Radio waves did odd things. It only needed freak conditions for some radio ham in Australia to pick up the message and pass it on to the newspapers. The whole operation could be blown wide open. He could imagine British intelligence services getting the White House seal of approval after that.

It had taken all the admiral's diplomatic know-how to

persuade the Americans to let him ride piggyback on that night's R/T run to bring him within range of Ross's transceiver. *Gorgeous Gussie* was the name painted on the side of the aircraft, under the command of Lieutenant-Colonel Muller who had been less than keen to carry unnecessary passengers, though once in the air he had co-operated briskly.

On their approach to Paikow the admiral had been up for'ard in the nose with a clear view through the plexiglass of the whole layout of the valley.

'Big fire down there,' he had reported over the intercom.

'Helluva big blaze,' Muller responded. 'But localized. Neighbouring buildings are still intact. We'll come round again in case your pal on the ground wants to talk.'

The B29 had climbed to a more comfortable height clear of the sporadic flak which spattered the sky around them and eventually it turned and levelled out. The admiral had gone back, squeezing past the navigator to join Higgins whose presence on board had been another cause of American resentment. Their own operators could handle any situation, they'd insisted, and they were certainly right. But Higgins was the Section's man. He had long experience of managing contacts with agents in the field besides being a technical wizard capable of coaxing a signal out of the ether with a bent hairpin and a metal foil chocolate bar wrapper.

'Ready with your message, sir?'

He must have finished enciphering Ross's report already. Taking the signal pad from him the admiral scribbled out his own brief note. He could only hope the prime minister was not overruled in Washington. Truman could be formidable.

Confirmation of the germ threat was no real surprise, nor the choice of aerosol dispersal; but Ross's news that

Soviet rockets were now operational would send shock-waves through the corridors. If it were true, of course. His previous report on V2 developments in Russia had been treated with scepticism by the London boffins, he recalled. It was not unknown for an agent's judgement to be distorted by some special bee in his bonnet.

But Washington's decision was inevitable either way, the admiral was convinced. They could no longer afford to take risks. MacArthur's rapid advance through North Korea had been rash and ill-advised. His troops had adhered to the coastal routes, leaving the more difficult inland terrain wide open for Chinese infiltration; now already they were being pushed back southwards. It was only a matter of a day or so before the reds recaptured the North Korean capital Pyongyang. A penumonic plague attack on Seoul, sufficiently concentrated, could decimate the exhausted UN forces along with half the civilian population and leave the south exposed, all gains from the Inchon landings lost.

The president had no choice but to authorize the bomb. All the prime minister could hope for was a brief delay. A pause for thought about the consequences on other fronts of any decision to start an atomic war.

'Say a mass for my soul?' Ross – odd man out as he was – must have understood something of the kind was in the wind. Not Baby Jane, of course; he'd no means of knowing anything about that. But his instincts seemed discomfortingly reliable.

14

Operation Nursery was authorized to go ahead.

The colonel indulged in a terse general announcement to that effect before he distributed their roles, behaving – Al Rossi's *sotto voce* comment – like some movie mogul directing a Hollywood spectacular. Delivery of Baby Jane was allocated to *Elaine* commanded by Major (previously Captain) Robert J. Schroder and *Gorgeous Gussie* was to fly weather scout. The next two B29s he named were ordered to stand by in readiness as understudies 'in the unlikely event that a last-minute substitution should prove necessary – got that?' Only the fifth crew in B29 Task Group T were left to retreat to the mess where they set up a poker school, unsure whether their complex personal feelings represented disappointment or relief.

Schroder ran into his first flak right away at the detailed briefing session.

'Goddam it, thirty-two thousand feet worked OK for Nagasaki!' the colonel's temper burst over him. 'What's gettin' you men, for Pete's sake?'

'If you'd taken a trip over Paikow valley you'd know. Sir.' Schroder tried to reason with him but failed. 'You've handed us a target that's tucked into that mountainside as tight as a chicken's ass-hole. From thirty-two thousand we'll never get it in there.'

'Seven thousand is too low, Major.' He could sense the colonel trying to hold back his wrath at being contradicted. 'You'd not get out in time. You'd be swallowed for breakfast by that radioactive mushroom – that's your plan, is it? Or fried alive.'

'I've reckoned it out, Colonel, and I know we can do it. Jesus, you've asked for a burst-point on impact as close to the cliff as we can place it. OK, so we're miracle workers – but not at thirty-two thousand. At that height we'd most likely miss and hit the town. Or the mountain up by that temple – is that what you want to tell the president? That we started an atomic war in order to wipe out a goddam temple?'

Even while yelling at the colonel he had a hunch this was one fight he was not going to win, but – shit! – what the hell did it matter? Once they began their run towards the aiming point no crap-packed colonel could tell him what to do. He'd be in command then at the controls of his B29 – the *Elaine*, as they all still called her, everyone but him.

'OK, we'll try it your way!' he called out on impulse, cutting the colonel's reply short. 'I'll hold the bitch at thirty-two thousand.'

But with daylight the weather reports from Manchuria north of Antung indicated thick cloud and snowstorms. The chances of an accurate drop were nil and the operation was postponed for twenty-four hours.

Bloody hell, he was still alive.

His mind drifted over cold snow, a speckled blizzard raging before his eyes. He was lying down – yes, he knew that much. Crouched defensively, half on his belly, on stone-hard snow.

Was it snow?

Limbs numbed. He avoided trying to move them, fearing the pain. Stay quite still and nothing will happen. Still . . .

Boots kicking into him, he remembered vividly. Rifle

butts too almost dislocating his shoulder. Was it dislocated? Dislo . . . lo . . . Snow in thick Father Christmas flakes floated around him like feathers, landing wetly on his face, melting on his lips, in his hair.

Another wave of consciousness crept up on him and this time he opened his eyes to blink, surprised, at greyness. No snow any longer; nothing but dull grey rock. His face pressed against it and he tasted dust on his lips. And the tang of blood. He was hurt, how badly he didn't know; the question nagged at him like a grumbling tooth.

Hurt but still bloody alive.

Apologies, Admiral. Blame the bloody Russkies, not me. Tried *my* best.

'Keep him alive!' Colonel Ivanov had ordered, the fat slug. Belly bulging over his belt. Traces of red bortsch in his whiskers. 'They want him alive for questioning. He'll talk all right before they've finished with him. They'll have him spilling it out like a priest with diarrhoea, no stopping him.'

His arms and legs seemed paralysed. He checked cautiously, first moving his fingers, left hand . . . right hand . . . Next, his toes. Left foot . . . right . . . No problems. Thing was to take his time. He tried lying differently, shifting his position to take his weight off his right arm; agonizingly the cramp pains shot through it.

'Hantu?'

His name was no more than breathed but the mere sound brought back an awareness of the objective world around him. He raised his head and immediately a violent aching hit him above the eyes like a hard fist. He dropped back again.

'Hantu?'

He attempted a reply but the noise his throat produced was more like a groan.

'Oh, I thought you were dead!' Even through the whisper her mixed distress and relief was unmistakable.

'Mei-lin?'

Slowly he lifted himself again, fighting down the wave of pain inside his skull. Whether or not he had spoken her name aloud he was uncertain. He was in a narrow cage of heavy mesh fencing around a framework of steel bars; beyond them he could see only more layers of mesh covering other cages. Above was a row of lamps whose intense light cast rhomboid shadow-patterns over everything.

'Can't see you.' He tasted the blood as he spoke; his cut lips smarted.

'Over here. But don't talk so loud. The guard'll be back any second. I swore I'd never met you before.'

'Good of you.' She was right, too; even the obese Colonel Ivanov would smell more than simple espionage when he learned his prisoner could also speak Chinese.

Smell. The rock stank of stale human body waste like some long-established, mature latrine. Hantu struggled to sit up and his cramp-locked muscles and bruises gave him hell. He wore only his long, Russian winter underwear, still clammy with blood and urine; his uniform they had stripped off him right at the start. Here in the cage someone had thrown a couple of layers of coarse sacking over him, perhaps to ensure he did not die of hypothermia before the State Security thugs arrived. Once in their elite hands he'd be better off dead.

'Where are we?' he asked, trying to whisper.

He could see her now, two cells farther along the row; at least they had let her keep her outdoor coat. Gradually he shifted to the side of the cage, moving very cautiously till he could sit leaning back against the bars while he massaged some life back into his arms.

'A kind of prison,' she said. 'There are two more caves

313

like this, only bigger. No one in them. No one here except for us two.' She suddenly tensed, listening; hurriedly she added: 'Guard's coming back.'

Hantu rolled over to lie down again, playing unconscious. The massaging had brought the blood pulsing back, making the pain worse. Blood still oozed too from some of his wounds, though sluggishly. He had bruises all over and the slightest movement was a punishment.

Along the full length of the bare rock walkway between the two rows of cages the guard's boots echoed. When they stopped, he was so close that Hantu could hear the breath wheezing in his nostrils. 'Still out; serve the bastard right.' It was a low muttering, hardly audible. 'Should've finished him off there an' then.' A vodka voice, grumbling at fate for choosing him to guard prisoners when he might be asleep.

As he moved away Hantu risked a quick look at him. Not a man to tackle even if he unlocked the cage and came in alone. He was tall, broad-shouldered, and probably as strong as a kulak's ox when sober. Stay out of reach, that was the only rule with his kind. A real bruiser – a stolid, stupid, obedient Stakhanovite at the craft of beating up prisoners. If the Russians historically understood anything it was how to run prisons. No escapes, and not too many survivors.

'He's gone,' came Mei-lin's whisper.

'Yeah, OK.' He pushed himself upright again and set about massaging the stiffness out of his legs, taking it slowly. 'What about you? Rough you up?'

'Questions, nothing else. I couldn't answer them. I speak no Russian, they speak no Chinese though one tried English. How much English did he expect from a Shanghai bar girl? Hey Johnny, you want jig-jig? Me nice clean girl, you see-no-see?'

'Wonder he didn't rape you. Rape everything in sight

314

when they're roused, those Ivans. Ask the Berlin women. Why the hell did you come here, Mei-lin? Fucked up the whole operation. You realize you'll not be let out alive?'

'Two visits to the Soviet Officers' Club, that's all it took, and they were falling over themselves to bring me here. Chuan said they never allowed Chinese civilians inside the base. I proved I could do it.'

'Bloody stupid.'

She flared up. 'You had your chances with me! Shanghai, the first night here – how d'you think I felt?'

'And that's why?' He didn't believe her. She must be deliberately needling him.

'Chuan agreed. We couldn't be sure you'd get into the base, or that you'd manage to get out again. At least I had a chance of taking a look round and getting out.'

'It wasn't your job. Now we're both in the shit. Chuan agreed, you said?'

'Whether he agreed or not I'd have done it.'

Stubborn bitch, he thought. Stubborn bloody bitch.

'If I hadn't put a stop to it,' he said, 'they'd have been queueing up for you with their pants round their ankles.'

'Would you have cared?' she shot back at him, raw, hurt.

'Yes.'

'In your eyes I'm just Chinese cunt.' She used a graphic Shanghai-ese word not found in the published thoughts of Chairman Mao Tse-tung. 'First Chou-fei, then you, so why not the whole Red Army – that's what you're thinking isn't it? Well?'

'Mei-lin, last night was more than bed-talk.' Oh Jesus, his legs ached viciously as he pulled himself to his feet, wanting to see her more clearly.

'That's all you can find to say?'

'Isn't it enough? Mei-lin?'

'Huh!'

She turned her back on him. A few minutes later, turning up her coat collar, she curled up on the ground to sleep.

The lights stayed switched on, offering no respite, and every half-hour a second guard came through to inspect the prisoners, though what he expected to find it was hard to imagine. Escape from these cages was impossible, and they had confiscated all means of suicide, even his belt containing the silk-printed cipher key. But suicide was no way out for him; as always, he had refused the L-pill Chubby had offered him.

During the next few hours he alternated periods of rest with exercise to keep his muscles from stiffening again. He envied Mei-lin her warm coat. She slept, her back towards him, and so quietly he could not hear her breathe. In that cave every sound, even the slightest whisper, amplified and echoed around the rocks, but she was so still that at times he wondered if she were dead.

At one point, to stir things up, he tried talking to the guard. The man stared blankly back but said nothing. Under orders perhaps; or maybe despite his uniform he was not Russian. Next time he came in Hantu put him to the test with a few choice Russian vulgarisms about his mother but they had no effect. Not even the stare now. No response of any kind. He gave up.

And the long hours dragged on, unending, with only the guard's regular inspections to punctuate them.

He had dozed off into a semi-sleep and didn't hear their approach when they came to fetch Mei-lin. Suddenly they were there when he opened his eyes, three men standing at her cage door, two in Soviet uniforms and one Chinese who told her if she made no trouble they could dispense with handcuffs. Her reply he was not able to catch but she walked past his cage without fetters, throwing him a quick glance, but expressionless.

With the clang of the heavy metal door as they slammed it shut behind them he felt deserted and alone. He would never see her again, he was sure. That throbbing soreness in his bones warned him what was to happen. Another few minutes and they would come for him too. Handcuffs. Leg shackles. And a long, freezing journey by rail across central Asia to a Siberian cell.

No announcements; no publicity. He would simply disappear. Not even death, not at first: not until they had tortured the last fluid ounce of information out of him.

And he would talk of course, in the end. Everyone did. The MGB recognized no heroism. They squashed heroes the way children swatted flies. Crushed them till they broke and the juices ran out.

When the guard returned – a new man this time, fresh-faced as though he had just come on duty – Hantu prepared himself. For a start he'd insist they gave him some clothes. But there was no escort, only the guard himself bringing drinking water and a tight hard ball which turned out to be boiled rice. Maybe laundry starch tasted something like this, he thought as he chewed stolidly before swallowing, but he took only half of it. The grains would swell in his stomach; besides, this must be intended as a twenty-four-hour ration. His gums froze as he sipped the water which was in a small, round cigarette tin whose edges were still sharp where it had been opened. State Express. How the hell had that found its way to Manchuria?

Mei-lin told him very little when she was returned to her cage. The guard brought her ration of rice and water but she didn't touch it. She sat there in a morose silence, staring at the steel bars; eventually when she did speak it was simply to tell him it was daylight outside, and snowing.

That meant the B29 flight would be grounded, probably

still on the tarmac at Okinawa Base, or Iwakuni, or whichever airfield they were using. They wouldn't risk bad weather, not over these mountains.

But what the hell, he had no transceiver anyway. His job was over, wasn't it? All he had to do now was somehow survive, though once they'd got him to Siberia, that British interrogation centre would seem like a Caribbean holiday home.

'The Russians asked the questions,' Mei-lin said abruptly, breaking another long silence. 'The Chinese official translated them, that's all.'

'An interpreter.'

'People's Security. He said inside the base I was on Russian ground and he could do nothing. Because of the Treaty.'

'Treaty ports again.'

'They asked most about you, but what do I know? First time I met you was when you saved me from those Soviet pigs who wanted to rape me. They said you were an imperialist spy here to sabotage the workers' revolution and the class struggle. I told them in that case they should shoot you.'

'Thank you. I'll enjoy that.'

'I want us both to live, Hantu. If we ever get out of here.'

He shrugged. With luck they *might* let her go. They would see her as a local whore who had accidentally strayed into the wrong place, no danger to the state. But his own chances were nil. Not even an exchange through Berlin. He could visualize how the admiral or HOS would react to that suggestion. The Section would be relieved to get rid of him.

He tried some knee-bends. He was as shaky as any rickety old man, but he persisted. From now on this was how it would have to be. Dumb persistence but devoid of hope.

Pride, some would call it.

Time moved slowly. The gaps between the guard's rounds stretched out like worn elastic. They made an effort to talk, he and Mei-lin, whenever they were alone, but for long periods they fell silent and were strangers to each other.

The lights never went out. Sleep, when it came, was only intermittent. But it must have been during one of these short snatches of sleep that he was disturbed by the sound of the metal door opening again. Still in a semi-stupor, he heard muffled footsteps, two men at least, treading furtively, coming for him. He stood up to receive them, unasked.

Then he recognized Siew. He was approaching cat-like between the cages with rags tied round his heavy boots to dull the sound. Loosely in one hand he carried a sub-machine gun: drum magazine, wooden stock. Possibly a Soviet PPSh.

Hantu stood motionless until Siew spotted him. Not a smile though. Only a quick stare of suspicion before he turned to signal to Chuan who was working his way along the other cages.

So what was intended? Rescue? Elimination once they had heard what he had to say? Siew had been hostile from the start and Chuan . . . well, Chuan had changed. Both were armed with the same type of PPSh – a reliable, workaday gun which had slaughtered more of Hitler's infantry on the Eastern Front than any other weapon. One burst through the mesh was all they would need. Who would know they'd ever been involved? The dead have sealed lips.

'Not pleased to see us, Hantu?' Chuan grinned at him,

fiddling with a bunch of keys. 'We heard they'd kept you alive. But you look a bloody mess. And you stink.'

'I stink. Too bloody right I stink! How the hell did you get in here?' His head cleared.

'Through the back door.' It was no explanation at all. 'One more notch on the tree, this one. How often have I saved your life now?'

'OK, I owe you. Now get this lock open and let's move. Job's done. I pray to God your bosses are satisfied when I tell them.'

'God has been abolished in the Chinese People's Republic.' At last Chuan found the right key and the gate swung open. 'All superstitions and fairy tales. What have you found out?'

Hantu wrapped the sacking round himself for warmth as he summarized the main points. It was too much to hope that Chuan would show any surprise, still less appreciation, even at the mention of rockets. Hadn't China invented them?

'If Seoul's attacked there'll be hell to pay,' he concluded.

'Could prevent it.'

'How? With two sub-machine guns, one walking wounded, and Mei-lin?'

'Plastic. Time fuses. Quality stuff left behind by the Yanks. I'll show you.'

While they were talking Siew had released Mei-lin and Chuan gave her a friendly pat on the shoulder, perhaps a gesture of secret understanding between them. Had she been expecting him all along?

Without boots, still in his filthy underwear but with the sacking round him, Hantu loped along behind them as they made for the metal door. Siew went through first while Chuan gave him cover. Seconds later he returned to beckon them on. In the next cave a section had been partitioned off as a guard room.

'If you want clothes,' Chuan said, 'help yourself.'

The two guards inside were both dead, their necks broken, each with a thin red necklace-cut which was Chuan's trade mark. Piano wire had always been his preferred method. The man on the bed was the tall bruiser who had been their first attendant. With distaste Hantu began to strip off his uniform – the other guard's clothes being too small – and clumsily put it on. It hung loosely, though the boots fitted well enough.

Chuan, watching him, asked: 'You up to going on?'

'I'll manage.' He winced as he bent down to pick up the dead man's belt. Every move hurt like hell.

'You could stay with the gear. We'll collect you later.'

'Fuck you! I said, walking wounded, not dead. Plastic's my trade. Leave it to you, you'd blow yourself up.'

The guard's holster contained a Makarov pistol. He checked the magazine. Eight rounds. Before leaving he took the other dead guard's Makarov too, dropping it into his pocket.

This cave was larger than the one where he and Mei-lin had been kept, but it too was filled with rows of unoccupied cages like a vast deserted menagerie – though for people, not animals.

'Japs built them.' Chuan's tone was hard and angry. 'For their human guinea pigs. Chinese. Though some others too – Koreans, Burmese, British and American POWs. In their eyes any non-Jap was sub-human, no better than dogs or pigs.'

'You've been here before,' Hantu said.

'No.' The denial was firm. 'Why else d'you think we needed you?'

He was lying. Had to be, Hantu was convinced. Which was why he had shown no surprise at the old monk's account of a route down inside the mountain, his 'back door'. But then why these elaborate arrangements to get one of the Section's agents involved?

A broad aisle between the rows of cages led to an opening wide enough to drive a truck through. 'Another guard room that way,' Chuan informed them, keeping his voice low. 'We go over to the left.'

Seconds later they had entered a narrow fissure in the rear wall which opened into a small, disused laboratory. Four waist-high rock tables, each large enough to take a human body, stood side by side; their drainage runnels fed a channel in the rock floor. Beyond them, several sets of shelves bore the carefully classified remains of those who had died: dozens of skulls, tibia, femurs, vertebrae, many distorted by disease, all labelled in Japanese script. And jars of internal organs, equally grotesque. The sight of them fed Hantu's own anger. Mei-lin grasped his arm, her fingers tightening.

Behind the shelves was the office area. The young monk who had first helped them at the monastery sat cross-legged on the desk in deep contemplation which he ended as they arrived.

'Our guide,' Chuan explained. 'He'll lead us back when we're ready. We lent him the PLA uniform to make the climbing easier for him.'

It was a gloomy corner, the electric fittings in this area of the cave were all torn out, but Chuan lit a small oil lamp which gave at least some light. From behind the desk he then produced two rucksacks, US Army issue; opening one, he took out some American chocolate bars.

'Best eat. We'll need the energy.' He gave them one each and put one down beside the monk. 'There's a water bottle, and more in those taps. It's one reason we decided on this place as our base, the water. No one comes here.'

'I'm not surprised,' said Mei-lin.

'Old bones hurt nobody, comrade.' It was a sharp rebuke, the New China stamping down on things that go bump in the night. 'Nor ghosts either. What you see is hard evidence of imperialism at work, don't forget it, comrade. Victims of Jap experiments.'

'Where's the plastic?' Hantu bit into the chocolate but immediately regretted it; the taste only reminded him how hungry he really was. 'Let's check it over first.'

On the desk Chuan laid out the contents of the two rucksacks. Mainly 500-gramme slabs of the stuff, though some were half that weight and there were a few small sticks. In the light of the oil lamp it looked like dirty yellow plasticine. Various time fuses, colour-coded, and a couple of small, round detonator dispensers. No incendiaries.

'We hit the rockets if we can get to them,' Hantu decided. 'If we can't we're in trouble. Anything else we destroy we only cause minimum damage. Rockets – well, every one is a potential bomb. A good charge of this stuff up their backsides to set them off, it's what we need. The question is how to get close enough.'

Taking another bar of chocolate, he carefully removed the paper wrapper and smoothed it out. On the blank side he sketched a diagram of the rocket workshop's layout.

'With the amount of fuel they have crammed inside them there's likely to be one almighty explosion. I reckon it could bring the cave roof down. Bury the lot.'

'How many working in there?' Chuan asked.

'Hard to say. Only the launch team once the rockets are ready to go, but we don't know when the attack's planned for. They'll need clear weather.'

They had done this so often before, he and Chuan, methodically checking every known detail, discussing each stage of the operation, aware that one mistake, one bit of bad luck, and their short stay on earth was over. Terminated. Yes, sabotage might be the only trade he had ever been taught, but he felt no confidence. It was suicidal this time. Too much guesswork. Inadequate reconnaissance. Not even the element of surprise once their escape from the cages was discovered.

One factor only was on their side: plague suits. Patiently he expounded their importance. Once past the guards, they were the priority.

Borrowing Siew's knife he sliced up two slabs of plastic explosive into narrow strips. Mei-lin looked on apprehensively. She moved the oil lamp farther away, but even if the stuff caught fire it would only burn, not explode. That was the joy of it. While he worked Chuan repacked the rucksacks, adding the yellow strips as they were ready. Chuan also pocketed one of the detonator containers, giving him the other; sixteen detonators in each. The pencil-thin time fuses they also divided between them.

It was Chuan and Siew who carried the rucksacks, staying out of sight between the cages until they were only feet away from the broad opening in the rocks which led to the guard room. There they slipped them off, leaving Mei-lin with the spare Makarov to keep an eye on them while they investigated.

Once inside the passage Siew went first, sticking close to the jagged rock wall. Chuan followed, with Hantu himself bringing up the rear. Despite the muffling cloth bound round their boots, every footstep seemed to reverberate throughout the entire cave. Ahead he could hear men's voices, Russians, but they noticed nothing to arouse their suspicions.

Two men, Siew signalled back from the door which stood open. Chuan took his place, handing his PPSh back to Hantu once he had checked out the situation. From a pocket he produced his coiled piano wire.

A brief nod, and Chuan went in. Quickly. Silently. The wire was already tightening round the first man's throat before either guard realized they were being attacked. By then the second one, Siew's pigeon, was starting to emit a dove-like rattle from the area of his tonsils. As his neck broke, his head lolled back inelegantly like an old rag doll's.

The scraping of heavy, nailed boots on the rock plus a tuneless, relaxed whistling warned Hantu of a third guard's presence. A door opened. Briefly he glimpsed a young, guileless Russian face before he brought him down with his gun-butt. It was Siew who cut the lad's throat, and he felt sick at the sight of it. Little more than a boy, that guard; some poor peasant babushka's favourite grandson.

Through the door he found a crude washroom, simply a cell carved out of the rock; the kid had been out to relieve himself, no more than that.

The guard room had two other doors which they checked. One led outside into the snow: it was a clear, moonless night, crisply cold. But the second took them into a store room, part cave, part concrete-walled, crammed with ammunition boxes, cases of medical gear, respirators, protective clothing, everything. On a row of hooks hung several white plague suits like so many sloughed-off skins: more were stacked, folded, on the shelves.

'Get Mei-lin and the rucksacks,' he instructed.

Without a word Siew went off to fetch her while he and Chuan checked the passage on the far side of the store room. A short way along it they came to the familiar overlapping rubber curtains of an air-lock, though this was not the entrance he had used with Captain Kim, he was sure of that.

Once Mei-lin had arrived, they chose fresh plague suits

325

from the stacks and tugged them on over their other clothes, adding gun belts stripped off the dead guards. Dressed like that, and with respirators, the three Chinese could easily pass for Koreans. The rucksacks were the next problem until Mei-lin suggested transferring the plastic into a couple of empty ammunition boxes which they then loaded on to a low, flat barrow they found in the store room. No lids – they would only get in the way – but on top of them he dumped a toolbag, thinking that no one ever challenged a maintenance crew.

'Right – respirators,' he said.

But then his eye fell on three bomblet canisters standing upright on a shelf near the door. Cautiously he picked one up, but then laughed and showed it to Mei-lin and Chuan. The guards had kept their stock of tea in it. He examined the other two; they were empty. Ready-made, he thought. Tipping out the tea, he stuffed each one with plastic explosive and then concealed them in the toolbag.

'OK, now listen.' He looked directly at Siew; if any of them caused trouble it would come from that quarter, he was convinced. 'We're going to walk through the workshop – wearing respirators, so no one will recognize us – and we're going to take our time, as if we work there. So don't stare around, don't show any curiosity. They'll spot us because this barrow squeaks, but we go straight on. Any challenge, let me handle it.'

'Hantu, just get us out alive,' said Chuan with one of his old grins. 'More I do not ask.'

Hantu hoped he had sounded more optimistic than he felt. They were going out into the unknown; improvising recklessly; taking risks every instructor would condemn out of hand. With luck they might achieve some damage before they were spotted, but already he had been more lucky than he deserved. This was his ninth life, and he was using it up fast.

With their respirators on and the draw-string around the hoods correctly tightened, they were at least well-disguised, that was something. Their sub-machine guns – four of them now – lay on the ammunition boxes partly hidden by the toolbag. Easily grabbed if necessary, though it would be suicidal.

He went ahead through the rubber curtains into the culture tank hall, then stood aside while the others followed with the barrow. Only two men working at the tanks, he saw; but they ignored him. 'Wear your respirator,' the wall posters screamed in Russian and Korean.

With Chuan beside him he strode purposefully, though not too fast, towards the passage leading into the second hall. The barrow, propelled by Mei-lin and Siew, produced a rhythmic and irritating *squeak-squeak-squeak-squeak* which should make it impossible for anyone to suspect they were saboteurs. Though he prayed to whatever God was still acknowledged in this outpost of the growing Communist empire that he was right.

They reached the second hall. Again only two men were visible, apparently servicing one of the hand-operated presses. Production work had stopped, all canisters filled, all warheads charged . . .

He went on, fearing they were too late and they would find the rockets gone. At the thought, his savage twinges of pain became more persistent, refusing to let him ignore them.

But the missiles were still there, bedded sleekly on their railway wagons, unattended. Six of them only, ready for use. Beyond them the massive gates stood open to reveal a floodlit area of hard snow scored with twin railway tracks which diverged to serve the two pyramids, now split open like segments of an orange. At first glance he did not understand what he was seeing; only after a moment or two did it become clear to him. The pyramids had been constructed in wheeled sections and could be pulled apart; the tractors were clearly visible under the harsh lighting. Housed inside each – possibly for protection from the weather – was a tall rocket-launching derrick.

Around one a cluster of twelve or more men were engaged in raising a rocket till it stood upright on its carrier-wagon. Another was already in place at the second derrick. Clearly if the attack was to be prevented, they had very little time.

Their barrow's constant squeaking grated on his nerves as he led his small sabotage team to the first row of rockets in the vast hall. No one was there to stop them, though he did notice some men busy at the far end in the shunting area.

They worked swiftly, he and Chuan, the 'old team' – packing plastic explosive into the nozzles in the tails of alternate rockets, ramming the stuff home while Mei-lin kept them supplied and Siew stood guard. Still no one came near to check on them.

Hantu himself inserted the thirty-minute time fuses, jerking out the tagged pin before plunging the pencil-like device deeply into the plastic. Whether he was right about the big bang he couldn't be sure, but at least these rockets would never fly. Four of the six he treated in this way. Then he stopped, standing in the shadows between two rockets, and gazed out at the two launch derricks. Commonsense said leave them, don't push your luck, lad.

But he couldn't leave them.

Mei-lin, beside him, touched his arm and briefly pulled the respirator away from her face. 'Isn't that the long railway shed we saw from the temple?'

He understood what she meant. Its track led directly into the shunting area at the back of the cave. If they followed it out they would emerge in the shadows just

328

beyond the left-hand derrick. But he would need covering fire from the cave in case they were spotted. Experienced marksmen. Chuan and Siew, one either side of the cave entrance. It might just work.

'You and me?' he suggested to Mei-lin. 'Crawl across the snow. One bomb under each wagon, then back. Ten minutes.'

'Five minutes,' she corrected him. Crisp and business-like, just the way he remembered her from Singapore. That pleased him.

Rapidly he explained the plan to Chuan and Siew while Mei-lin emptied the toolbag of everything except the three bomb canisters. He was replacing his respirator when he noticed Captain Kim on the other side of the cave near the offices and they wasted several minutes pretending to be absorbed in their work until he had wandered away again. Hantu felt relieved that they had not been forced to kill him. He had liked the man despite his precise, well-trained manner; in a civilian world he might have become a dentist.

'OK,' he nodded to Mei-lin. 'If you're ready.'

The men in the shunting section did not even glance at them as they entered the branch line tunnel which for most of its length was dimly lit by well-spaced-out lamps. Only for the last hundred yards or so were they plunged into darkness and had to place each foot carefully until they arrived in the open air.

'Stay back in the shadows,' he warned, pulling Mei-lin down. Against the snow their plague suits made them practically invisible.

The floodlighting began some three yards away. It was intensely white, almost a Christmas card scene save for the two missiles at their launch derricks, pointing sky-wards. Their launch pads were the same railway wagons on which they had been delivered and spaced out around them, offering useful cover, were the mobile pyramid segments and their tractors.

Hantu unscrewed the three canister bombs to insert ten-minute fuses; anything shorter and they risked blowing themselves up. He gave one to Mei-lin and returned the other two to the toolbag.

'We'll make our way round the edge of the light till we're directly behind the wagons,' he explained. 'Then it's a belly crawl towards them – one each, you take this side. Go underneath between the wheels, then work along the full length and leave your bomb exactly under the rocket. OK?'

'Understand. Same way back.'

'Same way back,' he confirmed. 'God willing.'

He could see the technicians were still busy around the right-hand derrick which he had reserved for himself. That was going to be the tricky one, but neither was easy. In case it all went wrong he had his PPSh, carrying it slung over one shoulder; Mei-lin had refused to bring one, saying it would only hamper her, but she seemed confident enough with a pistol.

'Then let's do it,' he said.

Sticking to the shadows meant walking, crouched, where the snow was thickest. It took longer than he had anticipated to get into position behind the wagons. With the technicians, he now saw, were several armed guards, though all their attention was on some difficulty with the rocket.

'Good luck, love!' he whispered as they lay side by side in the snow, ready to go.

It was the old army crawl which he had first encountered in the freezing mud of North Wales with a berserk training sergeant yelling at them to keep their arses down. The snow, colder, almost packed ice in some places, was at least clean. A sudden shout from the men warned him that their difficulty, whatever it might have been, had been overcome. Now was the danger point when they might start looking around.

He glanced over towards Mei-lin and was relieved to see she had already reached the wagon. Slowly her legs disappeared underneath it. But he still had several yards to cover with the toolbag clutched in one hand and the PPSh on his shoulder getting in the way. His bruises and pains were objecting rawly to this new mode of locomotion; if there were any justice he should be in hospital.

At last, under the wagon, he paused briefly to recover his breath. From the slight movement in the shadows beneath Mei-lin's wagon he noticed she had almost reached the rocket which was mounted immediately above the end bogey. He unslung the PPSh and began to edge his way forward over the sleepers.

Then he froze. Voices. Two pairs of legs. The bastards were standing within a couple of feet of him. He had no watch, no means of knowing how many minutes he had left before the two bombs in the toolbag exploded. Four perhaps? Three?

He shifted his position, trying to check how far Mei-lin had got, but his gun's barrel clinked against one of the metal wheels. The sound was sharp on the cold air.

His reaction was instinctive. Kicking hard against the sleeper, he propelled himself forward till he was clear of the wheel, then rolled across the rail on the opposite side from the two men. Had they heard him?

He pressed flat against the snow, saw the legs move, and then a head peered beneath the wagon. The man must have been blind not to notice him despite the white plague suit, but the head disappeared again and Hantu began to crawl away still in the direction of the rocket, this time alongside the wagon, exposed.

'I'd swear someone was there,' a Russian voice grumbled. 'Better go round and take another look. You stay this side.'

Another couple of yards and he'd be close enough to the end bogey to place the bombs, then his only problem would be how to get away. His ninth life, he reminded himself again.

From behind him came the crack of a pistol and the sound reverberated off the cliff face.

Mei-lin!

He dropped the toolbag and swung round in time to see her fire again, holding the pistol two-handed, crouching. From the top of the wagon a Russian dropped dead into the snow, his rifle thrown a couple of feet beyond his reach.

Then from around the far end the second man appeared running towards him and shouting an order. Hantu brought him down with a quick burst from the sub-machine gun.

'Get back!' he bawled at Mei-lin. Christ, this was it!

Quickly stooping, he grabbed the toolbag and shoved it directly beneath the rocket itself before dashing across the snow towards her, scrambling under her wagon and out on the other side where he hesitated, uncertain whether they could risk attempting to cross the wide stretch of brightly illuminated snow ahead of them. It was suicide, yet –

From the confusion of shouted orders, he gathered that none of the guards or technicians had yet understood what had happened. Then he heard Chuan open fire from the direction of the caves – that should really send their heads spinning, he thought. It offered a chance.

'Run!' he whispered urgently. 'Over to the railway shed!'

They sprinted as fast as the snow would permit and

were within feet of the entrance when – prompted by some sixth sense – he grabbed her, pulling her down to the ground. The shock wave from the first explosion passed over them like a gust of wind. They heard the crash as one rocket fell, and then a second, double explosion followed by a sudden shattering roar whipping up a gale of oven-hot air whirling around them.

No more shouts, only the fierce rasping of prolonged burning; and a male voice screaming in agony; and the crackling as timber caught fire.

Ahead, he saw how the long shed wall had parted from the sagging roof and leaned outwards ready to collapse. Had they reached it before the bombs went off they might not have survived.

By his side Mei-lin raised her head. The blast had ripped the white hood away from her head, leaving only torn strips. 'I'm still alive,' she said wonderingly.

'Must move, love. We've not much time.'

He helped her to her feet and started half-running, half-stumbling back to the cave, keeping to the borders of the floodlighting, though staying clear of the damaged wall. They had to get through the rocket hall and back to where they had left the young monk before those half-hour time fuses triggered off the plastic in the remaining missiles. His own fault, Hantu knew; his timing was too tight. Would he get Mei-lin through at all, he wondered, or would it all end with her as dead as Yen-hua?

'Not lost your touch, Hantu!' Chuan greeted him, coming out of the shadows, his sub-machine gun held ready to use.

He glanced back. The right-hand rocket, on its side, was burning with an intense ball of flame. With that heat the other, lying tipped over towards it, might explode any second.

'We must get out of here!' he yelled. He seized Mei-lin by the arm to hurry her on. 'Where the hell's Siew?'

But there was no time for an answer. In the rocket hall four guards appeared from the direction of the office where he had drunk vodka with Captain Kim. Before they could fire, Siew had stepped out from between the wagons and eliminated them with three bursts from his PPSh. He enjoyed killing, that was only too obvious from his smile.

More guards followed, another five or six at least, blocking the way through to the next hall. Mongolians, thought Hantu as he squeezed the trigger, taking two of them out. Not even their own war, poor sods.

Siew and Chuan dealt with the rest and their shots reverberated through the high cave like hammer blows.

The second hall where the bomblets had been filled was now completely deserted. In less than a minute they were through it and into the hall with the culture tanks. Two workers in plague suits and respirators were standing together nervously; slowly they retreated as Hantu led the way through.

'No!' he ordered sharply, sensing that Siew was about to shoot them. 'Let them live, for Chrissake!'

He remembered his own respirator, hanging by its straps around his neck, but it was damaged and so too was Mei-lin's. But he couldn't leave those tanks intact. Ordering the others out first through the overlapping rubber curtains, he spattered the tanks with bullets, punching holes in them through which the fluid began to drain out before making his own escape.

The young monk was waiting for them with the miners' lamps already lit. At the rear of the charnel house was a steel grille set in the rock, doctored to swing open once the catch was pulled back; the monastery must have known about this secret route into the base during the Jap occupation when locally rounded-up slave labour had been used to fit out these caves.

Once through, they secured the grille again behind them. They were in a rock passage but left it after only two or three yards when the monk indicated they were to climb up a fall of boulders to their right. This took them to an apparently blank wall which turned out to be a thin curtain of rock, like a hanging shawl, with a slit-opening to one side just wide enough to squeeze through.

It led into a chamber hung with stalactites, full of shadows and whispers. As Hantu raised his lamp to see better, the whole mountain came alive with the sound of rushing air punctuated by deep-throated echoing roars as though a long-dormant volcano were rousing itself to activity. The big bang had happened and the air swirled with dust.

'That's the end of the rockets,' he coughed, choking.

'The way you planned.' Mei-lin's voice was dry and factual.

'Planned, yes. I wasn't sure it would work. Listen to that!'

The mountain seemed to shake with the force of the next explosion and Hantu began to laugh to himself. He'd done it! He laughed loud and long, every muscle aching, his whole body protesting, dried-up wounds re-opening and oozing blood.

Then he became aware of Siew staring at him, bewildered, not understanding a damned thing.

15

The skies were clear as B29 *Gorgeous Gussie* crossed the coast alone heading for Paikow. Virgin snow sparkled white on the swathe of flat land bordering the sea. From the bombardier's seat in the aircraft's nose the admiral identified the airfield he had spotted on their previous sortie two days earlier.

'Some activity down there,' he told Lieutenant-Colonel Muller briefly on his intercom. 'Looks like they're clearing the runway ready for take-off. What d'you reckon those planes are? MiGs?'

On the ground they resembled tiny Dinky toys.

'Mebbe.' The reply crackled laconically in his ears. 'No bother from them last time. Guess so long as we don't drop eggs on the Yalu bridges we're OK.'

But already the B29 was over the mountains, still flying inland. It was a white Christmas card landscape that he saw below him, the smooth snow broken here and there by outcrops of dark rock, patches of forest or isolated villages tucked into the valleys. The patterns changed constantly, seemingly endless, till after some twenty minutes he noticed a long white smudge of dark smoke against the sky ahead.

Muller beat him to it. 'Guess some other bright-ass got in first,' came his metallic drawl through the headphones. 'Must be where we're heading.'

The co-pilot's voice broke in. 'Sure is. Bull's eye.'

Ross's handiwork, thought the admiral smugly. He should have known he could trust the man. They could pack up and go home. Party was over.

He made his way back to join Higgins who was already set up to transmit the identification code, his hand poised over the morse key as if about to caress it. The likelihood of Ross being alive still was remote. A good man too. Pity to lose him. Higgins glanced up, seeming to read his mind.

'All set, Sparks?'

'All set, sir.'

'Approaching target area,' Muller announced.

S-D TO N-T, Higgins tapped out in his neat, rapid morse, repeating the call three times before flicking the switch to 'Receive'.

'Say a mass for my soul', the admiral recalled his last message. It must have been a suicidal plan he'd worked out; Ross must have known then he could not survive. They had a fanatical degree of loyalty, these agents, verging on insanity. It *was* insanity by any normal standards. Quite different from a naval engagement, even one against hopeless odds, the quick stab in the dark as against Queensberry Rules.

'Acknowledging, sir,' Higgins reported.

'He's still alive! My God!' The admiral had been so certain that Ross was dead, his feelings now were confused. If he had not seen that billowing column of smoke with his own eyes he'd have been convinced the man was betraying them.

'Plain language, sir,' Higgins commented mildly. 'His grouping's a bit ragged.'

The admiral watched the signal pad as the radio operator wrote out the message letter by letter in precise capitals: HORNETS' NEST FLUSHED OUT STOP GUY FAWKES ATTACK WILL NOT REPEAT NOT PROCEED STOP ALL FIREWORKS EXTINGUISHED STOP AM DUE SICK LEAVE ENDS.

'Your man OK?' the headphones enquired.

'Wounded, but it seems he's done our job for us. If he's right Baby Jane won't be needed. Let's take a closer look.'

'OK, fellas, you heard what the sailor said. Bargain basement.'

He'd have been happier crash-diving inside a leaky submarine. The plane lurched, side-slipping to port, its engines roaring in protest, the bulkhead groaning. He grabbed the nearest strut to hold himself steady inside that claustrophobic container which Muller was throwing about like a maniac. It seemed as if a week passed before at last they straightened out, still losing height, and he was able to return with difficulty to his perch in the nose. The sight of the snow-bedecked ground through the plexiglass was like a return to harbour after that.

How low Muller brought the B29 he did not ask, for it was none of his business, but grey puffs of flak began to appear in the air around them and he heard a rattling like hailstones against the fuselage after one unusually close burst.

'Shrapnel, Captain.' He didn't recognize whose voice it was on the intercom.

'Damage?'

'No sign of any. All systems functioning normally.'

'Oxygen masks, fellas. Engineer to lower pressure.'

Muller held his course over Paikow township and straight up the main valley, giving the admiral a pigeon-eye view of the devastated research centre. The outer perimeter wall still stood and the buildings closest to it were apparently intact, though several others were on fire; but the main casualty resulting from Ross's work was the cliff face itself which had disintegrated into an avalanche of giant boulders, burying all the structures that had been built up against it and apparently sealing off the cave mouths. As for the twin pyramids it was difficult to judge their fate; no sign remained of where they had been.

'That completes the tour, fellas,' Muller's voice rasped in his ear. 'Now let's get the hell outa here.'

B29 *Gorgeous Gussie* began its long, agonizingly slow climb back to the comparative safety of 30,000 feet though every man on board was aware that the new MiG-15 hunters could follow them up to that altitude without difficulty. The cosy milk runs were over. Flak had been much heavier with many more guns involved; firing was now in earnest. As they neared the coast they could expect MiGs.

Meanwhile, the admiral knew that B29 *Elaine* would already be airborne, cradling Baby Jane in its bomb bay. One signal would be sufficient to turn them back, but that signal he was not permitted to send. General Corby, USAF, had explained the reason over lunch in Okinawa while attacking a blood-red porterhouse steak: it would constitute an order. The British were valued allies fighting alongside true-blooded Americans under the United Nations flag, but no US personnel could come under the command of a non-American. Besides, only the President of the United States of America was empowered to authorize use of the atomic bomb; only the president could countermand his own order.

In one hour at the most the world's first atomic war would either start or be narrowly avoided.

His first signal, twin-stage enciphered, was transmitted by Higgins the moment he established contact with Okinawa where it would be immediately relayed to the British Embassy, Washington, for prime minister's eyes only. It read simply: FERRET SUCCESSFUL VERMIN DESTROYED CRADLESONG UNNECESSARY

STOP SEA DOG. And to General Corby, USAF, Okinawa, he sent a four-word message using a simple code previously arranged between them: PAUSE FOR THOUGHT ADVISABLE. He could now only pray his advice would be accepted.

He was for'ard in the plexiglass nose when the first MiG-15s appeared to starboard and the B29's guns opened fire midships. It was to avoid this situation that he had originally been refused permission to overfly hostile territory. For a director of intelligence services the risks of being shot down and captured were too great, so the arguments ran. Stubbornly he had overruled them. He distrusted all backroom decisions including his own; he had to see for himself. Slipping his hand into his breast pocket he located the lethal pill, just in case.

'Admiral, git your ass outa this glass house, will ya?' he heard Muller drawl. 'Git through the tunnel to the rear compartment an' use your portable oxygen cylinder the way you were shown, OK? Not that I give a monkey's, but my orders say to bring you back alive.'

'You're in command, Colonel,' the admiral responded.

Why every room in Washington had to be heated to hothouse temperatures the prime minister could not understand. The White House was no exception. He passed his finger under his collar and wished someone would open a window.

Across the table the president took off his glasses and went through the motions of cleaning them while he thought through the implications of the signal on the blotter before him: FERRET SUCESSFUL VERMIN DESTROYED CRADLESONG UNNECESSARY STOP SEA DOG. It was clear enough. Unambiguous. Twenty-four hours earlier he'd not have hesitated to call off the attack, the prime minister thought.

But twenty-four hours is a long time. Long enough to add a new dimension to the arguments favouring the use of an A-bomb against Paikow. Then it had been a technical matter; an act of surgery to remove a defined threat. Now . . .?

The prime minister was uncertain what to expect.

His Washington trip had not been a success. The Americans had listened politely to his analysis, just as he had listened to theirs, but the gap remained. His suggestion, based on the best advice from knowledgeable experts, that a Tito element in China existed and that one day China might wish to tread its own path free from Moscow's shackles – well, to put it mildly, he was disbelieved. The advantages of trying to end the war by negotiation and the admission of Communist China to the United Nations were dismissed out of hand. Though in a friendly manner, he had to admit that. Despite the room temperatures there had never been anything heated about their discussions.

'We cannot negotiate from our present position of weakness,' the president had repeated more than once. 'If we get out of Korea someone will have to force us out, and we didn't get into this fight with the idea of getting licked.'

Their top brass were jittery, obsessed with the idea of defeat since China's intervention with twenty-six divisions already committed. General MacArthur, in the words of Secretary of State Dean Acheson, was in a 'blue funk' at how the situation had reversed almost over night. He was advising that the United States had only one choice: either atomic weapons or total withdrawal. Such an atmosphere did not make for sound political thinking; and nor did panics of the kind they had experienced the previous day when the president interrupted their meeting following the Pentagon's report of large formations of unidentified planes encroaching on US air space from the north. A mistake, it turned out later. Freak effects on radar screens caused by the weather in the Arctic Circle.

He cleared his throat, glancing at the wall-clock. The seconds ticked away and the president had still not pronounced. Somewhere over the Yellow Sea, perhaps by now crossing the cost of Manchuria, a United States Air Force B29 Superfortress was air-lifting the first A-bomb of World War Three to its target.

'Vermin destroyed', the admiral's signal assured them, and he knew the president had received a similar report from the weather scout's pilot. But what about this new military argument that an A-bomb on Paikow – a limited strike – would demonstrate US might sufficiently to halt the reds in their tracks? The prime minister's respect for the president had grown during this visit despite their disagreements; in politics he was as skilled a poker player as with cards. It was just possible he might take the risk.

'This British Sea Dog – you trust his judgement?' The president broke his long silence. 'One hundred per cent?'

'He's a very experienced man. Our best.'

'That right? I'll admit I'd feel more confident if our own US intelligence agencies could back up this information.'

The prime minister gave a vague smile but said nothing.

'If the slightest danger of a rocket attack on our boys still exists, whether germs or anything else . . .' The president stopped abruptly and banged the table with the flat of his hand. 'Hell, I've examined the evidence, listened to the arguments, taken advice, and now a decision must be made – with a fifty-fifty chance I'm gonna be wrong. OK, that's the job. Call the plane back. Abort the operation – and pray to God I'm right.'

With luck, Chuan thought, a Soviet radio operator would pick up Hantu's transmission and report it. That would be the finishing touch par excellence, the dealer's seal authenticating the forged scroll. Not even General Tai-li could have trumped that card, devious though he had been. Leaning over the Englishman's shoulder he switched off the suitcase transceiver. The man trembled like an autumn leaf in the wind. Where his arm had rested a spot of dark red blood the size of a silver dollar stained the table-top.

'Hantu, Comrade Siew will take care of you while I arrange transport. You're to stay inside – got that? Don't attempt anything on your own. They'll be watching every road.'

'Sleep, that's all I need.' The Englishman got to his feet, obviously in pain, weaving about like a drunk. 'Mean well, Chuan. Know that. Not've made it without you, an' all that. But Christ I need sleep.'

'You need a doctor. Siew will dress those wounds and give you something against infection. You can trust him, he had paramedic training before he joined the army.' He beckoned to Mei-lin. She looked no less exhausted but she could rest later. 'Comrade, a word outside. Put on your coat.'

Before going down through the caves he had arranged for all their things to be transferred to this woodcutter's stone hut, long unused, to avoid any suspicion being levelled at the Taoist monks for helping them. That temple was too handy as an intelligence base to risk it being closed down, at least while Ivan stayed in the area. But they couldn't stay hidden in the hut too long, not with their tracks in the snow leading directly to it.

'Comrade Fang, so far you have done very well,' he said, taking her by the arm and conducting her a little distance away among the trees. 'Now we reach stage two of our operation. By now our Soviet allies will have requested help from our own military commanders in tracking down the saboteurs, as they will call us. In particular they will want Hantu. Such requests cannot be refused, not between allies. Getting Hantu safely out of Manchuria will be that much more difficult.'

'He is not well.'

'Siew will make sure he recovers but we can't wait that long. We have to move today.' He stopped, wondering how far he could take her into his confidence. Perhaps even in so short a time she had become just as emotionally entangled with Hantu as previously with Ong Chou-fei. He made up his mind. 'Sick or not, we shall have to handcuff him. If we are stopped on the road it must appear that he is a prisoner being taken to Peking for trial. I rely on you to persuade him not to make difficulties.'

'The handcuffs will be locked?'

'Of course. You will have to help look after him. Feed him and so on. This is the safest way, comrade.'

'If he objects?'

'It will be more comfortable for him to collaborate.'

'Very well.' Her callous tone surprised him. 'What happens when we get to Peking? What do I tell him?'

'One step at a time, comrade. Certain arrangements have been requested.'

He accompanied her back to the stone hut, their feet sinking deeply into the snow as they walked. The sky was clear, a pale blue, offering no chance of fresh falls to obliterate their tracks.

Pausing at the doorway, she said: 'He did sabotage the germ warfare attack, we owe him something for that. Without him we might not have succeeded.'

'It will not be forgotten, comrade. Hantu is very valuable to us.' But as Chuan watched her entering the hut, he feared she might possibly have understood more than he intended.

* * *

Major Robert J. Schroder cursed at the sudden appearance of two MiG-15s dropping down on him out of the sun. These B29s were not built for aerobatics, but nevertheless he instinctively threw the *Elaine* into a side-slip to starboard and yelled out a warning to the crew. He heard his control gunner open fire, all turrets, then the obscenities as the streams of lead went wide.

'Christ, did you have to do that?' his bombardier's grumble carried over the intercom. 'Coulda woken up Baby, then we'd all be sitting on a cloud harping.'

The MiG-15s streaked away across the sky with three USAF F80s in pursuit. 'Better late than not at all, I guess,' Schroder commented to his replacement co-pilot Vince Kramer. He levelled out at 25,000 feet and settled back on course.

'F80s are too slow for those MiGs,' Kramer said. 'We collected a scratch – hear it?'

'Anyone else think we were hit? Damage report?'

No response came from the rest of the crew so Kramer shrugged and admitted he could be mistaken. 'Coulda been something falling inboard. Who knows what it was?'

Schroder nodded. He had not usually been lucky with his co-pilots. Over Germany he had lost more co-pilots than tail gunners, which was against all the odds, so it hadn't really surprised him when his regular man had been rushed off for an emergency appendectomy. But he felt confident with Kramer. The guy had a sense of humour; with Baby Jane on board that was reassuring.

'Guess those MiGs were off course,' Kramer was saying. 'Why bother with us? Reckon they were meant to be guarding the Sinuiju bridge.'

Below, the mountains were as sharp and clear as a table-top model, their slopes and ravines wedding cake white. Baby Jane's little fireball could change all that in seconds, throwing up thick steam clouds over Paikow and the valley, melting everything around, fusing rocks and dust into hard clinker, excising solid buildings as though they had never existed. The whole population of that small town around the marshalling yard would die, every last gook of them, leaving the B29 crew to live with their guilt for the rest of their days. And no one more so than Major Robert J. Schroder, commanding.

Guilt? Christ, who started the fucking war?

But he'd still have to live with it. That bomb was his baby now. Not even death could take that away from him. To think that without Elaine he might have been back in the States doing a socially useful job, like flying divorcees to Las Vegas. She could have tagged along.

'Baby Jane to be armed,' he instructed.

One pass over the target – their sole chance. If they goofed they'd not get another. Oh Jesus, why did it have to be him? One thing, it was a sure place in the history books. He initiated the slow descent. At 10,000 feet the bombardier might just hit the bull.

Odd how that snow on the mountains resembled cake icing. Elaine's mother had made their own wedding cake and never failed to remind them of it – how family and neighbours had clubbed together, sacrificing their sugar and margarine rations, and how she'd bought black market dried fruit, being too proud to accept his help from the PX Store. He should have known that was an omen.

'Ten minutes to aiming point, Bob.'

'Roger.'

'Signal from base, Captain,' the radio operator broke in. 'Just coming through now.'

Sergeant radio operator, seemingly happily married to a wife who resembled a blob of pink blancmange, three kids likewise. Would they boast how their father was one of the crew who started the Third World War?

But the message jolted him out of his bleak mood. It was short and brutal: OKINAWA TO ELAINE STOP ABORT REPEAT ABORT NURSERY STOP RETURN JANE INTACTA TO CRADLE STOP DON'T ASK ME WHY ENDS.

A pause of disbelief followed Schroder's announcement that they were turning back, mission aborted. Then a ragged cheer came from the crew, part sincere, perhaps also part ironic. He handed over to his co-pilot who brought the plane in a wide half-circle, climbing. On the ground he could see flashes of anti-aircraft fire, but the shell-bursts were well to their rear.

His own reaction was his biggest shock. He should have felt relief. Those gooks on the ground were going to live. The world's first genuine atomic war had been called off. At the last minute the ref. had cancelled the fight. But none of those feelings matched the emotional whirlpool going on inside him. He'd been robbed, that was the vicious truth. Subconsciously he'd wanted this fucking world to burn, and Elaine with her fat lawyer and stupid mother along with it. In that moment, for the first time, he came face to face with the depths of his own bitterness.

'Bob, we have trouble with number four engine,' the flight engineer reported. 'Fuel pressure's erratic.'

'OK.' It jolted him back to reality.

Then, seconds later: 'Best feather number four engine.'

Could be they had picked up a scratch from those MiGs, he guessed. In fifteen minutes they would be approaching the coast. They could still make Okinawa even on three engines – with or without five tons of Baby Jane in the B29's belly.

But Christ, he felt he had been ripped down the middle to become two separate people. Major Robert J. Schroder commanding the B29 was unchanged: a rational, instinctive pilot, man and machine meshing together as they had

347

always done. Yet lurking behind his active mind was this insane stranger he did not recognize, who day-dreamed of flying solo and bombing the shit out of humanity by simply operating one lever. With no crew to inhibit him, by Jesus he'd be capable of it. Not Paikow either, but somewhere to make them really scream. Tokyo . . . Vladivostok . . . Peking . . . He'd blow a hole in this universe so wide they'd all be sucked through it, every stinking treacherous sonofabitch who ever breathed.

'Airfield straight ahead,' the co-pilot mentioned. 'See that runway?'

'Yeah.'

On the horizon beyond the snow-blanched landscape a dark band of sea was already visible. Hell, he had to kick this brooding and get his thoughts straightened out. The entire crew was on edge; he could sense it. This oddball mission was getting at them all. After this, smashing hell out of German cities day after day, night after night, seemed like sanity. Hamburg, Berlin, the Ruhr, Dresden: witnessing your best friend – best man at the wedding – spiralling down in flames to his death; counting the empty places in the mess once you got back; and all the while his wife Elaine, his love, lustfully exercising her hips with that fucking lawyer – oh Jesus, her peaches and cream cheeks flushed scarlet with the effort as they always were after . . .

'F80s ahead!'

He forced himself back to the present and took over again from Kramer. Five he counted, approaching fast. That tight-assed colonel must have fixed an escort. Didn't want his Baby hurt. Considerate of him. Permission to jettison the bitch in the sea would be too much to wish for.

'On our tail, Captain!' the intercom screamed at him

suddenly, shattering the unreal calm. 'MiGs! One – two – three – Oh, Holy Mary, Mother of God!'

Their own guns' staccato response was lost in the general clatter of explosions and screams and ripping metal as the MiGs' fire punched holes through the B29's fuselage. Then – just as quickly – all was quiet again. Only the engines' coughing, uneven drone remained.

Vince Kramer, latest in his long line of co-pilots, sagged in his seat, dead, held upright by his straps. Intercom silent. Bombardier slumped forward in front of him. Flames licking at number one engine. He closed the fuel shut-off valve. The B29 was losing height rapidly. He had no alternative but to jettison the bomb.

'OK, Baby Jane – bathtime!' he muttered.

He reached for the emergency bomb release, expecting to sense the sudden lightening of the plane as Baby fell clear, but nothing happened. He tried again. The mechanism refused to budge. Through the shattered plexiglass he caught sight of an F80 dropping towards the sea, leaving behind it a long pall of black smoke like a funeral pyre.

One thousand feet.

Angrily he tore the oxygen mask away from his face and turned to bawl back through the aircraft. 'Any of you hear me? You can't all be fucking dead!' His voice seemed puny against the strained roar of the two spluttering inboard engines and the rush of wind against his face.

Behind him was Al Rossi, stirring uneasily over the navigator's table as the plane was buffeted by its rapid descent. His head lolled sideways. His mouth worked as though saying something through the blood and mess.

'What d'ya say?' Schroder yelled at him. 'What d'ya say, Al? Jesus, there's no time!' He tugged at the stick, trying to get the nose up.

'Elaine we'll call her!' Al boomed out at him, his

carcass-face red-gashed. 'Howsat grab you, fellas? Elaine!'

An explosion tore through the wing. Schroder was pitched forward to be given a crazy fairground view of the spinning sea as the B29 plunged towards it. Pain in his lungs. Intense heat. Flame surrounding him hungrily.

A man . . . somewhere . . . screaming.

16

Consciousness returned only slowly. His body felt unfamiliarly confined as if encased from shoulders to ankles in plaster, or was that merely illusion? Everything seemed so vague . . . so dark . . . To clear his mind he tried breathing deeply but the effort brought a sharp pain to his ribs. An iron lung, Ross puzzled; they've put me in an iron lung. He frowned, trying to recall what had happened, but his mind slipped away again into the caves where he was gradually engulfed by an oddly pleasurable mist.

Voices spoke without meaning, distant voices which didn't connect, voices without faces . . .

Then the violence started, the rocking which never ceased, the jolts throwing him one way then another, and he knew he must be in a boat at sea, crossing the English Channel in a storm, leave pass and travel voucher in his battledress pocket, yet for some reason they had strapped him to his bunk in the dark narrow cabin.

Strapped down, that was the explanation – but why?

'Hantu?' She shook him by the shoulder with her small hand but her fingers hurt as they dug into him. 'Hantu, open your eyes. I've brought you something to drink. Oh, can't you wake him?'

'Give him time. He'll wake in time. Wasn't a strong dose.'

A man's voice this time. Chinese. So he was in China, was he? But of course he was in China; remembered that much. Came to China to – oh hell, why? He came to China to . . . He opened his eyes, puzzled. A small flickering light threw shadows against canvas walls; to see them better he tried to sit up but he *was* confined, leather straps across his body holding him down as if in some madhouse, wrists shackled and – Jesus, his feet too. No illusion this time.

'What the hell's going on?' He croaked his words through a dry throat, but had anyone heard him? 'Mei-lin?'

'Wait, I'll unbuckle this strap. Let you sit up. We're stopping here for a while.'

'Here? Where's here?'

'Nowhere,' she said, releasing the buckle, then raising him with one arm around his sore shoulders. 'Trees, snow, everything dark. We left the road some time back. Now, careful! I'll hold the cup to your lips. It's tea. There's food as well if you feel up to it.'

In a few sips he had emptied the tiny cup. He asked for more, staring around while she poured it. His mind was confused, his thoughts like tiny pieces of coloured glass in a kaleidoscope, vivid patterns constantly changing, making no sense. Rockets – he remembered rockets – fire, explosions, wire mesh cage, treacherous rocks giving way as he climbed over them – but why? Why was he climbing? It was an oil lamp they had in here, a tiny oil lamp giving inadequate light; that would explain the smell. But then the handcuffs? Why?

'Where is he?' He turned his face away from the tea. 'The man who was here?'

'Siew? Oh, he's outside somewhere.'

'Siew.' He recalled Siew and his haunted, disgruntled expression. And Chuan – where was Chuan? Had Chuan ordered him to be handcuffed?

'Poor Hantu, you're thoroughly mixed up, aren't you?' Mei-lin laughed at him, not without sympathy. 'You've been ill.'

'Have I?' He was not certain he could believe her.

'After the way they beat you up it's not surprising. Siew cleaned your wounds. We had to strap you down to keep you on the stretcher.' She laughed again – brightly, as if trying to humour him. 'You look bewildered! This is an ambulance we're travelling in, a field ambulance borrowed from the People's Liberation Army. Supplied by the Americans. It has a big red cross on the sides.'

Held up by her, he stared around. All he could see in the patchy light from the small oil lamp was the bare interior of the truck which contained no special medical equipment other than a first-aid box and anchor points for stretchers on either side. A portable charcoal stove supplied some warmth and on it stood the kettle of hot water for the tea.

'I don't remember any of this.' But he realized now that she wore a uniform under that quilted coat. Her forage cap suited her the way she wore it, pushed back slightly over her black hair.

'Of course you don't. Siew gave you a drink to make you sleep before we carried you down to the road.'

Drugged, that was the explanation; he'd been drugged by them. He struggled to get up but the straps and handcuffs restrained him. 'What is it? What did he give me?'

'Nothing harmful, he said. Laudanum. Every time you seemed likely to wake up he gave you a drop more. That's probably why you feel so dazed, but it'll wear off.'

'When was the first time?' He lay back again. No need to panic, it never paid off. Take it quietly. Only way to find out. 'How long?'

'Yesterday.'

'I've been out twenty-four hours?'

'More than a day. Not really out, though. Peaceful. Hantu, I'll heat up some soup for you. Food'll help.'

353

'You could take these handcuffs off. I'm frozen.'

'I don't have the key.'

'You're not telling me the truth, are you?' His haziness was giving way to irritation. What she had said was lies. No one puts cuffs on a man's wrists and ankles to prevent him falling off a stretcher. He told her so.

It touched a nerve. Her face darkened with unexpected anger. 'We've risked our lives to get you away, Englishman. Three checkpoints we were stopped at. You'd be handed over to the Russkies by now if Chuan hadn't persuaded them we were taking you to Peking for interrogation.'

'As a prisoner.'

'Of course. How else could we convince them? We told them – *he* told them – that you'd been arrested in the Changpai Mountains, spying, and had no connection with the explosions at Paikow. They weren't too keen to believe him.'

'OK, but we're not at a checkpoint now, are we?' Hell, if only his head would clear properly he might be able to work it all out for himself. His limbs were numb too; no feeling in them. 'I know Chuan makes the decisions . . .'

'That's right,' she stopped him. 'He does.'

She was stirring something in an enamel pot on the little charcoal stove. It was already steaming and a vague smell reached his nostrils, nothing specific but it made him queasy. He hoped she wouldn't force him to eat it. Difficult to believe they had been lovers. Perhaps they hadn't; perhaps it had been an opium dream.

'Which direction are we taking?' he asked. 'When we move?'

'South.' She tasted the concoction. 'To an airfield in the plain. From there we fly to Peking. Chuan says . . .'

'Says what?'

'I've told you too much. Ask him when he gets here.

Now if we can prop you up somehow I'll feed you. Because it's true, Hantu. I have no key for the handcuffs.'

She loosened the straps across his waist and legs. His limbs were so stiff with cramp, pains shot through every sinew as she pushed and tugged at him till he was sitting upright, his back supported against the timber of the ambulance's side. 'Stay there, don't fall!' she warned, going to fetch the enamel pot. 'You'll feel better with some hot soup inside you.' She sat beside him and began feeding him like an invalid, waiting for him to open his mouth for each spoonful, then wiping away the fragments from his lips and stubbly chin. The broth was salty and almost scalded him, but his body responded to its spreading warmth. He chewed the tough vegetables and mushrooms, swallowing them down hastily as she held out the spoon yet again.

When he had finished she took the pot away, then knelt before him and began kneading his legs with strong fingers to stimulate the circulation, afterwards repeating the process on his arms and shoulders.

Hearing the rear door being opened and sensing a sudden cold breeze as someone came in, he was able to push himself up to glance around. Siew stood in the doorway, his back towards them, kicking the snow off his boots before coming fully inside.

'Still alive then, comrade?' Siew grunted. It was seldom he had addressed Hantu directly before; this time he sounded almost friendly. 'Miracle you didn't freeze to death lying on that stretcher. Can you stand up? If you can I'll take you outside, let you have a pee.'

'Why the sudden concern?'

'Chuan worries, not me. I couldn't give a fart. Wants to deliver you alive. You ready?'

'Deliver me where?'

'You'll find out. Don't try any tricks now when we take the cuffs off. You're not up to it.'

Freeing his ankles only, Siew pulled him roughly to his feet and held him steady till he found some sort of balance. With some anxious assistance from Mei-lin he managed to climb out of the ambulance without falling. His hands were useless because of the steel cuffs on his wrists which Siew refused to remove.

'Chuan may trust you. I don't.' With a series of shoves in the small of his back Siew propelled him across the snow towards a thick, gnarled tree-trunk and ordered him to get on with the job. 'I'd as soon trust you as a poisonous snake. You're finished, you whites. Who listens to you any more?'

He didn't argue. Siew seemed to resent his silence. Then, on the way back to the ambulance when he stooped to scoop up some snow from a deep drift beside the path, intending to rub it over his face to freshen himself up, Siew kicked him viciously, sending him sprawling into it.

'I said get back inside. Who told you to stop?'

Hantu struggled to his feet again, hampered by the handcuffs. 'OK . . . OK . . .'

'You do what *I* want – got that?' Siew insisted. 'You Europeans never listen.'

If Mei-lin had not objected vehemently Siew would have strapped him to the stretcher once more; as it was, he was effectively hobbled by the cuffs replaced on his ankles. But even if he had been able to walk he had nowhere to go. He had no idea even where they might be. If Mei-lin knew she refused to say. Till Chuan returned there would be no answers – and when they came they'd better be convincing. Christ, he'd kept his part of the agreement, hadn't he? Walked into that Soviet base to find out all they wanted, risked spending the rest of his life in a Siberian prison cell, destroyed the . . .

Think straight, he swore at himself. Get the facts in the right order. Chuan had been inside those caves before. He must have known what was going on in some detail – not Seoul, not the target perhaps, but all the rest. He had arrived with the explosives, prepared to sabotage the operation with Siew to help him, no need for anyone else, least of all some burned-out Englishman who would rather have been feeding the ducks in St James's Park.

Then why? For the reason he had given all along? Or was there another answer?

'I'm hungry,' he said suddenly. 'Any more to eat where that soup came from?'

'The soup did you good. You're looking your usual self again.' She foraged in the first-aid box and announced: 'There's this Manchurian bread the monks gave me, if you like it. And soup again. I can give you more beans in it. Build up your strength.'

'It'll do.'

'There's nothing else. Chuan should be back soon. He may bring something.'

'Where is he all this time?'

'You ask him.' The enamel bowl was on the charcoal stove again. 'I'm only a flea on the dog's back.'

'Beautiful flea,' he said, watching her as she tended the soup.

'Does it make you amorous, lying there shackled? Don't raise your hopes, Hantu. This is an ambulance and I'm your nurse. Concentrate on that.'

But his wounds still ached, more now he had thawed out; under the dressings his skin itched and throbbed. He added: 'Beautiful nurse.'

A very proficient nurse too, he thought when she brought his meal to the stretcher. She had warmed the bread over the charcoal and the soup this time was thicker, more like a bean stew. He tried spooning it

357

himself, handcuffed, but soon gave up and accepted her offer to feed him.

He was still eating when Chuan entered the ambulance, kicking his boots against the step and exuding a general air of coldness. Tossing his gloves and fur hat on to the spare stretcher, he went immediateley to the charcoal stove.

'That smells all right. What is it? Enough for me? It's like the North Pole outside.'

'Why the hell are you keeping me here?' Hantu demanded, but he kept his temper. He knew Chuan too well. He held up his manacled wrists. 'And what's the meaning of these?'

'Ah, you're awake, Hantu! Began to feel you wouldn't recover – isn't that right, comrade? Comrade Fang has been taking care of you.'

'You'd better explain, Chuan. And don't give me any shit.'

'You're number one on the wanted list, that's the explanation. On every road between Mukden and the Yellow Sea the Soviets are out looking for you aided by the Chinese People's Liberation Army.'

'And you are one of them.'

He helped himself to soup. 'I can pull enough rank to prevent them taking my prisoner away from me, but only if they're convinced you really *are* a prisoner.'

'You seem to have convinced Siew.'

'Has he been mistreating you? I apologize. Believe me, Hantu, this is necessary. If you're picked up they'll hand you over to the Russians. That wouldn't do either of us any good.'

'The Russians are your allies.'

'True. Barbarians, but they are our allies.'

Mei-lin scraped up a last stray bean and popped it into his mouth before he could reply. Her expression betrayed

358

nothing but in her eyes he read a warning to be careful what he said to Chuan. Lovely pure eyes . . . Oh Jesus, he *was* in love with her and it complicated matters. It was a weakness Chuan would not hesitate to exploit once he spotted it. Perhaps he already knew?

Swallowing down the bean he grumbled at Mei-lin that he could manage on his own now and this was a private conversation he was attempting to hold with Chuan, so why did she have to stay hanging around? He hoped it sounded convincing.

She flushed. 'Feed yourself next time, Englishman!' she snapped. 'Think I'm your amah?'

'Bloody woman!' He turned to Chuan as she stormed out. 'If she'd taken the handcuffs off at least I could've eaten on my own. What was the matter with her? Afraid I'd rape her?'

'I gave Siew the only key.'

'She could've asked him. We're off the road, aren't we? No danger of any patrols finding us here.'

'Perhaps, but why risk it?' Chuan's lips twisted into that odd, mirthless grin of his. 'Another day and we'll have reached the coast if there isn't another snowfall. Then you'll be on your way.'

'The old team, eh? Working together?'

'That's what you always used to say.'

'Chuan, you're a lousy liar. Always were. The inscrutable East, that was the term when I was a kid in Shanghai. Not for me, you weren't. I could read you like yesterday's newspaper.' He stretched out his hands in front of him. 'If I'm free to go you can take these bloody handcuffs off. Well?'

'Not yet.' Chuan's smile was broader, hiding his thoughts.

'Not before Peking, is that it?' He could sense he was right. But he'd have known even if Siew hadn't practically spelled it out to him. It was the only logical explanation, staring him in the face all along. He asked: 'So what happens in Peking?'

'Let's test how good you are, Hantu. You tell me.'

A depressive spasm coursed through him like a fever as he sat hunched on the edge of the stretcher, wrists and ankles shackled. 'Show trial, that's obvious. British agent arrested red-handed after sabotage at Soviet base. With you, Mei-lin and Siew in the witness box giving evidence against me.'

'You'll be on your own, Hantu. We shan't even exist. New identities, new names. Mention us and they'll accuse you of lying, though by then I doubt if you'll even remember us. For such trials prisoners are always very well prepared beforehand. And there's no shortage of evidence. Twice you used a false identity with forged papers – as Peter Bentley first, then as Colonel Gayev. Your childhood links with White Russians will explain your political motives. The clothes you wore when you arrived in China will be found. One jacket button concealed a British-made miniature compass. Your commando knife, your radio, your American-made explosives, the cipher chart concealed in your belt, the State Express cigarette tin, the chocolate wrapper bearing your handwriting . . . The case against you will be very convincing.'

'Congratulations. You've done better than I imagined.'

'I don't need your congratulations, nor your patronizing airs. You came into this operation with your eyes open but you were too blind to see. Weren't you warned that China couldn't openly act against the Soviet Union? You're the whipping boy.'

'Who was to be allowed to escape after it was all over.'

'You didn't really fall for that, Hantu, did you? Perhaps

you did. You always struck me as naïve. People over-estimated your abilities.'

That was turning out to be true enough, he thought moodily. He remained motionless on the stretcher, too numbed even to think straight any longer. Easy enough to let go at Chuan, he supposed, but what good would a display of bad temper do him? He was secured hand and foot, still weak, weaponless, and his only prospect till the end of his days was a series of prison cells.

'I was asked in Singapore if you were to be trusted,' he said. 'You were – once.'

'That was stupid, Hantu. We were never fighting on the same side, you and I, not even in the jungle. We had a temporary alliance, a matter of convenience. You're British, I'm Chinese – don't you realize that? Perhaps not. You British never think clearly.'

'The differences are smaller than you imagine.'

'Small or big, they exist.'

'You've changed. They've got at you. You're not even Communists, you people. No brotherhood of man for you lot. All non-Chinese are barbarians, isn't that what you think? You admitted as much just now. Middle Kingdom Nationalists, that's all you are. Jesus, you never used to be like that, Chuan. And these – ' indicating the handcuffs – 'wouldn't have been worthy of you, not in those days.'

'Those days, these days!' Chuan shrugged. 'I always despised you yet you never noticed. In the jungle it was your guns and ammunition we needed, not you. Your supply drops. Keeping you alive was the price we paid.'

'For the training I gave you.'

'Training? Fighting? We Chinese were winning wars while you British were still living in caves. Accept it, Hantu – it was the supply drops, that was the reason. Yet you had to be given command, better food than we needed, quinine, aspirin, all those medical supplies

361

intended for us. Oh yes, we made sure you stayed alive, our "liaison officer", because without you there'd have been no more parachutes mushrooming down. That was why.'

'And Yen-hua? You wanted her, didn't you?'

'Yen-hua was obeying orders but again you didn't notice. The same orders I gave Mei-lin.'

Hantu shook his head. 'Oh no. Yen-hua would never have obeyed such orders, nor would you have given them. You were far too idealistic in those days. Young and puritanical, that's how I remember you. And you lusted after Yen-hua yourself.' A quick thought surged into his mind; a suspicion he had long suppressed. 'Is that why you betrayed us to the Japs?'

Chuan jumped up, flushing with anger. 'Be careful, Hantu. Things can be made very unpleasant for you.'

'Then you did betray us. Wanted me out of the way, did you? Only Yen-hua and the others died instead. And as a reward the Japs let you dig her grave. You're pathetic.'

The back of Chuan's hand swept across his face, knocking him sprawling across the stretcher; then he was grabbed and jerked upright again. *Slap . . . slap . . .!* Hard, vicious blows which shook his brain inside his skull.

'Siew!' he heard Chuan yelling, but distantly through the distorting noises filling his head. 'Siew!'

The rear door of the ambulance was open again; the temperature seemed to drop several degrees. Siew pinned him down on the stretcher while Chuan replaced the straps, dodging his kicking legs. That last remark had really got under his skin, he thought; for the first time he'd suceeded in needling Chuan. That gave him some satisfaction.

'Another drink'll put him under.' Siew's voice.

362

'Let the bastard suffer,' Chuan responded with undisguised bitterness. 'When the cramps start he'll soon know what it's all about. In two hours we move.'

Hantu was left on his own lying on the stretcher with the straps so tight, it was difficult to breathe in. He was in almost total darkness. Before going, Chuan had blown out the oil lamp; a pungent odour of paraffin lingered on the air. He felt sick but couldn't move; if he brought anything up he'd spew all over himself. His mind went back to the clinical interrogation centre in Hampshire where they had strapped him to a chair for days at a time, shone their bloody lamps at him, *hammer-hammer-hammer-hammer* – sensory deprivation techniques: oh yes, they had names for all the tortures! – and he'd pee-ed himself; he'd shit himself; he'd done everything they had planned to reduce him to the most sordid, humiliating level like some disgusting lower form of life crawling about in primeval slime. Oh, Chuan was right! Chinese civilization was well over a thousand years older, their tortures were bound to be even more sophisticated, they'd had so much more time. Death is part of the cycle of life, the old monk had preached at him; and so too was gradual decay, the breakdown of bodily processes, a bacteriological field-day. Pneumonic plague would at least have been quicker.

Cramp-pains penetrated his legs and arms. Impossible to move them; impossible to black them out of his thoughts. Time will numb them, he tried to reassure himself; but time did nothing of the sort. Time only made the agony worse. He had a sudden vision of long tape-worms squirming inside his muscle fibre, slowly . . . lovingly . . . wanting him to suffer . . . But then his mind switched to frostbite and what would happen if they allowed the charcoal stove to burn out. Or simply tipped him into the snow for the rest of the night, manacled and bound as he was. Once in Russia he had seen a man's toes blackened by frostbite, a couple already missing; or it could happen to his fingers, his lips, the tip of his nose, oh Jesus even his prick. Chuan was quite capable of dreaming that one up, plotting his revenge – because that was what lay behind it all, wasn't it? Personal revenge.

'Hantu?' Mei-lin came quietly into the ambulance, lit the lamp and knelt down by the stretcher to ease the too-tight straps a notch or two, though she had a struggle to loosen them. 'Couldn't get away from Chuan till now.' She kept her voice low. 'He was boasting with Siew about how they'd made sure you couldn't move. He hates you, Hantu. I hadn't realized that before. Really hates you.'

He was so seized with cramp, he could hardly speak. 'Don't . . . understand . . .,' he whispered. But the truth was that he did, only too well.

'When he said these handcuffs were to help smuggle you through the checkpoints I believed him.'

'What . . . else?'

'That story about the airfield and flying you to Peking to stand trial – all that is true. Perhaps it's the correct line to take, I don't know.'

'You people . . . always worry . . . about the correct line. Do you have . . . no opinions of . . . your own?' He forced breath into his lungs, gasping at the pain across his rib cage.

'We are taught that we must not permit personal feelings to distract us from carrying out the will of the masses. You British think differently.'

'We express it differently.'

Leaving him strapped down – but more loosely now – she began to knead his muscles through his clothing to get some life back into his limbs. 'It's better you don't die before you get there.'

'Convince Siew of that,' he said pointedly. He tried to

think the situation through but came up with no solutions. He had played and lost. Checkmate. After a silence he asked, 'Where are my things? My bag and all that?'

'Your radio is here with us in the ambulance. So is your bag, I think, or else in the other truck which Chuan drives.'

'Could do with a change of clothing.'

'Ask him. He might permit it once we're on the plane.'

'And the airfield is in the south?'

'What does it matter to you?' She shrugged. 'If I undo this strap and let you bend your legs to get the circulation moving will you promise not to try anything on?'

'What could I try on?'

'I don't want any trouble with you, that's all. If they think I can't manage they'll forbid me to come here.' She let the buckle slip, releasing the strap across his thighs, then tucked her hands beneath his knees to raise them. 'The airfield is near the coast on the road to Ta-lien, that's all I know. He said the way we came wasn't possible because of snow, but I suspect he had this planned all along. He sounded too smug about it. He seems to think it a great triumph. Perhaps he's expecting to be promoted if it all works out.'

A quick bang of a fist was heard against the metal door. It opened and Siew peered in. 'Not dead yet, is he? That's right, Comrade Fang – keep the bastard alive! He'll regret it later on. We're moving on now. We take the lead and Chuan follows in the truck. Any trouble from this scum, give the partition a kick and I'll come round.'

The door was slammed shut again and a few seconds later he heard the whine of the self-starter. In the Section they wouldn't give a damn what happened to him, not unless he said something to swing the spotlight in their direction. But when it came to the crunch what did he really know that was worth telling? They had never exactly confided in him. No, Potts would write a neat little note in his file, 'Salaries' would freeze payments, and Richards would be too busy manipulating his next promotion even to be aware that he had lost an agent on the way. Only the admiral might give him a passing thought, a twinge of regret that he could not cross-examine him in person.

'This might keep you warmer.' Mei-lin unfolded a rough blanket from the other stretcher and spread it over him. 'I don't want to be blamed if anything happens to you.'

The ambulance jolted and slithered with noisy changes of gear and sudden violent swings as they reached bends in the road. On its hook the oil lamp danced about wildly and he suggested it might be safer to put it out. They seemed to be travelling downhill on a winding route studded with switchbacks and turns made more treacherous by the hard snow. Mei-lin waited for an apparently smoother stretch before turning down the lamp and joining him under the blanket, her fingers busy with the buckles to loosen the straps even further.

'Body warmth,' she murmured, nuzzling up to him. 'The most inviting words in Chinese, Chou-fei used to say. Do you mind me talking about Chou-fei?'

'Should I?'

'Yes.' But her voice sounded deliberately contrary, teasing him. 'Tell me about Yen-hua. Everything about her.'

'You're sure you don't have the key to these handcuffs?'

'You know I don't.'

'How many days have I been like this? That stuff Siew made me drink – how long did it knock me out?'

'Quite a few hours. This is the second night since we

left Paikow. Chuan says by daylight we'll reach the airfield; so this is our last chance, Hantu, to be together.'

'He said that too?'

'No. But I'm not sure he'll take me on the plane with you.'

The second night. That meant there was still time. They would be listening out for his signal if only he could find some way to free himself. But that didn't seem likely. Despite all her complexes and taste for luxury, Mei-lin was undeniably loyal to her own ideals, her attitude to Chuan showed that much. His motives disturbed her, not his methods. God, if only he could be convinced that at least one operative in the Section was capable of such idealism.

'Yen-hua,' she commanded gently. 'Tell me. Please.'

So he told her – what was there to hide? – and she listened without a word of criticism, seeming to understand. But of course she understood. For her it was only a story, wasn't it? Something she might read in a novel. Her only questions concerned Chuan. Where was he on this occasion or that? How did he react? Had they really been so close to each other?

For a long time they talked and perhaps afterwards they fell asleep together, he could not be absolutely sure, but when he woke up he found himself alone, strapped firmly to the stretcher. Thin strips of daylight outlined the shape of the double doors. The ambulance was stationary and it seemed warmer; perhaps the wind had dropped, giving the little charcoal stove a chance.

He lay there for half an hour or more, he reckoned; occasionally he heard a voice outside – Siew maybe – but then silence again. If he had arrived at the airfield he must be well away from the hangars or the mess; probably on the far perimeter, safe from inquisitive eyes. When they were ready they would come for him, flinging open the ambulance doors and lifting him down, still on the stretcher, to load him into some unmarked plane. War casualty, anyone chancing to witness the incident might think.

He was wrong of course; wasn't he always? When the door – one side only – at last opened, it was to admit Meilin. She nodded, apparently relieved when she saw he was awake.

'Siew's coming,' she said abruptly. 'You have to be ready. Get this out of sight.'

Into his hands she placed a knife, then pulled his extra blanket away and began folding it.

Pointed blade, he noted, exploring it with his fingers. He still wore the ample uniform trousers he had stolen from the dead Mongolian guard and he pressed the knife down between his thighs, holding it under the folds of cloth. Handcuffed as he was he could only risk one blow; if that didn't hit home he'd be finished.

'Where's Chuan?' he demanded.

'Airfield. Seeing about the arrangements.' She had just enough time to mutter her answer before Siew clattered in contemptuously, leaving the door open. 'You'd better take him outside, comrade. He wants to pee.'

'Let him pee where he is.'

'And have him in the plane with us all messed up? Don't be so disgusting. Chuan told you to take him out if he needed it.' She started to undo the strap over his legs. 'Well?'

'You're too fussy. He's only imperialist scum.' But he unbuckled the other two straps as he spoke. 'Teach him a lesson to lie in his own filth.'

Hantu slipped his fingers between his legs until he found the hilt of the knife. Siew leaned forward to grip his jacket to tug him upright. With whatever strength Hantu could summon up he plunged the knife into him

368

beneath his ribs. The point went home but not deeply enough; Siew's clothing was too thick. He staggered back and the blade came clear, bringing blood with it, his face showing surprise and rage. Before he could do anything Mei-lin shoved him forward again within reach. This time Hantu raised his arms as if in supplication and went for Siew's throat, slashing across it with so much force, he ended sprawled across the stretcher, the knife on the floor.

Siew crumbled slowly, the blood pouring over his hand as he clutched his neck, until at last he collapsed to the floor, dead.

Mei-lin backed away from him, her eyes filled with terror.

'The key, for God's sake!' Hantu gasped, hardly able to breathe. 'Get the key – right-hand pocket, isn't it?'

Reluctantly she went to Siew's corpse and fumbled in his pockets till she found the key to the handcuffs. She freed Hantu's hands first, then he took the key from her and clumsily dealt with his ankles himself. When he tried to stand his legs refused to obey and he almost fell.

'You'll have to help me.' Leaning on her, he pulled himself up and somehow got over to the open door, stepping over Siew's body. Outside he saw only trees with a light scattering of snow on the ground around them. 'Where are we? Where's the airfield?'

Mei-lin pushed past him to get out, leaving him holding on to the doorway. She supported herself against the side of the ambulance looking as though she was about to be sick, but she wasn't after all. She took one deep breath after another, her head down, trying to regain control of herself.

'The airport's two miles away over there.' She pointed. 'Chuan said we should stay under cover here till he's sure the plane is ready for boarding. Too many Russians around. We can't risk causing an incident over you.'

'Considerate of him.' He made no attempt to hide his bitterness. 'Didn't you say this was the main road to Ta-lien?'

'According to Chuan. We turned off along this track.'

'OK, let's move before he gets back. Siew first.'

He climbed into the ambulance, his limbs still aching, and emptied Siew's pockets, confiscating his identity documents, keys, and a Makarov pistol with a full clip. The rest he pushed back into the dead man's jacket while Mei-lin watched unmoved from the open door. Wrapping the body in his own blanket, now bloodstained, he strapped it to the stretcher which between them they carried deeper into the woods till they came to a spot where the uneven ground suddenly dipped into a natural gully. There they tipped it in and it landed with the stretcher uppermost, serving as a substitute gravestone to mark Comrade Siew's last resting place.

Next he checked over the ambulance. It was an American Dodge, built for rough country; secured to the outside was a shovel, a toolbox and a spare can of petrol, full. What bothered him most were the large white circles and red crosses on the vehicle's sides and bonnet, and no doubt also on top, which made it impossible to conceal. In the cab he located his suitcase transceiver tucked away behind the seats and with it were two of the Soviet PPSh sub-machine guns they had brought from the caves – but no maps, nothing to tell him where they really were.

'Want to drive?' he offered.

She shook her head. 'You drive. Where are we going?'

'As far away from Chuan as we can get, then we'll work it out.' The engine started without trouble and the petrol gauge told him there was plenty of fuel still in the tank. 'Ta-lien, if you like.'

It might not be such a bad idea if everything else failed, he thought as he reversed along the track. Ta-lien – the Japs had called it Dairen, the Russians Dalny – would be crawling with Soviets like maggots over prime steak. It would be the last place they would expect to find him; at least there he could hide out, passing himself off as a deserter.

'Main road ahead,' Mei-lin warned him.

He slowed down almost to a stop. The track at this point was wide enough to allow him to turn and it was only then – once the ambulance was facing forward – that he noticed the silver streak of the sea ahead, perhaps a couple of miles away across the sandhills. From his left came the roar of planes taking off: three MiG-15s climbing steeply, obligingly pinpointing the exact location of the airfield. He headed away in the opposite direction, westwards along the empty highway which cut through the landscape with a directness only a civil engineer could have conceived.

From time to time they ran through woodland where the trees on either side were bare of leaves though their gaunt, black branches carried a scattering of snow. Then the road emerged again alongside the belt of sandhills. Somewhere along this route he had to find a spot where he could park the ambulance out of sight, while he attempted to establish contact. Not too close to Ta-lien either, whatever he had said to Mei-lin. Nor, luckily, had he ever confided the details to Chuan.

'Chuan is ideologically wrong,' Mei-lin announced after they had been driving for the best part of an hour, mostly without speaking.

'Is he?' He was taken aback. She must have been brooding on it during their entire drive.

'These things mean nothing to you, do they? The fact

that he killed Ong Chou-fei, or ordered his death which is the same.'

'How d'you know that?'

'He was laughing about how he had deceived you into coming back to China and used Ong Chou-fei to make the first contact because you wouldn't be certain about him. Your people would be bound to know he was connected with the Kuomintang. That would intrigue you, he said. You enjoyed puzzles.'

'And he had him killed.'

'In case he was arrested and interrogated before you'd properly swallowed the hook. Chou-fei died in order to trap you. Chuan even explained it to me, imagining I'd be grateful.'

'Three people killed – Pereira, Susie Lim and Ong Chou-fei.'

'For his own selfish reasons. Working for the Revolution there are times when killing is unavoidable, and of course if the Party decides it is right then . . . But no, not this. This wasn't for the Party. This was for Chuan himself.'

'Don't men always act that way? You can't tell me you've only just found out. Chou-fei would be surprised at you.'

She started up angrily. 'You're too cynical, Hantu – or you pretend to be. Underneath I think you're soft, like an underboiled egg. It's all talk with you.'

They had been driving through yet another short wooded stretch and as they emerged he spotted several army vehicles on the road ahead. 'Down! Get down!' he ordered, bawling at her. 'On the floor where they can't see you.' It was a whole convoy, stationary, lining the side of the road, heavily laden trucks with a couple of staff cars for the officers. The men were sauntering up and down stretching their legs, smoking, or clustered together in little social groups.

'Tea break,' he commented as he drove past them keeping his gaze stolidly in front of him and ignoring the waved greeting from a couple of them. 'Russian supply column. They may be going to the airfield.'

He glanced down at Mei-lin crouched on the floor of the cab. In her hands she held a PPSh and looked ready to use it.

'Chuan will have discovered we've gone by now,' she said. 'He might even have found Siew's body. He'll request help from the PLA this time. He can't risk letting you escape.'

Once again the road passed between trees and he searched for a track where at least he might be able to conceal the ambulance till dark. Not a chance. The trees lined the route in unbroken ranks. When they emerged, the sandhills offered just as little hope. They were much higher now, with tangled scrub growing over them. They would need caterpillar tracks to get through them.

But then he saw a possible opening. 'Hold on tight!' he told Mei-lin. Slowing down to walking pace he turned off the road and drove towards a narrow gap in the hills, almost certainly man-made judging from the sheer walls on either side. Once through its purpose became obvious. The whole area was strewn with coils of rusting barbed wire, spent cartridge cases, sections of wall and a couple of badly scarred concrete pill-boxes. It looked like a battlefield but it wasn't.

'Training ground,' he guessed, jumping down from the ambulance. He examined some of the cartridge cases, scratching away the corrosion with his thumb nail. 'Jap. We can only hope they cleared up afterwards. Be ironic to tread on a Jap mine after all this.'

'We're not going to stay here?' Her face darkened

again; she was close to losing her temper. 'You were taking me to Ta-lien. Chuan must be reported.'

He glanced at her ironically. She was more naïve than he had imagined. 'We'll hide out here for a while. Our first job is to cover those tyre tracks. If you are right about Chuan the entire army will be out hunting for us.'

One of the concrete pill-boxes had been constructed snugly into the side of a high sandhill facing the sea and beside it enough space had been excavated to take the ambulance. He reversed into it, switched off the engine and jumped out. Away from the woods only remnants of snow were left, little more than occasional patches of white against the ochre sand. With the knife he had used to kill Siew, he hacked at the scrub till he had cut a bouquet of twigs as a broom for each of them. Returning on foot to the roadway, they began to sweep loose sand across the deep impressions left by the tyres; as they worked they retreated slowly backwards, obliterating their own footsteps at the same time. From the road at least no one would be able to guess where the ambulance was parked.

The next task was to deal with the red cross in the large white circle on top of the vehicle, but this proved easier than he had feared as – working from the pill-box roof – he was able to shovel sufficient sand over it to make it invisible from the air.

It was only then that he checked over his suitcase transceiver. Not only was it undamaged; the battery still had plenty of life in it. He ran the aerial up to the sandhill's peak where he secured it to the handle of the shovel which he left standing upright, pushed into the ground. Back in the ambulance he fitted the emergency frequency quartz crystal and prepared to transmit, praying that someone out there was listening.

N-T . . . N-T . . . N-T . . .

Miraculously he heard the faint bleeping reply in his headphones. It took a moment's adjustment before reception was clear enough. M-S . . . M-S . . . IDENTIFICATION REQUESTED . . . OVER.

He could almost visualize the unknown operator, probably some young Leading 'Sparks' with a pimply face, bless his bell-bottoms. Between the sandhills he caught glimpses of the sea but the horizon was hazy. Somewhere out there was the Royal Navy, just as Sea Dog had promised. He tapped out the agreed identification code and requested to be picked up. Affirmative. To let them get a fix on his position he held the key down, twenty seconds at a time, keeping it up for longer than the agreed duration despite the risk of the Chinese or Russians listening in.

The Navy would make one attempt only. He had to be sure there were no mistakes.

At last he broke off and transmitted his query. The pause before a reply came through seemed endless. Then the bleeps began: M-S . . . M-S . . . M-S . . . ROGER . . . RENDEZVOUS MUFFIN TIME . . . BEST OF REPEAT BEST OF . . . OVER AND OUT.

'They're coming tonight,' he told Mei-lin. She had stood watching him throughout, smiling at him as though able to read his relief in his face. For the first time he felt they had a chance to get out alive. 'Till then we wait here. Is there anything to eat?'

'Nothing left, not even Manchurian bread.'

'I'm hungry.'

Climbing to the top of the sandhill he dismantled the aerial, and began coiling it round his hand. That simple message out of the ether seemed like a rescue line fired from a lifeboat. His tensions slowly eased.

From far in the distance he heard what he took to be the rumble of an approaching lorry; then he realized he was wrong. Tugging the shovel out of the sand he tossed it down beside the pill-box.

'Plane!' he warned urgently. 'Mei-lin, get out of sight!'

Rolling and slithering, he managed to scramble into a hollow which gave him some cover. It was a small piston-engined aircraft, perhaps a trainer, and it flew westwards in the Ta-lien direction, following the road. Not too high, either.

'Searching for us,' came Mei-lin's whisper. 'That'll be Chuan. He's asked for air force help.'

'We can't be sure.'

'I'm sure. He's checking the road. On his way back he'll come over these sandhills. Perhaps I should give him a wave.'

But she went back into the ambulance to fetch the PPSh. 'Just in case,' she explained. 'And I do know how to use it.'

The plane did return, flying low overhead, and they ducked back under cover hoping no one had spotted them. Their attempts at camouflaging the ambulance must have been successful because it headed purposefully eastwards without circling, without doubling back. Soon they could no longer even hear the engine. He retrieved the aerial wire, coiled it up again and placed it in its compartment in the suitcase.

'You're bleeding again,' she said.

'It's nothing.' There was fresh blood on his sleeve; his tumble down the sandhill must have reopened a wound.

'Take off your coat. I'll look at it.'

He began to refuse but she insisted. Her attempts to change the dressing were inexpert and the bandage kept slipping but he said nothing. These might be their last moments alone together for a very long time, he realized. Once on board that submarine their fate would be in others' hands. He could not even be certain where they would be taken.

When she finally finished bandaging his arm she kissed him. 'I love you, Englishman. I love you more deeply than I want to, but I must think rationally. About who you are, and who I am. Don't assume I'm coming with you on your submarine. I'm not.'

'Mei-lin, you'll be shot if you stay here. That's crazy!' He held her hands, dismayed. A stubborn look crossed her face as he tried to persuade her. 'They know you're helping me to escape. It's a death sentence.'

'My dear one, calm down. You don't understand.'

'When I radioed I said you'd be coming along. It's all arranged. They agreed. They're expecting you.'

'Where will they take us? Singapore?'

'Perhaps. I can't be sure.'

'Where thousands of Chinese Communists are already held in British prisons. Without trial, or don't you know that?'

'Under emergency regulations.'

'Dear one, I am a Communist. What d'you imagine they will do to me? They'll offer me a choice. Go to prison, or work for them. Betray my own people. I can't do that.'

'Then I'll insist on England. Or Australia.'

'Would they take any notice? You can't really think you're that important to them.' She was laughing at him, but tenderly. 'I am staying here.'

To stop his protests she kissed him again and her tongue probed sensuously. He tried to break away, not wanting to leave the argument unsettled, but she twined herself around him till they both fell back on to the cold sand, and the painful nagging of his wounds no longer seemed important.

'Come,' she said, getting up and holding out her hand to him. 'No, don't say anything more.'

She drew him towards the ambulance. Inside it was warmer, sheltered from the cold wind, and they made love on the one remaining stretcher though without undressing, fumbling through layers of clothing to explore and touch and caress each other. 'This is to say goodbye,' she murmured. 'It has to be, dear one.' Perhaps for that reason their love-making seemed selfconscious at first, like a duty that had to be fulfilled; but gradually its urgency increased, blotting out everything else. Afterwards they lay together sharing each other's warmth and hardly speaking till without any conscious decision they joined once more, gently savouring their bodily love.

Sitting up at last, straightening her clothes, Mei-lin began to talk about Ong Chou-fei.

'Whatever Chuan said, I don't believe his death was necessary. Chou-fei accepted the Revolution. Even if he was ideologically a running dog of capitalism he was no danger to the Party. With his business contacts he was useful.'

'You were fond of him.'

'How could I not be?' she responded simply.

It was growing darker and he could hardly see her face as they talked. When he went to light the little oil lamp the flame spluttered briefly, then died. They had no more oil.

'Chuan must be stopped,' she said.

'You can't do it. Not by yourself.'

'He has no authority over me. We each report to our own departments. Of course, he has many friends on the most important committees.'

'And you don't,' he told her, guessing.

'I am nobody.'

A nobody who still clung to Maoist teachings and

regarded her own enjoyment of capitalist luxuries as a weakness, he thought. Ong Chou-fei had not lived long enough to wean her away from her fierce political puritanism.

'You don't stand a chance against Chuan,' he said. 'Not if you stay. You should get out now while you can. It'd be safer.'

'Safe!' She scorned the idea. 'We'll never be safe, neither of us. But I can make sure Chuan is punished, believe me. For plotting against the people.'

'I have to move the ambulance,' he announced abruptly. What she really wanted was old-fashioned revenge but she had to dress it up in Party jargon. Well, that was her business.

He helped her jump down from the ambulance and for a few seconds he held her close, wondering unhappily what other arguments he could use to coax her to go with him.

'You can get at Chuan better from outside China,' he suggested. 'We can make Peking think he is working for us. An occasional hint planted here and there, through their known agents, or via the Russians . . .'

'You don't understand, do you? Would you work for the People's Republic? Or for Moscow? Yet you think I can change sides like putting on a new *cheongsam*. I can't, dear one. You ask too much.'

The thick spread of stars across the clear sky gave a frost-hard light which was bright enough for them to see their way to the top of a sandhill near the road. A heavily laden truck trundled past, rattling, but it was the only one. It passed and everything was quiet. He asked Mei-lin to stay there and keep watch while he attended to the ambulance.

It was going to be risky using the headlights as a beacon to guide the Navy in, but the only alternative – to light a fire – was equally dangerous. After scouting around he decided to position the ambulance in a high gap between two sandhills where it would be visible from the sea, yet sheltered landward. Getting the ambulance up there in the dark, manoeuvring precariously over loose sand, took longer than he'd reckoned.

'Nothing has come along the road since that last truck,' Mei-lin reported, joining him as he jumped down from the cab.

The sea was invisible, a dark void. Only the distant whisper of lapping water told him he faced the right direction.

'I want you to hit me,' she ordered. 'Hard enough to bruise my face. I'll tell them I wasn't in the ambulance when you overpowered Siew and killed him with his own knife. I found you already free and tried to stop you, but you beat me up and handcuffed me. Then you forced me to come with you. You meant to use me as a hostage.'

'And you seriously expect them to believe that?'

'Why not? Isn't it just what you'd have done? Siew was the only witness, and he's dead.'

Before he could think up any more convincing objections, a small bright light on the horizon began flashing the identification code he was expecting. He got back into the cab and acknowledged, using the headlights, then left them switched on. He could only hope the People's Liberation Army slept well that night. At least the sandhills offered some concealment.

'I can't bruise you, not the way you ask.' They had maybe thirty minutes left together. Perhaps less.

She teased him. 'You're a born bruiser, Hantu. What's the problem?'

'A broken jaw. Teeth knocked out. It's too dangerous what you're asking. And it might be days before they find you. You'd never survive.'

'Now the ambulance is up here they'll spot it right away. Didn't I say you're only a soft-boiled egg? Hard outside, squashy inside. You're not tough at all.' She kissed his cheek, her fingers lingering over his skin. 'It's to save my life, dear one. It'll mean the firing squad if they think I helped you. This is the only way.'

'Come with me,' he tried one last time.

'No.'

'You don't give up, do you?'

'Nor do you.'

'OK, now you listen to me. I'll handcuff one wrist only to the steering wheel, and in case something goes wrong the key will be on the seat where you can reach it.'

'They're not fools, you know. If you make it too easy they'll know I'm lying.'

'When you hear someone coming you can drop it out of the window, or simply push it on to the floor. But if no one *does* come, at least you'll be able to release yourself. Oh Christ, Mei-lin, I don't like this. Change your mind – please?'

She shook her head, smiling.

This was the moment, he realized. He had no choice. His right fist shot out, catching her on the chin. She did not even see the blow coming. Her legs gave way as she stumbled backwards, then dropped on to the sand, unconscious. Pulling her upright, her body seemingly lifeless, he slapped her savagely across the face with the back of his hand, once in each direction, and hated himself for it.

Why not take her out against her will, he thought. Till they were on the submarine she would know nothing about it. A tempting idea, and she might well be grateful for it later. But he could not bring himself to do it. Trust was too rare a commodity. He handcuffed her to the steering wheel as agreed and left the key on the seat beside her where she was bound to see it.

Straightening up, he glimpsed the faint outline of a rubber dinghy approaching the shore. Hastily he switched off the ambulance's headlights and it disappeared. She stirred slightly, mumbling in her half-consciousness when he stooped to kiss her goodbye.

'No problems now, my love,' he reassured her softly. 'Just make sure you stick to your story, it's all you have to do.'

But that's not so easy, he thought as he left her. It needed only a skilled interrogator to tie her up in knots.

He went reluctantly, heading across the dark sandhills towards the beach with his suitcase transceiver in one hand and the PPSh in the other. The idea of leaving her unarmed made him uneasy, but her story would never stand up if he left it with her.

At the water's edge a voice called to him quietly across the breakers. 'You Ross?'

'Come to join the party,' he replied, using the agreed password. He made out two dark shapes in the inflatable dinghy and began wading out towards them. 'Good of you to drop in.'

'Did you have to use your bloody headlamps, Ross? Beach was lit up like it was Christmas.'

'Couldn't have you getting lost.'

'You're alone. We were told two bodies.'

'The other one died.' A lie was easier than the truth and the explanation seemed to satisfy them. 'Here, take the radio first, will you? No point in leaving it behind.'

They relieved him of the case and with their help he struggled on to the frail craft. Water dripped from the PPSh. He shouldn't have bothered bringing it.

'I'm Lieutenant Marsh, and with me here is Petty Officer Hicks,' the deeper voice said. 'The shallows on this coast run a long way out, so we've some distance to go before we reach the sub. You'd best relax till we get there. From now on, silent routine.'

'Lights to starboard,' Hicks reported.

'Still some way off. Let's go.'

Ross counted three vehicles – no, four – approaching along the coast road from the airfield direction, and travelling at some speed too. The two navy men were paddling with a strong, easy rhythm and slowly the rubber dinghy drew farther away from the shore, leaving Mei-lin on her own. Vulnerable. The sea's swell became more marked and as they dipped into each trough in the waves the entire coastline temporarily disappeared and all he could see was water and stars. It was like riding roller-coaster in a doughnut-shaped balloon, though it was straight at one end and equipped with an outboard motor which remained silent.

Then he saw the sweep of their headlights as three of the vehicles came down on the beach within yards of the hidden ambulance.

'Must have spotted your Blackpool illuminations, Mr Ross, from somewhere round the bay,' Hicks commented. 'Outboard, sir?'

A searchlight, obviously mounted on one of the trucks, was switched on, sending a long beam feeling its way across the water. Before the lieutenant could reply it passed slowly over them, then paused and focused on them. The ragged volley of rifle shots seemed distant, as though quite unconcerned about the dinghy.

'Yes, outboard!' the lieutenant snapped. 'No need for silence now they know we're here. Though we're out of range by now.'

'Depends what they're using,' Ross grunted. One hit in the wrong place and that inflatable dinghy would fart its way to oblivion, taking them with it.

But Hicks had already tugged the lanyard to start the

motor and they picked up speed, throwing Ross violently against the rubber side. He heard more shots, but they were wasting ammunition unless . . .

Mei-lin, he thought. If only there was a god he could pray to.

Epilogue 1952

The Malayan Airways Dakota took off from Kuala Lumpur half an hour late that evening. It was not full and Ross had a window seat giving him a clear view of the thick jungle 3,000 feet below, already gold-tinged by the setting sun. As usual Alun Browne had gone by an earlier flight, leaving him to travel alone. He preferred it that way.

Since Paikow he had experienced a change in his own character, or perhaps it was since meeting Mei-lin. She would hardly know him these days. He had become quieter, not so nervous, less likely to buck like a startled horse when things went wrong. So Tim Moody told him at any rate. 'It's Shangri-La!' he always declared. 'Got into your bloodstream, same as it did mine. Enjoy it while it lasts!' Maybe he was right, who could tell?

The Section had been pleased with him, which was astonishing enough in itself. On board the submarine he had turned over the possibilities in his mind, convinced he was heading straight for their interrogation centre again, only this time they'd throw away the key. But it hadn't turned out that way. After moving at maximum knots on the surface, the submarine had dipped under the waves to continue at snorkel depth for a further few hours before surfacing to rendezvous with the aircraft carrier HMS *Theseus*. The admiral was on board to welcome him and from that time onwards it had been plain sailing, all smiles and courtesy, impossible to put a foot wrong. They had not even forced him to return to Singapore: it had been a suggestion only. First New Zealand to get those wounds cleared up – 'you'll be out of sight there, which can't be said of London' – then maybe he'd like to run in harness with Tim Moody for a while before eventually taking over from him? Problems with that Internal Security chap Alun Browne? Play along with him, why not? Give yourself double cover.

He hadn't believed it but he hadn't argued either. It no longer seemed important. He spent two months in New Zealand during which a coy letter arrived from the Section's London office announcing that he had been awarded an additional increment. As soon as the quack pronounced him fit he travelled back to Singapore to take up permanent quarters with Tim Moody who greeted him on the veranda, his arm around Asiah for support. 'Shangri-La calls!' – his first words. 'No escaping it, old chap.' A few days later Asiah introduced her friend Minah, beautiful Minah who as the months passed helped him to accept the fact that – by her own choice – he would never see Mei-lin again.

Shangri-La.

From the window he saw a scattering of lights penetrating the thick darkness. By now not a glimmer of sunlight remained. He recalled how rapidly night fell in the jungle when there was no moon, though simultaneously the insect sounds had always seemed to get louder and the fireflies had appeared, flashing tantalizingly past their faces. He had spent the day locked in a top security prison with Alun Browne, checking through the latest batch of four guerrillas, poor sods. 'Guerrillas' was a term guaranteed to annoy the pipe-sucking Browne, but it was how Mei-lin would have seen them. All male Chinese, this lot, fished out of the jungle by an army patrol which for once had struck lucky. Nothing to be learned from them that the army interrogators hadn't already discovered. Browne had been disappointed.

He glanced at his watch. They must be just about to cross the Johore Straits. In a few minutes they would set down at Kallang. As agreed with Browne, these up-country trips were tied in always with the typewriter business; this time during his two days in Kuala Lumpur he had picked up a big order for the new model. The news would please Tim. Cover story or not, they were both ambitious to get the Singapore operation into profit. It would be like cocking a snook at those civil servants in the Section.

The Dakota touched down smoothly, racing along the runway and gradually losing speed till eventually it stopped close to the terminal building and the door was opened. At that stage he had no reason to suspect anything was wrong, not even when he noticed the uniformed Malay constable at the foot of the steps. As he reached the tarmac the constable saluted.

'Tuan Ross, please come. Message for you.'

'Of course.' He left the line of passengers. 'What is it?'

'Come.' A police car stood close to the aircraft's wing and the constable held open the door for him. 'Superintendent Winterton wants to speak to you.'

Ross got in. He recognized the constable now as the one who had driven him back to the hotel after he had identified Susie Lim in the police mortuary. But that was eighteen months ago. What could be bothering Winterton this time?

The drive lasted no longer than thirty seconds, just as far as the side entrance to one of the airport buildings. He was conducted into an office where Winterton and Browne waited for him. Their first glance as he went in warned him something was wrong.

'I'm afraid it's bad news, Ross.' Browne spoke first, fiddling with that damned pipe. 'Bandit attack. Thought

387

I'd better stick around and tell you myself. It's a bad show. Winterton here will take you out there.'

'Out where, for Chrissake?' But he knew already; he felt it in his guts.

'They've killed Moody. Attacked the house.'

'Details are still not too clear,' Winterton said, picking up his peaked cap from a desk. 'If I were you I'd stay in Singapore for tonight but Browne here said you'd want to check the house for yourself. I don't advise it, but if you insist you can travel in my car.'

'Thank you, Superintendent.' His voice seemed hoarse and unnatural. He didn't know what else to say. The news had left him so numb, his mind refused to function. 'I do insist.'

'Always welcome to stay at my place,' Browne volunteered. His concern seemed genuine. 'Any time tonight. Just turn up.'

Ross nodded.

In the car Winterton tried to explain what little was known but it was not much. It was less than an hour since the attack and he had only the telephoned reports from the local police station to rely on. Even the number of casualties was uncertain though it seemed either one or two of the Malay staff had died. Whether man or woman he couldn't say.

They were heading out of Singapore now along unlit roads. Their headlamps picked out neat plantations on either side and occasionally the darkness was broken by the faint, flickering light from a farmer's shack or a Malay kampong. He knew the route well enough, though it was not the way he usually took. His mouth dried as they turned off on to the rough track which – about a mile farther along – led to the house. A cordon had been thrown around the whole area, Winterton explained; already they had passed two army checkpoints.

So many army and police vehicles were parked in the drive going up to the house it was difficult to get through. The headlamps of several had been left switched on, projecting their harsh lights at the jungle thickets which made up the garden and where groups of soldiers could be seen thrashing the undergrowth with long lathis.

At the front door they met a young, harassed police lieutenant who betrayed undisguised relief at the arrival of a senior officer.

'Lieutenant McNeil,' Winterton introduced them. 'Ross lives here. Works for the same company.'

'Not too pleasant in there,' McNeil warned him.

Ross pushed past him and went in. The lower stairs were smeared with blood; so too was the wooden floor and part of a wall. Two bodies still lay there covered with sheets which had once been white. Automatic weapons, he guessed as he stared around at this place which had been his home, his Shangri-La; practically every piece of timber was pitted and splintered where the bullets had struck.

Winterton indicated the bodies. 'Feel up to identifying them?'

'It has to be done,' said Ross. The questions spun through his mind – why had they attacked here and not Alun Browne's place? Or had Moody been a random target, chosen because the house was isolated? No other reason?

Averting his face, McNeil lifted the sheet to reveal the shorter of the two bodies. Her sarong was bloodsoaked and her staring eyes did not recognize him. Four bullets at least, he reckoned. Not a clean killing; he ached at the thought of how much she must have suffered before dying.

'Know her?'

'Minah.' He pronounced her name as though blaming himself. But for him she would never have been there.

McNeil lowered the sheet over her again and turned to the second body. This was Tim Moody, his mouth settled into a vague smile of death. In his shoulder was a single bullet wound but a deep wire-cut circled his throat. Chuan's trade mark. The message was only too obvious.

No random target, then. After eighteen months of silence Chuan had resurfaced. Ross was in no doubt about that.

'That's Moody all right,' he said unnecessarily. Winterton knew him well enough from the Cricket Club. 'Where are the others? There must have been two more people in the house.'

'One other was found – a Malay, male, badly wounded.'

'Suleiman. He was the cook. Nobody else? Another Malay girl lived here. Name's Asiah.'

'Maybe she ran off, or they took her with them.' McNeil glanced at Winterton as if asking for a ruling. 'Three bandits, the wounded man said. Chinese. It was a miracle we got that out of him. He was unconscious again when the ambulance arrived. Oh, and there's something else you should see. Through here.'

In the next room was a tall, glass-fronted cupboard in which Tim had kept the three or four sporting trophies he had won before the Japs crippled him, and also a motley collection of glasses and a couple of jade figures he had recently bought. There was more blood here too and someone must have dipped a finger into it to write across one of the panes. A single word only: 'Hantu'.

'Any idea what this could mean?' McNeil asked.

'I'm Hantu. It's what they called me in the war.'

'Ross was a jungle-wallah,' Winterton explained. 'You've heard of Force 136?'

'Vaguely,' McNeil admitted. 'Bit before my time.'

From outside – some distance away – came the sound of a Sten gun firing two short bursts, then silence again. Army patrols, he thought; inexperienced conscripts shooting at their own shadows. If those bandits knew their job they could be well clear by now. No cordon was that tight.

Except for Chuan.

That was the meaning of his message without any doubt. Chuan would linger, waiting for the right moment.

The police departed immediately the bodies were removed. Ross refused Winterton's offer of transport back into Singapore, saying he wanted to stay in the house in case Asiah returned. It sounded unconvincing though it was partly true. He owed Tim more than that. The army unit – coolly commanded by a Captain Brewster – set up their operational headquarters on the ground floor, leaving him the second for himself.

Chuan had been thorough. In every room mirrors were smashed, doors were kicked in, beds and mosquito nets had been machine-gunned. Not unmotivated damage, any of it. This had been a manhunt, efficiently and ruthlessly conducted with the aim of flushing him out and killing him.

He went first to his own room, feeling under the bed-frame till his fingers encountered the commando knife he kept hidden there. It was his only weapon, placed so that he could reach it easily in the night. Slipping it into a leather sheath, he strapped it to his leg.

In Tim's room he lay on the bed and tried to work out where he might have concealed the Browning pistol he had once admitted having. It would be somewhere he could get hold of it simply by stretching out an arm – but where? It took half an hour before he discovered it was held in a spring clip beneath the bedside cupboard. Well cleaned and oiled. Full magazine.

At dawn he watched from his window as the army

patrols returned. Even from where he stood he could hear how much noise they made pushing through the undergrowth, and the men who came to relieve them did not seem any more experienced. Before Winterton left, Ross had suggested offering his help in the search but was advised against even mentioning it. 'Only create bad blood,' Winterton had said, 'whatever your war record. Leave it to those whose job it is.'

He went through the house to a rear veranda, climbed over the rail and shinned down the post. Through a window he glimpsed the glass-fronted cupboard still bearing the word 'Hantu' in brown scrawled letters of dried blood. It was his job after all, not the Army's, he thought as he dropped quietly to the ground. Seconds later he was among the trees which Tim had so often discussed clearing in order to extend the lawn.

Wherever Chuan was hiding out, it would be close to water and not too near the house. Water had always been a point Chuan had stressed; with fresh water at hand a cadre can hold out for days if necessary without betraying his whereabouts. But this was not jungle country. It was farming country with clumps of old trees here and there; plenty of secondary growth too, not as high but equally tough at ground level.

When he came to the lane he ducked down under cover, surveying the scene carefully before dashing lightly across and plunging into the next thick copse which was considerably more extensive. No need to hurry though. Eyes and ears open, as he had always preached in the training sessions. All senses alert. The old Hantu tricks.

Voices.

British – a fresh patrol doing their best to warn any lurking bandits of their presence. He pitied the cursing NCO with them. He could have reached out and touched

the man, he passed so close without noticing the motionless form watching him. If they ever found themselves
doing real jungle duty they'd be lucky to survive their first
day.

With no evidence to guide him other than a vague
hunch, he headed towards a freshwater stream they had
all explored one day – he and Tim, Minah and Asiah,
cooling off beneath a tiny waterfall only yards from the
point where it fed into the estuary. Among the rocks it
offered several hiding places. But long before he reached
it the trees began to thin out and he found himself skirting
an extensive coconut plantation. Through the tall, slender
palms he saw a man emerging from an atap house and
realized he'd been spotted. To dive back into cover would
only arouse his suspicion; he had no alternative but to
walk straight on.

'Tuan, *mari sini*! Come here!' A young boy appeared
and seized his hand, tugging him back towards a path
through the trees. 'Asiah, tuan!'

Beyond the trees, concealed from the coconut plantation, he discovered a Malay kampong whose atap rooftops
he must have observed a dozen times from his veranda.
The boy dragged him to one of the houses, repeating
urgently that Asiah wanted to see him. Kicking off his
shoes, he went up into the dark, cool house and found
her sitting there, cowering with fear. Getting her story
together was a long, slow process. First he had to reassure
her that he was alone and that no one had followed him.
But eventually she told him how three Chinese, all armed,
had suddenly appeared in front of the house and sent her
inside to fetch the white tuan. Tim. They had approached
so openly, she had imagined them to be police till she
heard the firing. How she escaped and hid was too
confused for him to make any sense of it.

'Do you know where they are now, these men?'

'Tuan, one man I see,' the boy interrupted eagerly. He had been standing all the while in the shadows, listening. 'One man I see. He look like this.'

He twisted his lips in an imitation of Chuan which was unmistakable.

'When did you see him?'

'Today. I take you there. He has gun. Ba-ba-ba-ba.'

'Asiah, stay where you are,' he said. 'Don't leave the kampong. I'll come back.'

The boy was a born tracker who seemed to know every root, bush and ditch in the area. After some fifteen minutes they emerged beside a slow-moving stream partly choked up by the long grasses trailing in it. He had been right about the fresh water but wrong on every other point. The boy turned upstream, taking care to stay under cover. On the far bank the line of trees was scant; beyond them was a banana plantation. Then the boy stopped and pointed out a tumbledown shed several yards away on the very edge of the water. One rusted sheet of corrugated metal still served as an incomplete roof.

Hantu left the boy crouching in the undergrowth and went on alone, moving back from the stream and circling the shed till he emerged on the far side. Once in position he could see Chuan clearly. He was dressed in a kind of greenish drill uniform and apparently preparing to eat.

Silently – ghost-like – Hantu began to glide between the trees to lessen the distance between them. Tim's Browning automatic fitted his grip as though made to measure. It felt reassuringly familiar. These Canadian Brownings had been favourites in the jungle. And he was glad it was going to be Tim's gun.

'Comrade Chuan,' he said softly. 'We meet again.'

Chuan swung around, instantaneously bringing up his Sten gun. Hantu waited only long enough to see a look of recognition cross his face before tightening his finger just a fraction, shooting him neatly through the centre of his forehead.

He returned to the house, Tim's Shangri-La, feeling as empty and desolate as during the Jap air raids of his Shanghai boyhood when he had wandered through the ruined streets too shattered even to mourn those he had lost. Killing Chuan gave him no pleasure. Revenge was not for him; it punished the avenger more than the victim. After a couple of days the Army left, abandoning the search for the remaining two bandits. Alone in the house with its stained and chipped woodwork, he took his sketch pad and pencils and began to draw.

Chuan's features as he remembered them from the days of the Three Star Army.

Mei-lin.

Then Alun Browne, his teeth clenched on his pipe-stem. Bastard.

A cold beer was placed on the table beside him and he glanced up. Asiah had returned, though he hadn't heard her coming into the house. She stood beside the chair, resting her hand on his shoulder, saying nothing.

Six months later a postcard turned up in the office mail. The stamp was Polish; the picture showed a view of Warsaw, pre-war. In careful textbook English it said simply: 'I like living here. It is a big town with many embassies. At Easter we have boiled eggs to eat. Do you keep well and remember friends? – Anna.' An innocent card from a foreign girl, the censors must have thought.

He propped it up against his desk calendar. How she had contrived to land a job at the Chinese Embassy in Warsaw he could not imagine, but – Yes, Mei-lin love, he did keep well and remember friends.

End Note

As the world knows, no atomic weapons were in the end used by either side in the Korean war though as time went on stockpiles grew and the means of delivery became more sophisticated. Already in the last months of 1950 the Soviet Union was conducting its first tests of submarine-launched rockets. Meanwhile, China accused the United States of germ warfare and in 1952 the Chinese Peace Committee and the Academia Sinica invited six internationally known scholars to join an International Scientific Commission to investigate these claims. The Commission's report implied a clear link with Japanese wartime experiments and appeared to support the Chinese allegations which the United States – with the full support of other Western powers – strongly denied.